David A. Rollins is a ~~former~~ ...or and copywriter who lives with his wife and three children in Sydney. He is currently working on his next novel.

ROGUE ELEMENT

DAVID A ROLLINS

PAN
Pan Macmillan Australia

First published 2003 in Macmillan by Pan Macmillan Australia Pty Limited
This Pan edition published 2004 by Pan Macmillan Australia Pty Limited
St Martins Tower, 31 Market Street, Sydney

Copyright © David A. Rollins 2003

National Library of Australia
cataloguing-in-publication data:

Rollins, David A.
Rogue element.

ISBN 0 330 36464 2.

I. Title

A823.4

Typeset in 10/13 pt Birka by Post Pre-press Group
Printed in Australia by McPherson's Printing Group

Author photograph: Samantha Rollins

For Sam

Acknowledgements

This novel is a work of fiction, written to sound like fact, the line between the two blurred so that you don't twig to where one stops and the other begins. Of course, whether I've succeeded in that is up to you, the reader, to decide.

I'm not a social scientist, a historian or a military specialist. Much of the material contained in this story was found in the public domain. That said, I did call on the services of a number of experts where the available information was either inadequate or when good old-fashioned experience was required. I would very much like to thank those people publicly, because they only get two rewards in this business. One is the satisfaction of knowing that, where their specialty is concerned, at least accuracy has been maintained. Two is acknowledgement that they'd probably rather be out playing golf than sitting on the phone to me, or correcting the manuscript yet again.

And so . . . Thank you Andy Bates for taking me on the wildest 747 ride ever. Thank you 'Woody', former USAF F-16 fighter pilot, for your patience and enthusiasm. Thank you Gideon Marshall for showing me one end of an M16 from the other. Thank you Neville Farley, SASR veteran, for making sure I wasn't completely off the planet. Thank you Chris Sherwood for the ins and outs on the Black Hawk. Thank you Mr Yuwono for the guided tour of Sulawesi. And thank you Bob Buick, Vietnam veteran and Military Medal winner, for your contacts and for your astonishing bravery under fire.

Also, thank you Patricia Rollins (me mum) for your tireless editing, suggestions and encouragement.

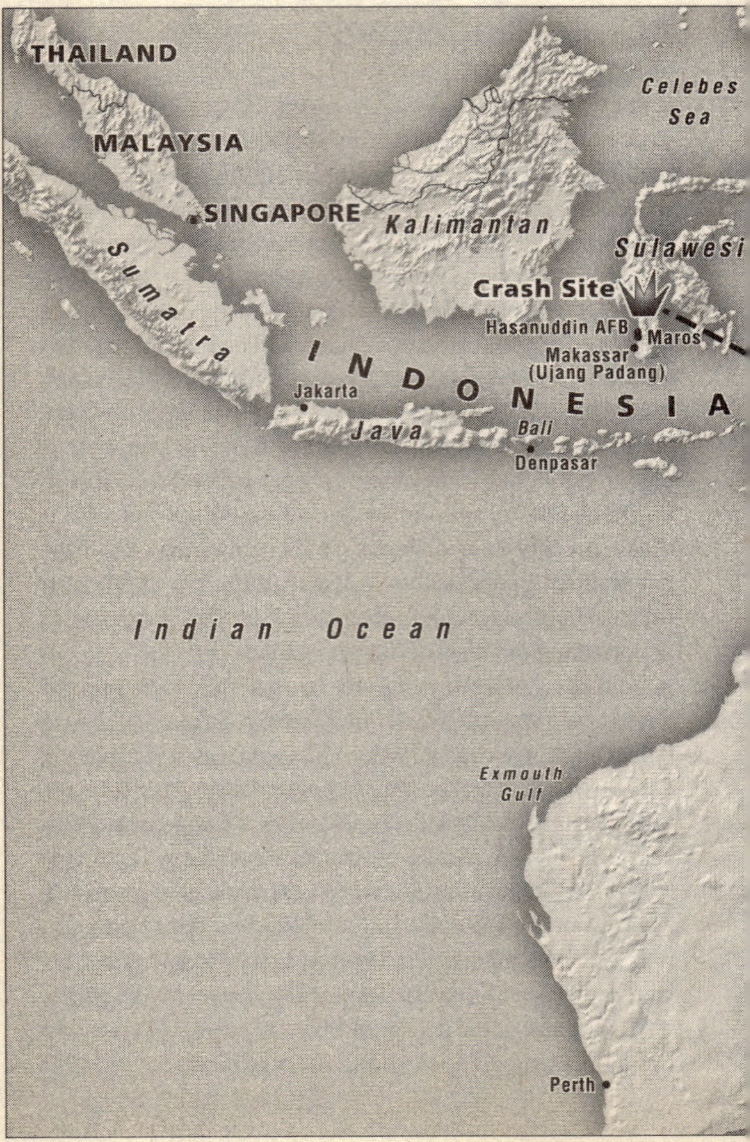
THAILAND
MALAYSIA
SINGAPORE
Kalimantan
Celebes Sea
Sulawesi
Sumatra
Crash Site
Hasanuddin AFB
Maros
Makassar
(Ujang Padang)
INDONESIA
Jakarta
Java
Bali
Denpasar
Indian Ocean
Exmouth Gulf
Perth

Pacific Ocean
Ambon
WEST PAPUA
(Irian Jaya)
PAPUA
NEW GUINEA
Banda
Sea
Arafura
Sea
AST
MOR
Darwin
Cairns
Townsville
AUSTRALIA
Brisbane
Sydney
Canberra

Glossary

ACI	Airborne Control Interception
ADF	Australian Defence Force
AFB	Air force base
AGL	Above ground level
AIM-9	Air-to-air heat-seeking missile
AMRAAM	Advanced medium range air-to-air missile
APC	Armoured patrol carrier
ASIS	Australian Secret Intelligence Service
ATC	Air traffic control
AV-8B	*Harrier* Jump Jet —vertical/short take off and landing aircraft
AV-TUR	Jet fuel
AWACS	Airborne warning and control system
BVR	Beyond visual range (missile)
C-130	*Hercules* transport aircraft
COMINT	Communications intelligence
COMPSTOMP	Computer Security, Tasking, Observation and Manipulation Protection
Cray XI	Super computer
CSAR	Combat Search and Rescue
DIO	(Australian) Defence Intelligence Organisation
DIGO	Defence Intelligence and Geospatial Organisation
DOD	(Australian) Department of Defence
DPRD	Dewan Perwakilan Rakjat Daerah – Indonesian parliament
E&E Bay	Electronics and Equipment Bay
EA-6B	*Prowler* electronic warfare aircraft
ELINT	Electronic intelligence
ETFOR	United Nations peacekeeping force, East Timor
EW	Electronic Warfare
F/A-18E	*Super Hornet* Fleet defence aircraft
F14	*Tomcat* Fleet defence aircraft
F16	*Fighting Falcon* fighter
FIR	Flight Information Region
FMC	Flight Management Computer
GPS	Global positioning system
H&K MP5SD	9 mm sub-machine gun
H&K USP	9 mm pistol
HE	High explosive
HE 463	High explosive M203-launched grenade

HUD	Head up display
Huey	UH-1D helecopter
IAE	Intelligence Assimilation Executive
INTERFET	Peacemaking force, East Timor
IRS	Inertial Reference System
KC-135	Air-to-air tanker
LM	Loadmaster
LSA	Lowest safe altitude
LZ	Landing zone
M16 A2	Military assault carbine
M203	Grenade launcher
M26 AI	Anti-personnel hand grenade
M34	*Willie Pete* white phosphorous hand grenade
M4	Military assault carbine
MAG	Mobile Assault Group
Minimi	Light machine gun
MLP	Marine landing platform
NSA	National Security Agency
NVG	Night vision goggles
OSCAR	Open systems core avionics requirement (weapons/stores computer)
PE	Plastic explosive
QNH	Area air pressure at sea level
RAAF	Royal Australian Air Force
ROE	Rules of engagement
RV	Rendezvous
S70 A9	*Black Hawk* helicopter
SAR	Search and Rescue
SASR	Special Air Service Regiment
SBS	Special Boat Service
SEA Section	South-East Asian Section
SIGINT	Signals intelligence
SRS	Special Recovery Squadron
Super Pumpa	Helicopter
TACBE	Tactical beacon (radio transceiver)
TNI	Tentara Nasional Indonesia (Indonesian army)
TNI-AU	Tentara Nasional Indonesia – Angkatan Udara (Indonesian airforce)
UH	Ultra high frequency
V22	*Osprey* Tiltrotor vertical/short takeoff and landing aircraft
VHF	Very high frequency
WAC	World Area Chart
Zulu	Universal Coordinated Time/Greenwich Mean Time

Prologue

General Suluang shook a toothpick from the holder. He dug out a piece of chicken that had lodged in the canyon left by a filling broken long ago. The waitress cleared away the meal eaten by the men hunched in the circle of dim light over the table. The general looked up when her scent reached his nostrils. She smiled. He admired the young woman's body, momentarily diverted from the discussion.

'Kalimantan is troublesome again,' said Lanti Rajasa, the head of Indonesia's security police. 'We kill the terrorists but the burnings persist.' His lips were stretched tight across yellow teeth, giving him the appearance of an animal baring its fangs.

The general nodded, relieved that the annoying piece of chicken had finally been dispatched. This was his favourite restaurant in Jakarta. The food was acceptable, the decor a mishmash of jungle themes and Indonesian mythology. The music softly piping through the restaurant's speakers was a *popular melody played on a continuous loop. The general found the familiarity of it reassuring. The room, though large, was dark and private. Thick brown carpet swallowed conversation and the muted light encouraged anonymity. It was the kind of place businessmen took their mistresses during the day, but it was one o'clock in the morning now and the last of the paying customers had long since left. He especially liked this restaurant because the owner was his cousin, a retired army major from a good regiment, so he didn't feel that he had to guard his conversation.*

Rajasa continued. 'Aceh is worsening. The police chief there is missing. We don't think we'll find him alive. Several government buildings have been torched. The army is on the streets, but the looting, as you know, goes on. The students are the worst. The people no longer wait for the soldiers to turn their backs before they steal. The army doesn't seem to be an effective deterrent any more.'

The general again nodded thoughtfully, 'Perhaps we should have had our men remove their red berets way back in the beginning. It would have been helpful having supporters in the area working behind the scenes. We've let things get out of hand. Lack of respect is a disease, Lanti, and it spreads. Aceh, Ambon, Kalimantan, Irian Jaya.'

'You mean West Papua, General,' said Colonel Javid Jayakatong, commanding officer of a mechanised infantry regiment. 'I still can't believe the government caved in to pressure from a few natives waving spears and allowed the place to be renamed.'

'They can call it what they like, Colonel. It'll always be Irian Jaya to me,' said Suluang.

'Even Bali is proving difficult,' said Rajasa, snorting in disbelief.

'Yes, it has never really recovered from those fanatics,' said Jayakatong, 'The Balinese resent us. They think we allowed it to happen because they're Hindu, rather than Muslim. Fools. Don't all of us here have assets there that rely on the tourists? Why would we hurt our own investments? Still, there is a bright side.'

'And that is . . .?' Rajasa was intrigued.

'The number of Australian flags burned across the country in support of the attacks,' said Jayakatong.

The men laughed heartily.

The general waited for the laughter to subside and let his face assume a hard, conspiratorial mien. He leaned forward. 'It started with East Timor. Now, every other island and province with the vaguest historical grudge against Java is moving towards secession. There are racial tensions, religious pressures. Gentlemen, we are sitting on the complete disintegration of Indonesia, nothing less.'

Blood flushed into Colonel Jayakatong's head at the mention of East Timor. He had been chased through a jungle trail there, humiliated by Australian soldiers, and he hit the table with a closed fist. 'Australians! Asia's white trash! They are to blame for so much unrest within our country.'

Lanti Rajasa spoke in a low voice, 'Many Indonesians feel as you do, Colonel.'

Suluang was pleased to see the anger on the colonel's face. That was good. It fed his resolve. He glanced quickly at Rajasa and received an imperceptible nod. 'We all know why we're here. Indonesia needs a strong hand. Together, united, we have the means at our disposal to act in Indonesia's interests.'

Rajasa's eyes flicked from Colonel Jayakatong to General Kukuh Masri, the man known as Mao, for his striking resemblance to the late Chinese leader. They'd all been thinking the

3

same thought. Indeed, it had been whispered often enough in barracks throughout Indonesia since Australia's invasion of East Timor. The impact of that blow was still echoing throughout the country, with each subsequent month seeming to bring a further diminution in the power and authority of the country's armed forces. Finally, someone had put the idea on the table and neither Jayakatong nor Masri had flinched.

General Masri had been silent, Rajasa noted, nodding occasionally but hardly the strident advocate of military intervention they were expecting. They needed him. He commanded a powerful regiment of crack paratroopers. 'Yes, it's time to stop killing our own people,' he said at last.

General Suluang raised his empty glass and saluted Masri's sentiment. 'You are absolutely right, Mao. We might be the shepherds, but our flock is wandering off. We need to regather them if Indonesia is to survive.'

The men looked at each other a little nervously. After the initial bluster, each man knew the course they were on was a dangerous one. 'And,' said Suluang after a pause, 'I have an idea that will almost guarantee there'll be no blood-letting on Indonesian soil.'

'What of the Americans? How would they react?' said Colonel Jayakatong. 'They are an unpredictable quantity.'

'Yes,' said Suluang, 'the Americans.' He seemed to be placing the question under scrutiny as he took another toothpick and examined its point. 'They do not want to see Indonesia disintegrate. They will appreciate the benefits of a strong hand holding the archipelago together. And we're not terrorists, or religious fanatics. We have a legitimate concern for our country's stability. If we say the right things about trade, promise a return to stability. Free elections, of course . . .' The general shrugged dismissively.

The officers chuckled, the tension relieved. Suluang's confidence was contagious. Of course the Americans would fall into line. And there was still so much occupying them in the Middle East. They'd be difficult at first, but they'd come around.

The young waitress again distracted Suluang. She was across the room folding napkins. A light from the kitchen behind her revealed long slender legs beneath the cotton sundress. Women: taking as many of them as possible to his bed was one of the advantages of power. Very few refused him. He caught his reflection in a mirror. He was a man of power and, at only forty-five, in the prime of life. He smiled to himself before calling her over on the pretence of ordering a drink.

'What's your name?' he enquired after placing an order.

'Elizabeth,' she said.

Elizabeth caught him staring at her breasts between the buttons as she leaned forward to remove some plates from the table. She moved to improve his view.

Joe Light was wired. His video screen was tuned to the news while his fingers worked the keyboard of his laptop. The title track from *Blood Soaked Earth* crashed through the earphones plugged into a DVD player by his side. He was nervous. He glanced around quickly to see if anyone had been watching. Satisfied, he closed the Internet connection and reopened the game minimised on the toolbar.

Within a few moments he was back in the world he was more comfortable with these days. His right hand gripped a vibrating joystick. On the computer's screen, millions of colours coalesced to form a grotesque being. Joe smiled as it ripped the head off another warrior. The freakish thing on screen looked familiar. Joe had patched the game with a parasite that allowed him to attach his features to the computer character. He tapped the keys and the monster flexed, swelling its exaggerated pecs, chest and arms to ridiculous proportions.

In the flesh Joe was strong, but he wasn't musclebound. An ex-girlfriend once described him as vaguely handsome in a wiry kind of way, adding that she thought he had a modem for a dick. Joe's other passion besides technology was boxing. Not the boxercise aerobics favoured by secretaries and marketing execs, but the real thing in real gyms where there wasn't any piped music or mirrors, and where the air smelled like a sour leather glove.

The game was a new one Joe was reviewing for *Dumb Thumb* magazine, an on-line/off-line rag that specialised in high-end computer entertainment and technology. Once he had worked his way through it, Joe would crack the cheat codes and post them on his own Internet site. Two sources of income for the one job. Cool. A sweet little earner. There were many streams to Joe's income, which was why, at twenty-seven, he could afford a holiday to England, flying first-class. Life was good. Yeah.

His fingers flicked over the keys. A hideous mutant flung gobs of its own dung at the warrior-Joe on screen. Instead of dissolving armour, fatigues and skin as it was supposed to, the lethal excretions passed straight through the computer character and melted the wall behind it. Joe noted the keystrokes on his palm pilot and went in search of more cheat codes.

'Can I get you something to drink, sir?' asked a flight attendant, leaning forward towards him to catch his answer. Joe had completely forgotten where he was. That often happened when he was on the computer. It was as if his mind became mated with the CPU when his fingers moved over the keys.

'No, thanks,' he said, slightly annoyed by the distraction, and went back to the screen.

The rest of the 747 was quiet when Joe woke from a short, fitful sleep, the overhead lights dimmed low. In economy, uncomfortable bundles in grey blankets filled the seats. Occasional arms and heads spilled into the aisles. Here and there passengers drowsily watched video screens. Sleep hung heavily in the warm cabin.

The flight deck was also dark, but nonetheless alert. Captain Andy Flemming, one of Qantas's most senior captains, wasn't on the flight deck. He was having a break, retired to the Crew Rest Facilities for a mandatory kip. First

Officer Luke Granger, a young-looking bloke with wiry red hair and a round face spattered with freckles, was in command. Second Officer Jenny Rivers was beside him, in the captain's seat, checking over the radio work that would be needed in the following Flight Information Region when they tracked out of Indonesian, and into Malaysian, airspace.

The door behind them opened. A flight attendant had come to see if they wanted refreshments. Luke turned. 'How's it going back there? Under control?'

'Yeah, since I drugged the coffee,' said the flight attendant. 'Get you guys anything?'

'I'll have one of those Korean massages where they walk on your back. Or a coffee, whatever's easiest,' grinned Luke, glancing over his shoulder.

Flemming pushed through the door behind the flight attendant. Rivers began to lever herself out of the seat. 'It's okay, Jenny. I'll just watch for a while. That weather delay in Sydney has really mucked up my sleep pattern,' he said, yawning.

The second officer eased back into the captain's chair. She liked the left-hand seat. She believed it would be hers one day.

'Tea for me please, Becky,' said the captain, noting the name on the flight attendant's lapel badge. 'And one of those cakes I saw you handing out at dinner to the first-class passengers, if you've got one left.' He reached up and adjusted the temperature on the flight deck down a couple of degrees.

'And a Coke, thanks,' mumbled Rivers into her paperwork. The flight attendant made a mental note of the order and left the crew silhouetted against a galaxy of cockpit instruments and switch lights.

Luke allowed himself the luxury of letting his mind wander and compared piloting the 747 to flying an F/A-18 in his alma mater, the Royal Australian Air Force. He had Blu-tacked a small plastic model of the fighter to the windscreen by his shoulder. He peeled it off and examined it – a beautiful, deadly shape. In reality, the commercial stuff was dull. Computers did everything. They flew the plane. They managed the engines. They monitored the frequencies. They maintained the life support system that pressurised the cabin and kept everyone alive. They found the airports the aircraft flew to. They kept a lookout for weather. And if that wasn't enough, hell, the 747-438 even had auto-landing capabilities. The plane could put itself on mother earth – and did so if the weather was exceptionally bad – touching down on the runway centreline when the computers considered the task beyond human ability.

Of course, the F/A-18 was a pretty smart plane too, but its intelligence was concentrated on finding and killing the enemy. He 'flew' the plastic model through the air before parking it back on the windscreen.

The 747 was no F/A-18 but flying one was still better than just about any other job he could think of in civvy street. Luke checked the altimeter. He was not surprised to see that it was reading exactly 35 000 feet. All engine gauges were synchronised and reading normal. It occurred to him that the 747 was like a big factory, and that the factory's product was lift. He was merely a foreman who monitored gauges and ensured that enough of that product was rolling off the production line to keep the factory in the black: flying.

They were tracking down the FIR loaded before takeoff

into the Flight Management Computer. The aircraft's track was checked automatically and constantly by three Inertial Reference Systems, backed up by two Global Positioning Systems. And if some slight error arose, the IRS would update itself against any and all ground-based radio navigation aids.

The concatenating technological wizardry meant that wandering off track was impossible. Getting from one place to another by the shortest possible route was what commercial flying was all about: minimising the burn of precious fuel. It was flying by the balance sheet. There was no need to double-check their heading but he did so anyway. Spot on. What do you expect? Granger asked himself.

He contemplated the moon just risen above the horizon. It was a dirty yellow dinner plate against a black curtain. The moon's light had dimmed the surrounding stars but it was a beautiful clear sky. Being up here was something he never tired of, even though there was really nothing to do on these long-haul flights except to concentrate on staying awake. You took in the view, kept checking the instruments you checked fifteen minutes ago, and counted the dollars accumulating in your bank account.

Money, or lack of it. That was the reason he'd left the RAAF. He wasn't sure it had been such a good decision. He'd been poor in uniform – enough money for beers with the boys and little else – but, shit, he was flying. Really flying. Punching military jets through the blue in vertical climbs that took him from sea level to the blurry edge of space in a couple of minutes. Being paid to dogfight in a multi-million dollar aircraft? Christ, he'd have done it for free.

His wife used to say that he *did* do it for free. That was

10

her problem. There was never enough money for her. Five years he'd been out of the RAAF now, divorced for three of them. His wife ran off with a stockbroker who earned over a quarter of a million dollars a year, not including bonuses. Karma had burst her little bubble, though. The Internet and the rise of on-line investing had put hundreds of brokers on the street, and his wife's second husband with them.

He'd heard they'd recently had to sell the Beemer. Luke was not a vengeful person, but he had to admit he was pleased. He'd loved the RAAF, and the fighter with his name stencilled on the fuselage. The woman deserved everything fate dealt her. His eyes unconsciously swept the panel for troublesome numbers but failed to find any.

NSA Pacific HQ, Helemanu, Oahu, Hawaii, 1843 Zulu, Tuesday, 28 April

Ruth Styles was a clerk but, as she often told herself, not just any clerk. She was an important cog in the machine of the United States' most powerful and secret intelligence arm, the National Security Agency. Indeed, the NSA registered her important contribution to the nation's defence with the grandiose title Intelligence Assimilation Executive. At fifty-four, Ruth was one of the most senior IAEs in the agency. Her stern, bloodshot eyes even made some of the section heads, beings ostensibly far above her on the public service treadmill, tremble.

Ruth had an imposing barrel chest and legs like tree trunks to support it. She had a penchant for severe suits and heavy powder that accentuated the pores on her face. She had joined the NSA as a secretary. Thirty years later, she was still hooked on the thrill her work gave her, because that was her life.

The contained underground complex Ruth Styles had joined as a young woman in 1970 had its entrance in the middle of a pineapple plantation. But it had grown like a living thing over time, adding appendages as the world became ever more complicated. There were now several towering wings above ground but, iceberg-like, that was nothing compared to the sprawling mass hidden below. It was certainly different from the old days. Now the pineapple plantation was gone, replaced by the ubiquitous car park.

The once ultra top-secret NSA had well and truly come in from the cold. It now even had its own website. The extent of the agency, the reach and impact of its power, astonishing even in the old days, was truly mind-blowing now.

Ruth's job in this world, while essential, was relatively simple. Despite the considerable advances in technology, the agency still relied on people to process the enormous volume of information that flooded in every minute of every day. This information was then passed to people – hopefully the correct ones – located at appropriate NSA nodes around the world, to analyse and act on.

Ruth had the eye or the nose, or whatever one chose to call it, for the job. She seemed to *know*, even when there were no apparent clues, when a signal was imperative and when it wasn't. Even some of the most innocuous signals could have far-reaching impact. Without people like Ruth, the NSA's multi-billion dollar infrastructure would be worthless. She knew it and, more importantly, so did everyone else.

Self-congratulation was far from her mind, though, when the B2-classified field opened automatically on her Hewlet Packard screen. A Watchdog installed in computer system CS982/Ind. was alerting the system. An intruder had been found.

Watchdogs were highly secret weapons in the war against computer hackers. It was a benign virus that followed intruders over the Internet, leaving snips of code at every switch the call passed through; in effect, just like a dog marking territory. The code snips thus became a trail that led to the hacker's point of origin. A hacker's computer could be plugged into a phone line in a country on the other side of the world. Alternatively, the break-in could originate in a house down the street and the call routed through half a dozen different countries. This subterfuge was useless when a Watchdog was on the trail.

Ruth had no idea where system CS982/Ind. resided, nor did she care. What she did care about was passing the information on quickly to the appropriate echelon, which in this instance, the B2 code told her, were both the owners of the system cracked and COMPSTOMP, the new super-secret group within the NSA established to counter computer terrorism. They could probably catch the computer terrorist in the act, Ruth observed, because this intrusion was happening now, in real time.

Ruth efficiently tapped the forwarding codes in the box provided and keyed enter. The slip disappeared from her screen, on its way to the appropriate analysts. There, she smiled. Another blow to the forces of darkness.

Captain Radit 'Raptor' Jatawaman was scrambled from Hasanuddin Air Force Base outside Mkassar, Sulawesi, one of the Indonesian air force's largest installations. Despite the early start, he was out of bed and into his flying suit before he realised it, his brain lagging behind his body. He was summoned to the briefing room and given the details of the mission he was about to fly by a high-ranking officer who was a stranger to him. The objective shocked him but he somehow managed to keep the surprise out of his face. Timing was tight. He grabbed his helmet from flight stores and ran to his Lockheed Martin F-16A, parked on the apron.

Ground engineers surrounded the aircraft. Ordnance officers checked that the AIM-9L sidewinder missiles, one on each wingtip rail, were correctly attached. The fuel cart drove off.

The F-16A was the premier front-line fighter of the Tentara Nasional Indonesia – Angkatan Udara, or TNI-AU, the Indonesian air force. Raptor was relatively new to the squadron, and he was proud to be one of the elite drivers. The aircraft had been pre-flighted and was ready to go. He hopped in, fastened his harness with the help of a ground crewman, jacked in his phones and began spooling up the Pratt & Whitney.

Once airborne, Captain Jatawaman received his interception coordinates. The F-16 climbed through 18 000 feet before Raptor turned sharply right. He levelled the aircraft out less than a minute later at 39 000 feet in clear, moonlit air. It wasn't long before he saw the 747 sitting in the sky four kilometres away in his three o'clock-low position, just where it should be. The seven-four appeared motionless, bobbing on an ocean of Indian ink, lit as if for a party.

The captain went to full military power and accelerated high over the 747. When he was fully twenty kilometres in front of the passenger jet, he dived back towards it on a bearing that would take the F-16 shooting down the 747's port side. It was a totally unnecessary manoeuvre but Raptor felt like playing. The game was cat and mouse.

Captain Jatawaman began the three-g pull-up on his F-16 the instant his aircraft rocketed past the giant kangaroo on the 747's tail.

Luke Granger yawned and lifted his eyes to the front windows as a ghostly dart blew past. 'Shit!' he exclaimed, his head spinning around in an attempt to keep it in view. The captain and second officer almost seemed to jump, even though they were both strapped in.

'What?' asked Flemming, craning his neck, eyes scanning the instruments in a reflex action.

'I . . . I'm not sure,' he said. 'I think something fast just went past us. Pretty close.'

'I didn't see anything. Are you sure?' asked Rivers, looking out the window, craning her neck to see down the 747's flank.

'No, but . . .' Granger wasn't sure. He'd been daydreaming, mind not really on the job. Was it possible that some kind of military fighter had just buzzed them?

He'd practised the manoeuvre himself hundreds of times. It was almost basic training for dogfighting: two aircraft flew head-on at each other, passing no more than fifty feet apart. Both aircraft would then pull up into inside climbing turns – known as high yo-yos – rolling out at the top to gain as much height as possible. The two aircraft would then continue turning in at each other in a succession of high and low yo-yos until one managed to turn inside the other and bring its guns/cannon/missiles to bear, or one of the aircraft ran out of sky and ploughed into the ground.

Have we just been challenged to a dogfight? No way, he decided. The outcome of such a thing overloaded his common sense. It could also have been . . . what? A bit of cloud?

Rivers relinquished the left-hand seat to her captain, climbing out of it as if it were quicksand. 'I have the aircraft,' said Flemming, once he'd strapped in.

'You have the aircraft,' Granger said, trying to recall exactly what it was he'd seen.

The jumbo, although a lumbering barge compared to Raptor's F-16, was cruising close to the speed of sound at .82 mach. If he was careless, the barge would slip outside his envelope of opportunity. Fuel reserves for this interception weren't unlimited.

Raptor rolled out of the yo-yo 1000 feet above the 747. He was positioned perfectly, high and behind the flying kangaroo. He hung there briefly, like a wasp poised for the kill. Raptor opened the throttle to close the distance. It was too easy.

Raptor's squadron had been flying almost constantly this last six months. It was a welcome relief after the years of only part-time flying. The financial crisis of '97 had hit his squadron hard. There was not enough money for spares. Not enough money for missiles. Not even enough money for fuel. The lowest point for his squadron was the realisation that only three F-16s were serviceable.

The country was falling apart. Morale was nonexistent. And then suddenly, virtually overnight, the money started pouring in. Spares and fuel became available, and he logged more hours in the next six months than over the previous three years. Flying, dogfighting, was why he joined the air force. Now he felt invincible. Let me go head-to-head with one of those Australian F/A-18s, he often wished. Shooting down a Qantas 747 was hardly the contest he'd hoped for. He reminded himself of the briefing officer's assertion that there were sound tactical reasons for the action.

The Indonesian pilot swooped behind the 747. He hung above his quarry's tail, keeping the distance between the two aircraft constant, and depressed the radio transmission button on the throttle a half dozen times, broadcasting clicks in a pre-agreed sequence that announced he was in position to make the shot. Raptor allowed his F-16 to fall back behind the 747; the AIM-9L sidewinder needed more air to get a lock on the Boeing's giant Rolls-Royce turbo fans.

He activated the missile's targeting system and watched the glowing red diamond float across the Head Up Display searching for prey. A tone sounded through his helmet phones. The missile's fire control system had locked on to the 747's right-hand, outboard engine. Raptor expected that. The AIM-9 was a heater. It was attracted to an object's infrared signature, its heat output, and an outboard engine had a greater heat differential between itself and the surrounding freezing high-altitude air than an inboard turbine snuggled against the warm fuselage.

Seconds later, he received the clicks from Hasanuddin AFB, confirmation that gave him permission, or rather the order, to fire the missile. A moment of doubt punctured

Raptor's conscience. But the uncertainty lasted for the briefest instant in a part of his brain that had long been subdued by hundreds of hours of training.

His finger depressed the fire button on his side stick controller. It was a subconscious reaction to the command, like the way a leg twitched when the knee was tapped with a hammer. The missile slid from its rail. He watched it snake until its guidance system stabilised the missile and delivered the warhead unerringly to the target. It flew up the tail pipe of the Rolls-Royce engine where the fragmentation warhead, packed with 3.6 kilos of HE, detonated. Red-hot metal spikes ripped through the engine and annihilated its delicate balance. The massive turbine, now with smashed bearings and spinning at 3 500 rpm, leapt out of its housings, blasting the shattered titanium fan blades into the thin air.

Raptor watched the destruction from his dress-circle position. The 747's outboard engine was utterly destroyed. The monster staggered, smoke trailing from the wound like a long piece of gauze dressing.

'Jesus, what the hell . . .' said Joe as the plane bucked and kicked unexpectedly, bouncing the Apple off his table and into his lap. The sleeping passengers woke, bewildered. The cabin was rapidly filling with engine noise and the smell of burning grease. Joe looked around to see what was happening. There was confusion on the faces of the passengers he could see. Their mouths were slightly open and they were looking around, like him, trying to establish what was going on.

Joe was immune to the usual aircraft noises and jolts he considered normal. He believed himself a comfortable flyer because he had done so much of it. The whirrs, pops and bangs that usually alarmed less seasoned travellers he took in his stride. But now that the plane was behaving in a manner outside his experience, Joe realised how genuinely afraid of flying he was. There was obviously something very wrong, only his conscious mind was refusing to accept the full and terrifying implications. Namely, that the aircraft was somehow poised on a knife's edge of destruction and that, as a consequence, so was he.

The groan of metal tearing and breaking underscored the vibration increasing in intensity. Joe realised then that the plane was ripping itself apart.

The last of the sleeping passengers woke. The quiet, vaguely uncomfortable environment they'd dozed off in was now filled with ear-splitting noise and a shaking that was jarring them out of their seats. Their reaction to this frightening new dawn was unanimous. They panicked.

The routine work of the flight deck suddenly became anything but. The sudden jolt followed by a high frequency vibration told them that there was a serious problem somewhere. Alarms began to sound. Both pilots scoured the sea of lights and dials to discover exactly what that problem was.

'Disengaging autopilot,' said Flemming.

'Autopilot disengaged,' confirmed Granger after the appropriate switch had been flicked. Flemming instantly felt an unusual weight on his control column.

The digital temperature readout for number four engine was unbelievably high, and climbing. While he watched it with a morbid interest, the Engine Overheat light illuminated, followed an instant later by the warning bell. The Fire Warning switch also glowed with an array of other lights that had, only moments before, been dim.

'Jesus Christ,' exclaimed Granger. 'Engine fire!' What the hell caused that? He hit the Bell Cutout switch on the glare shield, silencing the alarm that filled the cockpit and his 'phones.

'Identify fire,' said Flemming.

'Engine fire number four,' Granger replied.

Luke stared at the electronic dials on the panel between them. Temps in the right-hand outboard engine had climbed way into the danger zone. All the instruments for fuel flow, even temperatures, had been absolutely normal not five minutes ago. Whatever it was, it was catastrophic. From the vicious shaking of the aircraft, it was probably a severe engine failure caused by . . . ? What? Jet engines, while delicately balanced, were also extremely robust.

What they had here was not a phantom problem, neither was it a drill. A fire on an aircraft, no matter how big or small the plane, was a major concern. The temperatures produced inside a jet turbine were easily hot enough to melt aluminium, and that's exactly what the wing above the engine was made of.

'Number four thrust lever,' called Flemming.

'Confirmed,' said Granger, seeing his captain's hand on the correct lever.

Flemming responded by snapping closed the throttle lever for number four engine. 'Closed,' he said.

'Number four cut-off switch,' said Flemming. When he saw that Granger's hand was on the correct switch he commanded, 'Cut off!'

Granger shifted the switch to the appropriate position. 'Cut off,' he confirmed.

'Number four fire warning switch,' Flemming said. Granger had fallen behind the sequence. Granger quickly placed his hand on the glowing switch. He glanced at Flemming.

'Pull!' commanded the captain.

Granger tugged the switch. 'Pulled!'

Instantly, shut-off valves for the hydraulic, engine bleed air and fuel were activated, starving the fire of combustible mixtures.

Flemming and Granger both stared at the Fire Warning light. It remained illuminated.

'Fire the bottle,' said Flemming.

Granger rotated the switch that discharged a canister containing fire-suppressing foam in the engine nacelle. 'Bottle fired!' A light came on announcing that the bottle had indeed been discharged.

Luke found himself leaning forward in his seat, willing the array of illuminated fire warning lights in front of him to go out. They did not. The engine was shut down, starved of fuel, oil and air, covered in fire retardant foam but, according to the instrument lights, a fire still burned out there under the wing. Jesus!

'Fire the second bottle,' Flemming said.

Granger rotated the switch the opposite way. 'Bottle fired!'

Surely the fire would now be extinguished. The pilots focused on the warning light, willing it to wink off. It didn't.

Shockwaves pulsed through the 747. They shook the plane so hard that Granger's teeth clattered.

'We're going to have to land asap,' said Captain Flemming, busily setting the aircraft up for an orderly descent to an altitude where the 747 could fly slower in thicker air. 'What's the nearest airport?'

Granger knew every strip along his route sector, but

there was only one within range long enough to take a 747. 'Hasanuddin Air Force Base. Force landed there once before with the squadron. Doubles as a civilian airport. But we'll have to turn around. It's a twenty-minute backtrack.'

'Okay.' Flemming paused and added, 'I hate to think what's going on behind us.'

Luke nodded.

'Better let the poor buggers know what's going on,' Flemming said. 'Once we level off, Luke, go back and have a look out the window. You probably won't see much, but you never know.'

The intense heat of the fire burned through the bolts that fixed the engine under the wing and it dropped away like a bomb.

Joe had stopped panicking. He had retreated into shock, along with most of his fellow passengers. The plane felt like it was falling, sliding sideways and downwards. People around him were screaming, but Joe didn't hear them. Something caught his attention. There was a yellow glow coming from somewhere outside the cabin. He wondered if it was an angel come to their rescue. He looked out the small window, squashing his face against the cold Perspex to get a better view. Whatever it was, it was somewhere out on the end of the wing. He couldn't quite work out exactly what it was, but it wasn't an angel. Joe realised it was a fireball, just as it fell away from sight into the blackness below. Was that an engine? he wondered, before discounting the possibility.

Instantly the pitch of the vibration changed. It stopped almost completely, along with the loud rumble that sounded like a freight train running over points just beside his head.

Flight attendants were working the aisles, moving back and forth in an attempt to calm the inconsolable. But any reassurances they gave were at odds with the reality of the moment. Screams continued to fill the cabin. Some people, Joe saw, had already assumed the crash position. His stomach convulsed and he vomited onto the floor between his feet.

Raptor was vaguely disappointed. He had hoped a second missile wouldn't be needed. That was wasteful.

The F-16's fire control system was still activated. He toggled through the missile's target acquisition options, shifting the little red diamond presented on the HUD from one engine to another. He considered which engine to take out next. He let the diamond settle on the right-hand inboard turbine.

His F-16 was only carrying two AIM-9 sidewinders, so this one had to finish the job. He wondered if the 747 had self-sealing fuel cells. If not, a hot sliver of metal – perhaps a burning fan blade – puncturing a wing tank would do the job nicely. Tone sounded in his headphones and he depressed the firing button on the control column operated by his right hand. Raptor gave a mental shrug as the missile flew on its way. The animal was wounded. All he was doing was putting it out of its misery.

Flying at greater than Mach three, the AIM-9 closed the distance in an instant. The warhead smashed into the Rolls-Royce's exhaust. The explosion blew a large section of the engine's secondary compression rotor into the adjacent fuselage, ripping a hole more than a metre wide in the side of the plane. The 747's cabin instantly depressurised.

The titanium blades torn from the engine became shrapnel. The deadly cloud of spikes speared the fuselage in the economy section, shredding three friends sitting together, all of whom were so drunk that, thankfully, they had no idea what was going on. The three, still strapped in their row of seats, were blown out of the hole in the side of the 747 and into the freezing vacuum of the upper atmosphere.

There was an explosion followed by a shockwave that rippled down the skin of the plane, and the air turned instantly milky white with mist. Frost glazed the window beside Joe's face. He was startled, and frightened, but he felt removed from the scene at the same time, as if watching a movie. A roaring sound filled his ears, along with intense pain in his eardrums. The screams were all around him and the loudest of all, he realised, rose from his own throat.

Raptor saw what appeared to be a group of seats tumble out of the hole in the fuselage, but he wasn't sure. The jumbo's wounds now appeared mortal. It was falling away to the right. Slowly at first, then faster. The fall became a plunge. Raptor followed the 747 into the accelerating dive. The two aircraft picked up speed, engine thrust and gravity combining with frightening exuberance.

The F-16's altimeter wound down, counting back through the thousands of feet in a matter of seconds.

Granger and Flemming were checking their instruments, and Rivers was setting up the coordinates of Hasanuddin in the Flight Management Computer, when the second missile hit. The 747 yawed violently with the blow.

The flight deck instantly filled with mist as the rapid pressure change condensed all the water vapour out of the air. 'Jesus Christ!' shouted Granger as warning lights illuminated and flashed, lighting up the panel in front of him like a city after sunset. His ears popped viciously with the sudden change in pressure. The cabin rate-of-climb indicator was racing. A warning horn sounded. Granger hit the Alt Horn Cutout switch to silence it. The air pressure inside the 747 was rapidly equalising with the air pressure outside – at around 30 000 feet, an environment lethal to humans.

The flight crew immediately fitted their oxygen masks. Granger checked that the breathing system for the flight crew was correctly pressurised, and that the Pass. Oxygen On light was illuminated, indicating that the passengers were also getting theirs. The captain hit the switch that instructed the passengers to fasten their seatbelts. It was an odd thing to do in the circumstances, thought Granger, as if the passengers were all standing around in the aisles, unperturbed and unaware of the current critical situation. But it was procedure and couldn't be argued with.

'Emergency descent,' said Flemming loudly, his voice muffled by the oxygen mask. He selected the PA and announced as calmly as he could, 'This is the captain. Emergency descent.'

Granger immediately dialled up the frequency for Air Traffic Control to advise them of QF-1's intention to descend to 3000 metres, and obtain the QNH for the area – the correct local air pressure at sea level that would allow them to rescale their altimeters for an accurate altitude reading.

He made the call and listened. Nothing. He tried again. Nothing. He checked the communications panel quickly. Jesus! It was completely dead, not even receiving power. They had no communications. They were completely cut off. Adrift. He couldn't let that distract them so he kept the knowledge to himself.

Flemming relentlessly continued the checklist for an emergency descent. 'Engine start switches.'

The number three engine now had a fire. They shut it down and fired both bottles. Granger, Flemming and Rivers had punishing earaches and stomach cramps from the gases expanding inside them. They were in excruciating pain, as was everyone in the aircraft. At this altitude, their blood was almost at boiling point and there was intense pressure building up in the cavities in their heads. Blood flowed freely from Flemming's nostrils into his oxygen mask. Start switches for engines one and two were selected to the On position.

'Thrust levers.' Flemming pulled the levers to the closed position and announced it.

'Closed!' yelled Granger into his mask.

The captain and first officer were themselves operating on a kind of autopilot with routines ingrained through hours of simulator time. They continued through the checklist, setting up the aircraft for the emergency descent.

The 747 began to pick up speed as it dived steeply towards the earth. The numbers on the altimeter rolled off backwards.

The seatbelt across Joe's lap was done up so tightly that he was getting pins and needles in his feet. The mask dropped down in front of his face and he looked at it dumbly, not immediately knowing what it was for. Then he felt as if he was plunging over a waterfall. He grabbed the seat in front of him, reaching out to it in an attempt to stop the fall. The engine pitch increased to a wail. Joe believed the end was near.

Granger called out their altitude in increments of 5000 feet as the aircraft accelerated. 'Flight Level three-zero-zero!'

Their rate of descent increased to the near vertical and the big aircraft shook frighteningly. 'Two-five-zero!'

Raptor watched his prey lurch viciously in its dive. He had expected the aircraft to explode in a ball of flame and was disappointed that it hadn't.

Still, the fighter pilot had seen enough file footage from gun cameras to know a kill when he saw one. There was only one possible outcome for the stricken 747. He retarded the throttle and slipped back a safe distance behind the giant. If the 747 did explode and his F-16 was too close, he risked bits of the disintegrating Boeing being inhaled into his engine, with disastrous results.

Joe strained against his seatbelt as the 747 screamed in its dive. He sucked oxygen from the yellow cup, the tangle of masks hanging like jellyfish tentacles in front of his face. He blinked through the frigid mist. His window was glazed with frost. The pain in his ears was searing. His stomach cramped in agony.

Across the aisle a middle-aged man's face had turned blue, white froth bubbling from purple lips. Joe stretched over and tried to pull an oxygen mask over his nose and mouth, but his arm felt heavy, like it was strapped with weights. It took him several attempts to get the mask on. Every time he almost managed to secure the cup over the man's face, the aircraft's pitching jolted his hands, spoiling the attempt.

Joe could see people screaming, but he couldn't hear the sounds they made. He wondered whether he was experiencing some kind of sensory overload, then realised it was because the roar coming from somewhere inside the aircraft was deafening, obliterating everything else.

Some people weren't yelling, having retreated into a semiconscious, almost primal state. They cried or whimpered, rocking in their seats. Some were just clutching each other, even people who had been complete strangers only minutes before.

The aisles were blocked by the contents of the overhead lockers that had burst open. Two rows in front of Joe, a heavy briefcase fell from an overhead locker and clubbed a woman senseless.

Unidentifiable lumps were tumbling down the aisles. It dawned on Joe's slow, oxygen-starved brain that the objects were people whose seatbelts probably hadn't been buckled. The bodies accumulated at the forward bulkhead. Joe noted that most of the faces he could see in the growing pile of rags were blue. He stared at them as an observer removed from reality, in shock, disbelieving. Perhaps they're dead, he thought, and then he realised that they were.

The thin air provided little in the way of resistance and the 747's descent rate built frighteningly. 'Two-zero-zero!' shouted Granger. 'One-five-zero!' The aircraft shook and trembled. The speed increased. The air protested as the monster tore a hole through it. The cockpit filled with the shriek. The numbers winding backwards on the altimeter transfixed the three pilots. The 747 nudged its speed of maximum operation, 0.92 Mach. And then its rate of descent began to slow as the air thickened, just as the manual said it would.

Flemming pulled back on the control wheel and the aircraft's nose began to rise slowly.

'Three thousand feet to altitude.' Granger continued the countdown.

The g-forces built, driving the pilots and passengers into their seats.

'Two thousand feet to altitude.'

The aircraft rumbled and shook, angrily protesting against the loads acting on it.

'One thousand feet to altitude.'

The captain eased the control forward to the neutral position as the jumbo levelled out.

'At altitude!' announced Granger, sweating profusely.

The 747 sat on 10 000 feet, just above a blanket of stratus cloud.

'The Lowest Safe Altitude in these parts is around eight thousand feet!' Rivers said, yelling the information as she juggled a bunch of maps and charts. 'We've got Mount Kambuno with a spot height of around eight thousand nine hundred feet, but I think it's to the north of our position!' She checked the aircraft's FMC. She noticed for the first time that both the flight navigation and directional instrumentation were dead. Shit! There was no way of knowing for certain exactly where they were. Nevertheless, she was still reasonably sure of their position.

'LSA, eight thousand,' confirmed Granger. He checked the altimeter. They were at 10 000 feet. That meant just 2000 feet of air between them and the end of Qantas's perfect fatality-free record.

The hydraulics pressure warning light flashed. Granger and Flemming checked the pressure gauge. It was falling. Hydraulics – oil – was the aircraft's blood. The 747 had four redundant hydraulics systems. Something had taken them all out of operation. The aircraft only needed one of those systems to operate the flaps, ailerons, elevator and undercarriage. Without those control surfaces, the plane was not flyable. Or landable.

Flemming took his foot off the left rudder pedal. The 747 yawed to the right with the asymmetrical thrust provided by the two good engines on the left wing. The effect on the dropping hydraulics pressure was slight but significant. Mercifully, it decreased.

The 747 was capable of maintaining altitude on two engines, even climbing slowly, but with falling hydraulics pressure they were merely forestalling the inevitable.

The three pilots on the flight deck knew that their lives hung by the barest of threads. If they turned the plane around using the ailerons, elevator and rudder, the drain on the hydraulics system could mean there wouldn't be enough pressure left to lower the flaps or undercarriage for landing. And with both engines on one side of the plane inoperable, attempting to steer it with the throttles wasn't an option.

'The news gets worse,' said Rivers, ripping off her oxygen mask along with Granger and Flemming. They were now in a breathable atmosphere.

Thick, crimson blood slopped from the captain's mask. 'It's okay,' he assured them, waving his hand dismissively before wiping his nose with the sleeve of his white shirt.

Rivers checked the FMC. 'We've got no radios, no transponders, nothing.'

'Yeah, saw that,' nodded Granger.

All three of them looked at the displays, which were usually filled with numbers. Blank. The 747 carried two VHF (line-of-sight) radios, an HF (long distance) radio and two transponders, transmitters that painted their 747 on air traffic control screens on the ground. Surely they couldn't all be stuffed?

The 747 began to sink slowly through 10 000 feet, the LSA. Now that it was yawing due to unequal thrust provided by the two remaining engines on the left wing, the aircraft was presenting more of its surface area to the airflow. That meant more friction, and therefore more power was needed to overcome it if they were to continue flying level. Flemming goosed the throttles slightly. The added thrust stabilised the aircraft again at 10 000 feet. Soon, however, there would be no hydraulic pressure at all. The weight of the control surfaces themselves would force them to sag, and the 747 would begin an accelerating spiral into the ground.

A decision needed to be made. And fast.

'Opinions?' asked Flemming.

'Force land somewhere here,' said Granger. 'I don't know how much time we've got. At least if we put her down now, we'll be able to manoeuvre a little, and maybe get our flaps and gear lowered.'

'Agreed,' said Rivers, her voice tight. With no hydraulics, they had ceased to become pilots. They were now merely passengers at near-useless controls, riding in a 250 000 kilogram missile loaded with tonnes of fuel.

'Agreed,' echoed the captain. 'Dump as much gas as we can. And get off a Mayday call.'

Rivers looked blank. Their radios were dead. 'But captain, the –'

Flemming answered her expression. 'You never know.'

The nose of the 747 fell towards the soft, silver lake of stratus cloud spread out below them. But was a mountain hidden somewhere within it? Or did the cloud extend all the way to the ground? In either case they would simply drill a large hole in the earth and never see it coming. All three pilots on the flight deck held their breath as the first wisps of silver slid over their windows. In an instant, the stars were obliterated.

Raptor couldn't believe his eyes when the seven-four pulled out of its dive, seemingly in control, above the cloud. What do I have to do to score a kill? he asked himself.

His fuel pressure and contents were still okay so he decided to wait. There was plenty of smoke trailing from the 747. The drama was not over yet. He smiled with satisfaction when the 747 began to nose under the cloud. There was rugged country beneath. Lots of immovable things to fly into. No 747 pilot would dip below 10 000 around here. Unless there was no choice.

Raptor watched as the 747 slipped below the surface of the cloud like a torpedoed ship ploughing under a ghost sea. This was getting interesting. He beamed the jumbo with active radar and followed it down from a safe distance.

When the plane levelled out of the dive, Joe couldn't believe he was still alive and that the plane hadn't crashed. The stench of vomit filled his nostrils. Much of the vibration had stopped but there was still a fair amount of noise. His mind was starting to grapple successfully with reality. He tried to place the noise and decided it was both wind and engine roar. Most of the passengers were calm now, as if resigned to their fate, whatever it would be. That was certainly Joe's outlook. He reflected on the fact that death by plane crash was an awful, protracted way to die. It had been going on now for, he checked his watch, more than ten minutes. At least it gave you some time to say goodbye. 'Goodbye,' he said aloud, testing the realisation. No one said anything back.

Bali, 2036 Zulu, Tuesday, 28 April

Abe Niko, a Japanese traffic controller on contract at Denpasar Airport, blinked with surprise. At this hour of the morning the skies were pretty quiet. There were only four air-craft on his screen: a KLM 747 out of Melbourne, Australia, bound for Amsterdam via Singapore, a Garuda 767 en-route to Jakarta, a weather delayed Qantas 747 headed for London, and a private Beech Baron on an intra-island flight, inbound, sixteen miles from the Denpasar runway.

The Qantas plane was on the screen and then it wasn't. It had gone, vanished! The suddenness of the disappear-ance made him blink, as if he wasn't sure what he'd just seen. Qantas Flight 1. Abe's brain worked hard to lift itself out of the torpor induced by a combination of boredom and the early morning hour. Shit, that could mean only one of two things. The first was that the aircraft's transponders had become unserviceable. That was highly improbable. The second more likely possibility? Well, that was too ghastly to even contemplate. He noted the time – 4.36 am local time. Abe picked up the phone and hurriedly found a line out.

The radio clicks exchanged between the Indonesian pilot and his controller joined the traffic on Ruth Styles' desk-top at NSA Hawaii. There was a lot of activity going on there, she thought, given the time of day, or rather, night. She tagged it with an asterisk and sent it on.

QF-1 shot out of the cloud base, stratus swirling in a vor-tex behind it. The high country of central Sulawesi that filled the pilots' windshields was the antithesis of the friendly winking threshold strobe lights of a commercial runway.

Flemming, Granger and Rivers gaped at the rugged ridge lines below them, and the occasional mountain face that rose above them: they knew they only had a few minutes to live.

What was now uppermost in their minds was giving everyone as much chance as possible to survive the landing. Flemming and Granger trimmed the aircraft for a descent rate of 500 feet per minute. The aircraft shook and bucked in protest but obeyed the pilots' commands.

Flemming flicked the intercom switch and addressed his passengers and flight crew. 'This is Captain Flemming. Both the engines on the right-hand wing have failed. Without them, this aircraft cannot maintain level flight.' This was not strictly true but it wasn't the right time to give an aircraft systems lecture. 'We will be making a forced landing shortly.

'If you are not in the crash position with your head forward between your knees, adopt it now. Make sure your seatbelts are fastened tightly and that any children are also restrained in their seats.

'There is enough oxygen at this altitude so you no longer need the masks. Your flight attendants will assist you if you have problems.

'We have broadcast our difficulties and our position to the local authorities. Help is no doubt already on the way,' he lied.

Who was it that said, 'You don't find atheists in foxholes'? Flemming couldn't remember but at that moment, even though he never considered himself a religious man, he could see the truth in it. He concluded the announcement. 'If any of you pray to God, now is the time to do it.'

There was no point doing the laconic pilot routine. He had just brought four hundred people through a gutwrenching dive from 35 000 to 10 000 feet in a handful of minutes. Perhaps a word about rescue – even if it wasn't true – and the reassurance that they were in God's hands, would do some good. He didn't know and he had run out of time to think about it. The moonlit jungle was rising up to kill them. It was time to land.

The mist that had caked Joe's window had melted. He wiped away the remaining droplets with the palm of his hand and looked outside. He was sickened by what he saw. The plane was flying in a large bowl ringed by mountains and lit by the moon. The peaks topped out above the air-craft's altitude. There was only one possible outcome. He'd listened to the captain's address and decided that the people at the front of the aircraft had reached the same conclusion about their fate. There were no lights below. There was no runway waiting for them. This was it. He peered out the window harder, trying to see exactly what they would be landing on. They were going to land weren't they? The captain had just said so. They weren't going to crash, surely? The window didn't allow him a view down-wards. He was frightened, but he realised he had no control over anything that happened in his near future. A part of Joe's brain found that oddly comforting. It calmed him. There was absolutely nothing he could do to alter the situation. He just had to sit there and wait. He bent his head between his legs and breathed the warm sickly air rising from the vomit-soiled carpet under his feet – the kiss your arse goodbye position, he thought. A pain swelled in his chest as if an invisible hand was squeezing his heart. 'For Christ's sake, just get it over with,' he said to the god he rarely spoke with.

'I'm going to go for that ridge over in our ten o'clock,' shouted Flemming. Granger and Rivers agreed. From their angle, it appeared to present more of a plateau, although it was night and appearances could be deceptive. Putting the plane down on a ridge would be a better option than a valley. Rescuers would more easily spot the wreckage, for one thing. And for another, a valley would inevitably end with a mountain, and slamming into a solid rock wall would be utterly catastrophic.

There was no argument. 'Luke, you've got the flaps and the undercarriage. Jenny, read off our airspeed. We're only going to get one go at this so let's do it by the numbers.' Flemming wanted to say he thought they'd been a good crew, but the best he could manage was a crooked smile.

It was possibly the most forbidding landscape Luke Granger had ever seen. The fact that he was about to set down a fully loaded 747 on it didn't improve his impression any.

The flight deck was hot and humid. It didn't take much to figure out that they probably had a large hole blown in the side of the aircraft. The engine must have exploded and taken part of the fuselage with it. It was possible that shrapnel from that explosion had wrecked their E&E Bay, taking out their communications and hydraulics in the process. Then Granger remembered what he thought was a fighter's deadly pass down the side of the 747. No, surely not . . . Was it possible? Part of Granger's mind knew they'd been attacked and shot down. Another part refused to believe it. Knowing the answer wouldn't help the situation any. He couldn't even radio anyone with his suspicions. The disquiet evaporated almost the instant it formed. There was too much demanding his attention.

Despite the tropical heat, the sweat on Luke's body was cold, and he realised grimly that he'd pissed himself.

Moonlight washed through a break in the clouds, revealing a lumpy tree canopy. Jungle. They were almost on top of the equator, so it wouldn't be anything else. Not a single reassuring light winked through the expanse below them.

The ridge Captain Flemming had pointed out was now lined up in plain view. Granger scanned the instruments and tried to focus on anything other than his impending death. Their hydraulics pressure was virtually nonexistent. At least the flaps were fully extended and the undercarriage had locked. That was something. With luck, they'd slide along gently after the gear tore off, eating up much of the plane's energy, coming to rest peacefully with no lives lost, held aloft by the waving arms of friendly palm trees.

Who was he kidding? thought Granger. Murderously steep gorges ran off from either side, beckoning. There was only one possible outcome.

Joe couldn't help himself. He'd heard the familiar whirr and bump of the undercarriage coming down and locking in place, and he managed to convince himself, briefly, that they were about to settle on a smooth runway. Then there was the sickening screech of grinding metal as the flaps lowered and the hope evaporated. The big 747 was flying with its nose high in the air. Joe had tested all the top flight sims; he knew the pilots were trying to slow the aircraft down so that it would arrive at its point of impact with the ground just as the lift under its wings gave out. The desire to know what they were about to land on gripped him again. He realised it might be the last thing he ever saw. He looked out and down and saw the tops of trees flashing by at alarming speed. 'Shiiiiiit,' he said, throwing himself forward again into the crash position.

QF-1 slammed onto the ridge. The force of the impact fractured the fuselage behind the wings' trailing edge. The huge fin and tail section, split from the main body of the aircraft, was thrown high in the air. It began to spin like a child's toy as it fell, flinging chairs, people and luggage into the trees. It whirled down into a steep gorge where it shredded itself against volcanic rock like cheese against a grater.

The main body of the aircraft, now engulfed in a fireball, continued to plough through the jungle. A rock outcrop caught the leading edge of the port wing. The violence of the impact carved off the centre section of the fuselage. The remaining fuel in one of the wing tanks exploded, turning the centre section of the aircraft into burning shards of aluminium that rained down over the jungle.

The forward section of the fuselage spun into a small depression. Its mass combined with its speed, telescoping the nose in on itself. Flemming, Granger and Rivers were turned into paste.

Burning fuel caused small fires for a thousand metres around.

The savagery of the crash silenced the jungle. Smoke from the burning fires hung like a mist of death in the moist, pre-dawn air.

Raptor watched the 747 hit the ground. It didn't appear to be going very fast at all but it was difficult to make out any detail until the fireball lit the scene. The sight of the aircraft breaking up was gratifying and he congratulated himself on a job well done. He thumbed the Send button on his control column several times, broadcasting the agreed code for a successful mission. Raptor noted the lat and long coordinates on his thigh-pad from the GPS. He lit his afterburners and set a course for Hasanuddin AFB.

NSA Pacific HQ, Helemanu, Oahu, Hawaii, 2050 Zulu, Tuesday, 28 April

The NSA is the world's most sophisticated eavesdropper. It keeps the airwaves safe for Uncle Sam, gathering information any way that it can, mostly through an extensive battery of antennae dishes scattered around the world. The dishes harvest the low frequency signals, the frequency range generally preferred by the world's military. If atmospheric conditions are right, these can bounce off the biggest dish of all, the earth's ionosphere. The higher frequency transmissions are trickier, the line-of-sight comms. To patrol this frequency range, the NSA deploys all manner of assets, including a flotilla of spy ships masquerading as ocean survey vessels and, of course, spy planes.

The NSA monitors most frequencies in the radio and microwave spectra around the clock; phone and Internet lines are also filtered. Even general phone communications are regularly sampled. The bottom line is, very little communication escapes the NSA, especially when attempts are made to hide it. If you're Milly chatting to Maude in the suburbs of Atlanta, Georgia, there's a good chance the NSA knows your gossip. If you're a Russian tank commander positioning assets around a Chechen enclave, you can guarantee it.

Occasionally, the NSA picks up transmissions that are only meaningful in the context of hindsight, such as the radio clicks passed between an F-16 and a ground controller in Indonesian airspace in the early morning of Tuesday, 28 April.

Ruth Styles was aware that the Indonesian air force had been particularly active for some time, trying to regain its edge after the recession that gutted the Asian Tiger economies and the subsequent fiscal constraints imposed by the World Bank. Perhaps it was this knowledge that activated the IAE's personal radar. She had already passed on some recent interceptions from Indonesia to HQ in Maryland. There was something irregular about them. Why? Had she been asked, Ruth wouldn't have known, but she always listened to her inner voice, no matter how faint its call.

Ruth tried to remember who the analyst for South-East Asia was. Wasn't it Gioco? Hadn't she met him at one of the conferences held to foster interdepartmental cooperation within COMINT, the communications intelligence department of the NSA? She tapped the enquiry into the box. The answer was instantaneous. Yes, Bob Gioco: thoughtful, intelligent, hard-working. Unusual name for a black man though, she thought.

Sydney, 2150 Zulu, Tuesday, 28 April

ABC Radio 702: 'We interrupt this program to bring you a news flash. Qantas Flight 1, en-route from Sydney to London via Bangkok, is missing, feared crashed.

'Unconfirmed reports are that the 747-400 disappeared from Bali Air Traffic Control radar screens in the early hours of the morning, local time.

'Just repeating: fears are that Qantas Flight QF-1, the regular service from Sydney to London, has crashed. We will bring you more news on this as developments come to hand.'

Parliament House, Canberra, 2155 Zulu, Tuesday, 28 April

Another uncomfortable silence filled the room. The Prime Minister of Australia, The Right Honourable William (Bill) Blight, glanced at the window and allowed his eyes to focus beyond the raindrops spattering the glass pane. The trees in the grounds of Parliament House had lost most of their leaves, letting them go in a circle of gold on the emerald couch below. Autumn. It occurred to Blight that he didn't much care for the view. It was sentimental, almost soppy. He preferred the iron trunks of heavy lift cranes that had formed part of the vista of most of his working life, and the ordered ranks of rusting containers that clanged like giant bells when dropped. What the hell am I doing here in this place? he wondered, vaguely aware that the Indonesian ambassador, Parno Batuta, had begun to speak again. Blight blinked, waking from a daydream edged by the oily rainbows that filled the puddles on the docks.

'Once again, Mr Prime Minister, let me say how sorry I am,' said Batuta, eyes lowered.

'I appreciate your authorities informing us so quickly of this disaster. Do your people know yet exactly where the plane came down?' asked Blight.

'No. Our military and civil aviation authorities hold different opinions, but no one has had the time to review all the facts. The natural assumption is that the aircraft has come down where it disappeared from radar on the island of Sulawesi. But our military believes the plane could also have flown on outside Indonesian airspace. We are testing both theories. Our air force has pledged every available aircraft for the search and I have been assured that we will find it quickly.'

'Can we provide any assistance?'

'Thank you, Prime Minister. I will ask our air force people if there's anything Australia can do. Colonel Ari Ajirake, one of our most senior officers, is personally overseeing the search. I'm sure he would welcome your support to bring this tragedy to a speedy conclusion.'

Blight nodded. He was detached and distant. A frown deeply lined his forehead and the corners of his mouth were weighed down.

'Mr Prime Minister, I assure you my country has no residual enmity for Australia,' said Batuta, wringing his hands. 'East Timor is behind us and I promise you we will do absolutely everything we can to find the Qantas plane as quickly as possible.'

Blight realised that he had been cool, even cold, and that talking to him had probably been a bit like conversing with a wall, lengthy silences punctuating the conversation. Perhaps the ambassador had translated this difficulty as a sign that he felt Indonesia was in some way responsible for the crash. That was nonsense. Blight smiled wanly, apologetically, and did his best to reassure the envoy. 'I'm sorry, Mr Ambassador, I'm sure you will. And thank you. I appreciate you coming over. I'm sure Indonesia will do everything it can to help us in this dark hour. I'm just a bit preoccupied.'

'Not at all. Understandable,' replied Batuta, relieved and smiling with a tilt of his head that conveyed understanding, sympathy and sadness all at once.

There was nothing more that could be said. Blight stood and Batuta followed his lead. The ambassador usually found the Prime Minister loud and physically intimidating. But here, in this situation, Blight appeared much smaller than usual, almost life-size. Batuta preferred him that way.

The Prime Minister's PA popped her head around the door as soon as the ambassador departed. 'Shirley, tell the Air Vice Marshal to come in,' said the PM. Blight stood and stretched his thick arms out behind his broad back. He felt and heard a couple of bones pop and crack. 'Bloody hell, it's going to be a god-awful day,' he sighed as the Commander in Chief of the Australian Defence Forces walked in. 'Take a seat, Spike,' said the PM.

Blight sucked in a breath. There were no pleasantries. 'Okay, the Indonesians are doing everything they can. The question is, what can we do?'

The phone rang in the adjoining room. Shirley answered it. A moment later, there was a tap on the door as it swung quietly open. With her small, sharp-featured face and pinched mouth, Shirley could easily have passed for a disciplinary officer in a correctional facility for girls. 'Excuse me, Bill. Line two.'

'Yes?' he said into the receiver impatiently. What he

heard made the PM's face blench visibly. He hung up the phone slowly. 'Andrew Harris and his whole family – wife and four kids – were on QF-1.' Blight knew that Harry, the Minister for Industry and Workplace Relations, was taking his family to England on holiday, but he had refused to entertain the thought that his best mate and close colleague had chosen to fly Qantas, and was therefore probably on the missing flight. But there it was, the phone call he'd been dreading. The news gutted him and he needed to sit. Alone.

'Jesus . . . ' he said.

Central Sulawesi, 0130 Zulu, Wednesday, 29 April

Joe was caught in a tunnel. He knew there was an end to it but he couldn't see it. He was falling and the tunnel was swirling. It felt like he was in the centre of a tornado. The forces in its centre were powerful, pulling the skin on his face and pushing it into rolls, as if he was an astronaut in a centrifuge.

He found it hard to breathe. The pressure was sucking the air from his lungs. And then something changed. He found himself in the very centre of the tunnel. It was calm here and he began to float. The tugging stopped, remnants of it dragging lightly at his legs then at his toes and then, gone. Above, there was light.

Joe's eyes flickered. He was reluctant to open them. His head hurt. Every muscle in his body felt like it had been pummelled, beaten black and blue by an opponent a couple of weight divisions heavier than him. Something was pinning him down and he sensed that he should move with caution. He wondered why he should be feeling so sore, and then he remembered. Surely the crash had been a dream too? He reluctantly opened his eyes. The ground was fifteen to twenty metres below him. It hadn't been a dream. The blood pounded behind his eyeballs. He moved his head to better take in his surroundings and he discovered that he was in a tree, still strapped into his seat, only upside down. The whole thing must have been ripped out of the plane. His mind was working, but only just. *I'm alive. Jesus, I'm alive.*

Joe remained still for a time, pulse thumping in his head, and he marvelled at his astonishing good luck. He was suspended, secured by his lap restraint. If he unclipped it, he would fall to the ground and it was a long way down. Wouldn't that be ironic? *Survive the plane crash and get killed by my own stupidity.* He did a mental check of his body. He didn't think anything was broken, but the bruises were painful.

Joe hooked an arm around the back of the seat and carefully unclipped the restraint. He slid forward. The shift in weight destroyed the balance of the seat. It fell several metres before being caught in another fork. The fall was fortunate, though, because it brought Joe's feet into contact with a branch. His legs took his weight, but they were rubbery. He collapsed and fell the last five metres, landing on a canvas duffel bag full of air and clothes.

There was a large, torn sheet of aluminium lying not far from the tree. The tail of the letter Q filled one corner. Joe recognised it as a section of the plane's fuselage. He went over to the sheet and lifted it up. It was warm to the touch. A man, a woman and two young children were huddled beneath it. The man looked familiar. They had shared the first-class section with him. The children had been noisy, bugging him, pushing the back of his seat continually as they got up and down, came in and out. Now it looked like they were all asleep, peaceful. Joe bent down and nudged the man. 'Hey, mate,' he said quietly. The man didn't move. Neither did his wife or kids. It took a few more prods before Joe realised that they were dead.

He was briefly afraid of the bodies, wary that their death might somehow infect him with their lifelessness. A whole family. Gone.

Joe turned around slowly on the spot, and found it impossible to comprehend the world around him. It reminded him of a rubbish tip, but no tip he'd ever seen was as gruesome as this, for bits of human bodies were strewn around together with clothes and luggage and scrap metal. The clearing carved in the jungle by the 747 was an open wound. Leaf litter and splintered tree trunks were churned with the contents of hundreds of suitcases flung from the aircraft as it tumbled through its landing. Few bodies were intact. Arms and legs were ripped from hips and shoulders, and hands lay here and there like stiff blue spiders. Already, ants, flies and beetles had found paths to the gore. They probed through earth that looked like melted dark chocolate because of all the blood.

Everywhere, bits of metal and rubber burned and smoked. An enormous section of wing was engulfed in flame and billowed black clouds. Little of the 747's superstructure was recognisable. Joe couldn't see the tail section anywhere. The nose of the aircraft was flattened, punched inwards. Broken seats were scattered all over, some with passengers still strapped in. A few seats had been tossed high into the trees where they hung like ghoulish ornaments. Joe stumbled through the ragged piles of clothing, broken bodies and twisted metal as if in a dream. The obscene smell of hot kerosene and barbecuing flesh filled his nostrils.

Things like this did not happen to Joe. His mind rebelled and shut down, wrapping itself in cotton wool. A woman's arm, wrenched clean off a shoulder, complete with gold watch and painted red fingernails, lay on the dirt. The reality of it pierced Joe's defences. He fell to his knees and heaved yellow bile from his empty stomach.

Something moved under him. He felt it, then heard a groan. He scrabbled back and saw a foot shift in the debris. Joe ran forward and lifted back a row of seats. Underneath, an elderly man and woman untangled themselves from the debris. The old woman let out a sharp cry. The man, sobbing, held his wife's dirty face in his hands and kissed it over and over. Her leg was bent back on itself, badly broken. She shrieked as Joe lifted away a suitcase.

'I'm sorry,' said Joe in a dry, cracked voice that sounded alien to him. 'Your leg . . . '

The old man and woman ignored him. Joe searched the immediate area for something to use as a splint. He returned with a length of aluminium tubing and pantyhose taken from one of the hundreds of suitcases ripped open, the contents scattered across the ground. He didn't really know what he was doing, but he'd seen broken legs fixed on television often enough to know that he had to straighten and secure it somehow.

Joe knelt beside the couple and carefully pulled away the bits of suitcases, clothing, and a bloody foot in a boot. He wondered what had saved this couple. Maybe they were just lucky like him, plucked from certain death by a quirk of fate. The old man, he saw, was practically untouched. He wore an expensive suit and it was remarkably clean. The woman, also, was immaculately dressed. He vaguely recognised them. More fellow first-class passengers.

'Hey,' said Joe, giving the man's arm a gentle nudge. The old man looked up with moist, rheumy eyes. 'Your wife. We have to fix her leg.' It was obvious from the man's blank look that he hadn't heard him, or that shock had prevented him from understanding.

'Your wife's leg is broken,' Joe repeated, directing the man's gaze to the bizarre angle of the limb, poking up under her skirt. The old man nodded finally. He wrapped his arms around his wife's shoulders in a bear hug as they lay there on the ground. Joe held her lower leg, wrapping his arm firmly around her foot and slowly, firmly, pulled back.

The woman's scream launched a flock of birds come to watch the grim spectacle from the safety of a nearby tree. They flew off, squawking, into the humid, grey morning sky.

Maros, Sulawesi, 0350 Zulu, Wednesday, 29 April

The young woman manoeuvred her tricycle through the narrow street. It was difficult to see over the top of the oven perched on the front wheels, stuffed with ears of corn. She had to lean out far to one side to see. She moved from one side of the trike to the other, hanging out like a sailor on a trapeze, tapping at the horn continuously to warn the dogs that slept dangerously close to the edge of the road, or to someone ahead on another bike, that she was closing in on them from behind.

It was practically midday and she was very late, not that she had a boss she had to check in with. But the world she lived in had a good ten hours head start, frantically trying to keep its head above the poverty line. People were slicing fruit, carrying bricks, hacking open coconuts, selling, hawking, scrabbling, feeding children or pigs, mending clothes, making clothes, firing bricks and roof tiles, planting rice, fertilising, tilling, serving, sharpening, sweeping, living and dying – all by the roadside. Indonesia was the busiest, most industrious country on earth. It had to be, thought the young woman. Everyone had a job, except for the very young, the very old or the enfeebled. In fact, most people had two or three jobs, just to keep themselves clothed and fed. And they all helped each other, supported each other, and in a way that neighbours back home rarely did. There was a fellowship here, a genuine community. There had to be something going for Maros, because it certainly wasn't the town itself. It was hot, dusty, noisy and smelly. One would have to have been born here to love it, she thought. She still found it hard to believe that such a shithole could produce such a friendly people.

The young woman arrived at her usual spot and parked the trike. She dismounted and hurriedly set up her stall, tearing husks from the ears and placing the corn in the portable oven. She noted that a competitor a little further back down the road, Sekrit, had already sold about a third of his load. She waved to him. Half those sales should have been hers, she thought angrily.

And then she laughed. What did she care, really? She

wasn't in the hot corn business. She was so deep under cover that sometimes she forgot who she was, and what she was doing. There were some soldiers from the base meandering down the road on foot. She held up her corn, kernels burned black by the oven's heat, and shouted her singsong sales pitch at them. Her corn was the freshest. Her corn was the tastiest. Her corn was the cheapest. None of which was true but that hardly seemed important. Everyone exaggerated; it was part of the pitch.

There were more soldiers than usual on the road, and some of them seemed edgy, in a hurry. She tried to engage a soldier in conversation, but all she got was a terse, barked reply for her to hurry and to stop chattering like a monkey.

A-6, as her employers in Canberra knew her, was the perfect spy. Her skin said Indonesian, but her heart was Australian. Despite frantic attempts to remedy the situation, Australia didn't have enough HUMINT – spies – in Indonesia, certainly not enough to provide reliable intelligence on a nation that stretched across some 17 000 islands and embraced more than 219 million people. Most of the assets it did manage to have on the ground had a similar profile to A-6.

She didn't stand out. In many respects, she was unimpressive, being of average height and weight. She was neither ugly nor particularly attractive. She spoke Indonesian like a local. She also had a deep love of her adopted country, Australia, and an equally deep sadness for what she believed Indonesia had become. A-6 wrapped another ear in newsprint and handed it to the soldier, who rudely flicked a note at her.

A truck ground to a halt in front of her stall, blowing a cloud of road grit into her face. A couple of soldiers jumped down from the cabin. They were the Kopassus, the elite. She'd been wary of these men from the start. They were haughty, dangerous.

She knew one of them well. He put his face close to her so that she could smell his sour breath and demanded half a dozen cobs in that sneering way of his. She smiled helpfully, trying hard not to let her resentment or her fear show, and handed him the corn. He didn't pay; he never did. He just turned and swaggered back to the truck.

She cast her mind back to their first meeting. It had been at night and she had heard screams coming from an alley. She went to investigate and came upon a young woman lying naked on the ground, a Kopassus soldier holding her face in the mud as he rammed into her. A-6 started yelling at the man to get off. Another soldier came out of the shadows and grabbed her arm. A knife was under her throat. She felt the sharp edge against her skin and smelled the oil on the blade. She looked down and saw that his pants were undone and his fly was open. He'd either had his turn, or was about to have it.

The soldier with the knife recognised her as the woman who sold corn in front of the barracks. He forced her against a wall, grabbed a handful of hair and hacked away at it with his knife, pulling out whole handfuls of it by the roots. He did it smiling through her pleadings and then her screams.

He said it was fortunate for the woman under his corporal that the 'corn cob girl', as he called her, had happened along. They didn't have to kill her now, he said, waving the dagger at the woman on the ground, because each was a hostage for the other. A-6 suddenly realised that he was right. If she managed to find a sympathetic policeman prepared to investigate, someone who wasn't afraid of the army – and that was unlikely, she reminded herself – then the soldier would kill the woman in the mud, thereby disposing of the evidence. And if the victim complained, then she, the corn cob girl, would be killed. More than likely, in either event they'd both end up dead. Ripping out her hair was merely underlining the assertion that he meant what he said. But her intervention had been stupid because she'd ceased to be anonymous. But what could she have done, she admonished herself, ignored what was going on?

A-6 remembered that particular soldier, the sergeant with smallpox scars covering his round face. Her hair grew back but her fear of him remained. She learned from other soldiers that his name was Marturak, Sergeant Marturak. She called him 'Sergeant Melon' after the large, evil-smelling durian that had similarly rough skin. Every morning Sergeant Melon took corn from her stall, often taunting and jeering at her about her plain, unattractive appearance.

Indonesia seemed full of men like Sergeant Melon, men who had achieved power and used it as an excuse to threaten and bully others. She was sure, however, that her father, a colonel in the Indonesian army, had not been like this pig. He had commanded an artillery regiment. A-6 often talked to her mother about him. He had been a highly decorated soldier who had fought the Japanese during the war, and the Dutch imperialists after it. He was not a politician or a warmonger, he just believed in Indonesia, strong and independent.

Then things started to go wrong. The Communists in the army were getting bolder. The Soviets were filling the military's armoury with hardware and its head with idealistic rubbish. The army divided into factions. Her father was asked to join both and he declined both, which made him the friend of neither.

One night when her father was sleeping at the barracks, they came for him. No one knew whether it was the Communists or the Nationalists but a lot of men died that night when the old government was removed with bullets and knives.

Her mother had scooped her up from her cot and 'friendlies' had smuggled them to Singapore. From there they went to Australia and applied for refugee status. The colonel had been highly regarded by senior Australian army officers. That helped them win their refugee status and A-6 spent the next sixteen years of her life growing into a proud Australian woman.

And then one day, a young man, a total stranger, approached her. He showed her ghastly photographs of her father snapped after *they* had finished with him. The man asked her whether she wanted to avenge her father's death. Looking back on it, the whole episode had been unconvincing. Nevertheless, she'd fallen for it. Now, she couldn't even be sure the photos had been genuine. They could easily have been faked. They could also have been real and the man being tortured could have been anyone. But she had been vulnerable. She'd heard many stories about her father, how much he'd loved her when she was a baby. A-6 even believed that she remembered him as a large and friendly shadow in the most distant reaches of her memory. She had said to the man that she wanted time to think but she already knew that the answer was yes.

She spent the next three months learning basic spycraft,

self-defence, and how to pass herself off as a poor Indonesian. That was two years ago.

At first A-6 enjoyed the cloak and dagger stuff. It was easy being a spy in the new millennium. All she had to do was call in detailed reports of troop deployments in and around Hasanuddin AFB. For this she was given a satellite phone. The techies back home were a bit concerned about that at first. The handset was nothing special. It looked just like any old Nokia. The dish, however, was more obtrusive, even though it was small, about the size of a small dinner plate. A woman with an old mobile wasn't in the least unusual, but a satellite phone? It turned out not to be an issue. Satellite TV was everywhere in Sulawesi, or throughout Maros at least. It was cheap, easy entertainment. It was almost unusual *not* to have it and a dish sat on even the poorest roof.

The phone could be used as a normal mobile but to use it as a satellite phone, she had to key in a ten-digit code. The handset then scrambled her voice into a random binary code and transmitted it on a scattered frequency to a military communications satellite. It was important that her calls could not be intercepted, unscrambled or traced without considerable effort. It was just prudent to be out of sight when she phoned in her reports. No big deal, she'd thought, although finding privacy in Maros was difficult.

Her run-in with Sergeant Melon demonstrated how serious and dangerous espionage was. And the current amicable relationship between Australia and Indonesia could turn ugly in a heartbeat, as it had often enough in the past. If she was caught when things were tense, there was the likelihood that she would be taken away and shot, unless there was political mileage to be gained by parading her through the courts. And then they'd shoot her.

A-6 wondered what it would be like to be a normal woman again, going to parties, the beach, nightclubs. It would be nice to dance, meet boys and have a normal life. The danger was all getting a bit too close now, especially given the continued contact with Sergeant Melon.

A-6 gave herself another six months. After that, she would review her situation. But in the meantime, something unusual was definitely going on in town. She heard the choppers before she saw them: two large Super Pumas came in low and lifted the tiles off several roofs, flinging them into the narrow, dank lanes. They cruised unhurriedly overhead at barely a walking pace. A-6 put a hand over her nose and mouth to protect her lungs from the dust picked up by the powerful downwash of the rotor blades, and squinted up at the aircraft through the stinging cones of sandblast. She was just in time to see that the helo was full of Kopassus soldiers before Sergeant Melon pushed the door shut. The aircraft then accelerated quickly into a climb.

The thump of the Super Pumas faded to a distant beat before A-6 started up her trike. Something of interest was happening somewhere if two Super Pumas full of Indonesia's crack soldiers were hurriedly being airlifted to . . . where? She would try to find out, but didn't like her chances. The Kopassus weren't the most talkative people and asking direct questions could prove unhealthy.

Exmouth Gulf, 0455 Zulu, Wednesday, 29 April

The Joint US-Australian Facility at Exmouth Gulf in the far north of Australia received the transmission from A-6.

The report from the asset was brief and processed by one of the US Air Force Security Services Signals Intelligence personnel.

The report read: 'A-6 Stat. 39. 29040440/29040453/TM VS-K UN/S 20-30 H2 B360 ENQ/D U.' It came off the printer and the corporal looked at it blankly. The sequence was decoded, but it still might as well have been Latin for the Sig Op had no 'need to know', therefore the significance of the string of numbers and letters was opaque to him.

It had to be one of the most boring jobs in the world, he told himself. Right up there with working on an assembly line, sticking widgets in boxes all day long. From morning till night he looked at shit that meant nothing to him. Then, at the end of the day, he went home to fuck-all nothing out here in the desert. No bitches except for really ugly ones, but at least there was plenty of beer to improve their looks. Lots of flies, though. Sticky motherfuckers that wouldn't take no for an answer.

The corporal took another look at the sequence on his screen. The one thing he did know was that Stat. 39 meant Station 39, or 'somewhere in Indonesia'. Another godforsaken shithole, no doubt, he told himself.

So much for 'join the air force and see the world'. If he was outside, he would have spat.

He sent on the slip – the coded sequence – via sealed hardline intranet to NSA, Hawaii, and copied the information to the local intelligence services as per the standard operational bullshit.

NSA, Helemanu, Oahu, Hawaii, 0457 Zulu, Wednesday, 29 April

Ruth was now on the lookout for anything from Indonesia and had coded her etray accordingly. The slip popped into the box and launched a flashing red exclamation mark on her desktop. She read it. The message didn't clarify anything for her but it certainly added to her disquiet. Something was definitely going on down there, she thought. Ruth pondered the significance of the information for a minute before snapping out of the trance. She dragged and dropped it into the box she'd created especially for Bob Gioco. Ruth shook her head. That inner voice was screaming at her, but she couldn't make out what it was saying.

NSA Headquarters, Fort Meade, 0500 Zulu, Wednesday, 29 April

Bob Gioco, NSA Group Analyst for South-East Asia, was gazing sleepily at his computer screen when the slip arrived. One in the morning. It was time to go home and he was dead on his feet. It had been a shit of a day, and he had a headache squeezing his head like a tight helmet. The icon popped up yet again telling him something had arrived for his attention. He clicked on it and the slip came up in a box: 'A-6 Stat. 39. 29040440/29040453/TM VS-K UN/S 20-30 H2 B360 ENQ/D U.' It got his attention. Indonesia. Anything from that part of the world did at that moment. There was that Qantas plane down in the area. Perhaps it had been found.

Bob translated the figure groups in his mind: A-6, an asset shared with an Australian intelligence service, with a report from Station 39, that's Maros near Makassar (formerly Ujang Padang) in Indonesia – on the southern end of Sulawesi. A-6 made the observation on the 29th of the 4th at 0440 Zulu time, and thirteen minutes had passed before she made the report at 0453. He glanced at his watch to check the date and time. Maryland was five hours behind Greenwich Mean Time, or Universal Coordinated Time as it was now known – fourteen hours behind Sulawesi. Whatever this report was about had happened just twenty minutes ago in a small town on a forgotten island off the world's radar screen. In other words the system was working, thanks to intel sharing and this A-6 asset who was obviously one on-the-ball individual. Gioco ignored his headache, sipped his decaf cappuccino and considered the information contained in the string of numbers and letters.

Okay, A-6 has had a TM VS-K or a troop movement confirmed visually of Kopassus units. She was UN/S or unsure of numbers but 20-30 is the estimate. They are in H2, two helos, departing on a bearing of 360 (north). ENQ/D – enquire question/destination, which means she has no idea where the helos are going. The observation, she thinks, is U – unusual.

Yes it was a bit *U*, but only a little. The Indonesian forces had been active for months now. And besides, there were much more interesting things going on, like that missing Qantas jumbo. The activity A-6 was reporting was in the right area, he observed again. Perhaps the

Indonesians were sending in Kopassus troops to help find the thing. They were jungle-trained specialists. There was plenty of jungle on Sulawesi. It made sense. Kind of. But there was something . . .

The debate going on in Gioco's mind was whether this had anything to do with terrorism. Planes did occasionally crash for reasons that had nothing to do with nutters prepared to die for some cause and take as many innocent civilians with them as possible. Terror was now the prime suspect whenever and wherever a plane went down. Indonesia . . . Hmm . . . Gioco distractedly chewed the end of a pencil. He knew the Australians had always been leery of the place – a big, sprawling country with porous borders, a succession of less than democratic governments, a fractious military, and a questionable human rights record. And recently, the realisation that terrorist groups linked to al Qaeda were flourishing there, hiding out in Java's rugged mountains.

South-East Asia had been targeted by the US as a potential terrorist hotbed, but not so much Indonesia. It was more the Philippines people here were concerned about. Then Bali happened. Was this 747 thing more of the same? Gioco absently made popping sounds with his mouth while he mulled through things. He tapped the pencil on his desk, a syncopated beat. There was nothing solid here to go forward on. He decided to give this one the benefit of the doubt, unless something else turned up to change his mind, of course.

Gioco went back to his slips. He had another two hundred or so to review and analyse before his day was done. He wouldn't get home for at least another hour. No doubt there would be other interesting and relevant slips amongst the dross. He tapped the keystroke that fixed the slip from A-6 onto a desktop noticeboard, and attached a small flashing star to it. Bob found this system a good way to work. A lot of meaningless crap drifted into his etray. He took out the interesting or relevant slips from his pile and pinned them on the board for later review. The slip from Station 39 joined a couple of other unconnected slips forwarded by that old battleaxe in Hawaii. What was her name . . .?

Parliament House, Canberra, 0500 Zulu, Wednesday, 29 April

The PM sat at his desk with his head in his hands. Losing such a close friend made him physically ache. And Harry's entire family had perished with him. He wondered about the chances of surviving a plane crash. The only connection he'd had with such events in the past was, as for most people, through news reports. Do people walk away from such things? It occurred to Blight that the friends and family of the passengers aboard the Qantas flight were probably feeling every bit as confused as he was, switching between grief and hope. *What if my own kids were aboard that plane?* He was able to visualise their final moments filled with terror, and the picture almost made him feel ill.

Answers. Bloody answers, that's what we need.

Qantas confirmed that the aircraft had crashed. The wreckage hadn't been located yet but it had to have come down. It was only carrying enough fuel for the Bangkok leg and time was well and truly up.

The country was already in deep shock. There was disbelief on everyone's face. Was this the work of terrorists again? That was Blight's first thought, so it had to be everyone else's too. Australia had once enjoyed the benefits of being isolated, a backwater. Then those days had come to a bloody end in a couple of tourist bars on his favourite holiday island. On some level attributing the plane's disappearance to an act of terrorism made the situation easier to come to terms with. This was a Qantas plane and Qantas planes just *did not crash*. The thing couldn't have come down for no reason, surely? Qantas had suffered some embarrassing 'incidents' in recent years, but the carrier's unequalled safety record had been maintained, and so had the public's faith in the carrier.

To lose a 747 was bad enough. To have no idea *where* it had come down made things a damn sight worse. Somewhere out there, four hundred people, many of them Australian citizens, were dead or dying of their injuries.

The Chief of the Defence Force, Ted 'Spike' Niven, tapped on the open adjoining door.

'Come in, Spike,' said the PM, motioning the country's most senior officer towards the leather chesterfield opposite.

In his day, Niven had been one of Australia's top fighter pilots. He had a mind that was relentlessly calculating, even under the stress of battle, and his hand–eye coordination was phenomenal. Blight had previously reviewed the man's record. As a young flight lieutenant he'd been sent to the US by the RAAF as part of an exchange program. The RAAF wanted the best pilots and the US had the finest combat training programs, the most famous being the US Navy's Top Gun Academy. The Australian proved an apt pupil. Once he'd come to grips with the extra power available from the American-specification F/A-18, Squadron Leader Ted Niven was unbeatable. No matter what the instructors threw at him, the Australian could find a winning answer. And if he got on your tail, he waxed it and you lost.

The Yanks gave him the call sign 'Spike'. They joked that it had nothing to do with his flying – it was because once he had his teeth into you, he never let you go. The truth was that Niven looked disturbingly like Spike, the bulldog who featured in Warner Brothers' Sylvester cartoons. His dark eyes were set wide apart on a square face with a small button-nose underlined by an aggressive jaw with a slight overbite. He was also short, barrel-chested, and had slightly bowed legs. Spike he had been christened, and Spike he had remained.

Niven's tour of the States had been in the early eighties. Now, at forty-seven, he was the youngest-ever CDF. 'Sorry for the intrusion, Prime Minister, but I have a thought on how QF-1 could be located quickly,' he said, scowling. He'd just heard that one of the men from his former squadron had been a pilot on the ill-fated jumbo's flight deck. Niven hadn't met the man, but the connection still added a per-sonal element to the tragedy. 'I also think, if you don't mind, that it'd be worthwhile bringing Graeme Griffin into the loop.'

Griffin was the Director-General of the Australian Secret Intelligence Service, a man Niven could always rely on to play it straight. The two men had been to university together, played football together, and had even been out with a few of the same women.

'Ahead of you there, Spike. Shirley?' he said, raising his voice so it would carry over the thick carpet. 'Could you get Graeme Griffin in here? And ask Phil Sharpe to come over too.'

Niven scowled again, this time intentionally. He couldn't think of one issue he and Sharpe agreed on.

The PA appeared around the door. 'Anything else?'

'No thanks, mate,' said Blight, treating the woman who'd been his PA for twenty years no differently to one of the boys.

The two men made small talk for a couple of minutes while they waited for Griffin and the Minister for Foreign Affairs to arrive, but the conversation was awkward. Both men wanted action, not talk, and were soon lost in the silence of their own thoughts.

Shirley hurried in with a jug of water and some glasses and left saying, 'If you need anything, call.'

The Prime Minister nodded.

'Prime Minister, Spike,' Griffin said as he entered the office and sat beside the CDF. The ASIS chief was tall and wiry with hard blue eyes softened by deep laugh lines at the corners. He wore his grey hair cropped short, military style.

The Minister for Foreign Affairs, Phil Sharpe, followed, settling comfortably into a chair under the window. He ran his hands through the thick, mouse-coloured hair that hung down his tanned forehead like rope, repositioning it back on top of his head. He affected a hint of a smile, as if he'd just shared a witticism at someone else's expense before entering the room. Niven and the minister didn't get on. Neither man knew why, it was just chemistry, or lack of it. Griffin and Sharpe shook hands and were cordial to each other – ASIS answered to the Department of Foreign Affairs and Trade.

Niven noted that, as usual, Sharpe wore an imported, dark navy suit and a hard white shirt. His tie had been chosen to make a statement. On other occasions, Niven had joked to himself that the statement was probably something like, 'Hey, look at me, I'm an arsehole.' The CDF caught a whiff of the man's aftershave. It was the one he used. Niven made a mental note to pour the remains of his bottle down the sink.

'Prime Minister, if I may start?' asked the ADF chief. Blight nodded.

'I've been doing some checking with both my own people and Qantas.' He opened an atlas he had brought with him at the marked spread and pointed at Sulawesi in the Indonesian archipelago. He also pulled out a World Area Chart of Sulawesi, the kind of map aviators use to navigate visually over terrain. The track of the 747 had been drawn on the map with greasy red pencil. The track ended with a red cross. A semicircle, also drawn in red, about eight centimetres in diameter, fanned around from the X.

'The X represents the approximate coordinates of QF-1 at about the time it disappeared from ATC screens, taking into account wind and other factors. We're not exactly sure of the position because the Indons haven't released the ATC disks that would give us the precise latitude and longitude. Nevertheless, our people are pretty sure of the plane's position in the sky when it was reported to have gone missing.

'Now, the 747 will be somewhere within this circle. To suggest it might have come down elsewhere is ridiculous,' he said quietly but firmly.

Niven studied the red track that ended in a cross on the map, and massaged his chin in thought. 'All kinds of different communications link 747s with various traffic control systems and satellites and there's a shit-load of redundancy built in. These planes don't just go missing. So when that traffic controller in Denpasar says QF-1's transponder code went out, along with all its communications gear, well . . . I hate to say it, but there are a few things capable of doing that and most of them make a nasty mess of an aircraft when they go off.

'There is the remotest possibility that QF-1 could have been flying out of control in a wide but decreasing downward spiral, which is why I've drawn in this semicircle here,' he said, pointing to the pencilled area on the WAC. 'Whether it blew up in the sky or crash-landed, QF-1's somewhere here.' He tapped the X marked on the map with his index finger.

'I'm not sure what your point is, Spike,' Sharpe said. 'We're in Indonesia's hands. It's their territory, and they do have the men and equipment needed to locate the crash site. It's frustrating but we'll just have to wait and see what they turn up. Also, let's not forget that the plane only went down,' he checked his watch, 'maybe eight hours ago, so we can hardly accuse them of dragging the chain. Then there's the terrain it went down in. Sulawesi is not a very hospitable place; most of it's covered in jungle and volcanoes.'

Griffin agreed. 'A fair percentage of the island has been logged but there are still quite a few impenetrable pockets. It's the proverbial haystack.'

Sharpe nodded.

Niven was undeterred. 'All of which adds weight to my view. I want to ask the US to use one of their military satellites to scan the area I've indicated on the WAC. I can't believe the Indonesians would object to that. If we scanned five nautical mile segments, there'd be enough resolution to see a crashed 747 and cover around one hundred square miles in only twenty passes. The satellites I'm talking about have a two-hour period, so the entire area would be covered in around forty hours.

'And there was a lot of fuel on board the aircraft. Ground fires in this area would show up like searchlights on infrared film.'

Blight winced as the picture of people burning in firestorms flashed through his mind.

'Good idea. We might even find the site on the first or second pass,' said Griffin.

'Exactly,' said Niven. 'As I said, the Indonesians could hardly object. It would save them a hell of a lot of money and, of course, get the plane found as quickly as possible. Good for them. Good for us. Everyone wins.' Niven's enthusiasm was infectious.

'Alright,' said the PM. 'If there's one thing I hate, it's sitting around on my arse. Our ambassador in Washington can handle the liaison.'

'Okay, so what about the question of terror?' Niven asked. It was the thought on all their minds.

'What about it?' said Sharpe.

'I jumped to that conclusion too, Spike, but so far there's not a shred of evidence to support it,' said Griffin.

'And aside from that, terror just doesn't *feel* right,' said Blight, rubbing his temples. 'Not on this one. It's all too quiet. Terrorists make grand media statements, don't they? The USS *Cole*, the Pentagon, New York, Bali, that awful strike in London. A plane going down in the middle of the night, just disappearing like this . . . does it fit the terrorist model?'

'I know, Prime Minister, I don't want to believe the worst either, but until we hear otherwise, we can't eliminate it completely, can we?' Niven had national defence issues to consider and he wasn't going to turn his back on them.

'Christ,' Blight said, frowning. 'I guess not.' The PM had slumped into a ball behind his desk. He was short and thickset, his body fashioned by thirty years of hard labour on the waterfront. Large hands with fingers like sausages spoke of physical power, and his skin was leathery from the sun. Until recently, a robust belly had hung over his belt, the product of years of supporting local breweries, but the minders had worked on him for the sake of his television profile, employing trainers to reduce it.

The press called him 'Bloody-hell Blight', or 'Blue Blight', for his love of colourful language, and that was one characteristic the spin doctors had been unable to change. The average man in the street loved him for it, though. He was human, a welcome change from the years of cocky conservatism.

Central Sulawesi, 0600 Zulu, Wednesday, 29 April

Joe Light swatted ineffectually at the swarm of mosquitoes. Feeling nauseous and utterly helpless, he peered down on the crash site from his new vantage point on an adjacent hill. The plane was far enough away for the detail to be lost but the overall picture was still terrible. He put the compact Bausch & Lomb binoculars he'd found still tangled in their duty-free wrapping to his eyes and centred the old couple in the lenses. He waved exaggeratedly at the old bloke. The man and his wife were now propped under the shelter he'd built for them, scavenged from bits of aircraft aluminium.

Their names were Jim and Margaret. Jim had been in shock and it had taken a while to get his name out of him. Margaret was unconscious when he'd left, probably from the agony of her broken leg.

Joe had gone searching amongst the debris for other survivors, and for painkillers for Margaret. He hadn't found either. At first he'd been uncomfortable sifting through other people's luggage but the pangs quickly passed. The passengers had no further use for their things. That change in his outlook coincided with the find of the binoculars.

Joe took a deep breath, filling his lungs. The air here was hot and moist and mercifully clear of the smell of jet fuel and roasted flesh. The equatorial sun and high humidity were already going to work on the hundreds of broken bodies lying around. Down at the crash site, a sickly-sweet smell had begun to rise from the ground. The first signs of decay.

Joe looked up at the sky. Unbroken grey cloud sat overhead like dirty cotton wool. Where was help? Why wasn't this place swarming with rescue operations? He then realised he had no idea where 'this place' was. He knew that it certainly wasn't Australia – the captain had told them when the last of the Australian coastline slipped by beneath the plane. That had been quite a few hours before the jumbo fell out of the sky. Was he in Malaysia, or Indonesia? Burma, Thailand? Geography was never his strong suit.

The aircraft's landing had stripped the area of trees. He saw that their runway was actually a depression surrounded by hillocks and the plane was lucky not to have hit one. Lucky? Only three passengers had survived the crash out of . . . he didn't know how many. That was hardly lucky.

The terrain they had landed in was relatively low lying. He surveyed the horizon. Wherever they were, it was remote. He could see no smoke from fires, save from the bits of aircraft still smouldering. No signs of population or civilisation. If there were people in the vicinity they were doing a bloody good job of making themselves scarce.

He turned around, keeping the binoculars to his eyes. Off in the distance was the perfect conical base of a gigantic mountain that towered above the rest, its summit disappearing into haze and cloud. He let the rucksack slip from his shoulder and the bottles of water spilled out onto the ground. He'd found the bottles, along with some food in packaged trays, after rummaging through a section of the galley searching for other survivors. The galley that had been ripped from the fuselage and thrown 400 metres up a ravine.

He'd also found a piece of wing flap attached to an aluminium rib. The implement looked like an axe. He swung it through the air. Felt like one, too. Joe used it to pick through the debris. It was also pretty effective at hacking through the vegetation on the hillock. He wanted to clear away a section of it and set up a campsite for himself and the two old people, well away from the bodies and the aeroplane, although God only knew how they were going to lug Margaret up here with her broken leg.

The hillock wasn't far from the crash site – about six

hundred metres – but it was a difficult trek, much of it through tall, thick razor grass that did its best to flay the skin from his bones. He looked at the deep scratches cross-hatching the flesh on his forearms. A collection of bugs fought with flies and mosquitoes to get at his blood. Joe shuddered. At least I'm alive, he reminded himself again, and there wasn't a hell of a lot of that going on around here at the moment.

It was Joe's second trip to the hillock. It had taken a good half hour to reach it the first time, threading through the dense, clawing bush. It was easy to get lost in the gloom. The jungle was virtually impenetrable. A thick mat of wet leaves, fronds, grasses and vines fought with trees and saplings for any light blinking through the canopy overhead. It wasn't made for human passage, especially a human more at home in the cafés of Sydney's Paddington.

The best way through the jungle was on all fours, close to the ground, where there wasn't enough light for the vegetation to grow too thickly, or in the tops of the trees. Indeed, he thought he heard the chatter of monkeys overhead, but the sound stopped before he could get a fix on the origin. He came across a trail through the thick vegetation, more like a tunnel, and he tried using that for a while, but it led diagonally away from his intended destination.

It had quickly become obvious to Joe, and Jim, that they had to move away from all the death. Every section of the aircraft big enough to provide shelter was either too sooty, too oily, or covered in gore. Within a day, most of the dead would begin to bloat and the smell of decomposing flesh, already thick in the air, would be unbearable. The most obvious section of the aircraft for them to shelter in would have been the nose and forward fuselage, but it was like an abattoir in there and his mind recoiled with horror at the memory of it. He had checked out where his seat, 5A, had been. It was missing, of course, plucked out from the seats in front and behind, some of which still contained the bloody, torn remains of their occupants. He found his computer, but he had no use for it and so left it behind.

Within hours of the crash the jungle had started reclaiming the ground it had lost to the 250 tonne chunk of aluminium that had ploughed through it. Decomposition was good for the jungle. That was how it sustained itself, perpetuating its existence; plants and animals dying and rotting back into the soil to provide nutrients for future flora and fauna: a continuous cycle of life and death. The crash had provided this cycle with an enormous shot of blood and bone, fertiliser, and the jungle was hungry to make use of it. This was no place for the living. A feeding frenzy was in progress. Nature would surely kill them and add their flesh to the feast if they hung around. They had to leave, and quickly, despite the fact that there was also a logic to staying put: if rescue came, where else would it go but to the scene of the crash?

Joe parted the foliage in front of his face and the devastation of the crash below was plain to see. He scanned it with the binoculars again and steeled himself not to become nauseated by what he saw. Joe then lifted them to the haze beyond. A city could be out there for all he knew, but if there was, he couldn't see it. Joe felt alone, forgotten, marooned. What the hell to do next? Where to go? Where the fuck is everyone?

The jungle was comparatively sparse on top of the hillock. He'd found a couple of blankets and intended to use them as an awning strung between the saplings. There was plenty of cloud shielding them from the full strength of the sun, but he knew that strong equatorial ultraviolet rays were bouncing around under them. The blankets would provide more complete protection. Joe's skin was pale and he'd never been a beach-goer, preferring to spend his time bathed in the radiation from a computer screen, or practising his left/right combinations in the gym.

Using the makeshift axe, Joe dug a pit in the earth to keep the bottles of water cool. There were eleven 250 ml bottles. Nearly three litres. Joe tried to remember how much a person needed to drink each day to prevent dehydration. Was it one litre or two? Did your body weight make a difference? Joe had no real idea except that it was probably bound to be more than a cup when it was so bloody hot. He wondered if Jim would know.

Food was important too. He'd had the presence of mind to salvage a couple of trays while sifting through the wreckage. He'd forced himself to do it though the thought of eating made him feel sick.

While moving through the jungle, he'd come across a creek that separated the aircraft remains from the campsite. He was about to drink from it, scooping up a handful of water, when he smelled kerosene. He decided to try finding more bottled water amongst the wreckage instead.

Joe considered some of the other things he would need to make the new site a bit more 'liveable'. Then it occurred to him that help might be a simple phone call away, so a mobile phone would be a lifesaver, his, if they had come down in a service area. He imagined making the call. 'Hello, yes, can you please put me through to the people who handle crashed 747s . . . ' It was then that something in Joe gave way. Hot tears filled his eyes and he slumped to the ground.

Joe lay on his back and looked up through the leaves at the sky. He couldn't recognise the sound at first. And then the helicopters flew right over the top of him. After a moment's shock, he jumped up, waving and yelling.

The Super Pumas flew in a loose formation. They skimmed the hillock Joe was setting up camp on and then swooped low across the crash scene, the rotor downwash creating eddies of loose rubbish. They made several passes over the depression, probably scouting the best place to land, or perhaps looking for survivors from a higher vantage point. He continued to jump and throw his arms about in an attempt to catch their attention, but they were focused on the carnage below rather than the hills above.

Joe followed them with his binoculars, hands shaking. The giant choppers settled on the ground, rocking on their wheels. Doors slid open and soldiers in full camouflage gear jumped out. Joe wondered vaguely why they were carrying weapons, then dismissed the thought. They're soldiers, soldiers carry guns. He could hardly contain his excitement and his sense of relief. Rescue had arrived.

The soldiers fanned out into the wreckage, obviously looking for survivors. Joe lowered his binoculars and leaped about shouting desperately in the hope that someone might happen to glance up in his direction. No one did.

One of the soldiers discovered Jim and Margaret. Through his binoculars, Joe could see them talking. There were lots of animated arm movements. Jim was obviously excited at the arrival of the soldiers. He pointed to Joe's hillock. That's right, Jim, tell them there's one more of us. 'Up here! Here!' Joe waved as the soldier looked in his direction. He ran backwards and forwards across the hill, vaguely confused about what he should do next, stopping every time he lost the image of the rescue party in the binoculars to refocus it.

The soldier turned to face Jim and Margaret and fired his weapon into them. One long and lazy automatic burst. Joe didn't hear the weapon discharge but the recoil was unmistakable. Jim slid slowly sideways. Margaret convulsed briefly. The soldier changed magazines then pointed his rifle in Joe's direction. He took in the scene open-mouthed, unable to accept it as reality. What the hell was going on? Puffs of smoke chugged soundlessly from the small black hole sighted directly at him. Two bullets passed close enough for him to feel their pressure wave against his skin, leaving a pair of neat holes in a fleshy green frond beside his neck. Joe dropped the binoculars then froze, every muscle locked in a spasm of fear.

The helos rose from the ground on their swirling columns of rubbish and flew away, leaving behind the soldiers and their guns.

Denpasar, Bali, 0600 Zulu, Wednesday, 29 April

Working at the control tower at Denpasar Airport, Bali, was no different from working in the control tower of practically any airport in the world. It wasn't as busy as LAX, Narita, Schiphol or Heathrow, and it certainly wasn't as good on your resumé as any of those other

74

world-class facilities. But Denpasar had other advantages, especially when Japan was in the grip of winter, Abe Niko reminded himself.

Niko enjoyed sending tropical island paradise-style postcards home to Tokyo, just to annoy his friends grinding it out in the freezing rat race there. They all thought he was so fortunate to be living in such a place. And they were right. There'd been the bombings, of course, and that had changed things for a while, but life had returned to normal, especially with the European and Asian tourist trade. People had such short memories.

Through the week he didn't get to see much of the Bali he had fallen in love with as a tourist years before, but he knew it was there, spread out below his tower, and that made all the difference. Of course, Denpasar itself was hardly a paradise. It had to be one of the noisiest, dustiest, hottest and, he had to admit it, ugliest cities he'd ever seen. And that's why he lived far away from it, in the centre of Bali, where the grit gave way to the green of lush jungle, and a thousand feet of altitude took the edge off the heat and humidity.

Niko threaded his Honda Accord through a thicket of two-stroke motor scooters that meandered across the road, blowing blue smoke, ignoring the painted lanes. When he'd first arrived in Bali, he'd thought the traffic a living example of chaos theory. Very few road rules appeared to be obeyed, which offended his sense of order. Once a traffic controller, always a traffic controller, he had joked to himself.

But then, as he became used to it, he realised the rules of the road were *sensed*, as if by some form of telepathy. Riders on motor scooters seemed to *know* when a vehicle was approaching around a blind turn and would pull back onto the correct side of the road at the last moment. To survive, one just had to be in tune with it. Until one could do that confidently, driving in Bali was a dice with death.

Abe Niko made his way to the outskirts of the city, through the prawn farms and furniture factories, and only started to unwind when he turned his car off the main road and began the climb. The people up in the hills were more relaxed than the city dwellers. They had a calmness, a serenity about them, that was lacking in the population in Denpasar. They were more in touch with Balinese traditions and culture, embracing their animist beliefs. And it wasn't just a show put on for tourists either.

Niko was a romantic about Bali and its people, but when it came to his job, he was rigorous, rational and pragmatic. He sat in front of a screen and directed international air traffic, handing aircraft from his chunk of sky to the next controller's chunk of sky. That was his job. It was routine work in a sector that was rarely busy, and not exactly taxing if one had a systematic mind. And Abe Niko had such a mind. It was because of this that he was troubled. He really had no idea what was going on. Niko had immediately reviewed the disks from his control board after he had called the authorities. The seven-four was at Flight Level 350 (35 000 feet), and then it was gone. Blink, then nothing. QF-1 had vanished from his screen without warning, no radio calls – complete silence – in a way that suggested the worst.

Immediately, however, the police had confiscated his disks, the ones that recorded the information collected by the traffic control system displayed on his screen. That was bad. But what had really got under his skin was a news report that made him sound like he didn't know what the hell he was doing. In his view QF-1 had probably been blown out of the sky. Terror. Yet what the authorities were saying – and quoting him, apparently – was that QF-1 had suffered some kind of cataclysmic system failure and that it had probably come down outside Indonesian airspace. That was stupid. The Qantas plane would turn up pasted against a mountain in Sulawesi like a bug against a car radiator grille and everyone would look like amateurs. Especially him. Why would they say such rubbish? And who were 'they' anyhow? The more he thought about it, the more worked up he became. What possible motive would anyone have for trying to conceal a plane crash? Or delaying the discovery of the wreckage?

He turned off the main road and started to descend through the palms, tamarind and mango trees along the track that led to his home. Niko was tired. He wanted to get home, have a shower and go to bed. He'd sleep first and then call a friend of his who worked in the newsroom of a major TV station in Jakarta. The nameless authorities had gotten it totally wrong. Worse, they'd gotten it wrong in *his* name! Just thinking about it made him angry. And edgy. Maybe I shouldn't wait, he thought, and decided he'd phone his TV friend as soon as he arrived home, to set the record straight. Sometimes these second-world countries did and said the dumbest things, but what on earth was the motive for this stupidity? The question kept repeating itself in his head. And then, suddenly, he knew. The answer was obvious. The plane had been shot down. He wouldn't wait to get home, he'd make that call now.

Niko fumbled with his mobile phone, turning it on as he rounded a corner. An army truck blocked the road. He saw it too late, swerved and braked hard, locking up the wheels on the slick mud surface. The car slid and spun, almost in slow motion, but nothing Niko could do prevented it from slipping off the road's soft edges and down the steep gully. The Honda gathered speed slowly at first, then accelerated as it fell through the trees. A front wheel hit a large stone, caving in the front suspension. The car rolled, then flipped. The front doors were flung open, the mounting centrifugal forces ripping them off their hinges.

Niko was still conscious when the car came to rest upside down in the creek that ran rapidly through the gully at the base of the hill. He'd had the wind crushed out of him but his air-bag had saved his life. It started to deflate and he felt less restricted, but his leg was jammed somewhere under the dashboard. He tried to free it, but couldn't. Upside down, the blood rushed to his head and the pressure built. His eyes felt like they were being squeezed out of their sockets. He saw his phone. It was sitting on a bit of plastic under the passenger glove box. He tried to reach it, but it was just beyond his fingertips.

Water filled the upturned roof space below his head. He heard it first, then felt the cold wetness on his scalp. He tried to lift his head up towards the dashboard trapping his knees, but his stomach muscles gave out. He yelled for help, screamed for it, as the water gurgled relentlessly into his mouth, making him cough and hack. Silence. The water was nearly up to his eyes, which were bulging with panic.

Somewhere there was the hiss of steam as water ran over hot engine parts. He managed to get his mouth out of the water for one last desperate plea for help. Exhausted, the water invaded his nostrils. He gagged, spluttered. Niko registered that the hissing sound had changed pitch now that his ears were under the surface. The water was malevolent, a force with an almost conscious determination to kill. He struggled again, hopelessly, to free his legs.

Abe Niko's head was under water for a good two minutes before he stopped thrashing, his brain forcing him to inhale. The water was cooling as it flowed into his seared lungs and the air traffic controller felt happily light-headed. He wondered why he hadn't sensed the truck's presence around the corner. He slipped into a black blanket of unconsciousness, all fight removed by a calming euphoria. Within another minute, he was dead.

A starter motor for a large diesel whirred and the engine caught. The army truck ground its gears and slowly moved off.

Sydney, 0600 Zulu, Wednesday, 29 April

Excerpt from phone interview with Indonesian Ambassador Parno Batuta on ABC Radio 702:

ABC: What sort of terrain has the Qantas plane crashed in?

Batuta: We do not know where the plane has come down.

ABC: But you're searching the island of Sulawesi?

Batuta: Yes, we are concentrating our search there. It's a rugged place. Much jungle and volcanoes. And the plane could feasibly be anywhere within a very wide area.

ABC: There's a report coming out of Jakarta, attributed to the air traffic controller who raised the alarm, that the plane could have crashed outside Indonesian territory.

Batuta: We are operating on the advice of our air force and that is something being considered.

ABC: When will you broaden the search?

Batuta: I believe our air force is already doing that.

ABC: If you are also considering other possible areas, then the search must be vast. That being the case, what resources have been allocated?

Batuta: Every available aircraft has been committed.

ABC: Have you invited Australian aircraft to help search?

Batuta: No. Our air force is more than capable.

ABC: What will you do when you find the aircraft?

Batuta: We will allow experts to examine the crash site and try to find the causes, naturally.

ABC: Are there any suggestions yet of terrorism?

Batuta: I would ask you, please, not to ask such a question. We don't know anything about terrorism. A plane has come down and that is all anyone can say for certain at this moment. And certainly, all I will say. Thank you.

Sydney Airport, 0600 Zulu, Wednesday, 29 April

The void into which QF-1 had flown left a vacuum that needed to be filled. Everyone, but especially people close to the passengers, needed answers. Not the ones asked by the politicians and the media, but simpler, more real questions. What has happened to my son? Is my daughter alive? Is my husband dead? The questions were underpinned by a consistent belief that the plane had to be in the air some-where, still flying, because Qantas planes simply didn't crash. The government couldn't tell them anything new, and neither could Qantas. They were left to work it out for themselves.

The first of these bewildered people began to arrive at the departure lounge of Sydney Airport. They came in ones and twos, besieging the Qantas flight check-in desks with questions. By noon the crowd had swelled to over a hundred and the section had become unworkable. And as their numbers had grown, so had their mood changed. Sydney Airport management had called security and had the irate throng moved as calmly as possible out of the way, into a large section of vacant seating. Qantas staff drifted amongst them with tea, coffee and sandwiches but offered nothing more sustaining, namely, answers.

Central Sulawesi, 0635 Zulu, Wednesday, 29 April

A sonic boomlet cracked as a bullet going supersonic creased the air over Joe's head. His mind was grappling with his situation, and nothing about it figured.

Now they were coming for *him*! The last thing he remembered seeing, before throwing himself onto the ground, was the image of two soldiers racing across the crash site towards him. Bullets continued to slap through the bush beside and behind him. They wanted him to keep his head down. He complied.

Eventually, one of those bullets would get lucky. While Joe was sure they couldn't see him, his position on top of the hill was exposed. He had to leave. His problem was that he didn't have a clue where he should run to, only that he should move, and fast. His world had utterly collapsed. He hurriedly stuffed bottles of water and the axe into the rucksack and slipped into the bush on his belly, dragging the rucksack behind him.

At the crash 'site Sergeant Marturak surveyed the wreckage. It was an unpleasant scene with an equally unpleasant smell, and while he was pleased that he hadn't been one of the passengers, the devastation left him unaffected. Marturak and his Kopassus troops were no strangers to death and destruction. He was surprised that there had been survivors at all, given the obvious violence of the aircraft's impact, but survivors were easily turned into victims with an FNC80, the Indonesian army's standard issue carbine.

He moved cautiously to where the nose section of the aircraft had come to rest. A shot punctuated the quiet as a soldier made sure of another passenger. The noise did not distract the sergeant, who was comfortable around the sound of firearms. Marturak first inspected what was left of the cockpit. The force of the impact had concertinaed the section to around half its original size. There was nothing recognisable left of the flight crew. Something crunched under his boot – a small plastic model of an F/A-18.

Remarkably, some of the seats and lockers were still in place. The sergeant levered himself up inside the giant tube and, using the jagged ends of aluminium ribbing jutting from the severed end of the fuselage as footholds, climbed easily into the first-class section. Careful not to lose his footing on the slippery human remains, he made his way towards the seat he had been briefed to specifically search. He hoped to find the occupant still strapped in, and alive, so that he could learn the passenger's identity before killing him, but the seat was gone.

However, a computer and other electronic equipment had become entangled in the seat beside the one he was searching for. He freed it. The casing was cracked. He pressed the on button to see what would happen. Unbelievably, it booted, albeit noisily. The screen named the owner but required a password to continue. Sergeant Marturak checked the drives. There was a disk in the slot. He smashed the computer with the butt of his rifle, recovering the disk, then tossed the remnants into a nearby smouldering fire giving off the smell of rancid barbeque pork.

He placed the disk in his webbing and made his way to the open end of the fuselage. A knot of soldiers were standing around laughing, smoking pungent clove cigarettes as a defence against the stench of death that hung over the place. Marturak barked an order. The men jumped, making their way to the sergeant. The young men effortlessly swung up through the wreckage and into the nose section. Marturak issued another staccato command. The soldiers checked the corpses littering the area, looking through pockets for identification.

The sergeant climbed down to a point where he could jump to the ground. He then trotted up to a higher vantage point and squinted through his Persols at the hill being searched for the survivor. The jungle was thick but the hill didn't seem too far away. It wouldn't be long till his men reported from its crest that the last surviving passenger had been killed, and he would then be able to make his radio report that the crash site was secured.

Once the jungle had obscured his retreat, Joe got to his feet and charged into the bush that hemmed him in on three sides. There was nowhere to go but downhill *towards* the killers! He stopped several times to listen to the jungle through his own heavy panting. He sucked in the warm, damp air to settle his racing heartbeat, and then held his breath, reaching out with his senses.

The jungle was not a quiet place. There was a bird – he thought it was a bird but he couldn't be sure – making a sound like fingernails dragging across a blackboard. The sound filled the jungle, combining with the press of the foliage to give him a profound sense of claustrophobia. It made his head swim. He was close to panic. A few hours ago he was a first-class passenger. Now he was being hunted, part of the food chain.

He touched his cheek and felt the swollen, angry skin. The side of his face had puffed up like a soufflé. What had caused the itchy swelling? Then he saw the large spiky green caterpillar hanging from a thick thread centimetres from his face. He pinched off the grub's bungee and angrily swung it away into the leaf litter on the jungle floor.

He had to get moving again. But which way? Joe was disoriented. The hill's fall-line was his only signpost. He traversed across it as much as the jungle allowed, taking a bottle from his rucksack and throwing back the contents as he half ran, but mostly crawled, sweat pouring down his face and stinging his eyes. He broke a stick from a tree and held it in front of his face, guarding against further assaults from the wildlife.

Joe managed to find a rhythm as he moved through the clawing bush. A machete would have been helpful. Then he remembered his makeshift axe. He dropped the stick and removed the axe from his rucksack. He thought he was beginning to tell the difference between bush he could charge through and vegetation he had to go around. And then he ran through a clump of leaves and into the solid trunk of a tree. The force of the collision nearly knocked him out. He bounced off the tree and found himself on the ground. His nose hurt badly enough to make his eyes water but he knew it wasn't broken. He'd had plenty of bloody noses from boxing and the pain was reassuring, like meeting up with an old friend.

He pushed on through a mat of vines sheathed in fine needles that made his skin itch. A section gave way and he fell into water. He'd reached the creek at the base of the hill that separated it from the crash site. It smelled of kerosene, even stronger here. Then he heard something. He froze and listened, trying to isolate the sound of moving water from the alien snap of a stick. The jungle was just as noisy as it had been, except that his fall had disturbed ground-dwelling animals that scurried off like startled smugglers, back into their hidden caves. He thought that finding some thick scrub to hide in would probably be a good idea for himself too.

Joe crawled out of the creek. He was careful not to make any sound that might alert the soldiers. He'd badly bruised his shins in the fall into the creek and he grimaced when he put his weight on his feet. He slowly pulled himself up the bank and into the jungle's embrace. He forced his way through on all fours and found himself in the tunnel he had noted earlier. He peered into it in the diminished light. The tunnel carved through the jungle, remaining roughly parallel with the creek bank for a while before twisting back at right angles and heading (probably, he thought) back around the base of the hillock. Joe turned and backed into it, deciding that if he was shot at, he didn't want to take a bullet in the arse, or have his nuts blasted off.

The floor of the tunnel was made up of flattened grasses and leaf litter. The tunnel walls were remarkably uniform, as if they'd been woven. He continued reversing through the tunnel until it kinked right. Then he stopped. Something around him had changed. But what? Then he knew what it was. The world had suddenly fallen silent. What was that? Had he heard something? He held his breath.

The wall of the tunnel suddenly collapsed in front of him. Something large fell into the space. Joe was paralysed with fear. It was either some kind of wild animal, or one of the soldiers. Either way, things were about to get unpleasant. Before he could react with a scream or shout, he was head-butted on the point of his chin. The force concentrated in his head, orange planets exploding behind his eyes. His mind fought to maintain consciousness. Then a hand covered his nose and mouth, and a weight pressed on his chest. In front of his face were frightened eyes as wide as Frisbees. It was a woman lying on top of him, pressing the air out of his lungs. At least, he thought it was a woman. She put her finger to her lips for him to be quiet. He nodded.

A noise! She gestured at the hole in the side of the tunnel. And then Joe heard it too. Again, it wasn't a noise so much as a patch of unnaturally still air in the fabric of sound that enveloped them. There was something close, very close, and it was trying hard to be stealthy. Its presence was something he could feel rather than see. Joe's own heart pounded noisily in his ears. He tried in vain to control it. The boot came down quietly an arm's length from the matted wall of the tunnel.

Joe saw the disturbance in the pattern of greenery first, then the mud-covered leather of the boot itself. It was a soldier's boot. The camouflage pattern of the fatigues was so effective he could only see that it wasn't foliage when the leg moved. Joe's eyes were large in his head. Not a metre away was a man with a gun, trained to kill, hoping to put that training to good use on them. On top of him was a woman as scared rigid as he was, pressing the life out of him. The boot lifted and was gone. They waited for the bullets to rip through the tunnel wall. Nothing. The soldier had come close to stepping on them, but still hadn't seen them. After what seemed an age, the woman quietly, slowly, slid off to one side. Joe exhaled and silently blessed the creator of the tunnel.

He blessed too soon. A brown head appeared around the bend of the tunnel ahead. It was an animal, a large four-legged animal the size of a full-grown pig. It stopped, wrinkled its nose and moved its head quickly from side to side. Joe blinked dumbly, not knowing what to do. Something in the animal's brain decided, for whatever reason, that it should be afraid of the animals in its path. Maybe it was their reluctance to move, or it smelled their fear. Whatever the reason, the beast's legs suddenly started pumping. The animal charged through the wall of the tunnel and made off noisily into the undergrowth, grunting and squealing.

At last, the soldier had a target. Bullets zeroed in on the ruckus. A scream of surprise and death followed. The undergrowth came alive as countless snakes, lizards and small mammals decided they'd rather be somewhere else.

The cracks from the carbine launched monkeys and birds from the trees. They squealed their distress at the sudden disturbance. Joe and the woman scuttled on all fours through the tunnel until they reached the relatively open ground that sloped down to the creek. They stood for a few seconds to get their breath, and a section of tree centimetres from the woman's head suddenly split away from the trunk as bullets slammed into it. Joe had forgotten that *two* soldiers had been dispatched to his hill. The man stood, weapon coming up to his shoulder, in the middle of the creek. If they hesitated, the next shots wouldn't miss. The woman pulled Joe to the ground and they scrambled for the thicker growth. But the jungle was too dense to penetrate. Nowhere else to go, they were forced back to the creek. They hid behind a mound of mud pushed up by the monsoon floods. Joe snatched a look over it. The two soldiers had now joined together in the pursuit and were running through the creek bed towards their hiding place.

One of the men opened fire just as he tripped on a stone. The bullet spat from the muzzle with a downwards trajectory. The propellant that launched the round burned through a thin layer of tin and ignited phosphorus packed into a hollow at the base of the bullet. It was a tracer. The projectile glowed fiercely red on its brief flight, striking the creek bed not far from the woman's outstretched hand.

And then suddenly the flesh on Joe's face was seared as the very creek itself exploded into a twisting, orange snake of intense heat. The punch of the explosion knocked the air out of him. A ball of flame was deflected by the mud bank and rolled skywards.

The two soldiers became human torches. Joe lifted his head and saw them run blindly through the firestorm.

One of the men was discharging his weapon into the air, his finger convulsing on the trigger. Then they both dropped to their knees and fell forward into the river of fire, hissing like hot pans doused in a bucket. Their screams choked with a gurgle.

Sergeant Marturak's attention was captured by the familiar report of an FNC80. The shots came from the hill being searched. It had been helpful of the old man to give up the whereabouts of the only other survivor. And it was good of that last living passenger to present himself as such a willing target.

Did killing the old couple give him pleasure? Perhaps not, but it was reassuringly professional to be able to do his job well. There were to be no passengers left alive. Those were his orders. The general had been very specific on that point. He had even elaborated on the reason why, saying the security of Indonesia depended on it. That was both unusual and unnecessary. An order was good enough for Sergeant Marturak and reasons were not required; following orders was his job.

The shots: he estimated thirty rounds. One whole magazine. That was wasteful. He'd sent two trained soldiers to shoot an unarmed man. It was a simple task, one his men knew well enough. It didn't take thirty rounds. That smacked of panic. Other smaller bursts of gunfire followed. Odd. There was obviously something wrong.

Marturak saw the fireball before he heard the explosion. It took him completely by surprise and he felt the radiated heat of it on his face. There was another blast of gunfire and then a menacing, black mushroom cloud of smoke, forked with yellow and orange flame, rose out of the gully. What could have caused that? he wondered. Then the smell of burnt kerosene reached his nostrils and he put it together. One of the aircraft's tanks must have ruptured and spilled its contents, the fuel pooling on lower ground. But what had set it off? He hoped his men had not had a careless smoke. No, they were good soldiers, the best, despite the spray of firearms. They certainly weren't stupid. What had caused the explosion? He spat an order and four soldiers immediately jogged off to investigate.

'Jesus! What happened then?' Joe said, pulling himself up off the ground. The woman was dry retching. After she finished, she opened her hand and revealed a Bic disposable cigarette lighter. Her arms were bright red, burned by the heat.

'Couldn't you smell the kero?' she asked. 'It's pooling everywhere here.'

'Did you light it? With that?' said Joe, incredulous.

'I . . . I think so, yeah. There was some of the stuff – the kero – beside me.' She stared at the lighter, every bit as surprised as Joe.

Joe's breathing was short. He had just seen two men die a horrible death. They'd danced a ghastly jig as they'd tried to escape the flames that clung to them. If there'd been an opportunity to turn back, there was none now. Joe realised that killing, or being killed, was his only future.

NSA, Helemanu, Oahu, Hawaii, 0705 Zulu, Wednesday, April 29

In the cool underground cubicle, Ruth examined the brief report. Her radar and that inner voice of hers were working as one now. Was the air traffic controller murdered, or was it just an accident? Ruth didn't believe in coincidences. She sent on the report and wondered, what next?

Parliament House, Canberra, 0730 Zulu, Wednesday, April 29

There was a gentle tap on the door. A lance corporal entered and, with the grace of an excellent waiter at a three-hat restaurant, handed a sheet of paper to the ASIS chief.

Graeme Griffin read it and immediately snatched up the phone. 'Spike, just got something from our NSA friends at the US embassy here. They thought it might be of interest. The air traffic controller in Bali who first reported QF-1 missing was found dead in his car at the bottom of a gully a short while ago.'

'Shit . . .' Niven said.

'Yeah, I know. Look, I'm not sure what it means. Maybe nothing.' But the feeling in Griffin's gut told him it meant a hell of a lot of something.

Hasanuddin Airport, Maros, 0730 Zulu, Wednesday, April 29

After phoning in her earlier report, A-6 went home, parked her motor scooter, showered, changed, and took a taxi to Hasanuddin Airport. She had the appearance of any number of the welcoming friends and relatives milling about the airport. She noted that a few children besotted by aircraft even had binoculars, like her, with which to watch the takeoffs and landings, and that relaxed her a little. She doubted, though, that any of them had a satellite phone on them, as she did.

She further observed that there were quite a few police and security officers around, but there was really nothing about her outward appearance that would attract their attention. A couple of aircraft had been late, so even the fact that she had lingered for hours at the observation deck, watching through her binoculars, passed unnoticed.

A-6 kept her binoculars trained on the air force side of the facility, and even that failed to raise an eyebrow, although A-6 thought it might. She'd begun the stakeout nervously, but soon relaxed. There were at least a thousand people in the place, coming and going, and she was just one woman amongst them. No one special.

Eventually they arrived, as she knew they would. The Super Pumas came in low from the north and settled over the other side of the airport on the air force apron. The doors cracked open when the rotors started to slow, but only the crew jumped down onto the tarmac. Other than their crews, the helos were empty. They had gone out with soldiers and come back from places unknown without them. It might be nothing, she thought. But there was something about the urgency of their departure that had attracted her attention in the first place. The helos had been gone around three hours. Was it worth reporting or not? She decided to call it in anyway. Too much information was always better than not enough.

The Tannoy announced that a Garuda flight from Jakarta had been diverted due to weather. A-6 feigned disappointment and, shoulders hunched, joined the grumbling exodus from the terminal.

Central Sulawesi, 0730 Zulu, Wednesday, 29 April

None of this made any sense to Joe. Why were these people trying to kill him? It was bizarre. They should be bundling him up and taking him to a hospital so that he could start recovering from the shock of the air disaster. What the fuck was happening here? And who was this woman who'd appeared from, well, nowhere, and rescued them from certain death with her cigarette lighter, like some female McGiver?

'We'd better not hang around,' she said, interrupting his train of thought. 'They'll come to investigate for sure.' She stood, turned her back on Joe and the foul stench of sizzling flesh and kerosene, and made her way to the relative security of the tunnel. Joe got up and followed, somewhat dazed. It was mid-afternoon and surprisingly dark under the canopy, the light reduced further by the smoke. When the sun set it would be pitch black. Complete darkness would bring a mixed blessing. It would hide them, but it would also cover the approach of more soldiers.

The all-pervading screeching sound he assumed was made by some kind of bird had stopped. In its place was a vast number of chirps, squeaks, grunts, rustlings and chatterings. The jungle was waking from the sleep induced by the heat of the day.

Joe joined the woman in the tunnel. Given what had just happened, he was reluctant to crawl back into the

hole, but he had nowhere else to go. The gloom was suddenly lit by a glow. The woman was burning leeches off
her legs with the lighter. In the light provided by the single
flame he saw that his own legs were covered in the things,
as well as cuts and bruises.

'If I were you, I'd strip down,' she said. 'You've been in
the water. You've probably got these buggers all over you.'

Joe took off his shirt and pants in the confined space of
the tunnel and inspected his chest in the shifting yellow
glow. He counted a dozen leeches.

'There are more on your back. Here . . . ' The woman
carefully burned them off. 'You've probably got some
down there, too,' she said, gesturing at his underpants. 'But
you can get them off.' There was no smile accompanying
that. She was all business.

'Where did you come from?' he asked over the sizzling
and popping of the leeches.

'Same place you did. I was in economy, down the back. I
always travel down the back. Statistically gives you the best
chance of surviving a crash. I saw the part of the plane I was
seated in down the bottom of a gorge. I don't think there
would have been any survivors in it. So, so much for statistics,'
she said with the suggestion of a wry smile. 'Anyway, I got
lucky. I was thrown clear.' The woman ran her fingers gently
over the back of her skull, tracing the outline of a bump the
size of a golf ball. The swelling was tender. She spied another
crop of leeches behind her legs and the discovery distracted
her. She forgot about the bump and went after them.

'The noise of the choppers overhead woke me up. I
must have been unconscious, or asleep, or in shock –
whatever. When I saw those soldiers, I just couldn't believe
it. I was thrilled.'

Joe knew exactly how she'd felt.

'And then I saw them shoot a couple of people and I just ran into the jungle. I thought I was it, the last survivor.'

'In the tunnel . . . how did you know I wasn't one of them?' Joe asked, gesturing back behind him with a flick of his head.

'I didn't. You surprised me.'

Joe nodded. When the woman had broken through into the tunnel, he'd thought the worst too. 'So, what's your name?'

'Why do you want to know?' she asked.

'Um . . .' Joe was confused by her reluctance.

'Sorry. I'm just a bit . . . you know. I don't know what's going on. Why are we being shot at?'

'Don't ask me,' said Joe. 'I just keep thinking I'll wake up, that I'm having a nightmare – too much MSG in the food or something.'

'Why kill us? What possible reason . . . those poor people, shot in cold blood.'

Joe heard the woman take a deep breath.

'Well, my name's Joe. Joe Light.' He offered his hand.

She took it, forcing a smile. 'Suryei Hujan.'

Shaking her hand felt weird and reassuring at the same time. Introductions were gestures that belonged in the real world, like the pub or the office. But the contact felt good, like it was possible for things to return to normal.

'Pretty name. Mean anything?' he asked.

'Sun and rain, a yin and yang thing. My parents are romantics,' she said, checking around the tunnel walls.

Joe didn't know where to go from there. The small talk evaporated.

Suryei had kept the flame on her lighter burning during

this conversation. But now the flame had heated the lighter to a point where the metal was too hot to handle. She let out a quiet gasp. The light flicked off and she stuck her finger in her mouth to relieve the burning sensation. They were instantly swallowed by a blackness that swam with after-images of the flickering light. Night had fallen.

'Better not waste this,' she said, pocketing the Bic. 'We should get moving. The soldiers . . .' The sense of shared safety they'd felt huddled together in the friendly glow of the lighter was extinguished with the flame, and the atmosphere between them became strained and awkward.

'What do you do, Joe, when you're not dodging bullets?' asked Suryei quietly after they'd crawled some way in silence.

'Computer software. Games, mostly.'

'Great,' said Suryei, half under her breath. 'That'll come in handy here.'

Joe had never felt like apologising for his occupation before. Back in Sydney, it was mostly a pretty cool thing to do for a living.

Joe could hear Suryei breathing in the murk. He called up his last image of her before the lighter was extinguished. It was hard to tell exactly what she looked like with all the mud and gore that covered her face. With a name like Suryei Hujan, she had to be Asian.

'Got some water here,' he said, trying to be friendly. Despite the hot, close air, the ambience was frosty.

'Thanks,' she said, a little of the edge gone from her tone. 'You've got a rucksack. What's in it?'

He felt around inside it. 'Some bottles of water, a couple of trays of aeroplane food, and a sort of axe.' He rummaged through the contents again quickly. Something was missing. 'Had a pair of binoculars . . . must have left them somewhere.'

'More than I've got,' she said. 'The lighter. That's it.'

'Do you smoke?'

'Did. Ran out.'

Joe held out a bottle to her ghostly outline. She took it. He heard her open it and drink.

She handed him the empty. 'Put this back in your bag. We don't want to leave those bastards any signposts.'

'Sure . . . Hey, what was that thing that came down the tunnel?' Joe was not keen on meeting another of the animals in the darkness.

'A babirusa.'

'Strange looking thing.'

'Pretty rare.'

'What were those growths on its face?'

'Teeth.'

'Eh?'

'Its canines grow through its snout . . . God, I'm an idiot!' said Suryei suddenly. 'That tells us where we are!'

'Yeah?'

'The babirusa is native to Sulawesi.'

'Where's that?'

'Part of Indonesia, one of the larger islands.'

'How do you know all that?'

'I'm a photo-journalist. These days nature stuff, mostly. We're lucky to have seen one. Wish I'd had my camera.'

'The babirusa probably isn't feeling too lucky at the moment,' said Joe, remembering how it had died.

'No, guess not. Anyway, at least we know where we are now. This tunnel was its highway through the jungle. Probably leads to a favourite food or water source. Which reminds me, we're sweating heaps. We're going to have to drink three litres each a day at least. If we're here a while, we'll need a good, clean supply.'

Joe was glad she'd cleared up the water consumption question for him, but the thought of being 'here a while' filled him with dread.

Parliament House, Canberra, 0730 Zulu, Wednesday, 29 April

'Come in, you blokes,' the PM said to Niven, Griffin and Sharpe, who had been waiting outside. 'I've just briefed Hugh Greenway and he's up to speed.' The tall, stooped Minister of Defence, nicknamed 'Lurch' by the press, nodded at his colleagues as they filed through the door and took their seats in the small auditorium.

'I've booked a conference call with Byron Mills, our ambassador in Washington, and I thought it best if we all caught it, to save time and avoid the Chinese whispers.'

He picked up the handset and pressed a number. 'Shirl, get Byron on the line, would you, mate?'

The snow on the television coalesced to become a distinguished-looking, white-haired man.

'G'day, Byron,' said the PM.

'Bill, gentlemen,' began the ambassador in his sonorous baritone. 'Everyone here?'

'Yep,' Blight said. 'We're it.'

'Okay . . .' He paused to look down at his notes outside the camera's field of view. 'I've put our case through the appropriate channels here and, well, we've got a problem.'

'What's that?' said Niven.

'The Americans won't help us with a satellite.'

'Why not?'

'Because basically, they don't have enough assets to go around. They're keeping watch over a large part of the earth at the moment – the Middle East, the Gulf, Afghanistan, Pakistan, the Chinese, the Russians, the Korean peninsula, and there's that unfortunate business going on in East Africa.'

'Terrific,' Niven said.

'The feeling here is that the plane will turn up anyway before they can re-task a sat and get it on station. The Indonesians say they're putting a lot of effort into locating it and the Americans believe that. So do we, right?'

Blight looked at the other men in the room. 'Yes,' he said unconvincingly.

'They believe that if the plane crashed in the jungle, the chances of anyone surviving would be next to nil. So . . . look, they're saying it's a tragedy, but not one they're happy to take their eye off other balls to investigate. I reckon they'd probably think differently if terrorists claimed responsibility, and if the prospect of finding people alive was greater, but, well . . .'

There'd been reluctance to state the chances of survival so emphatically – there was always hope – but there it was: reality. Christ! thought the PM. 'So where does that leave us, Byron?' Blight asked, plainly disappointed.

'There is one avenue I'd like to investigate, but I'll keep that to myself for the moment because it mightn't go anywhere.'

'Fair enough. If something turns up?'

'Sure, get back to you straight away. I'm going to keep at

them anyway, Bill. If the plane doesn't turn up for a couple of days they might change their tune, especially if we're prepared to do a little horse trading over free-trade issues. Keep you posted.'

'Thanks, Byron.' The PM's deflated tone reflected everyone's disappointment.

Central Sulawesi, 0730 Zulu, Wednesday, 29 April

Sergeant Marturak walked towards his men as they appeared at the edge of the jungle. In their camouflage fatigues they were barely silhouettes, shadows on shadows. The corporal made his report quickly and pointed towards the area that had been engulfed by the fireball. He handed his sergeant a plastic bottle found by the creek. Marturak considered his corporal's view that it had belonged to the man they were hunting. No other wreckage or objects were found in the vicinity, just two very dead men. His men. He unscrewed the top and smelled the contents. Water. He poured it onto the ground before dropping the bottle.

Marturak didn't want to report that he was unable to perform to his general's expectations – that the site was unsecured, that two of his soldiers were dead, and that he was in pursuit of an unknown number of survivors. He decided to abbreviate it to something more innocuous like 'site unsecured'.

The operating procedure for this mission was that he would report within two hours of arrival, and give the go-ahead for the experts to come in, clean the area and recover the black boxes – the flight data and flight deck voice recorders. If the site was unsecured then he would have to report every subsequent twelve hours, or until the mission had been accomplished, whichever came first.

As if on cue, one of his men materialised and produced two metal cases painted a luminous orange, roughly the size of shoeboxes, marked with number sequences and letters. The aircraft's black boxes must have been exactly where they had been told to search for them because they'd turned up quickly. One of the heavy cases was badly dented. Marturak turned it over. It didn't appear to have been breached. He congratulated the soldier. Finding the black boxes was something good at least. Marturak told the man to guard them with his life. The soldier saluted, and retreated into the night.

Back at Maros, Marturak had scoffed at the notion that this operation might last more than a day. He had been given a maximum of three days to resolve the situation – their rations would expire then. Time was crucial on this one. That had been made very clear. He had expected to go in, quickly establish that there were no survivors, then get his men out within a few hours. How many people were likely to have survived a 747 ploughing into the hills? Answer: none. Simple, clean, easy. Marturak hawked up a gob of phlegm from deep in the back of his throat and aimed it at a frog resting on the splintered end of a tree stump. The frog jumped clear just as the spinning oyster plastered its perch.

He called his men together and laid out a plan. The troops then formed a line abreast, one hundred metres across, and began moving into the jungle. Sergeant Marturak was happy to be leaving the crash site. It smelled disgusting and it was virtually a bio-hazard zone – too much death and too many insects.

Marturak removed the night vision goggles from his pack, adjusted them to his head and switched on the power source. The NVGs turned the black, shapeless wall of jungle in front of them into clearly visible individual trees and bushes, picked out in various shades of green, the spectrum of visible light human eyes were most sensitive to. His men glowed lime as they moved out of the clearing and into the bush.

Sydney, 0900 Zulu, Wednesday, 29 April

News report, ABC radio: 'The Qantas 747 that crashed in the early hours of this morning has still not been located, despite a massive search. The aircraft, en-route from Sydney to London via Bangkok, was carrying a full complement of passengers. The focus of the search remains the island of Sulawesi, although Indonesian air force authorities are believed to be pushing for a widening of the search to Malaysia and Thailand.

'Experts still refuse to speculate on possible reasons for the crash until the wreckage is found. Qantas has announced that it will not release the passenger manifest until the relatives of all passengers have been located and informed.

'Authorities have become increasingly concerned with the mood of friends and family of the passengers on the doomed flight, who initially gathered at Sydney Airport in a vigil of hope. In the meantime, a hotline has been set up for relatives to contact for further information. The number is 1800 90 . . .'

Central Sulawesi, 0915 Zulu, Wednesday, 29 April

Suryei took the lead. Joe felt a bit uneasy about that. He thought it should have been him out front probing the tunnel, but Suryei just forged ahead and he was too exhausted to argue.

He'd managed to squeeze out a few more details from the woman, but they'd been given grudgingly. She lived in Richmond, a suburb of Melbourne, and she'd had some previous jungle experience. That was as far as he'd managed to get before meeting a wall of silence.

The going was slow but at least they were making progress. The tunnel walls guided them but it would have been nice to know where. They could be going around in circles for all they knew. It was getting darker by the minute. Occasionally he ran in to Suryei's backside and she once accidentally kicked him in the face. He sucked in his lip. It was swollen and split.

His back was now cramped from being doubled over and the skin on his hands was sliced by vegetation impossible to avoid on the tunnel floor. Joe didn't complain. He'd heard Suryei gasp in pain quite a few times, stop briefly, and then continue, but she wasn't whining either. Joe imagined her squeezing away the pain of another cut, wincing quietly while she sandwiched her hand under an armpit. She was a cool customer. But for her, Joe knew he'd already be dead.

Joe's watch didn't lie. They hadn't been in the tunnel long but it seemed like a lifetime. They'd briefly talked about leaving the security of the tunnel and striking off into the jungle, but his enthusiasm for this had been one-sided.

'Why?' Suryei asked. 'Neither of us has a compass. There are no landmarks to navigate by. We can't see any stars because of the cloud. The moon's not up yet. And we can't move nearly as freely through the undergrowth, as you've already discovered. And believe it or not, this tunnel is probably the safest way to get around. As I said earlier, it's like a freeway. The other, smaller animals know that too. They stay away.'

The question on Joe's lips slipped out before he could stop it. 'So what do we do then?' he whispered between short, hoarse breaths. He heard her stop just in time to avoid burying his head in her rear yet again.

'Jesus, how would I know? I'm just going in the opposite direction to the people with guns.' Joe was worried that they were being herded, and Suryei had just confirmed it.

'Look,' he whispered, sucking in wet oxygen. 'You said earlier you didn't really know where this was taking us. We could be heading back to the plane for all we know. We could just crawl right into those bastards.' In the almost complete darkness he could make out her shape, head bent, slumped against the side wall of the tunnel. But she was listening, so he continued. 'Also, just a guess, but I'd say those soldiers are pretty relaxed in the bush.' Joe took a breath. He felt like he was about to wade into deep, freezing water. 'I know this sounds crazy, but I once reviewed a computer game called *Nam*. The only way to evade the bad guys was to stay off the trails and yet here we are, heading down jungle main street.'

Silence.

Joe pressed on. Suryei was at least listening, keeping an open mind, even if he was talking about tactics featured in a computer game. 'If you stuck to the trails you'd always lose because there'd be ambushes and booby traps set by the enemy. The point was the enemy *expected* you to take the easy route, the trails. The only way to win was to stay off them and move through the untracked jungle.'

There was an unexpected pause. Joe wasn't sure whether she was about to laugh at him or just leave him behind. Her eventual response took him by surprise. 'Okay, I accept that,' she said quietly, intensely. 'So what do *you* think we should do?'

Joe thought, the now almost complete darkness hiding his insecurity. 'We should have something to eat and drink.' He rummaged through the rucksack and fetched out the trays of aeroplane food and two bottles of water. His fingers told him there were only three full bottles left amongst the empties. He thought he had six full bottles altogether. Have I dropped one somewhere? He hoped he'd made a mistake counting them in the first place. Joe handed her a tray and one of the bottles. 'And I don't know about you, but the other thing I need is sleep. I haven't slept in over thirty-six hours. Just an hour will do – I don't usually sleep much anyway.' He took a bite out of a stale ham and cheese sandwich with the crust cut off. 'Ugh,' he said, 'economy!'

'Sure, no problem. We can just find a nice hotel. I'd like a swim and room service,' she suggested sarcastically through a mouthful of sandwich.

Joe knew it sounded stupid. They were being hunted like animals and his big idea was to have a snooze. But the reality was that they were both physically and mentally exhausted.

'I'm finding it hard to concentrate. I'm not thinking about anything other than putting one hand in front of the other here. If we've got any chance of getting out of this alive, we'll need our wits about us. Simple as that.' Joe's conviction that he was right grew with every word. Sleep wasn't a luxury, it was mandatory.

Suryei surprised him. 'Okay, but only if you let me choose the hotel.'

'Fine,' he whispered. 'After you.' Then he paused while his tired mind ordered his thoughts. 'Suryei, any idea what sort of people we're up against?'

'Not really. All I know is what I learned when I was in East Timor.'

'What, taking wildlife shots?'

'No, back then I was doing hard news, covering the Indonesian military's handover after the elections in '99,' she said quietly. The tunnel reached a small clearing in the bush. She poked her head out tentatively and looked around. There was plenty of chirping from crickets and frogs – a good sign. She felt Joe bump into her. Again.

'Sorry,' he whispered. Suryei crawled out of the tunnel and stood in the small clearing, stretching, massaging the cramp out of the small of her back with her hands. Joe stood beside her quietly and did the same. They both then crouched, making themselves as small as possible.

'You said you were in East Timor,' Joe said after a minute of silence. 'Was it as terrible as the papers reported?'

'Worse.'

'I never really understood why. I mean, the place was a thorn in Indonesia's side from the beginning, wasn't it? Surely they'd have been pleased to be jack of it?'

Suryei was reluctant to talk. She wanted to save her breath, use it to get away from these people as fast as she could. But at the same time, talking helped them both imagine they were some place a long way from their current nightmare. 'Back home in Australia, the media went on about how giving up East Timor offended the pride of the TNI, the Indonesian army. That was often suggested as the reason behind the army's willingness to engage in violence and intimidation, and for arming and inciting the militias to do the same.'

'Yeah, I remember.'

Suryei was remembering now too, and vividly. 'The real motive for the death and destruction in East Timor was financial. There are 200 000 soldiers on the TNI's books but Indonesia can't afford that. They pay the soldiers a pittance. So the men are encouraged to augment what little the government pays them.'

'Shoot people in the morning, then sell oranges and lemons to the survivors in the afternoon?' Joe said.

'If you're not going to take this seriously then –'

'Sorry. But that's exactly what you're saying, isn't it?'

Suryei waved her hand dismissively in the darkness. 'I guess so, if you want to be flippant about it. In the light of that, what happened in East Timor made perfect sense. The army was entrenched in the economy of East Timor, from the bottom up and the top down. There was no way the TNI was ever going to happily turn its back and walk away from the businesses it had built up there over the previous twenty-five years. Once Indonesia lost control of East Timor – in other words, once the army gave up control of the economy of East Timor – all the hard work put in since the invasion in 1975 was for nothing.'

'Jesus, no wonder it got so nasty.'

'The TNI ends up controlling everything. And they drive tanks, so very few local communities argue,' Suryei said, summarising.

'Sounds like a hell of a recipe for graft and corruption. Are they good soldiers despite all that?'

Suryei put her hand on Joe's arm and squeezed gently. He stopped talking. The night creatures had suddenly fallen silent. Joe and Suryei listened hard, trying to discern the reason for the sudden stillness. Then, just as mysteriously, the night chorus chirped up again. After a while, Joe prompted, 'The Indonesian soldiers?'

'It depends who you ask, and on the unit you're referring to, and, for that matter, on what the government has sent them to do,' said Suryei. 'But, as individuals, there are good soldiers and bad ones, just as there are good people and bad people everywhere and in every walk of life.'

Suryei paused. 'There are some pretty awful things going on in Indonesia – Ambon, Aceh, Kalimantan and West Papua. We don't hear about a lot of it in Australia.'

'Why not, do you think?'

'Your average Australian isn't interested, for one thing, and for another, Canberra is reluctant to piss Jakarta off. I reckon the relationship between our two countries is shakier than they let on.'

Suryei suddenly felt nervous and vulnerable standing out in the open having a chat. Perhaps it was the subject matter. 'Come on. If we're going to get some rest, we'd better get moving. There are still a few hours left before the moon comes up and I think we should be hunkered down before it does.'

'Why is that?' asked Joe.

'I met a lot of different troops in East Timor, on both sides. The best – and worst – of the Indonesians were their Special Forces troops, the Kopassus. They're better trained and equipped than the average Indonesian foot-slogger. Meaner too. They do a lot of the real dirty work. If it is Kopassus out here, they might be carrying night vision goggles to help them see in the dark. When the moon comes out, it'll be like daylight for them but still pretty difficult for us to see. That'll give them a big advantage.'

Suryei threaded her way carefully across the clearing, staying low.

'Where did you pick up all this stuff?' asked Joe, genuinely impressed by the woman's general knowledge, particularly about military things.

'When I was in Dili, I had a friend. I met a soldier, a New Zealander.'

'Oh, what did he do?' Joe enquired, picking up on the subtle inflection on the word 'friend' that implied something more.

'Who said it was a he?' replied Suryei, distracted by the task of deciding which path through the jungle would provide the easiest passage. She quietly parted some fronds of a fleshy plant and slithered through the opening, staying low. Halfway through she stopped and quietly whispered behind her, 'Shh. Enough talk. Keep your eyes and ears open.'

The tunnel appeared to begin again on the other side of the clearing. Suryei's ghostly outline ignored it. She had decided to play the *Nam* way, disappearing into the wall of jungle.

It had taken Sergeant Marturak and his men at least fifteen minutes to advance in stealth to the creek. He had rarely seen such thick jungle. The current had carried the two soldiers gently downstream, scraping them occasionally along the bottom of the creek bed. They were not pretty corpses. His men quickly buried them under cairns of smooth black river stones.

The fact that two of his soldiers had perished in this way made Marturak angry. He wondered how the creek had been set alight. Was it an accident brought about by their own stupidity, or was there some kind of booby trap? Whoever it was had been close to his men when the explosion had killed them – the discarded empty water bottle proved that. Sergeant Marturak had not the slightest doubt that he would catch and kill the perpetrator, but who and what was he up against here? He found the entrance to a tunnel in the bush and sent two men into it.

The jungle was not an ideal environment for the NVGs. They worked best when there was some open space with large areas of contrast against which the distinctive shape of a human could be painted. In the thick bush, there were just too many confusing planes and shapes of green, and these often began inches from the lens of the goggles. Also, the NVGs cut peripheral vision down to a paltry twenty percent. It was like peering through a long black tunnel.

Sergeant Marturak swung his head slowly left and right. He couldn't see any of his men despite the fact that they were close, only five to seven metres on either side of him. He saw numerous pairs of astonishingly large, round eyes flashing bright green in the fork of a tree – tarsiers, small primates. He removed the goggles and fed them into a pouch off his webbing. The things were more trouble than they were worth. He concluded that he would be unlikely to catch his quarry at night unless he was lucky and they (yes, maybe it was a *they*) were stupid.

It was difficult to find anything in the complete darkness. Joe wondered what his hands must look like. They felt greasy, slick from the blood oozing from countless cuts. The pain almost didn't bother him any more. He was tired, a fog insulating his brain. They felt through the darkness with their hands, stopping every couple of metres to listen.

Unfortunately, noise was all around them. There were monkeys – he assumed they were monkeys – chattering high in the trees, coughs and snarls from the kind of animals that sounded as if they might like eating meat, and once there was the sound of something very large and heavy brushing aside the undergrowth. Suryei froze.

'Snake,' she said. That was a good reason to freeze in Joe's mind too. He wasn't phobic about them but they weren't exactly his best friends either.

Suryei whispered behind him, 'This place is crawling with them.'

'Don't you mean slithering?' Joe said quietly to himself, suddenly very careful about where he put his feet and hands.

After about half an hour of inching through the dense growth they stopped in a small clearing. 'I think this will do us,' said Suryei. 'Bed.'

Joe manoeuvred himself beside her and he reached out in front of him, into the darkness. The pain of the barb that immediately stabbed into his open palm made him cry out. 'Shit!'

'Careful,' said Suryei softly, and too late. It was impossible to see it in the darkness, but the bush Suryei was suggesting they sleep under seemed to be nature's answer to razor wire. It was tough and vine-like, with plenty of thick foliage, and lethal two-centimetre spikes protruding in every direction. The vine also bore some kind of bulb or fruit, and the spikes were obviously employed to protect it.

'I am not a bloody swami, Suryei. This is a bloody pin-cushion.' Joe stretched his hand into the dark again, more carefully this time. He isolated one of the barbs. It was a weapon, the kind of flora you gave a wide berth, not snuggled into. He'd been hoping for a pile of soft leaves at best, or maybe a fork in a tree at worst.

'We need protection and this bush will provide it. Have you seen those little fish that swim between sea urchin spines?' she asked condescendingly. 'Well, think like a little fish.'

He wondered how the hell they were going to get on the other side of those barbs without being skewered.

'Give me your shirt,' said Suryei. Joe was too tired to say anything smart about her request. He just did as he was asked. He could dimly see her wrap it around her hands, grab a section of the vine and lift it up. 'Come on,' she said impatiently. Joe wriggled under the mass of vine Suryei was hoisting. Once inside, he had to agree it made sense. No light whatsoever made it into the centre of the bush, and as there was no fruit on the inside, there wasn't a requirement to protect anything, which meant fewer thorns.

Once inside, Joe put his shirt back on and curled up on

the leaf litter. It was dry and soft and there weren't too many mosquitoes. All in all, a good idea. He vaguely heard Suryei say, 'You've got an hour, then it's my turn,' through the plunge into merciful sleep.

NSA HQ, Fort Meade, Maryland, 1210 Zulu, Wednesday, 29 April

Jesus, ten past eight. It was too early for serious brain-work, especially given the late finish the previous evening. Indeed, it felt like he'd never even left the joint at all. Bob Gioco's mind didn't function until he'd had at least two double espressos. The real stuff, full strength and black as sump oil. He had them both poured into the one Styrofoam cup. He sipped the hot, bitter liquid and felt it going to work on his synapses. This group was something special, and worth missing a couple of hours of sleep for.

The expertise gathered in the lecture theatre repre-sented a whole new ball game for the NSA. It was part of ELINT, the division once concerned only with the inter-ception and analysis of radar signals and missile telemetry, largely from the Soviet Union. After the dissolution of the Eastern Bloc, there was a proliferation of nuclear materials and other weapons of mass destruction, and of their deliv-ery systems. And now there was an insidious new threat to world peace: computer terrorism. It was now entirely pos-sible to bring a country to its knees, and cause widespread death and mayhem, simply by tampering with the appro-priate computer network. ELINT's new role was to provide early warning and counter-intelligence to prevent these dangerous new threats from ever coming to pass.

Gioco stifled a yawn while he settled into his chair and smoothed a hand across hair still wet from the shower, but an aberrant lock refused to obey the pressure and sprang up annoyingly.

Like all organisations, especially US government ones, the NSA had a passion for acronyms. The one for this gathering was COMPSTOMP: Computer Security, Tasking, Observation and Manipulation Protection. It was a fancy title for the NSA's new anti-cyberterrorist node. The group had its problems – too much intelligence dedicated to information anarchy in the one place, Bob often thought.

A young mathematician, indeed the one giving this morning's briefing, was the creator of COMPSTOMP, and a vindication of the NSA's policy of poaching the finest math brains in the country. She had followed a hunch that hackers left individual and distinctive signatures – fingerprints – when they entered systems. She thought it doubtful that hackers would crack computer systems with a one-day pad mentality, never using the same logic process twice. It was more likely they would find a key that worked for them, then use it over and over because, she assumed, even people with above-average intelligence were lazy. If her theory checked out, then those fingerprints could be identified, catalogued and tracked. As it happened, she was right. Hackers used consistent processes, rarely changing them, and no two processes were the same.

The NSA supported the theory with a budget, and COMPSTOMP winked into existence. Within six months it had quite a comprehensive database containing over 4000 fingerprints. Each rap sheet detailed a hacker's misdeeds, call sign, off-line name, address, employment records, all of which were continuously being updated and checked. It was a massive job, but it was paying dividends.

The overwhelming success of COMPSTOMP made the theory's author, the twenty-one year old woman sitting on the floor amongst her comrades, a hero within the NSA. But COMPSTOMP was super secret, so her fame was limited. Hackers weren't stupid. If they knew Big Brother was watching their every move, they would start employing their own counter-measures, such as altering their signatures, and the group's effectiveness would be drastically impaired.

As was normal practice with the NSA, COMPSTOMP had new detection software developed in-house to employ in the fight to keep information secure. The most successful of these was called Watchdog. Watchdog alerted COMPSTOMP of a computer break-in in progress. COMPSTOMP would then check the hacker's signature and determine his or her identity against the register. If the system was part of the nation's defence, or essential to its national security, the hacker would be tracked and arrested. If he or she was extremely good and managed to break through the internal firewalls that protected the core of these systems from outside interference, an ultimatum would be given – join the US government willingly or become a reluctant guest of it in a small, dark cell.

So far, no one had taken the latter option and COMP-STOMP was largely made up of people who had been caught with their hands in the cookie jar. Oddly, there seemed to be little resentment about being spirited out of their old life and given a new one. The pay was extremely good and the work immensely satisfying, not least because of the enormous resources at the NSA's disposal. COMPSTOMP was even encouraged to set up a dummy company, Fido Security, and lease the Watchdog database technology to other countries and large corporations. The income stream from this activity was now very healthy, which pleased the oversight committees on Capitol Hill no end. And, more importantly, it allowed the NSA to spread its information-gathering capabilities into unwitting rich new areas previously denied it.

Watchdogs were now patrolling the systems of companies as diverse as General Motors, IBM, Starbucks and Virgin. Quite a few countries had signed up – the Netherlands, Argentina, Indonesia and others. Not all these clients took the same level of protection. Watchdog could operate merely as an alarm system or a complete 'back-to-base' tracking system, although this latter option was extremely expensive because it made the NSA a de facto full-time employee. Of course, none of these customers had the slightest notion that, through Fido, the NSA was patrolling their hard-drives. Fido Security presented itself as a stand-alone high-end service company staffed by the best and brightest, one of the few Internet start-ups to survive the burst e-bubble because it had something unique and worthy to offer: total security.

Mostly the COMPSTOMP/Fido group discussed interesting ways to attack and defend systems, and the effects of any new technology coming on line. Gioco found these discussions exhilarating. Much of the talk was pure speculation but the air seemed to crackle when they were onto something new. Often, the consequences of their brainstorming brought real benefits to the NSA and its ability to meet its charter. They also discussed the fingerprints of the newcomers to cyberterrorism, most of whom had aggressive or obscure call signs like Howitzer and Pukeboy.

Today's COMPSTOMP gathering, though, was low key. The world's computers were enjoying a period of relative safety and security. There'd been a bit of a discussion about whether information should be contained by firewalls or set free to benefit mankind. Bob had heard it all before. There were good reasons to keep information free but, in his view, better reasons against it.

'In conclusion, then, over the last week all we've had is a bit of activity from one "Cee Squared",' said the brilliant young mathematician sitting in the lotus position on the carpeted floor. 'The system notified the client of the penetration – they have the full package – and action, if any, was theirs to take or not. It was a low-grade intrusion, a small server off the main system and hardly worth worrying about. Cee Squared hasn't been active for a long time. Thought he'd given the game away.

'Anyway, the details have gone to the South-East Asia section head – that's you, isn't it, Bob?' Bob held his finger up and gave a casual salute from the darkness at the back of the theatre. 'And that's it, really,' she said, snapping the folder closed.

The group broke up and the room cleared quickly, leaving Gioco alone with his thoughts. There was something troubling him, but he couldn't nail it.

Jakarta, 1210 Zulu, Wednesday, 29 April

General Suluang found himself exercising considerably more care. He was just being prudent. Listening devices guaranteed there were not many places, if any, that one's conversation could be kept confidential. The places he listed as unsecured now included his home, his office, his car. Indeed, thinking about it, the general wondered whether he could speak with anyone anywhere and be assured of keeping the exchange private.

Suluang speculated whether his caution was an indication that he was losing control of the situation, but he dismissed the thought instantly. The feeling of disquiet, however, once imbedded, was difficult to shake.

Lanti Rajasa, the head of the security police, was in the driver's seat of the battered old teal-coloured Toyota Kijang, one of many that rattled slowly up into the hills behind Jakarta. Motorcycles overtook them in a steady stream, blowing oily smoke that swirled in their headlights. The Kijang passed a poor village quietly announcing its existence to the world with a small soft-drinks stand and a pathetic stall that sold carved junk to tourists.

The location of the meeting place was Rajasa's choice but the general agreed to it. They drove in silence. The vehicle was unsafe. Rajasa had ordered it 'cleansed' beforehand and no bug had been found, but neither man was confident that Indonesia possessed technology equal to identifying the latest in listening devices.

Rajasa glanced regularly at the mirrors for following lights but this was Java, the most densely populated island on earth, and there would always be lights bobbing in the rear-vision mirrors.

The Toyota slowed and pulled off the crudely sealed road into a clearing past the small village. Both men got out and walked to the road, where they joined a steady stream of locals going about their business in the early hours of the evening. It was dark but for the constant glare from the lights of passing traffic and, with their heads lowered, it would be impossible for the casual passer-by to identify them, even though the general had one of the most recognised faces in Jakarta. 'A seat number on the aircraft was identified as the location of the thief. It was in our power to kill the occupant and neutralise the threat. I don't believe I had a choice,' Suluang said, shaking his head slowly.

'General, you did what was needed to protect Indonesia. We're just lucky the means to maintain secrecy was in your power,' said Rajasa.

Yes, but for how long? both men thought.

'You've located the wreckage?' Rajasa asked.

'Yes, and the mopping up has begun. Any leaks from your end?'

'No. Security has been tight. But for this one –' he cleared his throat for dramatic effect ' – incident.' Rajasa couldn't help himself. 'Incident' was a hell of a euphemism for the shooting down of a jumbo jet. 'How are you handling it with the government?'

'The parliament knows only what we tell them, and that's not very much. In fact, they're unwitting accomplices, spreading disinformation. They're telling the Australians that the 747 may or may not have come down in Indonesian airspace. Of course, the reasons for the crash are unknown. And we, Indonesia, are very sensitive about having foreigners telling us what to do. Etcetera, etcetera. You know, the usual line.

'It has been easy to manipulate the search procedure to exclude all but hand-picked military personnel – our people. I think, actually, that the parliament is enjoying the game. Causing Australia anxiety and frustration is giving them a secret pleasure, but they'd never admit it.'

A trike pulled off the road in front of them and three people jumped off to help right another trike that had broken an axle under a heavy load of chopped wood. The general waited until they'd walked past the noisy melee before continuing. 'All games aside, Rajasa, as I see it, we have two alternatives. But only one real choice.'

Rajasa nodded.

'One: we can clean up the site as best we can, then announce the aircraft has been located. The government can then graciously allow in an international investigation team. We hold our breath and maintain our original timetable.

'Two: we can move our plans forward and let the incident with the plane be seen in the context of the broader picture.'

'I see what you mean about only having one choice.'

'I knew you'd agree.'

General Suluang considered whether or not he should let Rajasa in on the fact that things were not going to plan at the crash site. Unfortunately, he was not exactly sure what the problem was. The Kopassus sergeant had communicated that the site was not secured but gave no other details in order to maintain mission secrecy. He was in the dark himself now, and that, given his exposure, was not a comfortable place to be. A particularly noisy two-stroke bike rattled past, piston slapping in its barrel, carrying mother, father, two young children and a baby. Suluang decided at that moment that there was already too much uncertainty and he would not pass on vagaries. Uncertainty bred nervousness.

Rajasa's mind was racing. If they weren't bold, everything would be lost. Obviously, the events of the last twenty-four hours had forced them to play their hand. They had to move, and fast.

'I assume the 747 was shot down with some kind of missile.'

'Heat-seekers.'

'They leave distinctive results.'

The general frowned.

'General, you did the right thing. The terrorist could easily have emailed the details around the world.'

That had occurred to the general too, and it had worried him considerably.

'But I don't think that happened,' continued Rajasa. 'We'd have all kinds of other pressures on us now if that were the case. We're not ready yet though, are we?'

'No, we need more time.'

'How much?'

'A month would be good, but three weeks minimum.'

'Can we hold out that long?'

'We'll have to.'

'What do you suggest, General?'

'Continue to say that we're searching thoroughly and that nothing has turned up. Aircraft from the Second World War are still being discovered after more than fifty years. It's not beyond belief that finding a 747 in such a remote place as Sulawesi could prove difficult.'

'How loyal are our troops at the scene?'

The general knew that the lives of his men would depend on his next words. 'I can speak for Sergeant Marturak, but of the rest, I can't be certain.' After a moment's pause, he continued. 'As for the pilot who fired the missiles . . . ' He shrugged. The unfinished sentence, together with the questioning tilt of the general's head, was a death sentence.

The police chief pulled a pad from his top pocket and

made a notation on it. Suluang found Rajasa's attention to detail reassuring. 'We'll need to keep security as tight as possible. I believe a certain Bali air traffic controller is no longer with us.'

'We had to act fast,' said the general.

'I agree. Have you heard from your men at the crash site yet?'

Here it was, the question Suluang had been dreading. 'No,' he lied. 'But they are due to report soon,' he said after checking his watch. 'I take your point about continuing the disinformation,' he said, changing the subject. 'But we can't control the knowledge of the crash site for too much longer.'

'Because?'

'Sulawesi is rugged and largely uninhabited, but it's not the moon. There are mining interests on the island – logging, tourists. But the main reason is spy satellites.'

'Australia doesn't have them.'

'No, but its allies do and they'll find the wreckage of a burning 747 in an instant. In the short term, though, we have a window,' said the general, thinking aloud. 'It is up to us to make the best use of that. But we'll have to be careful, and stay on our toes. Events are going to be difficult to control when the truth is known.'

'We should meet with our comrades,' said Rajasa, his tone resolute.

'Yes,' said the general. 'But if time allows, I would prefer to defer any debriefing until I have a report from the site. What about Mao? Is he committed?'

'I believe so.'

'That's not the emphatic answer I was hoping for.'

'General, you know Kukuh Masri better than me. He is

always considered, rarely excited or excitable. I'm as sure as I can be that he is with us one hundred percent.'

'Okay, Lanti, but do me a favour and keep an eye on him.'

'His driver is one of my people.'

The general patted him on the shoulder. 'As always, you're ahead of me in many things.'

'Doing my job, General.' Lanti felt energised. His fingers tingled. They were poised on the very knife-edge of history. 'So we go?'

'Yes, old friend. There is now no turning back.'

'God is great!' said Suluang

'Allah Akbar!' agreed Rajasa.

The two men paused at a satay stall and bought some sticks from a young man fanning the coals with a scrap of cardboard. They turned and began the walk back to the car, both, for a time, lost in the minutiae of their own plans. A woman drifting by on a Yamaha scooter wearing Western clothes caught the general's eye. She smiled at him, reminding him of Elizabeth, his mistress. There was something about her hair, or the dress she wore. He glanced at his Rolex. Plenty of time to make their rendezvous at the Hyatt. The other night she opened the door for him wearing something short and tight and vaguely transparent. Perhaps tonight she would greet him wearing nothing at all . . .

Parliament House, Canberra, 1325 Zulu, Wednesday, 29 April

Niven woke exhausted after a brief catnap and sat upright on his couch. He checked the time: almost half past

123

eleven. He'd desperately wanted to sleep, to curl up under the warmth of the covers at home, and wake up to find the whole Qantas mess a bad dream. But the situation was real, and he knew that he'd never get any worthwhile shut-eye so he hadn't bothered trying.

He'd requested a briefing on Sulawesi, but nothing much of practical use had turned up. It was an island covered in volcanoes, formerly known as Celebes, and very inhospitable. A small mountain of largely useless reference material sat on his desk and spilled onto the carpeted floor.

There was a knock on his door. 'Come,' he said. Griffin walked in, looking dishevelled, tie off and top button open, and flopped onto the CDF's sofa. 'Hey, Griff, I see you live here like me,' said Niven. 'What's up?'

The ASIS chief held up a folder and waggled it, expelling a lungful of air noisily as his body sank into the cushions. 'A DOD briefing on Hasanuddin AFB, Sulawesi, its strategic importance – the usual.' He tossed the cream manila folder onto the pile on Niven's desk. 'You turn up anything?'

'On Sulawesi? We've got nada on the place, and neither does Foreign Affairs. Can you believe I had to send someone down to the local library and travel shop? Once you leave the population centres on the coast, it's a mystery island. There's bugger-all on the place in these books. A bit of history – it was once the capital of the Dutch Spice Islands. There's the occasional picture of a prahu, a local teak schooner with a high sweeping bow, and a mug shot of a Bugis, the people who sail them. Oh, and the Toraja, a tribe who bury their dead in limestone caves tunnelled into cliff faces. That's about it.'

'The best source we found was this fifteen dollar tourist

guide.' Niven held up a thin, greeting card-sized publication. 'Get this. It says here, "Look at the maps and our texts on the island's central regions: you'll notice there is very little information available for most of the mountainous areas. If you travel to any of these parts, let us know if you survive and what you found." Great, huh?' he said, flipping the booklet into the bin.

'Yeah, I know. I've come up with pretty much the same from my people. But I do have something that'll interest you,' said Griffin. 'We have an asset on Sulawesi.'

'You're joking,' said Niven, suddenly focused.

'No, seriously. At a place called Maros, around twenty-five klicks north of Makassar. Near Hasanuddin AFB.'

Niven leaned forward. He sensed that Griffin had some news. 'C'mon, mate, you do drag things on. Spit it out.'

'We got something from our asset this morning. Apparently, a couple of Super Pumas loaded with Special Forces – Kopassus – took off heading north. The helos came back three hours later. Empty. It's all in the folder.' Griffin nodded at the sheaf he'd put on Niven's table.

The information didn't appear to be ground-breaking, but it could be the key to something major. 'What's the significance?' asked Niven.

'Apparently they were in a big hurry to go somewhere,' said Griffin.

'Do you think our Indonesian friends are keeping something from us?'

'No, but the asset there thought the behaviour unusual. The NSA also thinks there could be some significance in it. The question is, what?'

'So we are getting some cooperation from the Americans at last?'

'Spike, they've never been uncooperative. We're getting lots of NSA stuff. They just can't give us satellites. There's nothing sinister in it.'

'Hmm,' said Niven, thinking. 'Well, at least we've got someone up there on the ground. Can we get the asset more involved if we need to?'

'She's trained as an observer only, but she's good – thorough.'

'Got any ideas?' asked Niven.

'Not at the moment. What about the Kopassus? What do you think?'

'Not much to go on, is it? Special Forces guys move around on training exercises every second week, just to keep sharp. As you said, could be significant, or not,' Niven said, spinning a pencil around his thumb habitually, looking uncharacteristically lost. 'I can't believe we're still in the dark, Griff. Bloody frustrating.' He let the pencil fall to the desk with a clatter and wrung his hands. 'I'm going to hang around here tonight and see what turns up. Just as a matter of interest, did you know there are three hundred and forty-seven individual sites on the Net dedicated to aircraft crashes?'

The intelligence chief said no, he didn't know that. He stood to go. 'Okay, Spikey, if you need me you know where to reach me. And get some sleep yourself, or you'll be no use to anyone.'

'Sure,' said Niven, turning on his computer.

Yeah, sure, thought Griffin.

Joe was free-falling. Worse, he was being dragged down, accelerating backwards, arms and feet flailing as he fell. He was breathing hard, the oxygen being sucked from his lungs. The air pressure pushed into his back so that he felt squeezed by the forces above and the forces below – pressed meat in a sandwich. He opened his eyes with a start. The ghost light of pre-dawn had replaced the dark. They had overslept. And there was something else. Silence. That troubling, localised, eerie void he'd experienced in the tunnel. Suryei was also frozen beside him, except for her eyes. They were making a comical sideways motion. Again and again. He followed Suryei's exaggerated eye movements and then he saw it too. The peril of their immediate situation became clear. His heart stopped. Treading softly just on the other side of the bush was a soldier.

They were painfully cramped already, so Joe and Suryei didn't need to freeze. They followed the man with their eyes. He wasn't looking in their direction, but away from them. They had no idea whether he was alone, leading other soldiers, or bringing up the rear. By oversleeping, they had totally lost their position in relation to their pursuers. When they were in the tunnel, they knew not only that the soldiers were behind them, but also how much of a head start they had. Now, they had lost that perspective. The stress and strain of the crash and their subsequent flight had sapped their bodies of all reserves of strength. They'd only meant to sleep for an hour each, but the second they'd closed their eyes they fell not so much asleep as unconscious, their metabolisms working overtime to repair the mental and physical damage sustained.

Now they'd woken from their brief few hours of hibernation to discover themselves without any kind of tactical advantage whatsoever. The enemy was at the gate. All he had to do was turn, brush aside a few leaves, and the bush would present him with a prize. A spike from the vine had penetrated Joe's Converse shoes. He felt pinned like a moth to a board, vulnerable and pathetic.

Joe braced himself for the bullets, hypnotised by the sight of the soldier. A rabbit in the headlights. He held his breath and waited for death to spit from the muzzle of the man's rifle. But the bullets didn't come. Instead, the soldier propped his gun against a fern and urinated into the bush. He appeared to look everywhere but *at* them. Yellow fluid coursed down one of the vines. It ran down another branch, and dripped onto the ground. Eventually, a small puddle formed at Suryei's foot. She dared not move. The smell of the urine was sickening. Steam curled from it. Suryei felt like retching. Groaning occasionally with relief until he finished, the soldier buttoned his fly, picked up his rifle and rested the butt in the crook of his elbow, barrel pointing towards the jungle canopy high overhead. He then moved off, cautiously.

Joe began to say something but Suryei put her forefinger to her lips. They lay motionless and silent for at least half an hour. Suryei spoke first, in a whisper. 'We don't know whether that man was on his own. If we leave here now, we might walk straight into a whole bunch of them. We'll have to stay here till nightfall.'

A whole day . . . Joe frowned at that but he didn't have an alternative suggestion. 'Thought for sure he'd see us,' he said.

'Me too,' agreed Suryei in a low whisper. 'But it's darker in here than it is out there. Those little binocular things high on his head were those night vision goggles I told you about. If he'd been wearing them . . . ' She drew her finger across her throat.

Joe took his first good look at Suryei. He realised that he really didn't have a clue what she looked like. They'd met in the perpetual twilight under the jungle canopy and complete darkness had come down fast. She was curled in a loose foetal position beside him. He knew she was Asian but her accent was Australian. Her almond eyes were closed and he could see her abdomen rising and falling as she breathed. She was petite, smaller than he'd thought. Her face was covered in sweat-soaked mud and dust, and her black shoulder-length hair was matted with leaves, twigs and dirt. He imagined that she could be quite attractive, but it was difficult to tell. Given our current situation, why am I even wasting energy thinking about things like that? he wondered. Here I am, being hunted and shot at, starving, possibly about to die in the fucking jungle, for Christ's sake, considering whether or not this woman's hot. What did her looks have to do with anything anyway? She has saved my life at least once. Isn't that enough? Still, his mind wandered on. He concluded that she was between twenty and thirty, but even that was hard to be sure of.

Sergeant Marturak was as good as lost. He knew exactly where he was geographically, but he had not the slightest idea where his quarry had gone. It was as if the jungle had opened up and swallowed his objective whole, without a trace. Again he wondered who he was up against. An ordinary person with no jungle training would have been overtaken by now, no question about it. The jungle was a dangerous and inhospitable place for the inexperienced. He reminded himself that it also presented an almost infinite number and variety of hiding places. The man could be holed up somewhere, too frightened and scared to show himself. Marturak had initially hoped that the survivor may have gone to ground in the tunnel beaten into the jungle by the wildlife, but the two men he'd sent up into it had reported no contact.

He knew the young man on the hill had seen him kill the old couple. That's what had frightened him into the jungle, and the volley of automatic fire hadn't helped either. He now cursed his own lack of patience. He should have trawled for any and all survivors first, then killed them as a group. That way he could have then simply radioed for the pick-up and by now he would be back at the barracks. He'd been overconfident, and there was never any value in overconfidence. But it was too late to dwell on earlier tactical errors. The question now was how to make good on this mission.

It was an important operation, of that he had no doubt. The crashed aircraft was a Qantas 747-400 and it had come down here in secrecy. He could make a lot out of successfully completing this job and he was not about to let the opportunity slip through his fingers. He whistled softly, imitating a species of bird common to Java but not found on Sulawesi, and caught the attention of the soldiers on either side of him.

Hand signals told them to stop and have breakfast. The men dropped to their haunches immediately after communicating the order along the line, and broke into their rations. Sergeant Marturak considered his next move as he unconsciously waved off the cloud of insects surrounding him. They were right on the equator and the day was heating up fast. Soon it would be almost too hot to move in the still, steamy sauna under the jungle canopy. But he was used to it. He had trained for it and he liked it. What he didn't like was being made a fool of.

He considered it remote that any untrained person could have tracked this far into the jungle as his current position. Splitting his men into two troops, he decided, would be the best option now. He would have each force sweep the jungle at right angles to their current line of march for around three kilometres, and then turn again through ninety degrees and move back towards the crash site. In that way, he would have picked through almost fifteen square kilometres of jungle: fifteen square kilometres of one of the densest concentrations of plant life on the planet.

It was possible that the man could slip through his fingers, but improbable. Another soft bird-like whistle gathered his force together. Marturak got down on a knee, cleared a small patch of earth and outlined their tactics with his dagger. He then divided his men and told them they had five minutes to complete their breakfast. Few words were exchanged between the men. No one smoked, joked or laughed. The man they were hunting could be close by and no one wanted to compromise their position. Everyone wanted this mission over with.

Unseen, the snake silently parted the bush and made its way to its nest. Suryei shifted her weight, pulling one leg towards her. The snake instantly reacted, rearing up and flaring its distinctive hood.

'Jesus!' said Suryei when she saw it, louder than she'd intended.

'What!?' said Joe.

'Cobra!' For the first time, Suryei saw a bunch of leaves and twigs gathered on the ground just inside the leaf canopy. There were eggs in the centre of the nest and a couple had broken open.

The snake moved its head from side to side, sensitive to the slightest movements made by Joe and Suryei.

'It's seriously deadly.'

'Seriously pissed off too, by the looks of it,' said Joe under his breath, trying to disappear into the foliage behind him.

'It's a mother, see?'

Joe saw the smashed eggs in the nest.

'We have to go. Get ready.'

Joe sat up slowly and the snake reared higher, as if it found his movement a challenge to fight.

'Careful,' said Suryei quietly. It was difficult for both of them to move. They had cramped into their resting positions. Joe flexed his hands. Blood cracked and fresh, crimson rivulets appeared. He ignored the pain. He slowly and carefully took his axe out of his bag. Suryei moved her foot.

The snake raised its hooded head and reared back, tensing to strike. It looked at Suryei and then at Joe and then back at Suryei, as if uncertain who to bite first. Suryei moved her foot, shifting a section of vine which sprang back. The snake reacted, striking at Suryei's feet. It darted once, twice, advancing belligerently. Suryei screamed. Joe tried to fend it off with the head of his axe. Before she realised it, Suryei was up, pushing wildly through the vines, thrashing through the spikes that tore at her clothes and skin. Joe was right behind her. The snake moved its head aggressively from side to side as the threat retreated, and then returned to sentry duty, coiling around its eggs.

Joe found Suryei collapsed at the foot of an enormous teak. She was whimpering to herself. Her composure had evaporated. She wrenched the shoe off, examined it, and found two neat sets of punctures in the leather upper. She rapidly switched her attention to her foot, and then fell back against the tree, relieved.

'What? What?!' Joe found her anxiety contagious.

'Nothing, thank Christ!' Suryei rasped. 'The bastard didn't get me.'

'Bitch.'

'What?'

'Bitch. You said it was a female, remember?' Joe picked up the shoe and examined the punctures in it. 'Saved by Nike,' he said quietly.

Suryei stood up and hopped behind Joe. She rummaged in his rucksack and pulled out a bottle of water. 'Shouldn't we save that for later?' he said as he watched her pour it over the shoe.

'I knew a photographer once who was taking shots of one of those things in a snake park. He got cocky. Went right up close to take its photo. The flash and the noise angered the cobra and it struck. It missed the photographer but got the camera body instead. The photographer wiped the venom off with his finger. Within an hour, he was fighting for his life. So, I'm washing my shoe, okay?'

'Okay, okay . . .'

'Sorry. I'm just a bit freaked out at the moment.' Suryei sloshed the water onto the suspect area of the shoe.

'Save some of that water for your arm. You're bleeding.'
He ripped off the other sleeve, then poured the last of the
water into the deep gashes. The sleeve made do as a bandage, and he wound it around her arm a few times.

'So are you,' she said.

'My blood clots quickly.' Joe drank the remaining water.

Suryei noted his physique. 'I thought you said you were
a computer nerd. What's with the muscles?' Suryei was
instantly annoyed at herself for asking the question. She
played it back in her mind and she thought she'd sounded
like some boy-happy bimbo. All that had been missing
was the giggle.

Joe caught the rapid swings in Suryei's mood. He put
his shirt back on. 'I box. Strictly amateur stuff, but I've
been doing it since I was ten.'

'Great,' said Suryei.

'I don't do it to beat people up,' he said, sensing the sarcasm. 'I was bullied as a kid. You know, the weedy guy in
the playground. Now I just do it to keep fit. It's a sport.' He
shrugged.

She didn't like boxers, was that it? Joe shook his head to
clear it. There were more pressing issues at hand. They
couldn't just hide and wait for a rescue that might never
come, or come too late. They had no food left, virtually no
water and no survival training. They couldn't just walk out
– they had not the slightest idea what direction would
lead them to the nearest outpost of civilisation. All they
had was each other.

And then the unexpected happened. A soldier stepped
out from behind the bush they'd been hiding in, the stock
of the rifle at his cheek, eye positioned over the sight. The
scare with the cobra had made Joe and Suryei forget about

him completely. He sighted the barrel from one to the other. Joe's mouth was open. It was like a movie they were watching, rather than something that was actually happening to them.

The three people just looked at each other, wondering what to do next. The soldier was nervous, shouting something in a language Joe didn't understand. To his surprise, Suryei answered him. She put her hands behind her head and sank to her knees. The soldier gestured aggressively at Joe to do the same. He didn't move fast enough. The soldier reversed his rifle and drove the stock hard into Joe's stomach. The blow caught him by surprise, winding him, but a daily regimen of three hundred sit-ups prevented any real damage. Joe fought for breath, falling to his knees, gagging. The soldier still wasn't satisfied with his level of compliance. He lifted the barrel of his rifle and pressed the flash suppressor hard against Joe's cheek, prising his teeth apart.

'No!' yelled Suryei. The bastard was going to pull the trigger. 'No!'

And then the cobra struck. It lunged through the bush beside the soldier's leg and sank its fangs into his thigh. The man looked at the snake like he didn't believe it was happening, but then it bit again and again, ferociously, and the reality of the attack suddenly hit him. He screamed and emptied the magazine of his weapon into it.

Joe and Suryei ran.

Sergeant Marturak heard the scream and the spray of automatic fire. It took them seven minutes to reach the spot where their comrade was lying on the ground. The soldier was convulsing violently and white froth bubbled from his mouth. The cobra's shattered body writhed beside him. It wasn't dead. Bullets had broken its back in several places and it was coiling itself into a knot.

One of the soldiers gripped the snake from behind the head and sliced it off with his machete. Sergeant Marturak had once before seen a man die from a cobra bite. He felt pity for the private. Fortunately, they carried antivenom in their kit. One of the soldiers administered a double shot of the pale liquid with a disposable hypodermic. The man shaking uncontrollably on the jungle floor was in a bad way. Antivenom or not, it was by no means certain he would survive.

Marturak cursed softly. He would have to leave one man behind with the stricken soldier. Morale would suffer if he just left the man to his fate. His force was steadily shrinking. Including the two he'd lost in the fire, his squad was now effectively reduced by twenty percent, with four men either dead, wounded, or otherwise out of action. Again, he wondered whether this man convulsing on the ground had walked into some kind of booby trap set by the man he was hunting.

He questioned the soldier babbling at his feet, but got nothing coherent. One of his soldiers called Marturak over to the base of the tree that dominated the clearing. There was blood. Another found a piece of material hanging on some thorns. More blood. There had definitely been some kind of struggle here. With luck, the injuries would slow the target. Sergeant Marturak now had a rich, red trail to follow. He deployed his diminished forces for the pursuit. Things were looking up.

Joe and Suryei knew the soldiers were close behind. They heard an eerie, lone bird call carried on the still, early morning air. They moved quickly and carelessly through the living obstacle course of the jungle. Their passage alerted the local inhabitants of this world and sent them scurrying noisily from trees and bushes. The monkeys were the worst. It was almost as if they delighted in giving away Joe and Suryei's position, which, in fact, was true. The primates were the jungle's early warning system, and they were remarkably good at their job. The soldiers, however, knew how to thread through the jungle quickly, and relatively effortlessly, with little noise or disturbance. Although Joe and Suryei had several minutes head start, that advantage was whittled away with every step.

Suryei began to claw her way desperately through the foliage. Joe caught the urgency. The jungle was now full of sound. Bushes and ferns were moving, seemingly of their own accord, all around them. They were being surrounded.

A soldier appeared in front of them, stepping from behind the trunk of one of the jungle's giants, and barred their path. He raised his carbine to fire. Not fast enough. Joe swung his axe against the man's rifle. It discharged harmlessly into the air. Three of the man's fingers plopped like fat grubs to the jungle floor as the blade of his axe clinked against the weapon's metal barrel. The soldier looked at his hand in disbelief. He dropped to the ground and tried to pick up his digits with the hand that no longer had any fingers.

Joe dodged around the tree trunk as automatic fire cracked behind them and slugs fizzed past just centimetres from his body. Joe and Suryei ran blindly, oblivious to the thorns and spikes that tore at them as they raced. The fact that Joe was facing death was apparent to his subconscious. Base survival instincts overwhelmed him. He was merely an organism trying to stay alive, clawing through the kaleidoscope of green, running as a terrified animal might run from a predator.

Joe suddenly burst out of the bush and into a campsite where half a dozen tents were neatly arranged in a semi-circle in a clearing hacked out of the jungle. He stood there swaying, mouth open, brain fighting to come to grips with the sudden appearance of civilisation. Smoke curled from a few low breakfast fires. He smelled coffee. Joe would not have been more astonished if he'd found himself in a shopping mall. Suryei staggered into the clearing, panting, seconds behind him. She stopped in her tracks and looked around in shock.

They stood, sucking in air, in front of a group of men, all of whom were armed and wearing building-style hard hats. The men were obviously nervous, fingering a range of weapons including rifles and machetes. Their camp was in a slight depression, and the noise from the exploding 747 five kilometres away had apparently passed unnoticed, shielded as they were by a ridge. The few who had been woken by the distant rumble thought it nothing more than the last gasp of the monsoon thundering over the horizon. But all of them had heard the approaching gunfire. Nature was also in an uproar with macaques leaping and screeching in the treetops. The sight and state of the two people spat out by the jungle into their clearing took them totally by surprise. Swaying breathlessly in the middle of their camp were two wild and desperate-looking people, covered in dirt and bloody scratches.

The group of clean-shaven men, some Asian, some Caucasian, who were lined up opposite them, lowered their weapons in astonishment, mouths agape. There was a crack and the face of the man standing in front of Suryei disappeared in a spray of red.

Suryei and Joe were running out the other side of the clearing, into the bush, before they were aware of the soldiers charging in behind them. Automatic weapons fire and the screams of men filled the jungle around them. Two explosions boomed. Joe grabbed Suryei's hand as they ran, frantically looking for an escape from the hell erupting around them.

Sergeant Marturak now knew for sure that he was chasing two people, a man and a woman, both young. He had seen them. Where had the woman come from? he wondered. He'd taken cover with two of his men behind a conveniently sited berm of earth at the perimeter of the clearing, to assess the situation. His crash survivors had blundered into what must have been some kind of forward survey camp for a logging operation. Sulawesi was full of them. They came in, counted the trees to determine whether the effort required to build the roads and infrastructure needed to pull the logs out was economically viable, and then surveyed the terrain for the road crews to follow.

The sergeant had no particular view about the rights or wrongs associated with the practice that was stripping parts of his country bare, despite the fact that he thought of the virgin jungle as a second home. These particular people did present him with a problem, however. The loggers were in the wrong place at the wrong time. He couldn't allow the crash survivors access to the outside world, and these people contaminated the integrity of his mission. No survivors. No witnesses. These men had to be killed. Especially now that one of his soldiers had, in the excitement of the chase, blown one of the logger's heads clean off.

He unhitched a grenade from his chest webbing and lobbed it twenty metres into the centre of the clearing. It detonated in a hard pulse of grey smoke, disabling at least five of the men with flying shrapnel, while the concussion wave shook dust from the tents, trestle tables and trees that crowded the clearing. Marturak's eardrums rang with the noise. Another grenade landed to the left of the first, taking out three more loggers. Automatic fire then swept the clearing, cutting the legs out from any men left standing. None of the loggers had managed to get off a single shot, which was as it should be, thought Sergeant Marturak with satisfaction, as the violence of the exploding ordnance bellowed through the jungle.

Marturak stood and carefully walked into the clearing, safety catch off, ready to shoot. He was a good and careful soldier. Others in his command quickly went from corpse to corpse. Nine millimetre pistol rounds were pumped into the heads of men who showed the vaguest sign of life. The sergeant did a quick count of his section. All present. No deaths, no injuries amongst his own. A satisfying result. He patted a couple of his men warmly on the back.

He thought about the two people he had been chasing, and had seen at long last. Both were obviously unarmed. And frightened.

He had the main tent searched. This confirmed his first thought that this was indeed a survey party for a logging company. Several of the dead had blond hair and one was a redhead. It was a joint American–Indonesian venture apparently, according to the paperwork lying around. He shrugged mentally. What did the Americans call this?

That's right, collateral damage. Sometimes it was unavoid-able. He detailed five men to pack up the campsite, bury the tents and the bodies, and burn the trestle tables, chairs and papers.

The sergeant asked them to take particular notice of all communications equipment, instructing his men to smash them before placing them on the growing bonfire. It was important to keep the area cut off from the outside world.

He'd seen his quarry exit the clearing so he knew which way they were headed. And one of them was wounded, leaving a blood trail that could easily be picked up. They were mortal, after all. It was just a matter of time before he caught and killed them. Marturak allowed himself the hint of a smile. They'd be dead before lunch.

Sydney Airport, 2200 Zulu, Wednesday, 29 April

The crowd had not diminished overnight, rather it had swelled, supported now by friends of friends and relatives. Pillows and blankets, provided by Qantas and other air-lines, were strewn everywhere together with fast food packaging and empty coffee cups, many stuffed with ciga-rette butts.

The news went round like wildfire and soon the news-stand was cleaned out. The morning paper carried the headline 'Terror in the skies'. The accompanying story, based on hearsay and speculation rather than fact, sug-gested that Indonesian terrorists had blown QF-1 out of the sky with a bomb secreted in Sydney.

Mothers became frantic, sobbing and crying for their lost children. The men were angry. A Garuda flight to Denpasar was loading. Several people hyped up on coffee and lack of sleep started abusing the ticketing staff, accusing them of crimes they had nothing to do with and no knowledge of. It was something the crowd could focus on, and perhaps gain some obtuse meaning from. More people joined in. They began to tear down the airline's signage and throw what came to hand at the innocent staff: garbage cans, barricades, food scraps.

A television crew setting up to interview people for human interest fillers caught it all on camera and did a live cross to the morning news.

Security arrived again, this time less inclined to be understanding.

Parliament House, Canberra, 2200 Zulu, Wednesday, 29 April

Niven woke with a start. Six am. Jesus, must have dozed off. The phone was ringing beside him. He picked up the handset groggily.

'Morning, Griff. Yeah, went home and slept like a baby,' he lied. 'Sure, gimme five.' He hung up.

The air vice marshal almost did look as if he'd been home, had a good night's sleep and a hot shower when the ASIS director stepped in to his office trailing the Minister of Defence, Hugh Greenway.

Niven ran his eye over the minister. He hadn't yet decided whose team the man was on. Lurch was in his mid-fifties, very tall and stooped. His skin was pale and freckled. He had ginger hair and strong hands. A farm boy. Greenway had intense green eyes and his brow was fine, rather than overhanging like the character in the television show. But nicknames were rarely given to be flattering. Do I trust you? Greenway was a new appointment in a recent cabinet reshuffle. Niven just hadn't had enough experience with the man to make up his mind either way.

Barely in the CDF's office, the minister said, 'I've just got off the phone to Byron Mills. I wanted to tell you both at the same time, rather than double up. There's good news and bad news.'

Niven was an optimist. Even so, when offered the choice, he'd always go for the bad news first. It was like eating your greens before anything else, getting them over with and saving the best for last. 'Give us the bad,' he said.

'The ambassador has been on at the Yanks about the satellite but they haven't budged.'

'Okay, we've already taken that on the chin. What else?' said Niven, impatience creeping into his tone.

'Mills had a talk with the people down at DIGO.'

Niven raised his eyebrows. The Defence Imagery and Geospatial Organisation was the department charged with, amongst other things, photo intelligence. They were the obvious experts to talk to when it came to spy satellites.

'No specifics, Spike; don't worry,' said Greenway, reading the CDF's frown. They'd all agreed that it would be best not to bring anyone else into the loop, at least until something concrete turned up. 'They had a couple of ideas. He followed up on them and found us a private spy satellite. A company called SpaceEye.'

'Yeah, I've heard of them,' said Niven, his interest surging.

'Launched their first satellite in '99, then ran into problems with the US Congress. Issues about privacy, mainly. There was some attempt to have their technology limited.'

'Did Congress succeed?' Griffin asked.

'Publicly yes, privately no. The sats were built by Rockwell and Kodak, with pretty much the same technology available to the US military – keyhole imaging, infrared, x-ray . . .'

'How'd they manage that?' asked Griffin.

'Money, basically. Defence Intelligence prepared a circular on it last year. The satellite program was being funded by Mitsubishi, Hyundai and a few others, and they didn't want their investment compromised.'

'Look, guys, with respect, the investment strategy's secondary. Can the satellite do the job for us?' Niven said impatiently. The game of twenty questions was starting to annoy him. No one had rung to announce that the plane had been found. That meant the nightmare was continuing.

'It's being positioned as we speak,' said Greenway virtually without moving his lips, in a broad, flat Australian accent that reminded Niven of vast, dusty cattle stations. 'A mining company surveying the jungles of New Guinea has just finished using it. So the sat's pretty close, which is fortunate. It'll be in place over Sulawesi within three hours. Should be getting pictures by . . .' he checked his Seiko, '. . . by lunch.' Greenway stood.

'Hugh, thanks. That is good news,' said Niven, meaning it, his foul mood turned around.

Griffin also stood to go as the minister smiled and left.

'Actually, Graeme, if you wouldn't mind, could you stay for a bit? There are a few thoughts I want to run by you.'

'Sure.' Griffin sat back down and poured himself some

water from the glass pitcher on the low table in front of him.

'What's up?' Griffin knew the CDF well. When he'd left him last night, the man had had *that* look in his eye, a certain intensity that gripped Niven whenever there was danger in the air.

After some hesitation Niven said, 'What do you know about Flight 007?'

Here it is, thought Griffin. He resisted the temptation to say something trite about James Bond. Niven was obviously not in any mood for banter. 'Absolutely nothing,' he said instead.

'Then how about if I add Sakhalin Island?' Niven was leaning forward on his desk, fingers forming a triangle in front of his face, forehead creased.

'Okay, yes, as a matter of fact. The Korean Airlines 747 shot down by a Soviet rocket in . . . '85, I think, over Sakhalin Island. Soviet territory.'

'September 1, 1983. And it was an SU-15 tactical fighter that fired the missile, an Anab air-to-air.'

'Been doing some research have we?' The question was rhetorical.

'You remember before you left last night I mentioned that there were –'

'– three hundred and forty-seven sites dedicated to aeroplane crashes? Yes, I remember.'

'I was bullshitting you. There are far more than that. I was looking into the survivability of the Boeing 747.'

'And . . . ?'

'And I found out that they are one very difficult mother to bring down. Unless you plough into something, or have a mid-air, or knock a wing off, they'll keep flying until the

145

pilots, or the on-board computers, are good and ready to land it.'

'You forgot blowing it out of the sky with missiles,' added Griffin, interested in seeing where this would go. He knew Niven rarely went on wild goose chases.

'I'll get to that.' Niven consulted his notes. 'On May 2, 1988, a United Airlines Boeing 747 with 258 people on board landed safely at New Tokyo International Airport after three of its four engines failed. There were no deaths or injuries.'

Griffin nodded and tilted his head. Landing on just one engine! He had to admit that was impressive.

Niven continued reading aloud. 'The 747 has four separate hydraulic systems. Knock three of them out and the plane will keep flying.'

'And if you take all of them out?'

'Yeah, it'll crash, but get this.' Niven wagged his finger, almost in triumph, and rifled through a sheaf of notes. Eventually he found the scrap of paper he was searching for. 'August 12, 1985: a Japan Air Lines 747 suffered massive structural failure destroying all of its hydraulics systems. For more than thirty minutes, the pilots controlled the plane's stability with engine power alone!'

'Then what happened?'

'Well, it eventually flew into a mountain killing 520 out of 524 passengers and crew – the worst single plane accident in history.'

'Uh-huh. Do you mind if I ask a question?' Griffin interjected.

'Go right ahead.'

'Where's this leading?'

'I'm not sure yet, but it scares the hell out of me.'

'I'm listening,' said Griffin, who now had his professional hat well and truly on.

'From what I can discover, backed up by what the people at Boeing say, it takes a hell of a lot to knock down a 747. They just want to keep flying. So, conclusion one – there was a bomb on board QF-1. Conclusion two – the plane was shot down.'

Griffin scoffed. 'Oh, for Christ's sake, Spike, who would want to do that? Don't you think that's a bit of a massive leap into the unknown?'

'Who do you think the prime suspect would be, Griff?' said Niven, ignoring the questions.

'Now let's stop right there. What possible reason, what motive, would Indonesia have for doing that? Relations have been, well, a bit jumpy for a while, but . . . shooting down a 747? They're not exactly the Soviets, you know. For that matter not even the Soviets are the Soviets any more.'

The Commander in Chief leaned back in his chair with a vaguely triumphant smile. 'It's interesting, and telling, don't you think, that the Indonesians spring so quickly to your mind?'

Griffin was flustered. 'Look, Spikey, we have a plane that's gone missing for twenty-four hours. No doubt in my mind – or anyone else's in this building, for that matter – it has crashed somewhere on the island of Sulawesi, in Indonesia. That explains why Indonesia is my natural context for speculation. I think the hypothesis you're pushing is just a bit off the wall.'

'I agree it's a chilling thought, but the facts, what facts we have, do lead in a certain direction.'

'Yeah, and my problem is, we don't have any facts and

therefore any direction, just a lot of unanswered questions,' said Griffin.

'Okay, but we also have history. A 747 is a very large object. It weighs over a quarter of a million kilos or half a million pounds. If it did blow up at 35 000 feet, how large an area do you think the wreckage would be scattered over?'

'Very,' Griffin was drawn in despite himself.

Niven sifted through his notes again. 'On November 27, 1987, a South African Airways 747 crashed in the Indian Ocean near the island of Mauritius. Debris was scattered over *230 square kilometres*! If that Qantas plane blew apart at altitude over Sulawesi, it would be raining aeroplane from one end of the island to the other. Indonesia would know about it.'

'Hang on. Now you're arguing that the plane wasn't shot down?'

'No, I'm arguing that the Indonesians are playing dumb.'

'Okay, I see your point . . . I think,' Griffin added, cautiously piecing together the logic. 'You think QF-1 met with violence over Indonesia, because violence is the only thing that'll stop a 747 short of a mid-air or a mountain.'

'Correct.'

'You think the plane didn't blow up, but nevertheless eventually crashed.'

'Correct.'

'You also think that the Indonesians have found the wreckage already, but aren't admitting to that for some sinister reason.'

'Correct again.'

'It's the whole sinister bit I just can't buy. Sorry, Spike.'

Niven began shuffling papers, obviously annoyed at his friend's reluctance to see what he believed was readily apparent.

'Look,' said Griffin, 'there's another alternative, the one no one's taking seriously, that the plane flew on crippled by some massive systems malfunction and has crashed well outside the search area, which is why they haven't found it.'

'The line the Indons are pushing.'

'Is it really that ridiculous?'

Niven twirled a pencil around his thumb. 'In my view, yes. The 747-400 has two transponders. As I said, a transponder is something that belts out an aircraft's sign to air traffic radars. The controller at Bali central said both transponders went out at the same time. I believe that means disaster struck the plane. It came to earth somewhere near that point on Sulawesi.'

Griffin stood up and stretched. 'Call me when you get some hard evidence, mate,' he said.

'Would you settle for circumstantial corroboration?' asked Niven, smiling.

'No,' said Griffin, smiling back. 'But tell me anyway.'

'Okay, that report you gave me last night about the Super Pumas . . .' Niven sifted through the pile of books and notes on the table and pulled out the WAC of Sulawesi on which he'd marked the track of QF-1. He passed it to the ASIS Director-General.

'I've seen this, haven't I?' asked Griffin, frowning, concentrating.

'The report says the Pumas went somewhere with a load of Kopassus and came back three hours later, empty,' said Niven.

'Yes . . .'

'Those helos cruise between a hundred and twenty and a hundred and thirty knots. So, assuming nil wind, it could have flown a maximum distance outbound from Hasanuddin of around a hundred and eighty nautical miles before returning.'

Griffin was still frowning. 'You're grasping,' he said.

'The red grease pencil is QF-1. The black line is a possible track for those Pumas.'

Griffin saw that the black line ended with an X almost on top of the spot Niven had marked for the crash site of the Qantas plane. 'You really want to believe the worst, don't you?' he said.

'Griff, I know this is not something we want to face as a possibility, particularly as there's no supporting evidence yet, but the fact that the Indonesian air force wants to stop looking in Sulawesi and start looking somewhere else entirely . . . well, that *is* highly suspicious to my mind.'

'And I'd rather believe the tooth fairy spirited the plane away. Sulawesi is not Sakhalin Island. Those Pumas could just as easily have flown their load of Kopassus troops to a piss-up on some deserted beach twenty klicks down the coast and partied for a few hours before flying home.'

'Look, I know that. As I said, *circumstantial* corroboration.' Niven stretched his aching back and rolled his head a couple of times. There was a tickle in the back of his throat. He hoped he wasn't coming down with something. Not now. 'You think I'm just being a bloody hawk and, because we've known each other so long, I think you should know better. There's something smelly about this and while I hope I'm wrong . . .'

'Sorry, Spike. I don't want you to be right because, if you

are, well, we'd all be in one big fucking mess. Also, I can't believe you're right because we have absolutely no information to go on. And I'll remind you, I'm in the intelligence business, not the speculation business.' Griffin rose to leave.

'Before you go . . .'

Griffin raised his eyebrows, pausing at the door.

'There's a twist to the Sakhalin Island story.'

'Which is?' Griffin was drawn in despite himself.

'You'd expect that the Soviets would have denied shooting the plane down, but they didn't. They actually released the voice tapes from the fighter pilot's cockpit. The tapes from the air traffic controller in Japan were also released. You can hear the Korean pilots informing ATC that the plane had suffered rapid decompression and that they were descending to one-zero thousand feet – 10 000 feet. Then, nothing. Gone. The Russians said it crashed. The Americans hurried to agree. But strangely, out of 258 PAX on board, and over half a million pounds of weight, only two bodies and a few small bits and pieces of KAL Flight 007 were ever found. Those statistics were completely at odds with what the experts would expect from a plane supposedly blown out of the sky – there should have been bodies and wreckage everywhere.'

'So . . . what are you saying? The Soviets spirited the plane away somehow, in collusion with the US?'

'Strange that there was no Mayday call, nothing. Why? Because the plane was obviously still under control and still flying, despite the missile hit. I believe it landed on Russian soil.'

'The Americans do love a conspiracy,' said Griffin as he crossed to the door.

'And sometimes the facts shouldn't be ignored, no matter where they take you.'

Griffin shook his head.

'Griff, a bit of paranoia in these uncertain days is good for the health. Just keep an open mind. I think we're in for some turbulence on this one.'

The ASIS chief smiled, shook his head and closed the door.

The phone rang. Niven answered it. 'Okay,' he said, and hung up. Greenway had said to turn on the news. He tapped the button on the remote and the screen warmed, the picture resolving rapidly into focus. Virtually a full-blown riot was in progress at Sydney Airport. Terrified Indonesian staff from Garuda Airlines were being evacuated by security staff. One of the women had blood streaming from her nose.

Then the police began breaking up the crowd, dragging people away kicking and screaming. A repugnant scene.

'Shit,' Niven said aloud.

Hasanuddin Air Force Base, Sulawesi, 2305 Zulu, Wednesday, 29 April

Captain Radit 'Raptor' Jatawaman lit the afterburner and the F5 Tiger 11 sprang forward. The acceleration pushed the pilot back into his seat, taking some of the pressure off the tightly adjusted five-point harness. His eyes focused on a point at the end of the long runway as the world shooting past his peripheral vision became increasingly blurred. There were only a couple of knots of headwind floating down the airfield into the aircraft's nose, and the sky above was a cloudless blue; a beautiful day to fly. The sweep hand on the airspeed indicator hit the right number. Raptor fed some gentle back pressure on the stick and the F5 rotated off the strip.

His eyes scanned the dials that monitored the turbine's health. Everything was as it should be. The old fighter responded well to his input. It climbed away easily from the suck of gravity without any weapons or external fuel tanks attached to underwing hard points. Raptor cycled up the undercarriage quickly before the aircraft's airspeed exceeded the manufacturer's maximum limit for leaving those bits exposed to the airflow. He went through the checks listed on a thigh-pad on his g-suit. He deselected the afterburner. Without the additional savage thrust it provided, the F5 settled into its best rate of climb. Raptor called the tower to inform the controller that he was climbing to his cleared altitude before initiating the standard crosswind turn. The tower then cleared him out of controlled airspace and into restricted military airspace.

It had not been long since Raptor had flown the Tiger. He'd departed the squadron less than two months ago after getting the call to fly Falcons. F-16s. The Tiger was a good little fighter but it was starting to show its age, especially in its avionics suite, which had to be three or four generations behind the state-of-the-art. Although it was still one of his country's primary front-line fighters, Raptor, and everyone else in the air force, knew the Tigers would be merely target practice against the more advanced fighters of the region. The transfer to an F-16 squadron was like a gift from God. It was every Indonesian fighter pilot's dream to pilot the legendary Falcon. And he, Raptor, had been chosen.

The F5 he was flying had been in the workshop having some minor problems in its avionics package debugged, and was now ready to come back on the flight line. Surely one of the regular F5 pilots could have taken it for a test flight? It seemed odd to him that they'd asked him to do it. No one else available, they said. Still, he didn't really mind, and he was still current on the type. The F5 was a sweet aircraft and he was happy to take one out for a spin for old times' sake. He thought he'd probably pack in a few loops and rolls too. He applied pressure to the stick and felt the aircraft respond. Yes, it was light and nimble; a nice little package.

He lit the afterburner for the thrill of it. Fuel was instantly dumped in the turbine's tail pipe and ignited. The gas from the ensuing controlled explosion exited furiously in an orange cone, forcing Raptor back in his seat as the fighter leapt forward.

A little back pressure on the stick and the F-5 climbed vertically to 15 000 feet. Raptor deselected the burner and levelled out. He aileron-rolled the aircraft first, deflecting the stick slightly to the left. The Tiger's roll rate was so fast that the aircraft's nose was still slightly above the horizon, where it should be, when the wings returned to the level position. Next, he pulled back on the stick until four gs registered on the accelerometer. The aircraft's nose came up steadily, and then continued over until it was flying wings level with the horizon, inverted. Raptor kept the stick position constant and the Tiger continued to scribe a giant vertical circle in the air. The gs started building again as it dived back to its starting position at the base of the circle. The aircraft buffeted slightly, which brought a smile to Raptor's lips – he'd just flown through his own turbulence created at the loop's beginning, indicating a perfectly symmetrical manoeuvre.

Next, he joined high and low yo-yos together, pulling five and six-g climbing and descending turns, creeping up on clouds then blasting holes through them exuberantly. He was congratulating himself on having the best job in the world when a small explosion rocked the Tiger and filled the cabin with smoke. The smell of an electrical fire found its way into his oxygen mask. The stick felt heavy and he deflected it slightly to the right to see how the aircraft would respond. Something was very wrong. The Tiger continued to roll to the right once the stick was centred. Indeed, the stick position had no effect on the aileron's deflection. They had locked up solid. The fighter rolled once, twice, three times around its longitudinal axis before the nose started to dip, and the arc scribed by the nose became more elliptical.

Raptor tried to reduce the roll rate by using a little left rudder and retarding the throttle. This worked to some degree, but the plane continued to roll. Too much rudder input would cause a cascade of other stability problems he could well do without, so Raptor kept his foot pressure to a minimum. He found that he did have some control over the aircraft's pitch but not to a significant degree.

A Mayday call was made in the calmest voice he could muster, giving his position and a brief account of his difficulties. ATC responded that it would immediately dispatch SAR to his position.

Raptor wrestled the aircraft down to 3000 feet and still it rolled around its longitudinal axis. He kept his cool and his spatial orientation. Raptor was a good pilot, but this aircraft was determined to drill a hole in mother earth and there was nothing he could do to prevent it. Raptor waited until the Tiger was at the top of its roll before pulling the yellow and black striped rubber ejector release handles between his legs. He tugged hard. Nothing. He tried again. A sudden explosion should have sent him and his seat skywards to safety, away from the metal coffin spinning to its doom. Raptor fought the Tiger all the way to his death. The aircraft hit the sea nose low and inverted. The impact tore the aircraft, and his body, into very small chunks.

Air Force Colonel Ari Ajirake received the report of the death of one of his pilots at breakfast. The lieutenant, who phoned him with the news, thought his commanding officer took it well.

NSA HQ, Fort Meade, Maryland, 2330 Zulu, Wednesday, 29 April

Bob Gioco stared at the computer screen as he ate dinner.

A musical chord sounded on his computer announcing the arrival of another slip in his etray. He opened it and read the accompanying note. 'Hello, Bob. Add this to your Sulawesi jigsaw and see if the picture starts ringing your alarm bells too. Ruth S.'

It was not unheard of for an IAE to make a personal approach to an analyst, but it was not entirely regular either. Ruth Styles. That's right, Gioco remembered her now. Formidable old duck, but she seemed to like him and that made it easier for him to like her. He apologised to the ether for thinking of her as a battleaxe. He scanned the information troubling the woman sitting in a bunker on the other side of the world. A company called Tropical Pulp and Paper had lost one of its forward survey teams in the jungles of Sulawesi. Apparently, the campsite had made its routine report that morning and everything was fine. An hour later, they were off the air. Totally. Nothing from the camp's VHF or UH frequencies, the sat phones were dead as were all computer comms. Alright, so something was definitely rotten in Denmark. Or rather, Sulawesi.

Bob stared at the slip. He pinned it on his virtual noticeboard and read through some of the others. There were around thirty or so that he'd highlighted with a red electronic exclamation mark, the ones he thought he should keep an eye on to see what, if anything, developed.

There was something about a group of mercenaries training on the border between Vietnam and Cambodia. An unusual virus had again jumped from the pig population to humans in a remote part of Malaysia. Unionists had sabotaged some stevedoring gear in a port in Western Australia (but there was a counterclaim by them that the damage was actually caused by company thugs). A number of schools had been torched in a systematic attack in Sydney. There was plenty of military traffic, some interesting, some routine, some plain odd. There were the reports from A-6, the Australian agent in Sulawesi. Sulawesi . . . He reread her first one about a squad of Kopassus troops heading north. He then read the second report, as it seemed an addendum to the first. He decided on a whim to dig a little deeper into this one.

He checked the radio interceptions from the helos that transported the troops. They were buried amongst millions of small data files, which could nevertheless easily be found by the NSA's Cray X1 supercomputers. He read through the slips. Two helos out of Hasanuddin AFB asked for taxi and airways clearance, so as to deconflict with private and commercial traffic. There was no further radio work from the aircraft at all except for an airways clearance when they re-entered controlled airspace approximately 180 minutes later. It must have been a special ops sortie or there would have been at least some en-route radio work. Gioco thought about it while he fished some egg from his dinner. Indonesian noodles, by coincidence: Mee Hoon. Okay, so a couple of helos landed somewhere, disgorged their troops and returned empty. He absently picked out a ring of calamari, and remembered his earlier assumption that perhaps the soldiers were off to search for that downed Qantas plane.

Something clicked in Bob's brain. The report on the Qantas plane. Jumbo jets did not just vanish. He checked the time of the aircraft's disappearance: 2036 Zulu. The time rang a bell. He called up all relevant radio work from that time of the day and in that area of the world. The Crays crunched the numbers. It took less than a minute before the required information was on his desktop. He had an F-16 Falcon out of Hasanuddin at around 2015 Zulu on a sortie. It was airborne for around forty minutes before landing back at base. From takeoff to landing only minimal radio exchanges, all of them just radio clicks, which could have meant anything, including a faulty radio.

2036Z – 4.36 am local time: the precise time the 747 went off the screen. The event was right in the middle of some of those unusual 'clicks'. Was it possible? Things were starting to race in Gioco's head. A picture was coming together and it was a particularly nasty one. *Is this what Ruth's driving at?* Would Indonesia blow a civilian aircraft out of the sky? No. They wouldn't, would they? He put the lid back on his dinner and pushed it to one side.

He was sure the clue lay on his desktop somewhere. He reviewed all the slips for the last thirty-six hours, looking for anything to do with Indonesia, whether he'd flagged them with an exclamation mark or not. It took him a good two hours. There was the death of the air traffic controller, which, the way things were going, was looking a bit too coincidental to pass as an accident.

Then a reminder for his early morning meeting popped up on his desktop. He'd forgotten to dismiss it as 'done'. COMPSTOMP. He traced the unease that had started to gnaw away at him to the morning's meeting. He reviewed his notes: *Watchdog found intruder in CS982/Ind. server. Watchdog traced hacker, Cee Squared, and system notified server owners.*

He cross-referenced CS982/Ind. against the registry of Fido Security clients, COMPSTOMP's venture into the free market, and discovered, just as he had feared, that computer system CS982/Ind. belonged to the Indonesian army. Then he noticed the time of the intrusion. Around 1830 Zulu or – he added the eight hours for the time zone in his head – 3.45 am local time. Could it be . . . ?

Gioco got on the phone to Research. 'Hello, Gioco, SEA Section. Can you get me the passenger manifest for a commercial aeroplane flight? . . . You can? Qantas QF-1 departed Sydney, April 28 . . . Yes, the plane that's gone missing . . .' There was a pause while Gioco caught the response. 'Yeah, I know. Tragedy. Okay, great.' The list of passengers would be posted to him on the internal mail system. It would take around ten minutes. In the meantime, he contacted COMPSTOMP. He wanted Cee 'Squared's name; he wanted to know the name of the hacker responsible for setting off the Watchdog in the Indonesian army's server. He was known to them, they had his 'fingerprint'. That also meant they'd have his real name, address and probably even his favourite breakfast cereal on record.

Bob jotted the sequence of events down on a piece of paper. He hoped that something would be so totally out of place that his growing fear about the fate of QF-1 would dissolve. He wrote:

- April 28, 1830Z, Watchdog picks up intruder in TNI server
- April 28, 2015Z, Indonesian Air Force F-16 scrambled out of the base close to flight path of Qantas plane (odd radio work between F-16 and controller)
- April 28, 2036Z, 747 vanishes from ATC screen at Bali Centre
- April 29, 0440Z, Sulawesi – (following morning local time) Kopassus troops dispatched north
- April 29, Sulawesi – logging camp radio silence
- April 29, Bali, air traffic controller car accident – fatal
- 747 still missing

Gioco had to admit that the events listed could be circumstantial, especially the logging camp's radio silence. He appeared to have quite a few incidents happening within a suspiciously short period of time. The glue was missing, an element (or elements) that would tie all these loose incidents together into something cohesive and incontrovertible. Still, there was enough there, on paper at least, to raise his interest.

Gioco checked himself for an instant. Was it really possible that the Indonesians would splash a 747? He whistled quietly.

The phone rang. 'Thanks a lot,' was all he said as the identity of Cee Squared came down the line. The icon for internal mail appeared on his screen at the same instant. It was the passenger manifest of QF-1. He scanned the 394 passenger names on it.

Jesus H. Christ! He couldn't believe it. There it was! The implications of what he'd just discovered hit him like a pile-driver. The flimsy string of events he'd lined up instantly hardened into something more concrete. He had his glue. Gioco sat in his chair for a good five minutes blinking at his computer screen, in a mild state of shock, again hoping that a glaring inconsistency in his logic would put the facts in a less ominous light. None presented itself. Was this the work of religious fanatics? Was Indonesia in the grip of some kind of fundamentalist boil-over? Perhaps this was just the beginning. Shit!

What had Cee Squared found in the TNI server that the Indonesians were so desperate to keep quiet? He added the clincher, the hacker's real-world name and allocated seat number, to his notes:

- Cee Squared – Joseph Light
- Seat 5A – Joe Light

Was it possible that Joseph Light and Joe Light were different people? Yes, possible, but improbable. Gioco considered letting Ruth Styles in on his deductions. He never would have been able to piece it together without her. No, he realised, he couldn't. She would have to remain in the twilight – aware that something was going on but uncertain of exactly what it was. Instead, Gioco picked up his handset, heart in his mouth, and dialled the Director of SIGINT.

Central Sulawesi, 2330 Zulu, Thursday, 30 April

Joe and Suryei ran through the jungle as quickly as they dared, making just enough disturbance to alert any wildlife in their path and give it time to move out of the way but, hopefully, not enough noise to telegraph their whereabouts to the murderers somewhere behind them.

'Stop . . . stop,' she said eventually, exhausted, collapsing on a rotten, moss-covered log.

Joe fell beside her, shaking. He vomited onto the ground, panting as his stomach heaved uncontrollably. This was not his world. He didn't belong here. 'Shit,' he said when the convulsions stopped, a string of yellow bile hanging from his lips. 'What are we doing? What the fuck is going on?' His mind replayed the severing of the soldier's fingers and the back of his throat constricted, preparing itself for the arrival of more digestive juices.

'Come on,' said Suryei, dragging Joe to his feet. 'We have to keep moving.'

'I'm okay,' he said, knowing that he didn't feel okay at all.

Suryei turned and stepped through a hole in a low bush and let out a scream. She disappeared down a steep mudslide, plunging beneath the surface of a rivulet. She yelled in shock and took a mouthful of water, spluttering, choking.

The water could be brackish, stagnant, and a serious danger to her health. As it slid down her throat, she realised that it was sweet. Relieved, she put her health concerns away and gulped mouthfuls.

Joe appeared at the edge of the bank, anxious until he saw Suryei come to the surface. She waved at him to join her, but quietly. Joe ditched his rucksack and axe and eased himself into the water, careful not to splash. He sank into the cool depths, feeling the water sluice through his clothes. It soothed him, took away some of the tension. He drank deeply, not caring that the water invaded his nostrils. He shook his head beneath the water, running his fingers through his hair and rubbing his face, invigorated. He then quietly surfaced, again making as little noise as possible, aware that sound would travel far in the cooler, denser air above the water. He turned and caught a glimpse of Suryei climbing up the opposite bank. Her clothes clung to her skin like wet tissue paper. Her breasts were not large but they were firm and her shirt hung suspended from her nipples. Joe stopped himself from staring, but not before Suryei caught him at it.

He climbed out of the water soundlessly and sat on the bank. Joe felt better, still numb, but at least he felt back in his body again rather than remote from it in shock.

'You okay, Joe?' Suryei asked.

He nodded. 'Thanks.'

He took the empty water bottles from his rucksack. Filling one, Joe held it up to examine the contents. The water was clear and clean. He filled the other bottles, stuffed them back in his rucksack and reshouldered the load. Joe then picked his way carefully up the slippery mud, grabbing tufts of foliage to keep his balance as he went. He glanced up as Suryei looked around. He took another quick glimpse of the woman squeezing water out of her hair.

He'd half expected that she would sprain her ankle or something, and that he'd then have to carry her through the jungle. That old cliché, the helpless female. But it hadn't taken him long to realise that she was tough and that if anyone would be doing the carrying, it would probably be Suryei.

The bush did not appear to be quite so dense here. It seemed cooler too. Enormous trees, giant columns, appeared to support the massive green roof overhead. At their base was a carpet of lime-green ferns. Families of monkeys chattered high overhead.

And then something occurred to him. 'Hang on, Suryei,' he said quietly. He went back to the rivulet, crossed it, and found a broken branch. He scrubbed at his footprints and at the skid Suryei had made in the bank where she'd slipped into the water, until they ceased to look man-made. He then crossed the stream and did the same to their tracks on the other side.

He considered whether they should have travelled down or upstream a distance before leaving the water, so as to throw off their pursuers. But, he reasoned, providing they were careful and left no entry or exit footprints along the bank, their pursuers wouldn't have a clue whether they'd even been in the stream, let alone where they'd left it.

Joe wondered where they would end up. Certainly he had not the slightest idea where they were going. Neither did Suryei. They were just trying to stay ahead of the killers. Maybe they'd just step out of the jungle and into a dirty great car park with a Pizza Hut. He wondered whether he was getting delirious.

Their eyes and brains were growing accustomed to their environment now. The foliage wasn't scratching and tearing at them quite as often. Indeed, it was much easier going in this forest of giants. That had a downside, he realised. The soldiers would also move more quickly through it, and there were significantly fewer places in which to hide. Their world had been a misery of crawling in and around thickets of greens and browns through air so dense and heavy with water that it almost seemed to physically impede their progress. And always behind them, or beside them, or in front of them, the ever-present threat of death.

Then there was the rain. They heard it before they felt it, a hammering that battered the leaves in the treetops far overhead. Eventually, the weight of the water would make the leaves sag and it would then fall through the next layer of trees and bushes and so on, until it eventually hit the spongy ground as enormous bloated gobs. There was a lot of mud too, thick molasses mud that sucked at their shoes. Joe started walking on the smaller ferns to avoid it, which kept his legs wet and covered with fiery bites from caterpillars, insects and small spiders.

The ground began to rise and with it, a new dimension of misery was brought to their efforts. The incline steepened quickly and became slick with water and their legs burned with the extra exertion. The higher ground, however, soon afforded them a view of the valley below and occasional patches of sky above, a welcome change from the dark canopy overhead.

Joe could barely remember having another life before

the one he was now forced to endure. He was losing track of time. How many days, weeks, years ago since the plane crash? Was it a week ago that the cobra had helped them escape from certain capture and death? How long ago had they run into the logging camp? Joe trudged on behind Suryei as she climbed slowly, one heavy step at a time.

At first they didn't know whether the sound was behind them or in front of them. But it was man-made, an engine, and it was getting close. Then Suryei saw it and risked giving away their location to the soldiers. 'There,' she yelled, pointing and looking down as it circled low and slow over the trees in the valley, banking into figure eights. It was bright purple with a yellow and red striped propeller. An ultralight. It was discovery, rescue, a hot bath. So many wonderful things flashed through Joe's mind that he shouted for joy, like a fan at a grand final whose team has just scored the winning points.

But then the little aircraft shifted its pattern to a new part of the sky, gaining altitude, and Joe and Suryei were overcome by an enormous sense of loss. They jumped up and down and screamed, desperately waving their arms. The little aircraft gave no acknowledgement of their existence. They heard the clatter of a long burst of machine-gun fire. Suryei and Joe watched, horrified, as the ultralight flew into the dotted line of tracer reaching up from the jungle.

The pilot appeared to jump about in his seat and there was a puff of black smoke from the small rear engine. The propeller stopped and the aircraft's wing dipped steeply. They watched it spiral one and a half times before the craft vanished silently into the trees 500 metres away. Suryei was first to start walking, continuing her way up a steep incline. She had a grim expression on her face, one that didn't invite conversation or comfort.

Joe ignored that and caught up with her anyway. 'That's good,' he said, gasping for air.

'Yeah, right. Soldiers, ten. Suryei and Joe, zero.'

'There'll be more ultralights,' said Joe, trying to convince himself that rescue was nearer.

'What makes you think that?'

'It had to have been from another logging camp, or maybe a bigger base camp somewhere. Maybe they were checking things out, to see what had happened to their mates.'

Suryei nodded but kept walking. Whether Joe was right or not, there was nothing else they could do.

The little plane was soon forgotten. Before long, Joe and Suryei were back in their own spaces, together but apart, heading uncertainly to an unknown destination.

They climbed on for what seemed an eternity. Just when they thought they'd put the last hill behind them, another would rise out of a valley. And then there was food, or lack of it. It had been twenty-four hours since they'd eaten anything. Coconut trees abounded but, so far, they hadn't managed to find any coconuts on the ground. And climbing the trees was out of the question.

Suryei caught Joe picking at some fruit hanging from a low branch. 'I wouldn't, if I were you,' she said. 'They're brightly coloured. Nature's way of saying, "I'm poisonous".'

Joe let the berries fall to the ground. Things were bad enough already. He didn't want to make them worse by getting violent stomach cramps.

Lack of food was starting to slow them down, and so were the hills, again. They were getting steeper. Both Joe and Suryei now had legs of clay. Every step was an effort. Joe stopped to get his breath. The scree shifted under his feet and he slipped back a couple of metres. He bent forward and let the axe, propped on the ground, take his weight. Ants scurried over the scree looking for food. He wondered if they were as hungry as he was, and doubted it. He panted. The muscles in the front of his legs, his quads, were pulsing, twitching, like the flanks of a horse that had run a hard race. He didn't think he could go on, but at the same time he knew he had to.

He wondered how high they'd climbed. The trail behind disappeared after a hundred metres into the dark green melange of the bush beyond. The vegetation was not as dense here at the higher altitude. Above was blue sky. The sky! Joe hadn't seen that for a while. It had been obliterated by a continuous canopy, which had also thinned considerably.

Joe caught a movement from the corner of his eye. It was Suryei, further up the trail, standing on what appeared to be the summit, the crest of the ridge, but Joe wasn't being fooled by that mirage again. A couple of times he thought they'd reached the top but it was only the angle of the scree lessening briefly before steepening again maddeningly. Suryei gestured urgently. Her hand movements said, 'Haul your arse up here, quick. There's something you should see.' At least, he guessed that was what she meant. They hadn't actually talked for a good few hours. Talking took too much effort, and made the climb that much harder.

Joe got his legs moving again. He was surprised they agreed to cooperate. One foot in front of the other, that's all I ask, he assured them. Twenty or so agonising steps later, Joe pulled up beside Suryei. He was gratified to see that her chest was also heaving. She was out of breath too. He had been starting to think this girl was some kind of goddam superwoman.

Suryei said, 'Look,' gesturing with a slight nod of her head. Joe turned and saw, away in the distance, the massive, perfectly conical shape of a volcano. Like something from a prehistoric landscape. It was blue-grey with a fluffy white bib of cloud around the summit. Ridge lines rolled away from the base of the volcano like ripples in beach sand. He realised that they had spent several exhausting hours climbing one of those ripples and he suddenly felt small and insignificant.

The view made him forget his legs, his lungs, his stomach, and the fact that a bullet could whistle out of the bush at any minute and take the view, and everything else, away from him. And from Suryei.

'Come on,' said Suryei softly, breaking the spell. She turned away from the volcano and renewed the climb up the ridge's spine.

Parliament House, Canberra, 0436 Zulu, Thursday, 30 April

The President's National Security Advisor's face was etched with concern. He had nothing further to add to the bleak news and the videoconference was at an end. The picture on the television monitor flickered briefly before fading to a silent, implacable grey.

Prime Minister Blight swallowed dryly, his Adams

apple moving painfully in his throat. 'Christ all-bloody-mighty . . .' he said, the words coming out in a hoarse whisper, exhaled on the breath he'd been holding. His eyes were round and large. He'd just been told the single most horrifying thing of his entire life.

Herschel Zubinski, the US ambassador to Australia, stood. 'Yes, as the National Security Advisor has just said, these are our gravest *suspicions*. But while our intelligence sources have not fully confirmed much of this information, privately Washington just doesn't know what else it can all mean. If the worst comes to the worst, you know the American people do not tolerate state-sponsored terrorism.' He walked to the Prime Minister and placed a hand gently on his shoulder. 'Bill . . . gentlemen . . .' The short dark man with the heavy New York accent bowed slightly to the room and left.

Griffin and Niven exchanged an anxious glance. The Commander in Chief's fears had been proved right, but this was one occasion Niven wished he'd been wrong.

Phil Sharpe, the Foreign Minister, was strident. 'Where's the proof?' he said. 'The hard, concrete evidence. As the Americans have said, these are *suspicions* only. We don't know for sure that the Indonesians shot the plane down. It's just some analyst's assessment on the other side of the world – circumstantial bollocks.'

Every time Sharpe opened his mouth to speak, Niven felt uneasy. No, it was more basic than that. The CDF just plain didn't like the man. He was a true politician, always working the angles for what appeared to be personal advantage. And Niven found him an odd choice for the portfolio of Foreign Minister, where an open mind was essential. Blight and Sharpe had been unionists together and were obviously friends. But what, other than a shared history, did Blight see in him? The dislike between Niven and Sharpe was mutual and Niven had to exercise considerable control to stop his feelings bubbling to the surface.

The reality was that the US, using the world's most sophisticated listening network, had intercepted enough 'circumstantial bollocks' that no jury would have trouble convicting the suspect. The US uncertainty boiled down to the fact that the crashed plane hadn't been found, so experts were unable to physically confirm missile damage. But everyone knew the remains of the plane would turn up, and soon. In a sense, finding the plane was almost a mere formality. And then a thought formed in his brain that found its way out of his mouth before he'd had time to stop it. 'We'll have to go in and get that proof then, won't we?' he said.

Sharpe was stunned. 'What, invade Indonesia? That's what you're suggesting, isn't it?' he scoffed, looking for support.

Niven knew instantly that he'd been hasty, but he pursued the thought anyway. The situation required cool calculation, not testosterone. Certainly, the remains of the aircraft were on foreign soil and the evidence was therefore Indonesia's to manipulate if it chose to, but the consequences of going in uninvited to relieve them of that evidence was unthinkable. At best it would be a suicide mission and at worst touch off a deadly broader conflict.

'Sorry, Spike, I'm not with you. What are you suggesting exactly?' asked Blight, agreeing with Sharpe but finding a more diplomatic way of expressing his doubts.

'Prime Minister, we've just been told the plane was shot down and, despite what the Indonesian authorities are telling us, I'm pretty certain I know where it came down. I'm talking about a limited, covert operation to secure the site for an international inspection team, and retrieve the aircraft's black boxes.'

'And what – the Indonesians would just put out the welcome mat, I suppose?' said Sharpe smugly, certain the CDF had just hung himself.

Niven ignored him. 'What I'm suggesting here is that we take the initiative.' Blight and Griffin appeared doubtful. 'Look, Indonesia is unwilling to let us help locate QF-1. The question is, why? More planes in the air, more eyes searching, we'd find it quicker. And a little of the spirit of cooperation between our two countries wouldn't be a bad thing.'

The PM nodded slowly, tentatively buying the logic.

'Obviously because they don't want us picking over it. We'd know pretty much instantly that it was shot down. But what if there's another reason? They must know we're going to find out what happened to QF-1. What if they're just stalling for time? What if it's the *motive* for shooting down the plane that they're so reluctant to let us see? Could *that* be found in the wreckage?' This thought occurred to Niven while he spoke, yet the force of it hit him like a revelation.

'What about this Cee Squared/Joe Light bloke?' asked the Prime Minister, hoping to find another answer somewhere. Niven was suggesting an aggressive course of action that made him feel downright uncomfortable. 'He's obviously the key to this.'

'I'll get on that immediately, Bill,' said Griffin.

Blight felt queasy. He took a sip of water to calm his stomach. As much as he would have liked it otherwise, the air vice marshal's head-on approach was perhaps the only way through. 'I think I see your point, Spike,' said Blight. 'You're saying they shot the plane down for a reason, and that that's more important to keep secret than the crime itself.'

'Exactly,' said Niven.

'Jesus, what the hell could it be?' said Blight, rapidly finding himself infected with Niven's suspicions.

'With respect, Spike,' said Griffin cautiously, 'simple pride could have a lot to do with their reluctance to let us help. In accepting our assistance, it could be seen that they don't have adequate resources to do the job themselves.'

'C'mon, Griff. Wake up and smell the roses,' said Niven impatiently. 'The Americans have just finished telling us that they believe the Indonesians have shot down a civilian jetliner. A Qantas 747 with a full load of passengers. *They shot it down*, for Christ's sake. *Why?* It's the "why" that's important here. As tragic as the actual crime is, we have to forget about that now and concentrate on the motive.' Niven knew he'd hit on something fundamental.

'Okay, I get the picture,' said Griffin, wishing he hadn't got it at all. He didn't want the CDF to be right about this because of the horrendous consequences. If they shot the plane down on purpose, it could be a prelude to war.

Blight wondered what that motive could possibly be. Revenge over East Timor was the only one that came to mind, and a deep sense of foreboding filled him. The Australian actions in East Timor were not his administration's, but he'd read the departmental papers. While the press had largely presented it as a triumph of Australian foreign policy, in truth it wasn't a shining chapter. DIO's brief to the Department of Defence had concluded that

173

there could be a bloodbath if the TNI were pushed off the island before peacekeepers arrived. That advice had been ignored and, as a direct result, an unknown number of East Timorese had paid the price with their lives. The rapid deployment of Australian troops to the island had at least prevented prolonged and more widespread carnage, but it had been touch and go for a while. Could the events they were now facing have their roots in decisions made years ago? These thoughts circulated in his mind together with the image of hundreds of people falling like rag dolls through the sky to their deaths. He shuddered and forced his attention back into the room.

'The Indonesians won't be able to hide the crash site for long,' continued Niven. 'Experts tell us that if the plane exploded at high altitude, the wreckage could be spread over hundreds of square kilometres.'

'So you think the Indonesians have already found the plane?' said Greenway.

'Bet on it,' said Niven.

There was silence in the room, the calm in the centre of a cyclone.

'So let me get this straight,' said Sharpe with a sarcastic edge to his tone and a vague sneer on his face, 'you think we should just march into the biggest Muslim nation in the world, a country with hundreds of thousands of men at arms, and ask them to stand aside and let us through because we don't trust them?'

Niven smiled back sweetly. 'Actually, yes. And all this time I thought you were slow.'

'Fuck you, Niven.'

'Jesus, keep your bloody shirts on!' said Blight, the veins in his neck pulsing angrily. 'We don't need that crap here. We need teamwork.' Blight turned to Griffin. 'What do you think, Graeme?' The PM had been hoping that some kind of political solution might present itself, but so far none had.

'About going in to Sulawesi with troops?'

'Yes.'

'I don't think so. Spike says he's sure where the crash site is. But what if it's not there? Well, it's a recipe for disaster. As we all know, there are many people in Indonesia angry about our last invasion of their soil: East Timor. We need to be mindful of the consequences of doing it again.'

The room was silent.

'Look, things might change . . . I just don't think we know enough yet,' said Griffin, walking to the water cooler to pour himself a glass. 'As for the reasons why we should send in troops – the Commander in Chief's fear of a broader conspiracy – I'm not convinced about that either. But I would like to make a point that hasn't been touched on and that is, I think we can't assume the Indonesian *government* has any top-level knowledge of this.'

'Are you saying that all this could be happening *without* the government's knowledge?' asked the PM.

'Well, yes, basically,' said Griffin cautiously. 'The armed forces in Indonesia have a history of operating outside government control. Look at our own experience in East Timor. We knew more about what the TNI was cooking up there than Jakarta did – the Kopassus units arming and enlisting death squads, the training of militia, the silent executions, the standover tactics. The military treated its government like proverbial mushrooms.'

Blight swallowed drily.

'Maybe the government wanted to be kept out of the loop publicly, but was in on it privately,' said Niven.

'We know that's not true. Not strictly, anyway. The trouble is, the army – the TNI – has a large number of seats in the Indonesian parliament mandated by constitution. So, in a sense, the army *is* the government. And that's where it really gets difficult sorting out who knows what – there are factions within factions in the army guarding fiefdoms in provinces a long way from Jakarta. Indeed, there are plenty of precedents where troops within a battalion have got up to mischief without even their commander's knowledge, let alone Jakarta's,' Griffin said.

'If the Indonesian government has been kept in the dark and fed on shit, as you suggest with your mushroom theory, how does that then explain their reluctance to accept our help in the search for the plane?' asked Niven. 'You really believe it's just a matter of pride?' He didn't agree with Griffin's reasoning, but that didn't mean he wasn't interested in the Director-General's point of view.

Griffin considered before answering. 'Yes. Pride, ego, face. They've always been sensitive about anything they might consider outside interference or intervention. Especially now after the rash of terrorist scares has put the spotlight on them. They're keen to demonstrate to the world that Jakarta's in control. And, as I said, the TNI has all those seats in the government. Or perhaps it's an over-reaction to once being ruled by a colonial power. Top that off with the fact that the government thinks it's under siege . . . one, all, or a combination of these factors could explain their actions.

'Internally, there's plenty of dissatisfaction and frustration with the way things are going: Aceh, Ambon, Kalimantan,

West Papua, are all boiling over. They are worried about the Balkanisation of their country. East Timor has gone. There is a very strong groundswell for independence in West Papua, formerly Irian Jaya, where there are freedom fighters – the OPM – who've been exchanging shots with the TNI for more than twenty years. No doubt you've seen the DIO paper currently circulating?'

Sharpe shook his head to indicate he hadn't. The Foreign Minister had just returned from a lengthy United Nations forum on new international standards for the management and housing of refugees.

Niven snorted. In his view, Sharpe spent too much time in front of the TV cameras and being seen at restaurant openings to be an effective minister.

'Briefly, Phil, it looks like the Kopassus are back to their old tricks, building up local militia forces in Papua. They get trucked in wearing civvies, with crates full of weapons and money, and arm anyone with a grudge.

'Jakarta believes East Timor's departure has set the precedent for other disaffected provinces to follow. Throughout the archipelago there are racial, tribal and religious tensions all exacerbated by poverty. The general populace of Indonesia, considered moderate by Islamic standards, has been surprisingly tolerant of the fanatics and terrorists on the fringe of its society. You don't have to walk far on any Indonesian street before you see someone in an "I love bin Laden" t-shirt. If I were to put my black hat on, I'd say Indonesia can only travel down one of three possible paths in the future. One, as I've said, the place Balkanises – fractures into smaller, bolshy states that pursue their own national interests. Two, religious fundamentalism takes hold. Three, a military dictatorship takes over the place. How long before one of these predictions comes to pass?' Griffin shrugged. 'We know all this – none of it's new. We've all become involved in endless debates about our largest neighbour to the north after the disaster in Bali. What's the most likely path? I still believe it's the dictatorship. Lord knows there have been plenty of precedents for it in the country's past.

'The government is now engaged in a delicate balancing act and we know that's making the military nervous. And while I'm on the subject of the military, they've taken a hammering since the glory days under Soeharto came to an end. The government's stance towards us over this incident could be interpreted as Jakarta's sop to the military. Y'know, look tough, talk tough. Flex those independent muscles. Basically, unless we get concrete evidence to the contrary, I believe we should give the government the benefit of the doubt.'

'And point the finger at . . . ?' Blight was intrigued.

'The armed forces, or a faction within them?' said Niven, taking his lead from Griffin's logic.

'Could be,' said Griffin, nodding. 'But again, I'd caution against jumping to conclusions. There's so much going on up there it's impossible to know where this has come from. The least likely place, and this is ironic, is that it's the handiwork of religious fanatics.'

'The people we've spent so much time and effort putting under the microscope?' asked Blight.

'Exactly.'

'So we've set ourselves up for this sucker punch?' Blight massaged his chin as if that part of his face had taken the blow.

'I guess . . .' said Griffin, frowning. 'But again, I'd caution against jumping to conclusions till we know more.'

'Hear, hear!' said Sharpe.

'I don't think we can blame East Timor for this. I mean, let's face it, our relationship with Indonesia's never been exactly rosy,' added Greenway.

Griffin and Blight both nodded.

'I don't buy any of this,' said Sharpe, arms folded.

Blight appeared to be pondering the options. 'So where the hell does all that leave us?'

'I'm not sure, Bill,' said Griffin. 'If we announce publicly that Indonesia shot down the plane, all hell will break loose. There'll be riots here and in Indonesia. You can guarantee there'll be flat denials from the Indonesians and, without proof, demands for an apology from the rest of Asia. You just know how Malaysia will react. Add to that a march into Sulawesi?' The ASIS chief left the question open but shook his head doubtfully.

'Second that,' said Sharpe.

The room was silent again. There seemed no way forward.

'Prime Minister, it might seem like I'm jumping from pillar to post, but I've changed my mind,' said Niven. 'Phil's right. We probably don't have a military option. Yet.'

Sharpe eyed Niven suspiciously.

'But I don't think we should sit on our hands either,' continued the CDF.

'So what are you thinking?' Blight hadn't had too much to do with the air vice marshal since his appointment to the position of CDF. Niven came highly regarded, which was why Blight had handed him the job and, so far, he liked the man – he said what was on his mind.

'We ready a small force, SAS. We brief and prep them for a black operation in Indonesia just in case we need to put people at that crash site in a hurry once it's found. And we wait. There's more to this, I'm sure of it, and we should be prepared.

'It would also be prudent to cancel all leave and put the Ready Deployment Force in Townsville on alert. It might seem like an overreaction, but I'd start moving our air assets out of places like Williamtown, Pearce and Richmond, and send them to Darwin and Townsville.'

The PM scowled. He was not happy about how the Indonesians would read that.

'Prime Minister, there's just too much here we don't understand and, frankly, that scares me,' Niven said emphatically.

'Okay.' The PM massaged his temples. 'I agree that we need hard evidence that a crime was committed before we confront the Indonesians. Intelligence assessments alone won't do it for us. Griff, I hope your bloody hunch is right and the Indonesian government is in the dark about this, otherwise, Jesus Christ, I don't want to think about where this will end. Anyone got anything else cheery to add?'

Silence.

'Okay then. We should at least prepare ourselves for the worst.' The PM stood up and stretched and rolled his shoulders to ease the stress. He seemed to Niven to be suddenly frail. 'Spike, get our blokes ready. Redeploy assets as you see fit.'

There was a tentative knock on the door. A young woman poked her head in the room and, eyeballing the CDF, walked tentatively towards him. Niven recognised her and his heart skipped a beat. She was from DIGO – photo intelligence. In her hand was a mustard-coloured envelope. *The* envelope. The interruption silenced the room.

'Excuse me, sir. But this was a hand-to-hand delivery,' the woman said quietly as she nervously gave the envelope marked 'Secret – hand-to-hand only.' to the CDF, aware that her arrival was at once disturbing yet crucial.

Niven nodded his thanks and ripped it open impatiently. The woman turned and left as Niven flipped through the contents. *So soon . . . surely not . . .*

He looked up ashen-faced at the Prime Minister. 'QF-1. It's in Sulawesi.'

The seven-four was exactly where Niven said it would be. There were quite a few photos taken in sequence, each five seconds apart. The resolution was incredible. There were bodies . . . He swallowed the lump in his throat. There were other photos in the stack of some kind of camp in the jungle that was burning. It was difficult to tell exactly what was going on because the tree canopy obscured much of the detail. He wasn't sure why they had been included. He checked the latitude and longitude burned into the print and noted that it was close to the location of the 747.

Niven handed the sheaf of photos to the Prime Minister. 'A complete analysis of this has not been done. Griff, a note here says DIGO are working on a complete work-up in concert with your people.'

'Oh my God!' The PM shook his head in dismay as he examined the remains of the 747 smeared across the jungle. 'Have the Americans seen this?' he asked.

Niven shook his head. 'No, sir. Not yet.'

Blight was receiving a lesson in geopolitical realities from the US point of view and he wasn't enjoying it. 'What you're suggesting could have a frightful outcome, Bill,' said US Ambassador Herschel Zubinski as he shook his head dubiously. 'Indonesia would need to be treated very carefully. If you provoke Jakarta into reciprocal violence, who knows how other countries like Syria, Iran and even the moderates like the Saudis might react? I'm sure the Muslim world would try and make it all appear to be some plot hatched by the West – you know how touchy these people are. Might set off something much bigger and nastier.' The ambassador shook his head again. 'The Joint Chiefs, Sec Def and Sec State are fully briefed as you know. And now the President himself has been brought up to speed. He's apparently furious with the Indonesians. Nevertheless . . .'

The PM felt like he was being patronised. He wondered how calm the Americans would have been had citizens of theirs been on the doomed flight. 'Mr Ambassador, the Indonesians shot down a fully loaded 747. That's bad enough. What our intelligence people are concerned about now is *why* they did that. Surely that's something your people back home would also be interested in knowing?'

Zubinski nodded. The Australian Prime Minister's assumption was correct. They would indeed.

'Look, Herschel, at this point we are not asking the US for anything. I'm just keeping you up to speed on our thoughts and likely intentions.'

'Thanks, Bill, appreciate it.'

The ambassador flipped through the satellite photos again slowly, deliberately. Blight could see that he was genuinely affected by what he saw, but as a representative of the US government, there was nothing he could do about it. He was just Washington's messenger. 'Jesus, Bill, this is a great tragedy. But it's a great *local* tragedy. As much as it hurts, I can tell you now that the United States' first priority will be to keep this from spreading. For God's sake, just don't do anything of a military nature about this yet. We need more intelligence.'

Blight kept his frustration in check. America was the boss, and that was the fact Zubinski had just driven home. Nothing could be done unless the US green-lighted it. Maybe, if the chips were down, Australia could call on Washington for support, but America would weigh up its own self-interest well before siding with Australia against Indonesia.

'Do we have these too?' Zubinski said, waving the photos.

'Yes, reciprocal intelligence arrangements. You know what we know.'

'Let me talk to Washington again.'

Blight stood.

'Thanks, Bill.'

'Hersch.'

Blight left the ambassador's office feeling frustrated, like a schoolboy admonished by the headmaster for something someone else had done.

Jakarta, 1005 Zulu, Thursday, 30 April

The violent scenes at Sydney Airport had been picked up by the international news services. By mid-morning, Jakarta time, they had screened in Indonesian homes and on the televisions placed in electrical shop windows throughout the country.

By late afternoon, the forecourt of the Australian embassy was taking a battering from bottles and stones thrown by a mob incensed at the treatment of their citizens in Australia. A line of police kept the demonstrators off the fence. How long they would be able to succeed without the use of riot equipment was debatable, for the numbers of demonstrators were increasing at an alarming rate.

Again, a local news crews captured the passionate display live.

Suluang happened to catch the five o'clock bulletin and was delighted by what he saw. *At last, some good news* . . .

Central Sulawesi, 2136 Zulu, Thursday, 30 April

Joe and Suryei awoke in the darkness. They were stiff and sore and barely able to move. They had climbed for most of the previous day, continuing into the twilight. Joe had started to worry that they might walk straight off a cliff; there were plenty of them around. In the dying twilight, they had found an overhang surrounded by rocks. They needed sleep. Going further without it was impossible.

They were both frightened that they'd wake up blinking into a gun barrel again, or worse, not wake up at all. Exhaustion had got the better of them so they'd climbed into the hollow, covered themselves with ferns and relied on the camouflage for protection.

Both Joe and Suryei came awake warily, expecting the worst. They stayed motionless, listening to the sounds of the pre-morning, trying to sense if danger was near, but their ears still rang from the explosions of the day before.

When they were satisfied that they were alone, Joe and Suryei drank some water, and began the day's climb. It was mercifully short. They trudged wearily to the top of the ridge on cold, stiff legs and aching feet. Suryei stopped in her tracks and put her arm across to stop Joe taking another step. The smell made Suryei retch. Kerosene. It was now irrevocably mixed with the dreadful stench of burning flesh. Horrific shapes formed in her mind – black, contorted, ghastly.

Joe pondered whether they had tracked a giant circle through the jungle and ended back at the crash site, but the area didn't seem at all familiar. It was no longer wet and hot, but damp and cool. He wondered how high they'd climbed – perhaps a few thousand feet. Goosebumps made the hair on his forearms bristle. He pinched a few leeches off his chest and blood oozed freely from the bites. He'd become casual about them, and wondered while he squashed them how the buggers had managed to get there. The direction of the air shifted slightly and the stench of kerosene strengthened.

Joe and Suryei held their breath and tried to concentrate on the sounds of the jungle. They could hear nothing out of the ordinary. They warily picked their way through the smashed tree branches littering the jungle floor. Something had torn them from the canopy overhead.

The kerosene smell thickened with every step. There was a clearing ahead. Something black and grey sat amongst fallen branches and tangled vines. The object was totally out of context and it was difficult to place. But then it clicked and Joe knew what it was.

'Jesus, Suryei,' he whispered, 'one of our engines.' They approached it slowly, cautiously. They were not comfortable stepping onto the open ground. It made them easy targets.

They edged towards the twisted metal turbine. The smell made Suryei cringe. Joe walked around it, examining it. He stuck his head in the tail pipe for a closer look. The metal was shredded like the end of an exploding cigar. He ran his fingers across one of the torn edges of metal and quickly drew his hand away, blood oozing from a sliced finger. 'Shit! When am I going to stop doing that?!' He clenched his finger and rich, red blood flowed from the cut. He nursed his hand before continuing the inspection.

Joe recalled the intense fireball on the end of the 747's wing. At the time, he hadn't been sure what it was. Now the significance of it struck him immediately: the outboard engine. 'It must have dropped off the wing. Maybe this is what caused us to crash. See how the back of this pipe is splayed out? Looks like something blew up inside it.'

Suryei's curiosity overcame her fear and she moved closer. She put her head inside the tail pipe next to Joe's. Neither Joe nor Suryei had the experience to know how much of the damage had been caused by the impact with the earth, or by something else.

The sun still hadn't come up and there was only a dim

twilight. Some stencilled writing on an engine part drew Suryei's attention. 'Why would a Rolls-Royce engine have the words "secure here" inscribed in Indonesian on a part?' she asked.

'I don't think it would,' said Joe.

'Then how would you explain this?' She pointed to a section of tube that appeared fused to the internals of the turbine. Everything was coated with a film of dirty oil and it was difficult to tell where one part stopped and another began, but the writing was clear enough. 'What does that say?' asked Joe again.

'It's Indonesian. It says, "secure here".'

Joe wiped away the film of carbon and oil with the flat of his hand. The section of tube with the writing on it was painted olive drab and had embedded itself in the engine's tail pipe. Something began to trouble him. There were bits and pieces, fragments that made up a picture, swirling in his mind, trying to take shape. He was standing too close to it, like seeing the dots but not the whole. It didn't make a hell of a lot of sense. Joe took a mental step backwards. And then he collapsed, sitting heavily on his backside as if a chair had been whipped unexpectedly from under him.

'Oh, shit!' he said quietly. 'It's a missile!'

'What?' asked Suryei. 'What did you say?'

Joe didn't answer. He was sorting things out. He stared at the ground between his feet, his head between bloody, oily hands.

'Why in God's name would someone shoot down a passenger plane?' said Suryei. 'Joe?'

'What?' he asked, lost in his own world. *It's a missile!* The Internet connection in the plane. The Indonesian general . . . *Is it possible?*

'Joe, do you hear me?' she asked.

Joe had frozen, his muscles locked up solid. He didn't even appear to be breathing.

'Joe! What's going on here? Are you okay?'

Could this really be happening? Am I responsible for this? So many people?

'Suryei . . . I . . .' Joe looked up, horror in his eyes. 'I think I know what happened.' His voice was hoarse, constricted. 'It was . . . me . . .'

'What? What are you saying?' Suryei sat in front of him, lifting up his head so that she could see his face.

'It's my fault,' he said. 'The whole fucking thing.'

'What? The plane crash?'

'Yeah. All those people . . .'

Joe tried to take his mind back to the early hours of Wednesday morning, before the crash, but that wasn't easy. That world didn't seem real any more. His existence had become a brutal here-and-now, a life and death struggle that obscured the recent past, making it seem almost as if it was someone else's.

He closed his eyes. He remembered glancing at the video screen at his elbow. The news . . . a villager was pulling something out of a well . . . A town somewhere in West Papua. The memory of it gradually came back stronger, clearer. The man wore a dirty cloth tied around his nose and mouth. A desiccated, ancient woman stood off to one side, tears tracking down the dust on her face. Sobbing children were clutched to their parents in a separate group. Joe recalled pulling the plug from his DVD and jacking into the aircraft's entertainment system to hear what the story was about.

' . . . the separatist violence continues in West Papua,

formerly Irian Jaya, in a virtual repeat of East Timor,' reported the BBC correspondent. 'In this village, resistance was pointless. The male population was hunted down by local militia, some were hacked to pieces, then thrown down the village well. Some of the younger males were held down and had their teeth pulled by rusty pliers. This woman's four year old great grandson was just one of the victims, the boy torn from her arms by men she had once called friends from the neighbouring village, who then kicked her for resisting. Their gruesome job done, the marauders melted back into the jungle . . . ' The vision cut to a high-ranking Indonesian soldier shaking his head. 'The TNI denies any involvement. More Indonesian troops are due to arrive next week in an effort Jakarta says will help stabilise . . . '

Joe was surprised by the detail that came back, as if he was watching himself viewing the incident on the video back in first-class. Like all Australians, he'd seen plenty of images of the suffering of the East Timorese, the former twenty-fifth province of Indonesia. He had thought himself immune to them but there was something vividly pathetic about the old lady, standing by the well's edge, waiting for the body of the little boy to be retrieved. Joe had been deeply affected by it.

Joe hadn't believed for one moment the Indonesian army's assertion that they were ignorant of the carnage. He'd heard it all before. The general in the news piece had shiny, sweaty skin, wore old-fashioned Elvis-style sunglasses, and his uniform was so tight that the fabric at his shirt's buttonholes was scalloping with the strain. Joe took an instant dislike to the man. He wanted to strike a blow, even just a small one, for the old lady and her dead child.

'I was watching the news in the plane,' he said, almost whispering. 'There was a report of a mass grave in West Papua. One of the victims . . . a four year old child in a well. I wanted to get even, make someone pay. So I hacked into an Indonesian general's computer, copied a few files and left a virus. Nothing serious.'

'And for that, you think they shot the plane down?'

Joe didn't answer.

Suryei analysed what he was saying, chewing her lip. Civilian jets weren't blown out of the sky as a regular occurrence. Something had prompted the military into an act of desperation. Something terrible. 'What sort of virus?'

'Pretty childish, really.'

'And you think they traced you back to the plane?' she asked incredulously.

'No. Too many different networks, switches. And I decoy my own computer's IP broadcast.' He thought about that. It used to be impossible to trace a break-in, but he'd been out of hacking for a couple of years now, lost touch. Things move fast. Maybe . . . Joe felt an enormous weight settle on him. Guilt.

'I thought you did computer games.'

'I do. Now. But I used to do a bit of industrial spying. Nothing too serious . . . perfume formulas, carbon fibre applications, that sort of thing.' Joe sat slumped, round-shouldered.

'Do you remember what files you copied?'

'No.'

'Well, you must have taken something pretty bloody important.' Suryei's mind raced. Even then, would they shoot down a 747 full of innocent people to protect it?

'Think, Joe. Can you remember anything about the files? What the hell did you see? What did you take?'

Joe again forced his mind back to the recent past. He had checked the protocols available from the aircraft and noted that WASP was on tap, the new Wireless Application Satellite Protocol that allowed wireless Internet access anywhere under a satellite footprint. He'd opened up his browser, found the phone directory for Jakarta, and noted the forty different numbers for the TNI. They appeared to be grouped in five distinct number series. He had had his computer ring all the numbers. Within a few minutes he knew which were old analogue and which were newer, digital phone numbers. Joe's computer then called the digital numbers, adding and subtracting extra digits either side of the original phone numbers until his system noted the familiar return signal of a file server.

Joe easily cracked the server's low security files. He remembered noting with satisfaction that the four digits of the carpark space reserved for the Indonesian general also matched his internal office phone extension. Recurring patterns of numbers were good news for hackers. It meant that whoever set the system up was careless. The time he'd spent hunting around inside the server amounted to a handful of minutes. He certainly hadn't loitered.

To an observer on the plane, it would have appeared that Joe was merely tapping away at computer keys, perhaps writing a letter. But Joe's mind saw it differently. He didn't see the keyboard at all. He became melded with the computer's hard-drive, sucked into another dimension that blotted reality from his mind. This was a black, lightless world where he existed as pure thought. There were objects in the blackness that appeared only semi-visible, mere shapes shrouded in black velvet. These objects were program spurs. To find them, Joe had to *feel* around until he sensed the shapes as ripples in the void. Joe had quickly discovered what he was looking for – the sophisticated, secure software program that ran the Indonesian army's computer network.

Fortunately, the system was a good three years out of date. That kind of time frame was an eternity in the world of software design. But while the operating system was old, it was incredibly complex. He remembered thinking that he had no desire to spend the rest of the flight carefully picking the matrix apart. He'd been after something familiar. Sometimes companies low on funds would augment their old enterprise software with something relatively cheap and off the shelf, just to keep the system more or less current.

But while Joe had been inside the general's computer disturbing the regular flow of electrons, the system's Watchdog had picked up his 'scent' and it had padded off unseen, backtracking to the origin of the call barking its silent alarm.

And then Joe found what he was after; the ubiquitous operating system he knew like an old friend. It was running the Indonesian army's internal mail. He thanked the declining value of Indonesia's currency for the country's willingness to cut corners, and hitched a ride on an internal memo. An instant later, Joe found himself on the general's hard-drive, the place he'd gone looking for.

He remembered being confused by what he found because he couldn't speak or read any Indonesian, and so couldn't understand the unfamiliar language strings. He'd moved through the space, shouldering the unfamiliar words and sentences aside. That's when he'd seen the safe. Not a real safe, of course, but a virtual one. It had immediately captured his interest. A safe meant secrets. So the general had files he wanted to keep off the army's tailored operating system, for extra privacy and security?

This was what hacking was all about, Joe remembered thinking at the time. Secrets were extremely tempting, even now when he was no longer hacking. There was something sexy about revealing them. He'd examined the box, walked around it in the black room. In the real world, it would have been made of hardened tool steel. Indeed, even in the virtual world it had appeared formidable, unbreakable, impregnable. But to someone like Joe, the safe might as well have been carved from balsa. He'd tapped out a coded sequence, the equivalent of a virtual shaped charge, lit the fuse and stood back. The ensuing explosion peeled the door from its hinges.

Inside the vault, Joe had hoped to find more than the general's Christmas shopping list, but he'd not been able to make sense of any of it. Disappointed, he nevertheless thought what the hell and burned the lot onto a beer mat anyway.

Joe seemed to wake from a trance. 'There were a few papers.'

'Is that all?' asked Suryei.

'The general had made an attempt to keep them hidden. But, now I think about it, there was something weird.'

Joe stood and walked slowly about the small clearing, piecing the fragments of the memories together, shoulders hunched, drawn into himself. 'There was something . . . I didn't think much about it at the time. Australia was part of a map . . .'

'A map?'

'Yeah, it's odd.'

'Why? How?'

'The names of all the countries. I remember now because those names were the only words I could understand. They were written in English. Except Australia. It was called something-or-other Irian Jaya.'

'Okay,' said Suryei, standing up, hands on hips, facing him. 'Can you remember what that something-or-other was?'

'I'm trying.'

'Try harder.' The blood had drained from her face.

Joe ignored her impatience. 'There was another word that prefixed Irian Jaya. Like Salute, or Salami . . . '

Suryei's face felt cold yet hot at the same time. The tips of her ears burned. Could it possibly be . . . ? No way. The Indonesians would never conceive . . . It was too outrageous. Yet, they had been in a Qantas 747 that had been blown out of the sky. And now they were being hunted by Indonesian troops. Maybe it wasn't too far-fetched at all and Joe had actually found something incredible, something so big that perhaps a plane-load of people had to die to prevent it being brought to the world's attention. 'Joe, think hard now. Was the word possibly . . . Selatan?'

Joe tried to visualise the map. 'Yes,' he said hesitantly. 'I think that was it. Yeah, Selatan Irian Jaya. Why, what does that mean?'

Christ, thought Suryei, her stomach twisting. This was something she didn't want to make a mistake about. 'The word Irian means "high" in Indonesian. Jaya means "victory". And Selatan means "southern". Selatan Irian Jaya – Southern High Victory. Whose computer did you hack into?'

'A general. A bloke called Soo-ang.'

'You mean Suluang. He's the Mr Big of the TNI.' At that moment, Suryei saw it all clearly and a painful anxiety gripped her chest. She sat heavily on the ground, just as Joe had earlier. 'I think what you might have found was part of an invasion plan.'

'What . . . ?!'

'It seems bizarre, but the facts fit – the plane, the missile, the soldiers trying to kill us. The Indonesians trying to keep some sort of invasion of Australia secret. Something like that is big enough to make sense of everything.' Suryei stared at the ground at her feet, in shock.

'That's why there's been no rescue. I'll bet the Australian authorities don't even know where the plane is,' Suryei said.

'Then we're fucked,' said Joe quietly.

'Is it possible they – the soldiers – know they're chasing the person who uncovered the plan?'

'I don't know how they could.'

'But if they did, it would make them pretty damned determined to put a bullet in you . . . us.'

Joe paced nervously and started towards the trees. 'Come on. Let's get moving. We can't stay here.'

'Hang on a sec. What are we going to do? We need some sort of plan here,' she said to his back.

He stopped. 'You're right. We can't go much further this way.' Joe looked up at the escarpment towering above them.

'I think we should head back to the aeroplane,' she said.

'Sure. And let's put big red targets on our chests for those nice men in khaki.'

'We're not getting anywhere wandering around in circles,' said Suryei, allowing his sarcasm to pass over her.

'Aside from whether going back to the plane's a good idea or not, I don't know where we are, or where the plane is in relation to us. So how do you propose we find it?'

'I don't know, but we have to try. When rescue comes, it'll go there, not out here. And there are plenty of places we can hide close by the wreckage until it does.'

When rescue comes . . . Joe also wanted desperately to believe in rescue. *Someone* had to come and pluck them from this nightmare. It was the one thought keeping him going, except for the ever-present threat of a bullet between the eyes if they didn't. Perhaps a search was underway right now, only looking in the wrong area. That happened sometimes, didn't it? Okay, so Suryei was right. Again. They needed to get back to the plane. That in itself was troubling: not that Suryei always seemed to have the answers, but because if their only option was so obvious, the soldiers would probably come to the same conclusion about their likely movements. Joe looked around. He had no idea in which direction the plane lay. Somehow they had to get their bearings.

Joe imagined what it must smell like back at the 747 with all the bodies bloating in the tropical heat. The memory of that awful smell found its way back into his nostrils and it took all his will not to gag on it.

Parliament House, Canberra, 2145 Zulu, Thursday, 30 April

Blight hoped he wasn't overdoing it as he thumped the table a third time, but lack of sleep always made him more aggressive. The Indonesian ambassador flinched visibly.

'Our air force has committed every available resource to the search, Mr Prime Minister.' Parno Batuta was shaken. Receiving a summons at sunrise from a Prime Minister was usually a bad omen. He was right.

'It has now been two days. Why haven't you found the damn thing?' hammered Blight. He was tempted to shove the photographs in the man's face, just to see his reaction. But that was an ace Blight had decided was best played in another hand.

'I totally reject your tone and manner, sir,' said the Indonesian, trying to maintain his poise. 'Sulawesi, as you know, isn't like one of your deserts. If the plane has gone down in a valley, it may never be found.'

Interviewing Batuta had been Griffin's idea. Lean on the man, he'd suggested. Try to get a feeling for whether the ambassador knew what was going on back home.

'Mr Ambassador, I will say this just once. Guaranteeing the security of international passenger aircraft overflying your bloody airspace is one of the cornerstones of modern civilisation! If you don't do everything you can to search every square metre of that jungle until you find our plane, then you're setting a bloody dangerous precedent.

'If it was a Garuda plane – or any goddam plane for that matter – that had gone down over Australia, we wouldn't be having this bloody conversation because all our resources would be employed. And willingly!' Thump number four. The Prime Minister was shouting, his face puce.

Batuta found the Australian PM a prickly character at the best of times. The anger and the language the consul could handle, but not the accusation that Indonesia had something to hide on the issue of this plane crash. The suggestion that it might indeed do so caused the vessels in

197

his temples to pound. Having his country's integrity questioned was more than a diplomatic slight, it was a personal injury. 'This is not a case of Jakarta stalling! I am deeply troubled and personally offended by your assertion. I reiterate, we have no idea where the aircraft came down! You will have to accept that because it is the truth.' It was Batuta's turn to thump the table.

'Perhaps our experts are right and the plane has come down somewhere else, not in Sulawesi as was first thought. We have a possible time when the plane disappeared from one radar screen, but that information was not corroborated. Given the aircraft's height and speed, our air force people tell us the plane could just as easily have come down somewhere in Malaysia —'

'Mr Ambassador, someone's filling your head with crap,' Blight said, arms folded, emphatic and implacable. The notion of the 747 flying on to Malaysia was a fantasy. 'Get yourself some new experts. Aircraft do not just "wink" out of electronic existence, and then fly on into the sunset. Something on that plane went seriously and catastrophically wrong.

'Our plane is on your soil, so don't try and tell me otherwise. Obviously, we cannot go to Sulawesi and search for it without your permission. Now there's a thought — why don't you extend us that invitation?' Blight wasn't finished. There was something else he wanted to add, but he was nervous about doing so. *Don't overstep the mark.* Blight shrugged mentally. This was a game and he had to drive the ambassador to the brink if he was to be absolutely certain. 'Mr Ambassador, if the reason you won't extend us that invitation is because the majority of the people on that plane are Australian, then God help you.'

Personally, Blight didn't believe that racism was behind the reluctance to invite Australian participation in the search, but he was nonetheless keen to see the man's reaction to such a repugnant suggestion.

Batuta took several deep breaths to calm himself. It required willpower not to return the Australian's ugliness in kind, and this conversation was in danger of getting completely out of hand. 'I reiterate that we are looking for your plane with all available aircraft,' he said softly, his jowls quivering with the supreme effort required to stay in control.

The ambassador stood abruptly, his face flushed red. The Prime Minister's tone and manner were far too blunt. 'And I remind you that, as you have observed, we are a sovereign country and our airspace is not – I repeat not – open to the prying eyes of Australian search aircraft.' Batuta felt himself giving in to his own anger as a rising indignation took hold. The audacity of these people! The arrogance! It was better to leave before he said something he might later regret. 'Good morning, Mr Prime Minister.' With that, he flung open the door and stormed out.

Blight was relieved. He sat heavily and replayed the meeting in his mind. He thought himself a good judge of character and his gut told him Batuta was ignorant. He'd pushed the man. Hard. If anything, the ambassador had been disinformed. And if that was the case, then it followed that the whole Indonesian government probably was too. Blight continued the logic and his relief was quickly replaced by anxiety. That disinformation had to be coming from somewhere. Who or what was the source? And the biggest question of all was still unanswered – why?

Joe and Suryei's presence disturbed a large family of monkeys in the trees overhead. They reacted by screeching, whooping and leaping about the canopy, thrashing leaves, baring their teeth and carrying their young into the highest branches. And then objects like footballs covered in small spikes rained down.

'Jackfruit!' said Suryei. She laughed and picked one up. It was rotten, covered in thousands of tiny brown ants. She hunted about until one came to hand that had the right firmness. She checked by flicking it with a fingernail. 'They make a special sound when they're ripe,' she said in response to the puzzled look on Joe's face. Suryei dug her thumb in under the skin and peeled off the spikes. She bit into the pale orange fruit and juice dribbled down her chin and she gave a grunt of satisfaction.

'What's it taste like?' asked Joe.

'Heaven!'

Joe picked one up that looked about right and smelled it. He reminded himself that he was hungry enough to eat bark. He peeled it and bit deeply into the flesh, the sweetness enveloping his senses.

After he finished, Joe began filling his rucksack with them.

'What are you doing?' asked Suryei.

'Lunch.' The rucksack bulged and sagged heavily on its straps.

'Forget it. They'll only get mashed up. Besides, these things have probably been all around us – we just haven't been looking in the right places.'

Joe unzipped the rucksack and let the heavy fruit fall to the ground with successive thuds. 'Can you find a yoghurt tree too, please?'

Suryei allowed herself to smile openly. He was good company, or would be if the circumstances were different. Joe returned her smile. The whiteness of her teeth contrasted with her dirty brown skin, making them seem almost fluorescent.

'You need another bath,' she said.

Joe was caked in grime, and his hair was matted against his head. Jackfruit juice and pulp coloured yellow the dark stubble on his chin. 'Have you looked in a mirror lately?'

'Let's go,' said Suryei turning away, smiling, her fingertips tingling.

Sergeant Marturak had made a mistake. They should have overtaken the two survivors by now. Certainly by morning. He was now sure he'd lost them. The blood trail that had been so generous had quickly disappeared. Their wounds must have been superficial. The men had found no footsteps, no faeces, no broken vegetation and certainly no more empty water bottles to indicate their passage. It was too easy to miss people in the dark, even with the NVGs. The jungle had given way to forest and there had been enough light to use them but there were still far too many places to hide. The last thing he wanted was for the fugitives to slip around to their rear.

He stopped his men beside a small stream and took out a map of the area. The plane wreckage was marked on it, as was the loggers' camp and their course through the bush. The two survivors had headed away from the hills, towards the low country.

Could they have doubled back and made for the escarpment instead? Even climbed it? He cursed their lack of personal radio comms. If he'd had them, this job would've been over. He'd have sent a few men forward to track the man and woman and then easily coordinated an ambush. Instead, he'd had to keep his force together and virtually within line of sight of each other. And the camp had had to be effectively dismantled – they couldn't have left it intact behind them. That had given the people he was tracking a head start. And they didn't seem to be playing by the rules, stumbling and bumbling along the established trails, leaving signposts of their passage. This whole business was getting frustrating. He swore and spat on the ground. His men tried to ignore his anger. But they too were getting edgy, feeling the tension.

The sergeant took a deep breath to steady his temper and surveyed the map again, attempting to see it with fresh eyes. The stream wasn't indicated on the map but that didn't mean anything. There were hundreds of millions of litres of water still draining off the mountains and hills after the monsoon. Water was everywhere.

He took out his GPS and marked their position on the map. A fresh plan was forming in his head. He interrogated it and decided it was sound. They would set up an ambush . . . here.

At their backs was the plane wreck. Away in front and to the left was the high, rugged country. It was an obstacle that only well-equipped, experienced climbers could tackle. Desperation and determination could overcome many equipment deficiencies, but he seriously doubted that his two adversaries, wounded from the crash or their exertions in the jungle, would attempt sheer volcanic faces.

There was an extremely good chance that they would stroll into his trap if he set it right.

Then, once contact was made, his men could pull back and converge to form a funnel that would catch his quarry in a killing zone. Marturak deployed lookouts, ordered his men to have their rations and take several hours rest. It would be a long day and an even longer night.

He checked the time. Allah! He was due to make a situation report. It was not something he could avoid any longer. His superiors back in Jakarta needed to know what was going on. The message he would send was in his head. Marturak knew it wouldn't be welcomed: site unsecured, two survivors, in pursuit. No, the general would not be pleased.

East Timor, 0155 Zulu, Friday, 1 May

Sergeant Tom Wilkes's section was patrolling the West Timor border when the call came over the VHF. They immediately broke off the patrol, found a spot under a tree and made a brew. It was time for smoko anyway. The light was grey and cool in the hill shadow.

Long after its independence from Indonesia, East Timor was still quietly hosting soldiers from Australia's Special Air Services Regiment, men like Wilkes and his section. Neither East Timor nor Australia entirely trusted the Indonesian military to live up to its government's word of nonintervention in the new nation.

'In country' was the ideal advanced training facility, great for the sharpening of battle senses. The bullets were real and border tensions regularly ebbed and flowed. Those tensions had lately increased somewhat since the proclamation of independence. The East Timor militia, now no longer supported by the TNI, had splintered into bandit groups that conducted vicious raids across the border from the old refugee camps in Indonesian West Timor. They had lost their war but continued the battle, a spiteful murderous rabble.

The United Nations soldiers of ETFOR on the ground knew what needed to be done to end the menace once and for all, but didn't have the mandate. Where the UN soldiers had rules of engagement under which they could fire only when fired upon, the local fighters had a Swiss cheese of opportunity. That was how the United Nations men and women saw it anyway – Swiss cheese because it was full of holes and it stank. Still, Wilkes's Warriors were having fun. This was what you joined up for. Exercising with the Yanks or one of 'our Asian neighbours' or the Kiwis in the north of Australia was clean and tidy compared to some of the things that had to be done when there was ordnance pointing in your direction that could put holes in you. Wilkes's Warriors had learned plenty up in these hills.

It was different up here, away from the cameras that sent mostly sanitised images back home, if they sent anything at all. The world had largely forgotten about East Timor, only someone had forgotten to tell the desperados along the border that the cause was lost. Wilkes and his men had seen plenty of action that was never reported. The battles were often a one-sided affair. The bandits sprayed their bullets, often just holding their weapons out from a wall or a tree while firing off a full clip without looking where or what they were shooting at. The tactic had worked perfectly effectively against unarmed civilians. Wilkes's Warriors liked to be more frugal. Pick a target and launch a round humming on its way. One target, one bullet. Ammo lasted longer that way.

Just recently, though, several lone UN soldiers had been ambushed and killed by gunmen who got lucky. Something subtle had changed in the attitude of the other side. It was like going back to the bad old days at the beginning of the conflict. It was becoming an increasingly dangerous world, and it didn't pay to be cocky.

The cooler morning air lifted the thump of the rotors, carrying it echoing up the valley – a harbinger of decent food and a shower. It belted up through the trees and throbbed in their heads like a pulse. The helo's dark green paint scheme appeared black in the frail light of the morning as the Black Hawk swung out from behind a ravine.

This Black Hawk was a gunship. It had a nasty sting with rocket launchers (empty) and mini guns on either side. The mini gun's rate of fire was so rapid and intense that at night it appeared as a solid spike of yellow-white metal. As the helo orbited the target, it seemed tethered to the ground by the glowing spike. The Black Hawk was a frightening piece of hardware to be on the wrong side of, which, in this instance, wasn't the case.

The helo passed through the green smoke of the flare that marked the RV, and settled on the gently sloping grass of the hill's crest. The men swung aboard with practised ease. The loadmaster handed Sergeant Wilkes a pair of 'phones which he slipped over his head. 'Wilkes's Wankers, eh? Welcome aboard, ladies!' The LM flashed the sergeant a phoney smile and batted his eyelids.

Wilkes gave him the finger in return and shouted, 'This

is for you, now.' Then he made a fist and added, 'And you can use this later in the privacy of your home.'

The banter was good-natured between the small numbers of Yanks and the Aussies in the UN force. Occasionally it became aggro but there wasn't enough nightlife in Dili – women or alcohol – for anything serious to develop. The Americans regarded the Aussies highly for their craft in the field. They also appreciated the fact that, for once, another country's armed forces were first on the beaches, getting their hands dirty, something the Americans were usually stuck with as the world's policemen.

There was a fair bit of mutual admiration between the two countries' soldiers – the American equipment and resupply particularly impressed the Australians. Those guys didn't want for anything. The only thing that gave Sergeant Wilkes the shits was the way the Yanks said 'mate'. They just couldn't get it right. It always sounded forced and try-hard. 'Mai-yt' was the way the Yanks said it, somehow managing to put extra syllables into it that he couldn't identify. When they added a 'Ger'daiy' to it, well, that was the fucking end. For Wilkes, it was like someone dragging their nails across a blackboard, which he didn't mind half as much.

Wilkes and his men sat in silence and watched the countryside slip by beneath them. Remnants of villages trashed by the militia back in '99 could still be seen. The weeds had reclaimed some of them, particularly those built with wood, fibro and dried grasses that had been burned to the ground. Other villages were still just a mess of broken buildings, abandoned to scavengers. From altitude, they had the appearance of smashed teeth set in rotting green gums. The poor countryside eventually gave way to the relative order of Dili, which had been transformed over the initial occupation by INTERFET and subsequent UN forces.

The leaders of Dili's independence movement had returned soon after the Australians had secured the country from the militia attacks. The capital of East Timor quickly regained the daily routine of a country at peace, despite the thousands of East Timorese reportedly slaughtered by the TNI-backed militia. Now there were friendly soldiers in town, and soldiers meant money and money meant commerce. Trade was a wonderful balm for the country's wounds.

But lately the bombings had started anew, along with what appeared to be organised raids. UN forces would secure an area and then leave. Soon after, the bandits would march back in and make horrific examples of the locals who 'cooperated' with the foreigners. Rather than pulling back, it soon became apparent that, if anything, the UN command would have to step up its operations. Of course, the Indonesian military denied publicly that they were assisting the militia from West Timor, but the Australian DIO thought differently. Factions within the Indonesian military appeared to want to cause trouble. East Timor could not be allowed to go quietly into nationhood. It had set an example for other disgruntled peoples within the sprawling archipelago to follow.

The Black Hawk landed at the airport and a couple of Land Rovers took Wilkes and his section back into Dili. The men all had showers and some food at the mess tent. Ratpacks were okay but nowhere near as good as tucker cooked on a proper stove. They then headed off to the briefing. The men laid bets on what their next mission would be. No one would pocket the money.

They entered the demountable and felt the tension in the air. There were a number of grim-faced officers present who they'd seen about Dili but never met, and a few types in civilian clobber who had to be spooks – CIA or possibly ASIS. No one had to tell the SAS section that what they were about to hear was highly classified, because just about everything the SAS did was black. Even the fact that they were in East Timor was supposed to be a secret, albeit one of the ADF's worst kept. The lights flicked off and a satellite photograph of an aircraft crash site illuminated a wall.

Wilkes's mouth dropped open. The briefing left all the men stunned, and that was not easily done. They had no mission, but they were told the situation might change. They had to familiarise themselves with the crash site of the Qantas plane and the terrain surrounding the area so that if they were called in, they would know it intimately. When the spooks and officers had cleared out, they were given the briefing tent in which to spread out WACs of the area and hard copies of the satellite pass. They discussed their equipment needs for a two-day infiltration, made lists of ammunition, communications, first aid, food and other bits and pieces and discussed the situation. A Qantas 747 shot down by Indonesia with more than 400 people aboard . . . all dead? Wilkes whistled silently.

Central Sulawesi, 0230 Zulu, Friday, 1 May

Suryei and Joe knew they would find a stream or a creek, flowing water at least, in the bottom of the steep valley.

They edged their way down to it, weak from lack of food. Their desire for a drink was powerful, a catalyst for mistakes. Joe stretched out for a crack in the rock face before he had secured his foothold. He reached for thin air and fell the last twenty metres upside down, clawing the air like a beetle on its back.

Suryei saw Joe fall and the emotions cascaded in on her; anger at his lack of care, desperation that she might lose him, fear for his life, and then anxiety about being left on her own. The feelings rushed around her system like a series of electric shocks, each fighting for ascendancy. She was afraid to look around the black basalt crag that obscured her view of the final moments of his fall. She did not want to see Joe's broken body lying at the base of the cliff, not after what they'd both been through and survived. She found herself crying as she made her way across and down to the spot where she thought Joe would be lying.

The impact with mother earth felt like hitting concrete and the force of it crushed the air from his lungs. And then the concrete dissolved and became water. Deep water. He'd had a moment to think he was dead before he became aware that he wasn't. Joe had landed in a pool. Far below the surface, the water was cool, even cold. Joe was aware of the light overhead as he floated towards it. The coolness became warmth, and then heat, a wafer biscuit of cold on cool, cool on warm and warm on hot. Joe burst to the surface with a searing pain in his lungs. He needed to breathe.

As Suryei came around the edge of the rock, a wide, black pool of water that had been hidden from her view opened out before her. The surface steamed like a large cauldron. Joe lay in the middle of it, floating face down.

Suryei carefully negotiated the sharp rocks at the edge of the pool, then jumped into the black water.

She didn't call out, didn't say anything. She just swam towards Joe, and when she reached him and found him unhurt, she punched him, softly at first and then harder and harder. Finally, exhausted, she rested, sobbing against his chest, arms around his shoulders. Dimly, she felt him growing against her belly in the warm water. She wasn't aware of it at first and then the feel of his penis against her skin shocked her. The sudden realisation that she had that effect on Joe aroused her. Before she knew what she was doing, Suryei reached down and freed him from his pants. His body was lean and terribly scratched, etched by their passage through the unwilling environment. She squeezed him to her, treading water.

Joe was stunned by Suryei's display of emotion. She'd been so in control. He felt her embrace, her warmth, and his hormones took control, flowing through his body. Her closeness to him had a powerful effect, no matter how much he tried to suppress it. He was aware of her hands searching hungrily. He slid his hand inside the remains of her shirt and felt the soft skin of her breasts, her nipples hardening under his fingertips. Suryei reached down and unzipped her fly. She bucked in the water until her pants slid from her legs, removed by the water's gentle caress. His own pants seemed somehow to have dissolved away.

They were suddenly naked together. Suryei needed this. Perhaps it was a reaction to the constant danger. She had never wanted a man inside her so badly. His heat entered her. For the first time in her life the intensity and the imminence of sex drugged her, overcoming her inhibitions. She wrapped her legs around his torso and pulled

210

him deep inside her. They kissed, sucking each other's lips, biting, hungry.

They moved together in the pool, probing, accepting, lifting each other to orgasm. There was desperation in their rhythm, an intensity to the urgency between them. And when they were spent, they stayed together, embracing, sinking slowly beneath the warm water, into the cool layers below.

'Listen, Joe, don't flatter yourself, okay?' Suryei said as she slipped on her wet cargo pants. Was that a smirk she'd caught on his lips? Suryei had already done a good job of justifying their fucking – that's what it was, fucking – in her mind. Nine months after life-threatening earthquakes and floods, she reminded herself, a spurt in the local birth rate is not unusual. She'd read about incidents where total strangers had coupled during such events. Even some plants flowered as they withered and died, in the hope of attracting bees and other insects, in one last death-defying attempt to pass on their genetic material. It was species survival, the force of nature. Feelings had nothing to do with it.

'What we did was just some primal thing. You could have been any "Joe", Joe.' Joe's face clouded and the realisation that she'd hurt him tightened her stomach.

'Look, Joe,' she said, wringing the excess water from her hair. 'We've done a good job of staying alive here, but we could be dead in a few minutes for all we know. The only reason we've made it this far is because we've kept ourselves single-mindedly focused on surviving. If we turn this into a sequel to *Blue Lagoon* or something, we won't get out.'

Joe examined her for a moment.

'What?' she asked, feeling uncomfortable.

There was nothing much Joe could say. Their situation looked pretty grim and their chances of getting out alive were slender and shrinking with every passing hour. This was hardly the setting for a budding romance. So he said nothing and just put his arm around her. 'Come on,' he said after a minute of silence.

Joe helped her across the rocks as they began the climb out. For the first time, it was help she accepted readily. He looked up and took in their surroundings. The massive volcano towered skywards, the upper reaches of its cone disappearing in cloud. A sheer escarpment rose vertically between them and the base of the volcano. The rock pool he'd fallen into lay at the bottom of a valley, carved by the lava flow from the brooding giant beyond. Small plumes of sulphurous steam puffed from fissures in the rock here and there and gave an unpleasant tang to the air.

It was a forbidding place, yet their relationship had changed fundamentally and the terrain no longer seemed to Joe quite so threatening.

Jakarta, 0230 Zulu, Friday, 1 May

Suluang had risen early from a fitful sleep, the demons of failure destroying any chance of genuine rest. So he'd been awake for hours, his mind parrying and counter thrusting through the range of options and issues that threatened to overwhelm the scheme. An empty bed was not a particularly inviting place to be when action was required. Only, what was the right action? The unknowns were building and soon, Suluang knew, they would burst forth into the public domain. And for that reason alone he regretted the act of shooting down the aircraft. The moral issues didn't trouble him. In retrospect and with a favourable spin, it would be seen in the right context: that of the rebirth of a nation rather than a desperate attempt to maintain secrecy. Suluang's mobile phone rang. He glanced at the number on screen before deciding whether to answer it. 'Lanti.'

'General,' said Lanti Rajsa. 'We cannot forestall the meeting any longer. The plane. Our partners are asking questions.'

'We need more time, Lanti. Even half a day.' Suluang had not had an update from the men in the field.

'We don't have half a day, General.'

Diesel and grease fumes hung heavily in the vast work-shop. The garage was clear of men, unusual given that it was ten-thirty in the morning, but being able to command privacy was one of the privileges of being a general. APCs stood stiffly in rows, massive slab-sided guardians, mus-cles fashioned in drab green steel.

Suluang felt comfortable here. He wore simple battle fatigues with the weight of his rank plainly embroidered in black on the wings of his shirt collar. This was his real home, his regimental barracks, and here he was king. He ruled his kingdom with strength and his subjects loved him. They were prepared to die for him and, one day, they would probably have to. This was how the world should be, thought the general. Here, life was simple and straight-forward. You followed orders. If you followed orders well, you would ultimately be given the responsibility of giving orders for others to follow. It was only outside the regiment that life became complicated.

The officers, his partners in the enterprise, sat nervously at the table. In the centre was a large pitcher of water and an equally large bucket of rapidly melting ice. There was also an impressive, oversized bottle of Remy Martin XO brandy, the sort usually reserved for display purposes in duty-free stores. Each man had a glass. Some sort of toast or celebration was on the agenda. The men wondered what the occasion could possibly be. Morning was not the best time to drink brandy, notwithstanding the fact that they had all been summoned well before sunrise and had therefore been up for hours. Unusually for a gathering of senior officers, there were no adjutants hovering about, and no pads of paper were supplied on which the men could scribble notes. There was tension in the air.

The general watched a droplet of oil slowly grow on the bottom edge of an enormous engine hanging from a greasy chain. The black pearl grew until its weight overcame its viscosity and it dropped with a gentle 'boing' into a large tray, filled almost to the brim with the motor's inky blood.

General Suluang had just finished debriefing the officers on the 747, and for most the news was a bombshell. A stunned silence charged the air with electricity. And he was yet to inform them that there were survivors of the crash, potential witnesses, who were running around on Indonesian soil.

Lanti Rajasa watched the men carefully to gauge their individual reactions. The future of the enterprise depended on the next few minutes.

'I don't know where to begin, General. I think shooting

down the 747 was regrettable,' said General Kukuh 'Mao' Masri, resisting the desire to say 'stupid', and trying hard not to reveal on his face the doubt seeping into every cell of his being. 'Whether you had a choice in the matter or not is debatable, but what is done is done. Insha' Allah. Have you heard from your Kopassus?'

'Yes, Mao. Twice,' replied Suluang. 'There were two survivors from the crash. The sergeant commanding the section says there will be no survivors by . . .' he glanced up at a clock on the wall and lied, '. . . around now in fact.'

There it was, the other bombshell, delivered in a most casual way. Both Lanti Rajasa and Suluang braced themselves for the reaction.

'Have these survivors been pursued by our men?' Colonel Javid Jayakatong enquired in a remarkably even tone.

That was promising, thought Rajasa, relaxing slightly. Jayakatong had said 'our men', which *could* mean that he was unconsciously taking some ownership of the situation.

'Yes,' confirmed Suluang. 'But they have evaded our men since the morning of the crash.' That was not something he knew as a fact, but had deduced. Somehow the survivors had managed to slip away from the ill-fated 747, but they would surely not be able to avoid a reckoning with the Kopassus for long.

Jayakatong frowned while he massaged his cheeks.

'There is a report in the newspaper this morning about a logging camp that appears to have been swallowed by the jungle. The owners, which include the Indonesian government, have not been able to communicate with the camp for twenty-four hours. Could this have some connection with your men in Sulawesi?' asked Admiral

Sampurno Siwalette, the newcomer surprising everyone with his bluntness.

'I have no information on that, Admiral,' said General Suluang truthfully.

'You put a lot of trust in your Kopassus leader. And you say he is what, a sergeant?' interjected Colonel Jayakatong.

The general surveyed the gathering. Support was sounding increasingly . . . questioning. 'He is one of my best and most loyal men, of any rank.'

General Kukuh Masri listened intently while he considered his options. He was in a mild state of panic. It was astonishing that none of the other men seemed even remotely concerned that a civilian 747 had been blasted out of the sky by one of their own fighters. This was not something he felt comfortable with at all. 'You have been quiet, Colonel Ajirake. Did you know about the shooting down of the Qantas jet?'

'It could not have been done otherwise, General,' said the air force man casually, leaning back in his seat, hands clasped arrogantly behind his head.

'Can you trust the man who pulled the trigger?' asked Masri, feeling all at once that he needed to put some distance between himself and these men but knowing, at the same time, that he had helped create the situation he now suddenly wanted no part of.

'A fighter pilot's life is dangerous. Unfortunately, he was killed in a tragic accident.'

Masri noted the barest shadow of a sneer on the officer's fleshy lips. A recent addition to their group, the colonel had obviously embraced its plan wholeheartedly. It was always going to come to this, thought Masri. Men would be killed to make their new Indonesia. So why was he squeamish about it all of a sudden? Perhaps he wasn't upset at all but just afraid. No, it was more than just fear. He had agreed to join originally because he was fed up using the army, his men, against the citizens of his country. But shooting down a civilian plane? That was brutal – mass murder – and the fact that it was another country's airliner didn't lessen the barbarity any. He still believed in their original goals, but the way they were being achieved did not sit at all well with him. Events had hijacked all honour, he realised, and he was now a prisoner of them. He wanted nothing more to do with the scheme, but the question uppermost in his mind was what it would take to guarantee his own safety. How could he back out and still live to reach old age? He had tanks, APCs, artillery and several thousand soldiers at his disposal, but hardware would not be enough.

General Suluang realised that something subtle but irrevocable had shifted within the delicate balance of the enormous military and intelligence resources he had brought together, not because of what had been said by these men in response to recent events, but by what had not been reaffirmed. 'This is not the way forward I would have chosen for our course of action,' he said. 'Fate has intervened. But whether we like the way it has begun or not, it most certainly has begun.

'Between us we command a sizable portion of our country's military might. We just need the will and the determination to wield it. As for the current situation in Sulawesi, Rajasa and I have discussed it at length. There will be no survivors of the crash. Within a few days, Australia will be invited to inspect the wreckage, as part of an international team, after our own experts have muddied the water a little on the reasons for the crash. In the meantime, our government will continue to say all the right things, offering the olive branch, smoothing the waters diplomatically until we are ready to go. But go we must, and soon.'

The men at the table were silent.

Suluang continued: 'There have been no real setbacks here, merely an operational replan which, as military men, you all know can happen and are trained for.

'Your men are ready and your equipment has been stockpiled. We will launch ten days from now.'

A yawning pit of fear opened in Masri's gut. Ten days? That was sheer madness. It was not possible to push the button on many aspects of their strategy in such a short time. The amphibious assault alone required a good month of careful recruitment and fastidious attention to detail. Without it, many people would be killed. Indonesian blood would stain the sea red. He saw clearly all of a sudden that the coup would fail. He considered saying as much outright, but decided against it. Suluang and Rajasa had the mien of fanatics about them now. Obviously they were committed no matter what the cost. Masri wondered whether any of the others sitting at the table could see that to continue with the plan would be suicide. Not just for them individually, but for Indonesia.

'We will meet here again in two days time, at 0030, to go over the details. Our time is nearly here. There is only one way for us to go, and that is forward,' said Suluang.

No, there is another way, thought Masri.

General Suluang stood, ceremoniously removed the top from the large bottle of XO, and poured each man a generous tot. 'Gentlemen. Success.'

All six men stood and raised their glasses in a silent

toast. Masri's eyes were frozen in their sockets. He walked out of the humid, grease-heavy atmosphere of the garage and stepped quickly into the air-conditioned comfort of his chauffeur-driven Benz. 'Home,' he snapped at the attractive female, a lieutenant, behind the wheel. They drove in silence to the general's residence. The forty-six year old man looked nervously over his shoulder at the following traffic several times, which, the lieutenant noted, was something he had never done before.

The lieutenant could sense the general's nervousness. After their six-month affair, she was attuned to his many moods. She had been hoping that they would go to a hotel in the evening as usual and play their special games. Her favourite was a role reversal in which she was the general and he the junior officer. In this game she gave orders commanding him to do silly, sensual things. From the man's anxiety, she knew there weren't going to be any such games that night.

They arrived at the general's home and he asked her to wait, leaving the motor running. Again, unusual. He dashed out of the car while it was still rolling to a stop and tripped up the stairs to the front door.

The lieutenant received a call on her cell phone. The staccato instructions she received instantly sobered her. She knew, now, why the general was tense. He had good reason to be.

Ten minutes later, the general's wife, with a bag under one arm and a small boy under the other, burst through the front door and ran down the steps to the car. The woman dumped the crying child in the rear seat and raced back up the steps and into the old residence that dated from Dutch colonial times. Seconds later, both the woman and the general came out carrying medium-sized suit-cases. The general didn't give the lieutenant a destination. He just told her to drive, and fast. The anxiety and stress exuded by his parents, coupled with the violent motion of the car, made the young boy cry louder.

Masri told the lieutenant to take a left and then a right. He kept looking behind them, craning his neck, examining the following headlights. The lieutenant drove as fast as the traffic allowed. A motorcycle accelerated out of a side street. It darted through a gap in the traffic and pulled up behind the limousine. The pillion passenger pulled a machine pistol from his jacket and hosed the rear of the car.

Bullets ricocheted off the bitumen in a ballet of danc-ing sparks. The general's wife had time to scream once before she died as a slug drilled through the top of her shoulder and spun a channel through her lungs and heart, bursting its chambers. The driver reacted as anyone might in such a situation, despite the fact that she knew the attack was coming. She turned the car away from danger. The rear of the vehicle flicked out with the weight trans-ference and removed the front wheel from under the motorcycle. The bike instantly slid on its side, spilling its rider and passenger under the wheels of a truck trundling heavily in the opposite direction.

The general screamed at the lieutenant to take another left. She complied. He then screamed again for her to stop. The lieutenant ignored the second command and instead pushed the accelerator pedal to the floor. She could not stop at this pace.

Masri jammed a pistol into the back of her head with such force that her forehead hit the horn. The general flicked the gun to the left and fired a warning shot. He meant business. The blast of the round erupting from the muzzle perforated her eardrum and blood spurted from her ear hole. She dazedly saw the road passing under the car, through the fissure drilled by the round in the floor beside her feet. She got the message and stood on the brakes.

The car skidded up and over a kerb, crashing heavily into a solid brick and cast iron fence. The firearm discharged a second time, accidentally, the bullet removing a large portion of the back of the lieutenant's head and spraying it on the footpath.

Unlike the child's, the general's seatbelt had not been fastened. The impact catapulted him over the front passenger seat and smashed him through the front windscreen. He came to rest, bloody and unconscious, on the ground. A restrained brass plaque on top of a cracked pillar read 'Australian Embassy'.

The Indonesian embassy guards raced from their checkpoint to the scene of the crash after a few seconds transfixed by disbelief. They hesitated again, vaguely fearful when they saw that the vehicle was a government one and there was much blood. Moments later the four Australian soldiers on extended guard duty following the previous day's ruckus arrived and took charge of the scene. 'This one's alive,' said a lance corporal, examining the man spread-eagled across the broken brickwork.

Sydney, 0420 Zulu, Friday, 1 May

ABC radio report: 'The streets of Jakarta turned into a battlefield a short while ago when tanks and troops loyal to General Suluang, Indonesia's top military man, attacked the barracks occupied by units loyal to General Kukuh Masri.

'Observers here are surprised because Masri was regarded as one of General Suluang's most ardent supporters. After Suluang positioned tanks at the gates of Masri's compound, the besieged troops briefly responded with small-arms fire. Soon after, a negotiator from General Suluang's forces convinced Masri's troops to holster their weapons.

'The skirmish comes as a real surprise to authorities in Jakarta. Indeed, security is tightening all over the city with helicopters patrolling the skies overhead. General Masri himself has not, so far, made an appearance and unconfirmed sources report that the officer has deserted his command. General Suluang is unavailable for comment.'

Parliament House, Canberra, 0425 Zulu, Friday, 1 May

Niven hurried to the Prime Minister's office. It was raining in Canberra and unseasonably cold. He was coming down with the flu. Perhaps it was just the stress. Flying over Baghdad at night in a non-stealthy aircraft with tracer fanning up from the blackness below searching for his arse was nothing compared to this Commander-in-Chief gig. Niven tried to shake the germs out of his head but only succeeded in having a subsequent desperate need for a tissue to stem the outpouring from his nose. A cold had finally caught up with him.

He barged through the security station at Parliament House. It was barely five minutes since he'd received a call from Blight telling him to get to his office, pronto. Niven had nearly caused a pile-up when he'd braked in the middle of the expressway, mounting the kerb and snaking across a wet grass median strip to join the traffic heading back into the city centre.

He waved quickly to Shirley as he strode through her anteroom. 'You're expected, Spike. Get you anything?'

'Thanks, Shirley. How about something for a headache? Besides a shot of single malt?'

He was through the door before she could acknowledge his request. Once inside, he noted that the team was already there – Griffin, Greenway and bloody Sharpe.

Shirley quietly entered the PM's office and placed a tray with water, glasses and a packet of paracetamols on the sideboard. The room was dark and a videoconference call was in progress. The atmosphere was dour. She gently closed the door on her way out.

The image of Roger Bowman, the Australian Ambassador to Indonesia, filled the large rear-projected screen. Niven thought he looked tired and anxious.

'Saw things got a bit rough for you last night,' said the Prime Minister.

Bowman took a deep breath. 'And it just keeps getting better, Bill. Anything come to light on QF-1 at your end?'

The men in Canberra exchanged glances. From the ambassador's body language, it was obvious that he had news.

'What you got there, Roger?' asked Blight.

'Do any of you know a General Masri? He's often referred to as "Mao".'

'Yes,' said Griffin. 'He's one of the TNI's major league players.'

Bowman nodded and continued. 'There was an attempt on his life earlier today. His wife was shot dead. The man's car crashed through our front gates here in Jakarta a short time ago.' The ambassador took a sip of water, his hand shaking so badly that water slopped over the brim.

Niven and Griffin exchanged worried glances.

'When we picked him off the pavement, Masri babbled something about being part of a group led by General Suluang that shot our plane down. He also said that a Kopassus unit was at the crash scene hunting down survivors.'

The room in Canberra was suddenly in an uproar.

Niven felt like he'd been slapped. Here was confirmation of the NSA's belief that QF-1 had been shot down. That was bad enough! But putting troops into the area to finish off any survivors?! It was unthinkable. 'What? To kill them?!' he said, aghast.

'Apparently.'

'Mother in hell!' exclaimed Blight.

'Do you know how many people that is?' asked Niven.

'Masri said there were two.'

'Jesus!' said Sharpe, head swimming.

'Did he say why the plane was shot down?' Niven asked, surprised at his own calmness. Perhaps because he'd prepared himself for the worst, he was better equipped to cope with it.

'No. Masri wasn't exactly coherent after the car accident. I believe he was on his way here to the embassy for protection. In the car were bags packed with essentials that included passports. The general also had his child with him who, I might add, is the only person besides the general to survive the attack.'

'How bad is he?' asked Greenway.

'Bad. The neurologist is not prepared to give a prognosis,' said Bowman. 'He has a depressed fracture of the skull. They're operating on him as we speak. Apparently he's pretty fit, so you never know.'

'Assuming he does come through okay, is there any idea when he'll be up to questioning?' continued the Defence Minister.

'That's the sixty-four thousand dollar question. None, unfortunately, Hugh. And if he does come around, there are no guarantees what he'll remember.'

Niven's mind raced. 'What about witnesses? Is there a guard on him?'

'Yes, the same four-man detail out the front when Masri rearranged the fence. But we've got no one to relieve them. We couldn't keep Masri at the embassy. Injuries were too serious. He's in the top expat hospital under an assumed name. Fortunately, his facial injuries are pretty bad, and so no one has recognised him, not even the local Indonesian embassy guards who were first on the scene.'

'What about Masri's troops?' Niven wasn't at all happy with the lack of security.

'They're preoccupied at the moment. If you haven't seen CNN this morning, turn it on. I can't tell you more than the news services are reporting. Obviously it has something to do with the reasons behind Masri's flight to our embassy, which is linked to the attack on QF-1 – none of which, I might add, is part of any news report that I've heard this morning. I'd be more worried about Suluang's men, frankly.'

'Sorry to jump back, Roger, but what's the Indonesian media saying about the crash?' asked Greenway.

'Masri's disappearance is something they're running around trying to unearth. We've been lucky. Only the local guards witnessed the crash and we got Masri and his son inside and cleaned up the mess before the police showed up. The media are reporting the crash, the bullet-riddled car and the death of Masri's wife. They're saying it's connected somehow with the standoff between Masri and Suluang's troops, and there are all kinds of bizarre theories being offered. It's all going to come out soon, though. We've got maybe a day – two at the most.'

'I'll get you Special Forces protection for Masri within two hours.' Niven calculated the time it would take to get some men across from East Timor. 'Can you handle the paperwork at your end?'

The ambassador nodded.

'So how are you keeping those Indonesian guards quiet, Roger?' asked Greenway.

'They are . . . er . . . heavily sedated . . . at the embassy.' Bowman was obviously distressed.

'You did the right thing, Rog,' said the PM, realising the ambassador had little choice. Sharpe ran his fingers through his hair. 'Christ Almighty.'

The Prime Minister quickly briefed the ambassador on the intelligence delivered by the Americans and the connection was terminated. Both parties had things to get on with.

Someone whistled quietly.

Greenway's forehead glistened with sweat.

No one spoke. No one knew what to say.

Griffin broke the silence. 'The problem is, we still don't know enough. So let's concentrate on what we do know,' he said. 'We know that a passenger on the plane, one Cee

Squared, broke into General Suluang's computer and saw something or took something or both. Shortly after that the plane was blown out of the sky. From that we can deduce Suluang, Masri and an unknown number of other high-ranking officers do, in fact, have something very big they want to hide.'

'How does the situation in Jakarta between Masri and Suluang's troops fit in to all this?' asked Greenway.

Griffin's face was blank. 'No idea.'

'We also now know that, despite protests to the contrary, the Indonesian military have located the plane,' added Niven, his cold making his speech a little difficult to understand, 'and that they're doing their damnedest to make sure there are no survivors. No doubt the soldiers will also be searching for the aircraft's black boxes.'

'You still think it's possible that the Indonesian government is ignorant of all this?' asked Blight, fingertips at his temples.

Griffin felt like he was standing at the water's edge, the ebb and tow of the surf undermining his footing so that he kept having to dig his toes into the sand to remain standing. 'I know it's hard to believe, Bill but, yes, we should continue to give them the benefit of the doubt.'

Blight wasn't sure. The contact he'd had with the Indonesian ambassador seemed to bear up the Director-General's view, but then, what if Batuta had been cut off by Jakarta and his ignorance was part of some deception? Jesus, so many uncertainties . . .

Niven shook his head in dismay. Two passengers on QF-1 had survived a missile attack and a crash landing, only to be hunted down by trained killers. In all likelihood, they were probably now dead. He fought back a sneeze and just managed to get a tissue to his nose in time. 'Anything turn up on this Cee Squared fellow, Griff?'

'Not a lot,' replied the ASIS chief, opening a folder on his Palm Pilot. 'Twenty-seven years of age. A computer software engineer. A games expert. He's well off. Not an active hacker. Lives alone in Paddington, Sydney. Father in Perth. Mother ran off when he was three. No brothers or sisters. The police are still investigating, but so far . . .' Griffin shrugged.

'Frankly, I think it's time we pulled the bloody Indonesian government's head out of its arse,' said Blight.

Sharpe nodded. 'But if we go charging up there with a lot of unsubstantiated accusations, we'll get nowhere.'

'We've got General Masri. He's an ace in our hand,' said Greenway.

'Who's absolutely no use to us unless he can talk.' Niven shook his head. 'But we also have the satellite intel, the photos, which is a hell of a lot more than anyone else seems to have at the moment.'

'What about the survivors?' asked Griffin.

'It's our job to protect them.' Greenway was adamant.

Niven caught the Defence Minister's eye and nodded. *Damn right!*

'Even though they'll be dead for sure by the time we get in there, if they aren't already?' countered Sharpe.

'I don't see how we can argue about it. There's no choice now. We have to go in,' said Niven, jaw set, the muscles in his face flexing.

'And why's that?' Blight sat back in his chair, fingers interlocked under his chin, pondering the options.

'For both emotional and strategic reasons, Bill,' said Niven, the Flight 007/Sakhalin Island incident swimming in his head. 'Because, as Hugh said, they're probably Australian citizens and it's our job to protect them. Because there's a remote chance we might find out at the crash site what these bastards are so anxious to hide. Because if General Masri never comes round, he'll be no use to us whatsoever. And because it's just the right bloody thing to do.'

Blight nodded. Sound reasons.

'The risks will be enormous,' said Sharpe. 'If you're to get there in time to do any good, you'll have to send troops now, with virtually no planning whatsoever. That's a recipe for disaster. The political fallout will rebound and –'

'But we also can't afford to sit around on our arses and do nothing, Phil, so, quite frankly, fuck the political fallout.' The Prime Minister's tone had finality about it. Blight was tired of the indecision and the inaction. It was time to Do Something. It was not likely that they would get too much more information on this situation before things – whatever they might be – got worse.

'We've already lost more than four hundred people. And that's enough bodies for one day. So tell me, Spike, what do you need? Do we have the resources to do this?'

'Bill, I won't lie to you – it's risky, and there are never any guarantees of success. Our Special Forces are amongst the best in the world. And, thanks to East Timor, Afghanistan, the War against Terror, they're razor sharp. The insertion and extraction will be tricky. Despite all the tough talk in recent years, our military is still a defensive force and we're not in the power projection business. We'll need help.'

'What kind of help?' enquired the Prime Minister, who suspected Niven knew exactly what he wanted.

The ADF chief tried to breathe through his nose but couldn't. He eyed the pack of paracetamols on the table in front of him and considered taking the lot.

US Embassy, Canberra, 0510 Zulu, Friday, 1 May

Blight again felt like a naughty schoolboy being interviewed by the headmaster. Herschel Zubinski always had that effect on him. That didn't stop Blight from liking the man; it was the situation, coupled with the fact that the ambassador's high, intelligent brow, deep voice and crinkled white hair made him look the part.

This was to be Zubinski's last stop before retirement. The man had made millions on the US bond market in the mid-eighties before switching to politics. One stint in Congress where Zubinski's integrity made things difficult for his own party was enough to convince the previous president that his own interests would be best served if Zubinski was kept far away from Washington. He had served as US envoy in France, the United Kingdom and now Australia. Zubinski liked his latest position but he missed the windy corridors of New York City. It was time to retire and spend some quality time with his grandchildren.

Herschel Zubinski drummed his fingers quietly on the tabletop. It was a habit he'd had all his life that displayed itself when he was concentrating. He listened to the Prime Minister. 'I know, Bill, I've just finished reading the summary from the NSA. The President is outraged. He's genuinely angry about this, and his anger is your best ally.'

'We can't do this without your help, Hersch,' said Blight. 'We're impotent and they, whoever *they* are, know it.'

'What about the Indonesian government? Forget the intel reports, what's your gut tell you?'

'To be frank, my gut's arguing with itself on this. I can't believe that a legitimate government would behave in this way, but at the same time I find it difficult to conceive that all this could be going on behind Jakarta's back.'

'It does seem unlikely, but Indonesia is that kind of country. And its armed forces have historically been a little on the maverick side.'

The phone rang.

'Excuse me, Bill.' The ambassador listened and nodded several times, saying, 'Yes sir,' and, 'Thank you, sir, I'll pass that on,' before hanging up.

'That was the President himself, Bill. The Joint Chiefs and the Sec Def have come round to the President's thinking on this. They want to know what's going on quickly. They have authorised me to let you know that our resources are to be put at your disposal during this crisis. When a Muslim nation, any Muslim nation, starts behaving erratically, it makes everyone nervous.' Zubinski opened the sheet of writing paper on which the Prime Minister had listed his requests. 'Are you sure this is *all* you want, Bill?'

'Thanks, Hersch. Please pass on our gratitude to the President. Our Commander in Chief, Ted Niven, believes this can be done quietly. I have to go with his advice. So, yes, I believe what's on the list will do nicely.'

Zubinski ran his eye down the paper again. He snorted to himself. 'Since when was a Carrier Battle Group and an MLP, a marine landing platform, doing things quietly?'

The PM smiled and opened his hands as if to say, 'beats me'.

Dili, East Timor, 0515 Zulu, Friday, 1 May

SGT Wilkes and his men had spent most of the morning poring over maps and photographs of the crash site and the surrounding area. It was difficult planning for a mission that didn't exist, but that wasn't unheard of in the SAS. Lance Corporal Gary Ellis and Private Al Coombs were out scrounging for extras. Wilkes liked to have backups of backups. Radios that worked perfectly well inside the barracks sometimes went mysteriously dead in the bush. And, of course, a radio was useless junk without batteries. They also needed a few extra NVGs because some arsewipe had lifted some of theirs. Gear had a habit of making the rounds like that – the stuff you nicked sometimes got nicked back – and with so many troops from so many different countries in Dili making up the UN force, there was some pretty tasty gear lying around for the taking.

Scrounging was not something the SAS needed to do. They had access to equipment other regiments only dreamed about. But the feeling in the group was that pinching articles from under the noses of some of the toughest hombres in the world kept them sharp. It was also just plain good fun.

Ellis and Coombs swaggered back with a couple of bulging duffel bags.

'Gather round, fuck-knuckles, and see what Santa

brung you,' said Coombs in his best imitation of a London barrow-boy, lowering his bag gently to the table.

He unzipped it and disgorged a whole range of booty from compact sleeping bags to radios, knives, webbing and a scoped and silenced full-automatic H&K carbine, which he began stripping down. 'Ooh, this is nice,' he said, squinting down the barrel's rifling. PTE Coombs had no intention of using the new prize in the field. Interchangeability was important on the job and he wouldn't put his life in the hands of weaponry he didn't know inside out, and trust unreservedly. He even felt a touch guilty stealing the rifle but it served the owner right. The soldier concerned would take more care of his next one.

'Do these work?' asked Wilkes, picking up the radios.

'Best of British, mate,' said Ellis happily, 'so probably, no,' he joked. 'We nicked most of this stuff from those tough-shit SBS pricks. Like candy from a baby. Hang on a sec,' he said, after examining the radios more closely. 'These are Kraut-made. Maybe the Poms have been a bit light-fingered themselves.'

'They'll be spitting fucking chips when they find them missing. Serves them right for leaving it all lying around. Well done, blokes,' said Wilkes as he turned the radios' switches to the standby mode and got green lights and plenty of static until he tuned them to the ETFOR base frequency.

'Spare batteries?' he enquired.

'Two sets,' said Coombs, digging around in the other duffel bag and coming up with the trophies. 'Plus TACBEs,' he added holding up three smaller tactical beacons, radios that sent out a constant radio signal that could be picked up by satellites and aircraft monitoring the distress frequency. The TACBEs could also be modified to broadcast low-power radio messages to aircraft circling overhead – good for keeping your whereabouts discreet. Not all of the gear had been pilfered. Most of it had come from Supply.

'And look at all this sexy shit,' exclaimed Coombs, pulling assorted Cordura magazine holders and chest webbing for 40 mm grenades from the duffel bags. 'What all the best SpecWarries are wearing this autumn.' He threw them to PTEs Chris Ferris, Smell Morgan and James Littlemore to sort and hand around. PTEs Greg Curry, Stu Beck, Kevin 'Gibbo' Gibson and Mac Robson mooched around the table to see what treasures they could claim.

'I bet none of you losers have seen one of these babies before.' Coombs pulled a small, unusual-looking machine pistol out of a thigh pocket. The weapon had a carbon fibre handle and a ceramic barrel. He removed the magazine. Polymer-cased ceramic projectiles. Real black stuff. The pistol was extremely light and appeared to contain no metal parts. A nasty little toy designed to foil X-ray machines at places like airports and embassies.

'South African?' enquired Curry.

Coombs nodded. 'Where else? God knows what something like this is intended for here. Probably just some wanker's toy.'

'Any hairdryers?' asked Gibson playfully. He'd recently shaved his head to get rid of a bad case of lice.

At that moment an Australian major walked into the demountable with a couple of men in nondescript uniforms – the spooks. The informal atmosphere within the room instantly dissolved, not because there was an officer present or because he had company but because the men could tell from their guests' body language that there was news. 'You're going in,' the major said as he loaded a disk into the laptop attached to a projector on the table, and turned it on. The computer booted up and the overhead light went off.

The now familiar overhead view of the remains of the 747 appeared on the wall. It was replaced quickly by a view from a similar angle of the logging camp. Both shots were slightly different to the ones Wilkes and his men had seen earlier, because they were more recent and taken at a different hour of the day. The camp had obviously been destroyed with the tents and other structures all burned.

'We've just got word from Canberra. There are Indonesian troops – we think it's our Kopassus friends – in the jungle. And they're hunting for crash survivors,' said one of the spooks. An electricity filled the room. Wilkes's Warriors exchanged glances. Not much shocked them any more, but this news was beyond even their experience.

A new satellite image flashed up on the wall. A number of bright green dots floated on the darker green chaos of the vegetation. 'Precisely which of these dots are Kopassus and which are our survivors is uncertain, although we do have a point of view. Initial reports suggested around twenty unfriendlies, plus two survivors. Unfortunately, we can only locate twenty contacts in total, rather than twenty-two. That could mean any number of things, including the worst – that our survivors have already been eliminated. However, the deployment of these forces would suggest something different.'

Another image was projected on top of the previous

slide. 'Now, if we superimpose a topographical map over the satellite view, the picture gets clearer.'

'An ambush,' said Wilkes.

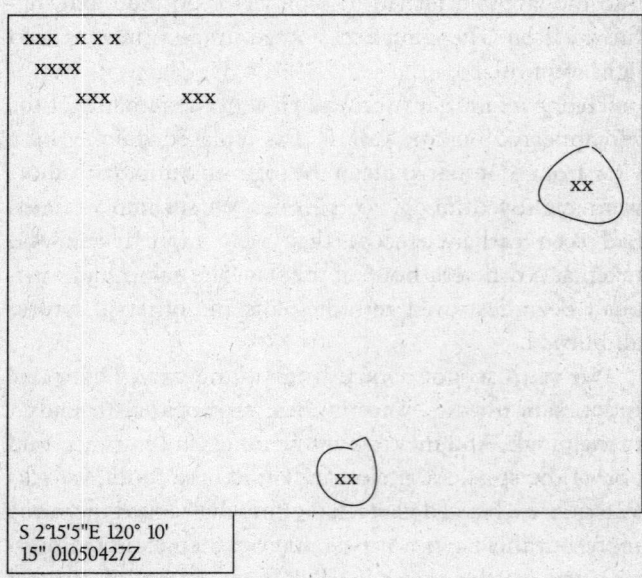

'Classic,' nodded the spook. 'The way the Indon soldiers are deployed makes their intentions obvious. That leaves two separate pairs of contacts away from the main group.' He circled them with a laser pencil. 'One of those sets is our pair of survivors. Obviously we can't be sure which is which but this pair here appears to be static,' he said pointing to the contacts at the base of the image. 'They could well be in hiding, which could explain their lack of movement. This couple up here appears to be on the move. One interpretation is that they could be forward scouts.'

The major stepped in. 'As has been said, we can't be sure which set of contacts are the survivors. These photos are less than half an hour old. The satellite we have on this is taking shots of the area at every pass, so we'll hopefully be able to freshen the intel at least once before you go in.

'These two people have lived through a plane crash and survived three days in the jungle. You're tasked to get to them before the Indons do, and bring them out.'

'Just two questions, Major,' Wilkes said after considering the presentation. 'Dili's a good 500 nautical miles from there. If we load now, and I assume we'll be in Black Hawks flying nap of the earth for most of it, we'll be pushing shit uphill to get there within four, but more likely six, hours from now.

'And with an educated guess about the kind of terrain they're in, I'd say these contacts here, the ones on the move, are only a few hours walk away from strolling into the known Kopassus placements indicated here.' Wilkes stuck his finger into the projected light, turning it into a pointer. 'You suspect these moving dots are also Kopassus troops. What if you're wrong? What if they're our survivors? Unless we're certain, we might get put down in completely the wrong place to do any good. So, question one – how do we get there before it's too late? And second question, sir, what are the ROEs here?'

'The rules of engagement are straightforward, Sarge. Go in, get our people out and don't take no for an answer.'

Wilkes nodded. This could be a tough one to pull off and he didn't want his hands tied with any niceties. 'Okay, so we're not sure which of these other contacts are our survivors, but we do know what this large group is and what they're up to.' He indicated the ambush placements. 'My suggestion is we take them out first – the large group – and then sort through who's friend or foe amongst the rest.'

'Fair enough,' agreed the major. 'The mission details are your call, Sarge.' The men in the SAS, even the lowest private, were selected on a number of criteria, not the least being resourcefulness and intelligence. They were all bloody tough bastards too. They knew what they were doing and they now knew what had to be done. It was not the major's job to tell them how to do theirs.

'Your assessment of the time constraints is spot-on. Fast transport is the primary issue. We're working on it with some help from the Americans. RV at Dili heliport within the next twenty minutes.'

'What medical expertise you got here, Wilkes?'

'Trooper Beck has done all the battlefield courses and knows a thing or two about tropical diseases,' said Wilkes, tipping his head in Stu Beck's direction. Beck raised his finger in acknowledgement.

'Well then, I suggest you go over to the hospital, Beck. I know you don't have nearly enough time but talk with the doctors about the kind of condition you're likely to find these survivors in. They've been through hell and they're not going to be in a good way.' The major's eyes flicked around the room and found it question-free. 'Okay then, if we're all done, good luck. This is an important one, you blokes.'

'We'll need a passenger manifest of QF-1 so that we can identify the survivors,' said Wilkes.

'Of course,' said the major.

'Also, we don't have any native speakers amongst us.'

'Yeah, not ideal, but then if our intelligence is accurate, I don't suppose you'll be doing too much negotiating, Sarge.'

Wilkes frowned. The major's comment was ill informed. When going into a foreign, and most likely hostile, land it made good practical sense to be able to speak the language, in this instance, Bahasa–Indonesian.

The major sensed Wilkes's disquiet. 'You've gotten by okay here on East Timor, haven't you?'

The more Wilkes listened to this major, the less he was impressed with him. Language hadn't been a big issue on East Timor because multilingual forces surrounded them. In the middle of Sulawesi, they'd be well and truly on their own. But there was nothing Wilkes could do about it, and obviously nothing the major could help with either. Wilkes let it go.

There was something else far darker niggling at the sergeant. 'Major, do we know why the Indons shot the aircraft down?'

'We're kind of hoping you'll be able to answer that one for us once you've been out there. Have you got everything you need?'

'Pretty much, sir.'

'So I see,' said the major with a hint of a smile, surveying the collection of goods on the table in the centre of the room before stepping out into another stinking hot day in East Timor.

Parliament House, Canberra, 0515 Zulu, Friday, 1 May

Griffin burst into Niven's office, obviously excited.

'What?' asked Niven.

'We have another useful asset besides the one in Maros,

Sulawesi. We have someone in Jakarta. I just found out. Real deep cover. A woman – Mata Hari type.'

Niven raised his eyebrows.

'You're not gonna believe whose bed she's been lying in. Bloody Suluang's!'

Dili, East Timor, 0530 Zulu, Friday, 1 May

The Mobile Assault Group, hauling heavy packs on bent backs, made its way across the Dili heliport apron towards the Black Hawk. There was a deceptively large space inside the chopper, but there wasn't much of it left once the ten men and their gear were stowed and secured.

SGT Wilkes found a position of relative comfort against the forward bulkhead, pack at his feet. The floor of the Black Hawk was bare alloy, and no matter how comfortable he was now, Wilkes knew the bones in his butt would soon ache against the unforgiving surface. But it was a minor discomfort. He was far more concerned about the job at hand.

There had been fuck-all planning on this op. Usually, every detail within reason would be thought through and shit still happened often enough even then. Shit happening looked likely on this one from beginning to end.

Lack of knowledge was the biggest killer in the field and a severe lack of it was gnawing away at the pit of his stomach. He felt like doing a nervous crap but couldn't. Black Hawks were lacking in passenger comforts. Questions swam around in his brain that he knew he'd get no answers to. He didn't even know how they were going to get into the middle of Indonesia in time, let alone get out in one piece. The whole business was one big shitty question mark.

He jacked into the helo's intercom and tipped his forefinger to his brow in a casual salute at the LM securing the Black Hawk's human cargo. The LM checked Wilkes's seatbelt, no more than webbing fastened into the floor of the aircraft, and then went on to secure the next trooper. When the soldiers and their kit were secured, the LM indicated as much to the two pilots on the flight deck, and the pitch on the rotor blades changed, carving deep into the air. The Black Hawk lifted positively, climbing rapidly, nose low. The helo banked as it climbed and turned through a steep 180-degree arc. Wilkes felt his cheeks being sucked down and his arms grow heavy with the gs.

As the helo gained altitude, Wilkes forced his mind to focus on the immediate issues. He scanned his men, receiving grins from most. But there was tension in the hot, cramped confines of the Black Hawk. Not the usual tension before a mission, the sort of fear checked by an innate belief in their training and ability. The atmosphere here was one of uncertainty, coupled with a sense of being up against it – time, stupid odds, and a situation that seemed, to put it bluntly, plainly fucking bizarre.

A voice in the headphones pierced Wilkes's concentration. 'Hey, Sarge. Lieutenant Harvey. I've been your taxi before. Up in the hills? I medivacked you and your mate after that firefight back in '99. How's your shoulder?'

'Yeah, that's right,' said Wilkes, recalling the pilot's face as he turned around and waved. 'Never got to thank you.'

'No wukkas.'

'Well, thanks anyway,' said Wilkes, dialling his brain back to the skirmish with the militia.

'What about the other bloke?'

'He lived.'

'Looked pretty bad.'

'Bad enough.' Wilkes changed the subject. 'So what you doing back here?'

'Exchange program with the States. Six months into it my Yank squadron got seconded to UN duty and here I am, back where I started.'

'Groundhog Day,' said Wilkes.

'You know it, girlfriend,' said the Royal Australian Army lieutenant in his best white trash American accent. 'Only there's probably some American lying in my bed back home screwing my missus, while I'm up here chewing dirt.'

Wilkes laughed.

'Nice to see you guys back to your old tricks. Ever landed on an aircraft carrier?'

'Nope.'

'Well, today's your lucky day.' The lieutenant didn't bother asking specifically what mischief these SAS boys were up to because he knew it was none of his business, and trying to make it so would get him nowhere.

'What's the flight time, ace?'

'There's a touch of headwind so, providing that's constant, I give us twenty-five minutes airtime.'

'Thanks.'

'Sweet. Just sit back and enjoy the kind of service our competitors shoot at us for.'

Wilkes smiled and let his mind wander.

On a mission, the rigid formalities and observances of rank dissolved. They were just men doing a job, a job that could get them killed. On this kind of sortie, the SAS carried no rank or indication of nationality. They were going in to a foreign country, one considered friendly, yet they would very likely leave a number of dead Indonesians behind them. In the event of capture, all hell would break loose. It would be highly embarrassing for both countries. Australia would cut them adrift. What they were about to do never happened. It was a hazard of the job – not all jobs he'd done as a member of the SAS, but definitely a hazard of this one.

Wilkes reflected on that, and the new information just passed to him through his phones from the flight deck. The Americans were involved. An aircraft carrier, for Christ's sake! Somehow the Yanks were going to get them into the middle of Indonesia in double-quick time. That kind of joint operation was rare, especially when the op had been put together on the fly as this one obviously was. So the S70 A9 Black Hawk wouldn't be making the insertion. He wondered what would.

The sergeant closed his eyes and let his head fall back against the bulkhead and he tried to separate the known from the speculation. Indonesia had shot down a Qantas 747 and denied doing it. Why? It made sense to lie about something so heinous. They had then sent in Special Forces troops to kill any survivors. Again, why? That fitted with something they wanted to keep hidden.

Australia was sending in a MAG to protect the survivors and get them out. Nothing odd there – they were probably Australian citizens. But if this was such an important mission, as it undoubtedly was, why not send in a Special Recovery Squadron? Because sending in a full thirty-man SRS would require three times the logistics and it would be unlikely they'd manage that with any stealth.

Wilkes had to admit to himself again that he didn't know much at all. He also had to admit that he was intrigued, but no less nervous. The MAG was going in armed to the teeth and ready to wreak serious havoc. They knew they were outnumbered almost two to one by the Indon forces, but they did have surprise on their side.

Being SAS, the men were permitted to take in weapons of their own personal choice. The US-made M4 was popular, a development of the 5.65 mm M16 A2 carbine, with 14.5 inch barrel and collapsible stock. The M4 was ideal for engaging multiple targets. It had low recoil, making it easier to keep the gun pointing in the right direction, and it was also very light, feeling more like a toy. Yet at three hundred metres and in the hands of a skilled shooter, the M4 was a devastating weapon. Excellent ergonomics also made it simple and reliable in the field, and hard to fuck up in a high-stress situation.

The M203 was a separate weapon slung under the M4. It hurled a grenade, which looked like a miniature artillery shell, up to four hundred metres. It was a useful weapon in open territory but Wilkes thought it was of questionable value in a jungle environment, where branches and other foliage could easily deflect the grenade's trajectory with possibly disastrous results. Also, once fired, the grenade required a minimum distance before it would arm itself and it was unlikely that the jungle would provide the open air necessary. It packed a powerful punch, though, and, who knows, might come in handy anyway. Most of the men favoured the HE 463 round. It was smokeless and trackless and so didn't give away the firer's position. Troopers with 203s had at least a dozen of these rounds.

Wilkes preferred the 5.56 mm Minimi light machine

gun. He'd had the barrel shortened, and a silencer fitted. The weapon still made a healthy racket but the silencer eliminated muzzle flash, reducing the chance of giving his position away in a firefight. PTE Mac Robson also carried the Minimi, and with the same improvements. The Minimi could fire up to sixteen rounds per second from an underslung box containing two hundred rounds, so it was the ideal weapon when covering fire was needed. And if the weapon ran out of ammo, the M4 magazine slotted right in. If the Minimi did have an Achilles heel, it was the ammo box. It was not as easy to replace in the heat of battle as an M4's magazine. Wilkes's insurance policy covering him against being caught between magazines was a butt-ugly, sawn-off pump-action Remington loaded with heavy #4 buckshot. Extra cartridges were held on the outside of the weapon with clips. It looked like it had been run up in the garage, probably because it was, but it comforted Wilkes enormously to have the weapon along for the ride. Wilkes carried the Minimi and had the shotgun strapped to the outside of his pack, so that it could be readily reached and deployed.

Robson snatched at a fly that had been caught in the dead air of the cockpit. He opened his hand in front of PTE Gibson's face. Empty. He'd missed.

'Wanker,' said Gibson, shouting over the helo's massive whirling blades and punching Robson solidly in the arm.

Wilkes smiled. At thirty, Gibbo was the grandfather of the section. A former secondary school maths teacher at a tough western Sydney state school, Gibbo had attended a presentation given by the Australian Defence Forces during Vocation Week. He'd sat through the presentation open-mouthed at the opportunities in the forces presented by the army lieutenant. Barely halfway through the one-hour presentation, Gibbo had been convinced. The lecture broke for lunch and Gibbo went AWOL from the school, taking a bus to the city to enlist. The love affair with the regular army hadn't lasted long, though. The life of a regular army trooper was dull between exercises. He wanted to be training full-time. That's when Special Forces caught his eye. Gibbo failed at his first attempt, the rigorous and difficult selection processes for the SAS taking him by surprise. But he'd succeeded at his second.

Gibson laid his M4 on the deck briefly and adjusted the pistol on his hip. It was his backup weapon – the same one they all carried – the H&K USP, the 9 mm self-loading pistol commonly in use in the Australian army.

Wilkes looked around, trying to read the state of his men. Morgan had his head back, resting against the bulkhead. It moved slightly as the helo rode the air currents. He appeared relaxed. In the crook of his arm was the H&K MP5SD, a 9 mm sub-machine gun, silenced, of course; the expelling rounds made no more noise than a baby farting. On his chest webbing were four M26A1 defensive hand grenades and four M34 'Willie Pete' incendiary/fragmentation hand grenades. The M26A1 had been in service with the US forces since the Korean War. The body was of thin sheet metal lined with a prefragmented spirally wound steel coil, and filled with 155 gm of composition B. On detonation, the M26A1 created a casualty zone with a radius of fifteen metres. A blunt instrument, but effective.

PTE Morgan could toss a grenade fifty metres and land it in a garbage can. He'd won lots of beers from dubious visitors on the firing range with that trick. The point was, he was damn accurate, and with a weapon like a Willie

Pete grenade, you needed to be because it had been known to kill quite a few of the good guys. It was filled with white phosphorus that burned at 2700 degrees Celsius, on contact with air, for around sixty seconds. The phosphorus particles were scattered over an area of around thirty-five metres. Get that stuff on you and it burned clear through to China.

Between them, the group also packed a dozen claymore mines, very common, nasty and cheap-to-buy little devices that held ball bearings encased in PE. The claymore was designed to fire its load of ball bearings in a specific direction so that its killing zone could be tightly controlled. It was the ideal sentry to place in a narrow defile or track you knew the enemy would take. The mine could be triggered remotely or by trip wire. And it was easy to deploy. One face of the casing instructed matter-of-factly, 'This side to enemy'.

For communications, the MAG was equipped with two Raven 11A HF sets, the extra one for backup. Ellis had one, Morgan the other. TACBEs, three carried for the sake of redundancy, had made the trip. More communications were always better than less. The Raven 11A, a development of the original and much-vaunted Raven, had a theoretical range of 200 nautical miles with 120 metres of aerial deployed, and was also capable of sending and receiving secure, scrambled short-burst transmissions. Two satellite phones were also carried, one as backup, with receiving equipment for image viewing. Two sets of backup batteries were carried for each.

The helo had quickly reached a cruising altitude of around 5000 feet. Wilkes peered out at the green water flecked with whitecaps below. A movement caught his eye.

It was PTE Littlemore, fiddling with his patrol radio, the type that allowed each man to stay in contact with the rest of the section. He was slapping the receiver in the palm of one hand, then checking the connections. Whatever the problem, it seemed to have been fixed. The trooper repositioned the tiny boom mike in front of his mouth, adjusted the earpiece then, satisfied, moved on to his pack, checking the tightness of the straps. Littlemore was a fiddler. Always checking and rechecking. Like all the men, Littlemore wore thick camouflage paint on his face, which, in his case, only served to highlight the shock of carrot-coloured hair on his head. Red hair also sprouted profusely from the top of the t-shirt at his neck.

Water had been scarce and they were thirsty. Joe and Suryei made their way cautiously into a gully, listening for suspicious sounds. They scooped handfuls of the cold, clear water into their mouths and then Joe quietly filled the bottles. A small yellow frog drifted across the surface of the slow-moving pool, stroking for the far side. Just as it reached the bank, a slender, bright green viper darted from the grass and snatched it up. The frog's legs quivered either side of the snake's jaws briefly and then were still. The reptile briefly held its prize above the water, as if in triumph, then carried it into the tall grass where it quickly disappeared.

Another movement in the grass caught Joe's eye – a large black scorpion stinging a beetle into submission with the wicked-looking barb on its tail. It occurred to Joe that he was witnessing metaphors for their own situation. Waiting somewhere were their killers – determined, ruthless and committed. That they'd managed to avoid their fate was nothing short of a miracle. He wondered whether he should share this pleasant thought with Suryei and instantly decided against it. Suryei's determination, her will to survive, had been their defence against the soldiers. Best not to undermine it, he thought. Something large pushed aside the bush on the far bank. Whatever it was it was making its way to the creek. Suryei placed her hand on Joe's shoulder and they slid back silently from the water's edge on their bellies into the thick of the jungle.

Wilkes shifted his weight against his pack – something was digging into his ribs and his butt was already sore. The insertion flight was always the worst aspect of any op, the helo flight out the best. His stomach rumbled. There'd been no time to grab something from the mess. He wondered what had been stuffed into the 'ratpacks', their primary food source for the duration. Ratpacks – ration packs – had been developed by nutritionists to provide all the calories and essential vitamins required to keep a soldier out in the field killing for twenty-four hours. They weren't exactly gourmet, but they weren't bad either, containing precooked meals, chilli powder, salt, pepper, Vegemite, peanut butter, cheese, crackers, coffee, tea, condensed milk, sweet biscuits, sugar and chocolate. They had each taken enough ratpacks for a two-day insertion. Wilkes added a satchel of coriander powder to his kit to enliven the flavour of the precooked meals.

Like all SAS soldiers, Wilkes and his men were more than capable of living off the land, especially the jungle, which Wilkes thought of as part kitchen, part garden shed. There was food literally growing on trees, as well as underground in the form of roots and tubers. There were also plenty of animals that could be eaten – mammals and reptiles. That was the kitchen part. A veritable smorgas-bord of berries and fruits that looked edible but were, in fact, lethal was the garden shed part. But while Wilkes and his men could all live indefinitely on the food nature pro-vided around them, it was a hell of a lot easier to just rip into a ratpack. Foraging for food could take hours and sig-nificantly reduce their effectiveness as a fighting force.

Each man also carried a light sleeping bag, mosquito netting, groundsheet and silk hammock, which could be strung between trees to provide a comfortable resting place no matter what the angle of the ground, as well as keeping the trooper out of range of the ants, scorpions and other biting nasties. The groundsheet was thrown over the top to keep the rain off. And the mossie net's use was obvi-ous. In the morning, the whole lot could be packed away leaving no trace of their presence.

Finally, the soldiers each had a survival kit that included a map of the area printed on fine silk fabric that could also be used as a water filter, a needle and thread, water purification tablets, a flint and steel with which to start a fire, a length of fishing line and a hook that could be used both to catch fish and as a snare for capturing small animals, a basic first aid kit complete with bandages, disinfectant powder, antibiotics, liquid sutures, a scalpel, gauze, codeine tablets, lock-ties and three one-shot ampoules of morphine with hypodermic syringe built in.

Floppy hat, Kevlar helmet, camouflage face paint, trenching tool, a dagger, and a machete to hack away the dense foliage once their cover was blown, when stealth and secrecy were no longer on their side, completed the approximately eighty-five kilogram pack each man was lugging into the jungle. It was like hauling a full-grown man on your back. It could have been worse, thought Wilkes, if they'd expected the operation to last a week rather than a couple of days. Once they arrived and had scouted the surrounding terrain, they would cache most of this gear, returning as needed for ammunition, spare comms, batteries and rations, carrying only what was needed to keep them as light and as mobile as possible.

Wilkes looked at the nine men jammed in around him: Ellis, Coombs, Littlemore, Beck, Curry, Robson, Gibbo, Morgan and Ferris. They seemed okay – almost comfortable – but the risks they were about to face were enormous. Wilkes reflected on his own mortality. If death came to him, well, no fucking worries, mate. He was by no means a fatalist, nor did he have a death wish, but you could hardly be a member of the SAS and not be at least a little ambivalent about your own life and death. If you bought it, tough shit. Sure, there were people who would miss him and cry at his passing and he felt a pang of sorrow for them but, for himself, this was the only way to live.

He'd done a lot of very dangerous shit over the years: served in Bougainville advising the Papua New Guinea regulars fighting the guerrillas; he'd been inserted into the Congo with US Marine Recon to eradicate the organised gangs of gorilla poachers; he'd helped rescue a couple of CIA men who'd been captured and held to ransom in Bosnia; he'd been dropped into Kosovo scouting for targets for the UN pilots. And, of course, East Timor. He'd missed Afghanistan, Iraq and Iran – he was a jungle expert.

Each job had had its own unique brace of problems. With this one, the big question was how they were going to penetrate Indonesian airspace and get to their RV, a ridge behind the two contacts Wilkes had assumed were the friendlies on the infrared photos, without stirring up a hornet's nest of trouble – and in time. Perhaps the Americans would have the answer. They had some pretty specialised gear for this sort of thing.

The Sea King helo from the USS *Kitty Hawk* appeared out of the haze at the appointed time. Lieutenant Harvey followed standard procedure for approaching a US Navy Battle Group and did not transmit his call sign or intentions to the American helo. The Black Hawk was expected. Harvey merely lined up behind the Sea King and followed abeam of its slipstream. The Sea King banked to starboard and altered its heading forty-five degrees. A large guided missile destroyer drifted by beneath them while the enormous grey-blue bulk of the carrier loomed out of the haze-obscured horizon.

The *Kitty Hawk* grew as they approached the fantail and Harvey saw the deck as an F-14 Tomcat pilot on short finals would. Although it was four and a half acres of black non-skid steel, it appeared as small as a domino, a minute target to hit with a fighter jet weighing four tons screaming earthwards in a controlled crash at 280 kilometres an hour.

Fighter ops on the carrier were in full swing. The deck bristled with F-14 Tomcats and F/A-18E Super Hornets. One of the Super Hornets was waiting on the catapult for launch. The Sea King held its station, hovering three hundred metres abeam the port side of the carrier. Harvey did the same astern of the US navy helo. The F/A-18E squatted down briefly on its undercarriage as it started to move. A river of steam exhausted from the side of the ship as the cat shot the jet down the absurdly short runway. The catapult flicked the fighter off the end of the threshold and the jet lurched away to port staggering, struggling for height, twin turbofans grinding out 40 000 pounds of thrust in full afterburner.

A paddle-wielding 'yellow shirt' on the deck of the carrier waved the Black Hawk and its escort towards the forward deck. Fighter operations were suspended briefly while the two choppers manoeuvred for landing, rotors whirring, over American sovereign territory suspended in the milky Arafura Sea.

The smell of AV-TUR, rubber and hot grease filled Wilkes's nostrils and cleared his sinuses. It was a heady brew, the smell of hard, high-powered military muscle. Perfume. He breathed it in deep as he loosened his floor safety strap. He grabbed his pack and shuffled to the door on his arse. Once outside, he glanced back through the Plexiglass side window and got a thumb's-up salute from Harvey. The Black Hawk had kept its revs up. This was to be a quick letdown. Once his troops were offloaded, the helo rose from the deck. No fuel stop. Wilkes made a quick mental calculation and concluded that the Black Hawk would probably get its tanks filled mid-air on the flight back to Dili.

The Sea King's rotors drooped with their own weight as they spun down. When stationary, the rotors would be folded back. A small vehicle had already tethered to the front of the helo in preparation for the short haul to one of the massive elevators that would take it below decks.

'Captain Chuck McBride, US Marine Recon. You must be Sergeant Wilkes,' shouted the tall black man over jet noise as he walked briskly up to the Australians.

The marine towered over him. Wilkes saluted and the officer returned it crisply, strong white teeth showing in a smile of genuine warmth. He wondered how the officer knew which one of the ten foreign soldiers that spilled from the American Black Hawk was Sergeant Wilkes, given that none of the SAS wore any badges of rank. He forgot about it and continued to gawk about like a dazed schoolkid at the activity on the carrier deck.

'Follow me, Sarge, and I'll get you out of harm's way.' The captain and two other marines in lightweight aviation overalls herded the Australians towards the looming shadow of the carrier's control island. Wilkes was happy to follow. He was aware that the deck of an aircraft carrier was the most dangerous workplace in the world, with any number of objects that could kill a man – from jet blasts to thick, grease-covered arrestor cables that slithered across the surface.

A shriek with a completely different tone filled the air as two US Marine AV-8B Harrier 11s, Jump Jets, rocketed down the dead side of the carrier's traffic pattern and lined up two nautical miles abeam of the fantail for landing. Gary Ellis caught Wilkes's eye as they watched the spectacle and gave a soft whistle. This was impressive shit they were watching, a well-oiled machine.

The AV-8s came in slow and didn't bother 'trapping', picking up one of the four heavy cables strung across the deck that brought jets like the Tomcat from 130 knots to zero in a neck-breaking three seconds. They came in over the fantail with drooping wings and dangling landing gear and hung in mid-air above the deck like giant mechanical gnats. The AV-8s appeared to defy gravity, descending slowly on invisible columns of air. They taxied to the space vacated by the jungle-camouflaged Black Hawk, which had slipped away unnoticed by most of the Australians during the show put on by the new arrivals.

Refuelling carts raced to the Harriers in a practised ballet. The pilots opened their canopies, loosened their harnesses and oxygen masks, and pushed themselves up and out of their ejection seats. Aircraft handlers wheeled over ladders to help the pilots down from their aircraft. The two officer pilots then trotted over to the 'island', disappearing inside the hatch.

'They're yours,' shouted the marine captain over the shriek of turbines, indicating the AV-8s. 'And so is that.' He directed Wilkes's gaze to the large hole in the deck that had opened up. An aircraft levitated up from the blackness. It looked like a mutant helicopter, or a genetic experiment gone horribly wrong, with two enormous black propellers sitting across the top of the fuselage. The cockpit area was heavily glassed and looked similar to the front end of a Huey, the UH-IB, the helo most people associated with the war in Vietnam. The back half of the aircraft was reminiscent of the Hercules, except that a C-130 didn't have its horizontal stabiliser between two vertical fins like this aircraft. It couldn't possibly fly. It was, without doubt, the most unusual-looking aircraft Wilkes and his men had ever seen.

The puzzled look on the combined faces of the Australians indicated an explanation was needed. McBride provided it. 'It's called a V22 Osprey, made by Bell and Boeing!' shouted the captain. That didn't seem to help. 'The new Tiltrotor – part aeroplane, part helo and better than both. Cruises at 270 knots with a self-deploying range of over 2100 nautical miles. Designed to get us in and out of trouble spots before the enemy knows what's going on.'

Wilkes nodded, liking the sound of that.

Recognition spread on Ellis's face. 'Weren't these things grounded?' he shouted.

'Yeah, but we think we've nailed the problem – a glitch in the software that ran the flight control computers.'

The words 'we think' and 'glitch' were not very reassuring and Wilkes couldn't stop himself eyeing the aircraft suspiciously.

'Don't worry, Sarge,' said the captain, smile gone. 'This is one safe motherfucker. We wouldn't be putting you and your men on it if it weren't. A successful mission under combat conditions is what the V22 program needs.'

It distinctly sounded to Wilkes and Ellis like they were being used as guinea pigs. But what option did they have?

'It's lucky for you, actually. The V22's been on a limited joint navy/marine shakedown trail. You know, to re-prove the concept that had been proven the last time we re-proved it,' he laughed, as if sharing an in-joke. 'That's why we happen to be here in the right place at the right time for you guys. That baby there's how we're going to do this thing.' The marine captain spoke as if the mission was in the bag already.

'What's our flight time, sir?' asked Wilkes.

The captain checked his watch. 'We've got some pretty hefty tailwinds. Around two hours will see you on the ground at your drop-off point, but we'll know precisely when we're airborne. We've got extensive comms on board this baby and we're expecting satellite intel to come through en-route to make sure you let down on the right spot.'

'You coming along, Chuck?' asked Wilkes.

'Wouldn't miss it for the world,' the captain laughed.

Wilkes didn't see the humour.

The Australians watched as the V22's wing swung from its storage position, lying along the top of the fuselage, to the place where a wing should be on an aeroplane. At least now it looked like something that could fly. Maybe.

Jakarta, 0600 Zulu, Friday, 1 May

Elizabeth surveyed the room, looking for errant belongings. The disturbing satellite photo was on the bed. She placed it in the envelope and reread the instructions on her laptop. The people back home were convinced the general was somehow responsible for the crash, and that seriously pissed her off.

It was Elizabeth's job to get close to high-placed military figures, but she'd never expected to land one of the biggest fishes of all. The restaurant she waited at was known to Australian intelligence as one of the haunts of TNI officers. It was also known that the owner was closely related to General Suluang. It had been surprisingly easy to gain employment there, and to catch the general's eye, and that worried her. Perhaps *she'd* been the person who'd been set up. No, that was unlikely, she thought, dismissing her suspicions. Very few restaurateurs would turn away such an attractive potential employee. And Suluang was a known ladies' man. She hadn't slept with him that first night, or the second or third – he would have thought her a slut. But she'd tantalised him enough to be certain he'd come back.

Elizabeth checked through the room once more, satisfying herself that nothing had been left behind. She then made her way to the lift. Suluang had turned out to be a difficult customer. On military matters, he was a model of discretion. She was angry that her efforts had gone unrewarded, gleaning precisely nothing of interest from Suluang. When the news came through that he was possibly responsible for the disappearance of the Qantas plane, Elizabeth felt she'd been ripped off. Suluang could have been a motor mechanic or an usher at the local cinema for all the worthwhile intelligence he'd divulged.

Elizabeth walked past a couple of hotel guests, a Japanese couple. She didn't notice the man's eyes grow large as they devoured her.

Suluang was a good fuck, but not a good talker. For him, women were either sex objects or servants. The assignment was beginning to frustrate her. And then yesterday, she'd received a drop in her etray. Up till now, interest in him back home had been routine. But now he was suddenly big news.

She replayed the previous twelve hours in her mind. He'd been distracted in their lovemaking and he hadn't slept much, leaving for the barracks early in the morning. As usual, he'd deflected her questions, preferring to talk about the quality of her skin or the shine of her hair. Bloody annoying.

Elizabeth swept past the front desk in the foyer, the morning light making her thin cotton dress vaguely transparent. She had to hurry. She fingered the A4-size envelope, reassuring herself that she hadn't left it back in the room. The concierge watched her walk through the revolving glass door out into the hot grit of another Jakarta morning and noted that she had no luggage. Whore, he thought, and unconsciously licked his lips as the sun outlined her long straight legs.

Timor Sea, 0605 Zulu, Friday, 1 May

One of the V22's enormous propellers whirled overhead, hot gases exhausting onto the baking steel deck from the 6100 horsepower Allison turboshafts. Its identical partner on the opposite wingtip began to turn slowly. The AV-8 pilots were back in the saddle, helmets on and heads down, going through their pre-flight checks.

The operation now had an audience. The unusual sight of what were patently foreign special ops troops milling about on deck, fully camouflaged and bristling with firepower, had attracted spectators. The fact that they were about to leave in the United States Marines' newest toy to an exotic and obviously troubled place fired the collective imagination. The attention made Wilkes uncomfortable. The SAS preferred anonymity.

The LM appeared on the ramp at the back of the V22 and waved the troops in. The Australians shouldered their heavy packs and weapons and, bending forward under the load, walked out of the tropical sun and into the shade of the aircraft's belly.

Captain McBride put his mouth close to Wilkes's ear and shouted above the jet whine, 'We're set up to fast-rope you in.' Wilkes nodded his understanding. Where they were going, there were no open grassy hills for the V22 to land on. Most likely they would put down over the tree-tops. They would have to abseil off the back of the aircraft's loading ramp, which could be lowered in flight, down into the canopy and the unscouted terrain below it. It was a dangerous way to deploy, but the SAS trained for it. All in a day's work. It was best, however, to get all the ropes organised now, beforehand. There might, for example, be a firefight going on in the drop zone that required their immediate attention and it would not do to fiddle around in the confined space of the aircraft's interior at the last minute, organising ropes with bullets flying about.

Inside the V22 there was significantly more room than in the Black Hawk. The LM showed them where to stow and secure their packs and weapons and directed them to the rows of surprisingly comfortable seats, which reminded Wilkes more of a commercial aeroplane than a military one. Now this is luxury. By comparison, the seats in a Herc, their usual mode of transport, were crude benches running down both sides of the aircraft's fuselage.

There was room for thirty or more soldiers in the cavernous space. The aircraft had been well thought out. It could airlift a platoon-size force plus gear. And it didn't require a landing strip at its destination because it could land and take off vertically. Wilkes saw the sense in such an aircraft immediately. With its range and speed, the V22 also gave the US marine and navy ships the ability to stand off a troubled coastline further than ever before, way out of the destructive reach of the enemy's missile envelope. And, with its obvious cargo-carrying ability, the V22 would make an ideal resupply vehicle. It allowed the marines to get in and out quick, and hit harder and more effectively when and where it counted.

The LM handed Wilkes and his men abseil harnesses. Wilkes climbed into the webbing, fastened the straps comfortably, and then checked the assembly for error. He identified the rope on which he would exit the rear of the V22. It was colour-coded to the wrap-rack on the harness and already fastened to a hard point over the rear door.

Wilkes was directed towards a seat. Ellis sat on his right with a place for McBride on his left. McBride handed out headphones with boom mikes to the soldiers. Low-powered interior lights winked on as the tail ramp closed shut on heavy hydraulic struts.

Wilkes and Ellis glanced around. 'Do you think they'll be serving snacks?' enquired someone through the phones. The seats were almost luxurious. And it was relatively quiet. The Black Hawk was god-awful noisy and, with the sliding doors opened, windy. Being inside a Herc was like someone putting a metal garbage can over your head and beating it with a stick. The V22, however, felt almost like travelling first-class. It was even air-conditioned!

The vibration through the seat coupled with the change in sound pitch that he could feel rather than hear told Wilkes that the giant propellers whirling overhead were synchronised. There were only a couple of small porthole-style windows in the side of the fuselage so there wasn't much of a view. Wilkes felt the aircraft rock gently from side to side on its undercarriage, settling back on the deck of the carrier before it lifted clear.

The feeling in the pit of his stomach and the pressure popping in his ears told him the aircraft was going straight up. On the flight deck, the pilot took the Osprey from heli-copter to aircraft mode with the flick of a switch. The wingtip nacelles rotated through ninety degrees until they were aligned with the plane's longitudinal axis. Wilkes felt the change of direction in the muscles of his neck as the air-craft accelerated briskly towards its cruising speed. One moment it was a helo, the next a fast transport aircraft. Bloody Yanks had all the good shit, thought Wilkes. A few babies like this would give the SAS real kick-arseability.

The captain's voice through the phones interrupted Wilkes's train of thought. 'We're going to climb to 18 000 feet and hold that cruise altitude over East Timor. Then we'll drop down to wave height under Indon radar. The AV-8s will ride shotgun for us.

'We're going to skirt around to the east of Sulawesi. We'll have to RV with a KC-135 tanker out of the Philippines a couple of times – those AV-8s are thirsty mothers. When we do pop up to refuel, there'll be an EA-6B Prowler orbiting to fry any hostile radar and keep us stealthy, 'cause you can never be too careful on these kinds of ops. We've also got an AWACS bird to direct the whole show when we get closer to Sulawesi.

'And if things really go to shit, we've got a flight of three Super Hornets on station with the tanker that we can call in on fifteen minutes notice,' the captain added reassuringly, reading off a computer printout.

Christ, thought Wilkes. This is a covert mission? It sounded like the whole goddam United States cavalry was riding on in. But this was something the Yanks had a lot of practice doing in theatres all around the world – they called it CSAR, Combat Search and Rescue – and he wasn't going to argue.

'What about when we get to Sulawesi?'

'Okay, as I said, we plan to come in from the east rather than the south. That way, we can ride the wave tops for longer and stay under their noses. Also, we want to avoid Hasanuddin AFB in the south of the island.

'Once we get abeam of the plane crash site we'll turn inland flying nap of the earth. It'll get bumpy. We're not sure exactly where we're gonna put you down just yet. We're hoping for more up-to-date intel. That should come through about an hour and twenty into our flight time. We'll go over deployments then.

'Total flight time to insertion is updated to one hour, fifty-four minutes, plus or minus one minute.'

Jesus, that was quick, thought Wilkes. 'Comms?'

'I've talked to your radio guy already. You've got HF, sat phones and TACBEs?'

Wilkes nodded.

'Okay. An AWACS will stay on station at all times to relay communications. Your call sign is Ferret, 'cause we're stickin' you down a dirty black hole. That okay?'

Wilkes gave the captain a thumb's up. This was slick. Getting in unannounced and in double time was *the* major issue. 'What about getting us out?' he asked, another concern on a long list of them.

'Okay, that's a bit trickier. The only place we know of for sure where there's enough space to put the V22 down is the area cleared by the 747. We'll make that our RV, unless you tell us different when you call us back in. Transmit the coordinates indicated on your GPS and set off a TACBE when we're two minutes out. We'll track in on that. We'll let you know when to turn it on.

'This bird can get in and out pretty damn quick. Once we get you and your guests secured, we'll make for the USS *Pellieu*, an MLP cruising in the Celebes. We'll be no more than an hour away. And don't forget you can call in those Super Hornets on fifteen minutes notice, maybe less. You need anything, just ask,' said the captain, smiling.

Wilkes returned the good news with another thumb's up. He let his head fall back against the padded headrest. He set his internal clock to wake him in an hour and ten, allowing time to go over the refreshed intel before arriving

263

at the LZ. Within two minutes he was asleep. Sleep was good for stress. Two of his men were already snoring.

Jakarta, 0655 Zulu, Friday, 1 May

Achmad Reza allowed his eyes to drift over the Dewan Perwakilan Rakjat Daerah, the People's Assembly of Indonesia. He knew all the men and women in the giant hall by reputation. It was his business to know them. Quite a few were known to him socially, even some outside his own party. Many of the men and women in the house had chosen a career in politics because they had wanted to do some good. A significant number had lost sight of the ambitions of their youth. For these the party itself had become the focus, rather than the desire to achieve something beneficial for Indonesia. Reza had little time for them.

Reza had absolutely no time, however, for the parliamentarians who enjoyed and sought power for its own sake from the very beginning. An outsider might think that the latter group contained all the military men who, by law, occupied thirty-five percent of the seats in the Indonesian parliament. But that was not, in fact, the case. In the course of his career, he had met many soldiers whose politics, and whose loyalty to the people of Indonesia, he had admired. But a dangerous game was being played here. He had absolutely no idea what that game was, why it was being played, or by whom, but his gut told him that when the answers to those questions were known, Indonesia would never be the same again.

Reza sat quietly in his seat. So far, proceedings had been taken up with the military's explanation of the inter-regimental squabbling and the exchange of fire in the streets of Jakarta that morning. It was a waste of time, but unavoidable. What should have been the focus were issues like finding ways to ease the ethnic tensions in Kalimantan, or even fixing the deplorable lack of sewage treatment in southern Sumatra because it was adversely affecting the fish catch. That was what government was really about; improving the lives of the people, not wasting time putting the personalities within the military establishment under the microscope. But perhaps this time it was necessary.

He listened attentively to the claims and counterclaims. He sat with the bombshell in his lap, drummed his fingers on the plain brown A4-size envelope, and waited his turn.

He wondered who had sent him the envelope in the first place and why he had been chosen. Everything about this was a mystery to him. He knew he was being used but somehow that didn't seem to matter so much. If anything, it had increased his interest. He was a little-known politician from the Gille Isles. He had no weight, no influence. But the envelope on his lap might well change all that.

He wondered about his own motives and was brought back to reality by a dig in his ribs. He glanced at the owner of the elbow and met an impatient gaze. His name was being called. Again. He stood and uttered the usual pleasantries. He then removed the bomb from its envelope and dropped it.

'This morning I took possession of this, a satellite photograph of the Australian Qantas aeroplane that has been missing these past couple of days. It's shown here crashed on a ridge line. The time indicated on the photograph is 12.30 pm local time yesterday. The latitude and longitude are also shown, placing the crash in central Sulawesi –' Everyone in the DPRD was now on their feet, shouting. At the top of his voice, he yelled above the chaos, 'It is due to be released to the Australian media within the next fifteen minutes. My question to the house is why has the crash site been kept a secret from the people of Indonesia, and the people of Australia?'

Achmad Reza then sat quietly and waited for the storm raging about him to subside. It took some considerable time. He was jostled and pushed by people trying to get at him, and others trying to keep them away. Eventually, when a semblance of calm returned, he again stood. 'How can the TNI not know of the existence of this crashed aircraft in our own country, when other sources have obviously known of it for at least a day? I do not think that possible. I suggest the TNI has been in possession of this photo all along, but has kept it a secret from this house. I would like to know why.'

Again the parliament was in uproar. Nearly all of the military officers were on their feet, outraged, pointing at Reza accusingly and shouting denials. He could not hear what they were saying above the din and so he bore on regardless. 'A lot has been said this morning about the fighting in the streets of Jakarta, just a few hours ago, by rival regiments. We have been told it was nothing of consequence. I do not believe it. Does this photo have anything to do with the disgraceful squabbling? And what of the untimely disappearance of General Kukuh Masri? What is the real story? Tell us truthfully!'

He had received the envelope containing the photo in

the internal mail. There was no postmark, the envelope itself was unremarkable, but there was an accompanying note with one simple instruction: that the photo be released in the parliament. It further stated that the photo would be released immediately thereafter to the Australian media.

The aircraft Australia insisted was on Indonesian soil was indeed where they said it would be. A single overflight by the TNI-AU would have confirmed it. That flight had been performed, he was sure of it. Yet the military, for its own obscure reasons, had insisted that the jumbo had not been found. But here it was, plain as anything, on top of a kind of plateau and not hidden in a jungle valley.

He squinted at the photo again, lifting his glasses above his eyes to improve the focus. The picture was sickening in its detail. No one could possibly have survived such a catastrophe. He realised he was probably looking at the bodies of at least four hundred people, and the thought deeply saddened him.

It had taken a supreme effort of will, but Suluang didn't jump to his feet when the little-known minister who represented a rock in the ocean tabled the photo. Somehow, he'd also managed to keep the look of concerned serenity on his face – the one he always wore when in this place – despite the fact that his heart had immediately jammed itself into his throat. He knew this moment would come, but he was surprised at how quickly it had arrived. The 747 had been found, just as he thought it would. But by whom? The politician stated that the photo would now be released to the Australian media. Did that mean the source was Indonesian? If so, who could that be? Masri, perhaps? Before any questions could be put to him,

Suluang rose and hurriedly made his way to an exit, leaving the chaos behind.

The mayhem in the large hall had a violent edge to it. Reza suddenly realised that his life was very much at risk. He got up from his seat and hurried out, leaving the photo. A man immediately picked it up and, waving it aloft, demanded that the military come clean.

The overwhelming majority of Indonesian parliamentarians had been dismayed at the implications of the photograph. That much was obvious. The fact that an Indonesian government spokesman had been suggesting that the plane might not even have come down on their soil, despite indications to the contrary, and refused permission for an international search effort, could be misconstrued as having something to hide. That 'something' being the truth. And that's what Reza found so disturbing. Once the satellite photo of the downed aircraft went out over the world's news services and the Internet, as it no doubt would, millions of other people would reach the same conclusion. What have I done? he wondered.

Reza felt regret. And fear. He did not want to personally bring dishonour on his country but, he realised, that's what many Indonesians would think he had done. But what option did he have? He had no idea who he could and couldn't trust. Airing the photo in the biggest possible public forum would get things moving quickest while bringing him some form of protection. Perhaps that's why the note with the photo had instructed him to do exactly that. The news was out – there was no point silencing him. And, of course, the truth was by now also released to the Australian media. Only time would prove his actions right. Or disastrous. At least he'd saved some national face by revealing the scandal before outsiders did. What troubled him now was just how far the knowledge of that photo went within the TNI.

Ordinarily, Reza was not a man of action. He wondered what he should do next. The feeling that his life was at risk had subsided almost as soon as he'd left the anger of the parliament behind. Nevertheless, a soft tap on his door made him start. He had a small office near the parliament where he conducted the daily business of serving his constituency. He was not independently wealthy, and could not afford a permanent secretary. This was one of his casual secretary's many days off. He'd removed the phone from its cradle and turned off his mobile in an attempt to clear some space to think. But interruptions, if they were determined enough, would always find a way to get through.

He eased himself up and out of the chair to answer the knock and noticed a plain brown A4-size envelope had been pushed under the door. It was the same kind of envelope that had contained the photo. He got to the door quickly and opened it wide. There were a dozen people rushing along the hallway in both directions. Any one of them could have delivered it. His annoyance at being disturbed vanished. He closed the door and picked up the envelope expectantly.

Reza examined it. It was identical to the last one. There was no stamp or postmark, not even a name on the front to confirm the intended recipient. He carefully broke the seal and examined the contents. It was a plain sheet of white A4 paper with a number laser-printed in small characters: a phone number. The number was for a digital cell-phone. He picked up his mobile, turned it on and ignored the message bank beeping. He punched in the number.

A woman's voice answered. No 'hello', no pleasantries. All business. 'Are you calling from a digital mobile?'

Reza was aware that calls made from digital mobiles could not easily be scanned. 'Yes,' he said. 'Who are you?'

She said, 'Someone you need to see.'

'Did you send me the photo?' Of course it had to be her, the owner of the voice on the other end of the line, but he also felt he had to ask to be absolutely certain.

'Yes.'

Reza thought about his next question carefully. 'Why me?'

'Picked your name out of a hat,' said the woman calmly.

She gave him a map reference and told him to meet her there in an hour. As a precaution, she advised him to claim that his mobile had been stolen. The call finished. He sat back in his chair. This was without a doubt the strangest day of his life.

Reza took a street directory from his desk drawer and looked up the map reference. It was a small village. It would take him at least an hour to reach it. He wondered what he'd find there. The frosted window in his office door shattered loudly and half a roof tile clattered to the floor amongst a shower of glass. A scrum of people burst through the doorway jostling each other, shouting angrily. The notion of mortality and his tentative hold on it again overcame Reza and he hurried out unseen through an adjoining office.

Joe and Suryei struggled up the steep incline. The vegetation was too thick to penetrate so they trudged up a cut left by an eon of monsoonal rains. Joe pushed aside a clump of bamboo overhanging their path and his hand erupted in pain. He peered at the bamboo and saw that it was covered in white hairs. On closer inspection, the hairs turned out to be fine needles that undoubtedly carried poison. He swore and held his hand at the wrist, squeezing it. He slid backwards. The ground was unstable, black mud and they both stumbled as they struggled against the sucking at their feet. Their legs and arms were black, and their faces were streaked with mud from their attempts to wipe away the stinging sweat that constantly dribbled into their eyes.

Their lungs were dry and their breathing hoarse with the effort of keeping muscles supplied with oxygen. Suryei rasped with every painful step. One step forward, half a step back as their feet lost purchase. They paused halfway up the ravine to catch their breath and give their legs a rest, chests heaving. The sun winked through the sparse covering overhead, sending the temperature soaring every time the direct light struck them.

Joe's axe had become heavy with the caked mud. He found a stick to prise it off, but the wood was rotten and the stick buckled and splintered. He used his fingers instead.

Suryei reached inside the rucksack on Joe's back and removed two bottles of water, now at body temperature. Handing one to Joe, she guzzled the tepid contents and wanted more. Joe did the same, but insisted they preserve the rest of their supply.

Despite the exertion required to climb, it had been Joe's decision to again strike for the higher ground. He had his reasons and he still thought that they were sound. They had no compass and therefore no means of orientation. Beneath the jungle canopy it was easy to wander around in circles. If they were to arrive at a specific point in the jungle, namely, the 747 crash site, they would need to continually check their bearings against features that rose above the canopy, such as the volcano and the escarpment now at their back and curving around to the right.

The visibility was very much better than it had been when he had first opened his eyes in the middle of this bad dream. The clouds had rolled away and the air was clear of the mist that had shrouded the horizon. They were a good 500 metres below the crest of the ridge so there was still plenty of climbing to be done. The realisation made him light-headed with frustration. He wondered what they would see when they reached the top. He hoped they would be looking down on the remains of QF-1 and a rescue team sifting through it, rather than the bunch of killers trying to turn them into fertiliser.

He wondered what had happened to the soldiers. If the theory he and Suryei had pieced together was true, very likely they were still on their trail. But where the fuck were the bastards? He wished he'd had some military training, some kind of knowledge that would allow him to predict the soldiers' behaviour.

'They're still out there looking for us,' said Suryei, reading his thoughts.

Joe nodded while he stared, trying to pierce the canopy

spread out around them with the force of his gaze. Somehow, they had managed to slip away from professional killers, men who were no doubt trained in jungle warfare and survival. It was pure fluke. But they couldn't just continue to blunder around, and perhaps making a beeline for the 747 wreckage wasn't so smart either. It was difficult to think straight with, among other things, the cloud of mosquitoes swarming about him, buzzing, humming, biting, distracting him, pissing him off.

What to do, what the fuck to do? And where, exactly, was the plane? They could guess, but that was all. The soldiers had seemed to know the general bearing Joe and Suryei were taking. They probably knew that their quarry would run into the mountains and that scaling them would be impossible. Would they then assume that they would double back and make for the wreckage? Without maps, guides or supplies there were really no other alternatives. It was likely, then, that the soldiers would just lie in wait for them somewhere.

'Suryei, where do *you* think the plane is from here?' Joe asked.

Suryei thought about it for a few seconds. She raised her arm and pointed in a direction roughly forty-five degrees to the left of their current line of march, up and over the ridge. 'Over there, I reckon, but I'm not a hundred percent sure.'

Joe didn't agree. Before the soldiers arrived and added to this nightmare, he remembered surveying the horizon with binoculars. A flash of memory, like a moving postcard, flared in his mind. In the picture he clearly saw the volcano and the escarpment, and suddenly he knew exactly where the plane was. He just had to reverse the positions of those two dominating features, and put them behind his back. 'I think it's more in that direction,' he said, holding his arm out like a street sign forty-five degrees to the right of Suryei's reckoning. 'You're going to have to trust me, but I'm sure I'm right.'

'I'm worried that we're not on the same page about this,' said Suryei.

'I know, but I'm ninety-nine percent sure.' He squatted on his heels and smoothed a square metre of mud with his hand, flicking off the excess that stuck to his palm. He then sketched out a map using a small stick.

Suryei crouched and scowled at the ground.

'Look, we've been wandering around in a natural kind of bowl with the plane wreckage here. The snake and camp we ran into was here and here,' he said, marking various points with crude icons. 'And this is our track so far.' Joe etched their wanderings with a dotted line. 'All of it's contained within this escarpment, the hot springs, and there's the volcano.' Their situation presented by the mud map was suddenly obvious.

'If you were to set an ambush for us,' Joe continued, 'where would it be?'

Suryei considered the lines and squiggles in the mud. Then she took Joe's axe and scratched a few Xs on it. 'Here,' she said, simply.

'I agree.'

'How nice. Only, we're trapped,' she said.

'Well, the scale of things on this map is deceptive, but I think if we're not careful we could walk into one.'

Suryei nodded.

'Those mountains, the volcano, they're a natural barrier. The soldiers must realise that. We're just edging around the base of the really difficult steep country because we don't have any other options.' Joe stood before continuing. 'Those soldiers are just waiting for us.'

'Okay, assuming you're right, and I think you are, what do you suggest?'

'Fucked if I know, to be honest,' said Joe, scratching his head vigorously with both hands, scraping crawling things off his scalp with broken fingernails. 'We can stay more or less here, go back, go sideways, just any way but forwards.'

'What if we move in a big circle, an opposite circle to the one we're making now?' said Suryei.

'Double back?'

Suryei rubbed out Joe's track and replaced it with her alternative suggestion. 'I know it sounds obvious but, yes, basically. Cut across here at right angles and rejoin our original path out from the crash. Then, we should be able to come up on the 747 from behind.'

Joe thought about it. It made sense and was perhaps their only option. 'Okay, sounds reasonable. We'll continue to the top of this ravine and confirm our bearings, then slip across hard left.'

'But what if those assassins think we'll do that and set a trap for us?'

'Jesus, Suryei –'

'I know. I'm just asking what *you* think. I don't want to die here, you know.'

'Okay, well, we can double think this, or double-double think the options, but no matter what we decide to do, we could think ourselves into a trap.'

'I know that too, okay?' Suryei's shoulders had slumped.

'Suryei, I –'

'Look, whatever. Let's just get it fucking over with.'

Joe was too tired to argue.

Despite her exhaustion Suryei did feel less anxious about their revised plan. Their last one, simply making a beeline for the plane wreckage, didn't take into account the people with guns. She felt a little more confident now and it took some of the heaviness out of her step. Still, it was a wickedly steep climb. Sheer determination kept them going, just one more step. Half an hour's near vertical climbing brought them exhausted to the summit.

It did them no good. The canopy closed in overhead and any view of the surrounding country below them was obliterated. Joe flopped to the ground with disappointment and exhaustion. He was filled with self-pity until he saw that Suryei had continued to move into the trees. She was no better off, but she wasn't complaining. She just kept going. He caught up to her. Suryei looked at him and smiled – albeit wanly. They walked in silence along the ridge for a time. The low ground rose to meet them and they found themselves back in the thick of the jungle. Maddeningly, the climb had been for nothing. They hadn't managed to catch even the barest glimpse of the surrounding terrain.

Joe found a tree he thought he might be able to shin up. Around ten minutes later he was back beside Suryei, panting and weak with exhaustion from the climb and lack of food. 'We're okay. Our track is about right.' He shouldered his rucksack and they walked slowly.

'Do you do a lot of computer hacking?' asked Suryei after they had regained their rhythm. They did their best to pick the path of least resistance through the jungle but, now that they were back on low ground, the jungle pressed in on them from every side.

'A bit. It's a sideline.'

'It's stealing, though, isn't it?'

Joe looked at Suryei's back. She didn't turn her head when she spoke. He wondered how much was conversation, and how much was accusation. Probably both. Talk was dangerous. He had no idea how far noise carried but, without conversation, he felt alone. Perhaps Suryei felt the same. Her question, if it was an accusation, was almost impossible to defend because he knew she was right.

At seventeen, he had gone to work for a software giant in the States, because that was the Mecca if you were seriously gifted. Joe was regarded as one of its brightest stars, but he was easily distracted. Within a few months he'd decided that the money the giant corporation earned was obscene. He created a virus he called Ethiopia which, when activated, consumed any word on the hard disk that was even remotely reminiscent of food, and left a small thumbnail image of a young black child with a distended belly in the space. Joe incorporated the virus into the operating system he was helping to write. The trigger for Ethiopia was keying the word 'lunch' into the system's appointments book. Over 50 000 copies of the new operating system had been shipped before the virus revealed itself.

Joe was quietly but forcefully shown the back door, while the corporation went into damage control. That's when Joe also discovered that he had a talent for hacking, particularly as the giant's employees had designed so many systems in use. He knew the way these people thought, and that was the key, getting inside the mind of the programmers. So Joe went to work as a freelancer, spying for companies wanting information from competitors.

The pay was good. And the conditions were great, because he could work from anywhere. Joe wasn't an information anarchist, an idealist. It just started out as a way to make a buck, nothing more. But then his conscience had kicked in. He was taking something that didn't belong to him, and that was wrong. So he stopped hacking and started authoring games, and providing critiques on others for various magazines. Most of the people who created computer games were maverick types like him, and he enjoyed their company. It was a more benevolent way to make a living, and one that didn't keep him awake nights.

'Yes, it's theft. That's why I don't do it any more.' Joe pushed a fern frond out of their way, careful to use his axe and not his hand or arm.

'So why'd you hack into Suluang's computer?'

'That was different. I had the chance to strike back at those thugs . . . I should have thought about it a bit harder before I dived in.'

'Hey, I'm not having a go at you. There aren't many individuals who get the chance to strike back at a whole system. You're lucky, you had a weapon. In Dili, I thought I had that too – a weapon – being a journalist, keen to write the truth. And then reality hit.'

'What do you mean?'

'I landed with the first troops to secure Dili airport. There was a ute burned out behind a hangar. In the back were half a dozen blackened human skeletons. On the side of the ute, someone had painted, "Welcome to East Timor". I wasn't prepared for that.' Suryei bit her lip and tasted blood as the brutal memory crashed into her mind.

'The authorities didn't regard the scene as a mass grave. That seemed ridiculous to me. I mean, how many murdered

278

people have to be dumped in a confined space before it's considered a mass grave?'

'Sounds like a sick riddle,' said Joe. He looked at Suryei and saw that the memory was still fresh and that it upset her.

'Yeah . . . anyway, I didn't have to wait long to find out the answer. There was a grave of over thirty bodies outside one village I visited. The people were so scared they didn't tell anyone about it till months after we arrived. These stories, and many others like them, were embargoed,' Suryei said bitterly.

'We heard rumours of mass graves wherever we went. Mostly, they were just that – stories. But every now and then . . . The village well you mentioned was nothing special. In East Timor, it was the militia's favourite dumping place for bodies because a rotting corpse or two also poisoned the water. And if it didn't physically, it sure as hell poisoned the well in people's minds. It's hard to drink from a place that's your family's grave.'

The picture of the old lady and her dead grandson flashed into Joe's head. 'Did you end up hating the Indonesians?' he asked quietly.

'No. It's not just the Indonesians, it's humans. Us. All of us. We're an incredibly brutal species.'

'It must have been rough coping with what you saw and heard.'

'I toughened up.'

Joe thought about Suryei's determination, her will to survive. Yes, she'd toughened up. 'Why East Timor? Why'd you go there?'

'My fiancé . . . I haven't told you.' Suryei swallowed hard and Joe regretted the question.

'You don't have to tell me.'

'It's okay. I can talk about it now.' Suryei took a deep breath, as if she was about to plunge into turbulent water. 'My fiancé and I were in the car together, coming back from a weekend away – a skiing holiday. It was night and I was dozing, listening to music on the radio. Then I heard Ric, my fiancé, say, "What's this guy doing?"

'I opened my eyes and a set of headlights was coming up over the crest, on the wrong side of the road. Everything slowed down. The approaching car was swerving about from his lane to ours. There was nowhere to go. A cliff face to the right, a big drop to a river on the left. In the last second, it was like our two cars were tied together, destined to crash.'

Suryei's breathing was heavy, her body reacting visibly to the traumatic memory. 'At the last instant, Ric turned *in to* the oncoming car. He saved my life. Instead of a head-on, the other car slammed into Ric's door. The last thing I remember about it was the glare from the headlights sparkling through our shattered windscreen. I thought I was going to die.'

Suryei cleared her throat, snapping out of a trance. She flashed Joe a nervous smile to let him know that she was alright. 'I spent a month in hospital – broke my pelvis. Then lots of physio. Missed Ric's funeral. I had amnesia for a while and didn't remember anyone or anything. My mother stayed with me in hospital. Had no idea who she was.'

'What about the other driver?'

'Eighteen months in prison. He was asleep at the wheel. The bastard was drunk. Anyway, you asked me about East Timor.'

Joe nodded.

'At the time, I was working for a big metro daily newspaper. After the accident, when I came back to work, the editor asked me if I wanted a change, do something different to take my mind off things. He was talking about sending me to East Timor. He thought I could give the paper's readers an interesting perspective – you know the sort of thing, an Asian-Australian torn between homeland and heartland . . . Sounds a bit trite now, but I jumped at it.

'First day there, I met a New Zealand soldier – just a rifleman. We became friends. I went out on patrol with his section a couple of times. The guys showed me a few survival techniques . . .'

Joe smiled. 'Oh, so it was a "he".' That explained a lot, he thought. Her apparent confidence in the jungle for one thing.

'He was killed in an ambush,' Suryei said abruptly. 'Dead. Gone. Again, no goodbyes. Nothing.'

'Jesus . . .'

'Happened up on the border. They were in an area known for militia activity when his patrol was fired on.' Suryei was mentally back in East Timor, staring into the middle distance. 'Witnesses said it was a strange, weird moment. According to the other guys in the patrol, there were Indonesian soldiers in the area, and other militia too, who were watching the firefight and laughing and cheering. When it all started, and even during the shooting, militia soldiers would step in from the wings, start firing, then withdraw. Like a game of tag-team wrestling or something.

'The rules of engagement meant the UN soldiers couldn't fire unless the enemy aimed their weapons at them, so they couldn't do anything about the enemy on the sidelines. It sounds like bullshit, but that's modern warfare for you.

'A couple of militiamen were killed. Nearly a thousand rounds were fired. Two UN soldiers, my friend and his buddy, were wounded. My friend died soon after of his wounds. The TNI soldiers watching from the West Timor border thought it was lots of fun. They were shouting and laughing through it all.

'It was only after he'd gone that I realised how important he was to me. Anyway . . .' she said, breathing deeply, realising that her eyes were moist.

'What was it like, going into Dili at the beginning?' asked Joe. He found the questions difficult to ask, because remembering seemed to affect Suryei profoundly. But somehow, he knew she wanted to talk, exorcise some of the demons.

'Tragic,' she said, shaking her head. 'The people were terrified and the place was a mess. Ransacked. Just about everything that wasn't nailed down was carted off by the TNI. You couldn't find a window that hadn't been smashed, or a door that hadn't been kicked off its hinges. The smell of human faeces was everywhere – it was disgusting and pathetic. The streets were filled with broken tiles and glass and rubbish. Any kind of infrastructure had been torched or torn down. But the worst part of it was the fear – that was as much a part of the smell of the place as anything.'

'What about the Indonesian army?'

'Everyone was tense. No one was really sure how the Indonesians would react after the vote. At first, they were pushy. There was a real swagger about them. I don't think they realised that the battle had been fought at the ballot box.

'Seventy-eight percent of East Timor voted for independence, rather than for autonomy within Indonesia, despite the intimidation and the killing going on before the ballot. Indonesia lost.'

'The soldiers take it bad?'

'Take it bad?' she said, snorting. 'When it looked likely that the poll wouldn't go Indonesia's way, the TNI and the militia just went bananas,' Suryei said, the memories still so vivid.

'The Indonesians had been stomping around East Timor since 1975, don't forget. This territory had become their plaything. The army had money and time invested there and it didn't want to lose that investment. And neither did a small but very determined band of East Timorese who were doing very nicely out of the TNI. Neither the militia nor the TNI were prepared to lose that without a fight. That's what was so amazing about the people of East Timor. They bore the brunt of the TNI/militia rage. They endured the looting, the murder and the rape and quietly, resolutely, voted Indonesia off their soil.'

'You think they're heroes, the people of East Timor?' said Joe, breaking into her trance.

'Yes I do,' she said, crouching to remove a small stone from her shoe.

'From what you saw, do you think the media did a good job there?'

'I guess, only Australians now find it impossible to draw any distinction between the people of Indonesia and its politics. Yet our democracy isn't exactly perfect either. We have our share of crooks and scandals.'

'Yeah, but we don't shoot our own people, and we don't blow passenger aircraft out of the sky.'

'On that first point, I'm pretty sure the Aboriginals wouldn't agree with you. And on the second . . . okay, I'll give you that.' They walked in silence while they negotiated a particularly boggy section. Clouds of mosquitoes rose from the thick mud and flew into their nostrils, mouths, ears and eyes. They ran through the last few sucking puddles, half blind, scooping the insects out of their mouths. Suryei lost her shoe in the mud. Joe volunteered to go back and get it for her. Suryei refused. She tied some fabric saved from Joe's shirt around her nose and mouth, went back and freed it from the bog herself.

'Look, I don't think the media are the bad guys but they have a serious flaw,' said Suryei, picking up where she'd left off.

'And that is?'

'The news media can only handle information in a certain way.'

'What do you mean?'

'It's not good with grey.'

'Eh?' Joe was not sure he understood the point. He pulled aside a branch that threatened to whip back into Suryei's face.

'Well, you know the expression, "it's all there in black and white"?'

Joe nodded.

'Well, it's never there in grey. Newspapers, the media generally, they take a side of a story, one that can be dealt with unequivocally, and report on it more or less accurately.

'And the news sources may – not always, but sometimes – give the other side of a story, providing the issues are clear. But it's not very adept at dealing with issues that have black and white mixed in equal parts. Like I said, it's not very good with grey. The bad guys are always bad and the good guys are always good. But life is rarely so ordered and people, issues – whatever – are never, in truth, so perfectly one dimensional and transparent.'

'You've obviously thought about this a bit.'

'Haven't you? Or do you just accept everything you're spoon-fed without question?'

'I wouldn't say that, but I don't think my levels of cynicism are up to yours. Probably because I haven't seen as much,' Joe added. Suryei had certainly been exposed to more *life* than he had.

'But it's always been like this. Take wars. The media dehumanises the opposition. That makes things worse because people are then more prepared to do things, cruel things, when they don't think the other side is as "human" and "civilised" as they are. That's what happened in Vietnam, and in the Second World War with Japan, and probably every war in human history . . .' Suryei gathered her thoughts. She stopped and surveyed the jungle hemming them in.

'Anyway, it's easy to see how the media works when there are extreme examples, such as when there are confrontations between nations, but the principle, the way the media simplifies things, is the same no matter what the issue.'

'Okay, but you can't blame just the media,' Joe interjected. 'It's been fashioned by the people who buy newspapers and listen to the news. News is presented the way it is because that's what sells. People want the facts delivered that way – simply.'

'That, Joe, is an incredibly simplistic view,' said Suryei, stopping. Her hands were on her hips, like she was ready to fight. 'The public believes getting the facts is the same as getting the truth, and one is not the same as the other. Those embargoed stories back in East Timor – the truth was managed, massaged, put through the blender.'

Joe quietly entered a small clearing. A family of macaques occupying a large tree, its roots dangling into the space below it like a matted screen, chattered and screeched and whirled quickly up and down the branches. Joe noticed the discarded fruit on the ground and nudged one over with his toe. It looked familiar – green on the outside with rich crimson flesh full of seeds inside. He picked one off the tree's trunk, peeled it open and took a bite. It tasted sweet. He ate it quickly and had another. He tossed a couple to Suryei. She joined him beside the tree, picking the fruit that sprouted from its bark.

'This is what the babirusa eats,' said Suryei, diverted, the journo again. 'It's a fig, unique to Sulawesi. Evolved just for the babirusa's dinner. The fruits are low, see, and easily reached.'

'Can you imagine what must be going on back home in Australia?' said Joe, almost incoherently, talking with his mouth full. 'Do you think the authorities – the government – know what's going on?'

'They must. Think about it. QF-I has gone missing,' Suryei said, hunting for a branch that hadn't been stripped. 'They must know it's crashed somewhere in Indonesia. The relatives of the passengers – your parents and friends – the whole bloody country's probably in mourning. And shock. And if it appears the Indonesians are up to no good . . .'

Joe whistled softly. 'Jesus, the shit-fight that must be going on . . . My guess is that if the Indonesians aren't letting our blokes in to help with the search – and why would they, given what we know? – then Australia will probably put it on the Yanks to get a spy satellite on the case. It's the obvious thing to do. But if they know the plane was *shot down* by Indonesia then, shit . . . maybe we're already at war with them!' Joe thought about that and shuddered.

'Maybe that explains the soldiers shooting at us,' said Suryei.

'Or maybe they're trying to stop us because we're just loose ends.'

Selatan Irian Jaya. Joe thought about what they knew for sure, and what was pure speculation. 'It's unlikely they'll know the whole story back home. I just hope they know enough to send our own people here with guns to come get us.'

Sydney, 0705 Zulu, Friday, 1 May

ABC Radio 702: 'And something just to hand . . . The crash site of Qantas Flight 1 has been located. A spy satellite photo, showing the 747 crashed on a ridge line in central Sulawesi, Indonesia, has just been released in a joint press conference given by the Minister for Defence, Hugh Greenway, the Australian Defence Forces Commander, Air Vice Marshal Ted Niven, the Australian Secret Intelligence Service Director-General, Graeme Griffin, and the Indonesian Ambassador Parno Batuta.

'It is believed the photo was released a short time earlier to a stunned Indonesian parliament. Questions were raised in the Indonesian parliament about whether the Indonesian army had prior knowledge of the existence of the photo.

'The Indonesian air force officer heading up the search, Colonel Ari Ajirake, has denied that the military had been keeping the photo secret. He said that, now the exact coordinates of the downed plane were known, a rescue team could immediately be dispatched to the site. He also said it wasn't surprising that the site hadn't been located sooner, given the remote nature of the plane's location.

'Just to repeat the news: the crash site of the Qantas 747 that went missing in the early hours of last Wednesday morning Eastern Australian time in Indonesian airspace, has been located . . .'

Central Sulawesi, 0705 Zulu, Friday, 1 May

That uneasy feeling was again building within Sergeant Marturak. He had deployed his men and the waiting game had begun. At the core of his concern was a complete lack of intelligence. He had absolutely no idea what the two survivors were up to. For all he knew, they were indeed trying to scale the impossible heights of the almost vertical escarpment rising like a painted blue wall from the jungle beyond. He knew he was up against just two people – a man and a woman – but who were they? He doubted that two ordinary civilians would have been capable of enduring three days in the jungle, let alone be able to outmanoeuvre and escape him and his men, and on more than just one occasion.

He dredged those moments of contact up from his memory and replayed them. He would have liked to believe that surviving the encounters with his men was pure chance, and if that's all it was then the survivors were extraordinarily lucky indeed. It was not reasonable to assume that people with no training could keep themselves alive for three days and two nights in an environment that was as dangerous and inhospitable as Sulawesi. Especially when one or both were wounded, had no food, no shelter, and were probably in shock.

Perhaps they weren't alive. Perhaps they were already dead, or dying somewhere of exposure, a fall, dehydration or poisoning, or any one of countless ways the jungle could take a human life. If they hadn't walked into his ambush by the appointed time at around four hours from now, he would assume them dead and notify Jakarta of the fact, then sweep the jungle for their bodies.

The unexpected boom of an explosion interrupted this thought, followed by another thunderous blow. His men were up and racing towards the area mined by the claymores. The jungle filled with automatic fire. Marturak began constructing the radio message in his head, one that would please the general, as he ran towards the source of the noise, all self-doubt erased by the deafening thunder of the exploding PE.

The staccato automatic fire petered out just as the sergeant converged on the narrow passage formed by the trunks of two massive hardwoods. On the floor of the jungle between the two giants, carpeted by leaves and mosses and spongy fungi, was a large four-legged black body with a thick crimson pool where the head should have been. One of Marturak's men walked into the clearing with the missing part of the animal – its head – one side of it a stew of red flesh, white bone and congealing blood. The soldier smiled as he held the head high. His expression of delight changed when Marturak caught his eye. The soldier dropped the trophy on top of the carcass and melted back amongst his comrades.

Marturak spat an order and three men went off to check the remaining claymores. Marturak felt like screaming. This was without doubt the most frustrating op he'd ever undertaken. The animal, some sort of wild cow or deer the size of a large dog, had obviously been running down the trail and tripped the first and second wires, discharging the mines. The first claymore had probably been set too high for the ball bearings to do their job. The second mine had effectively decapitated the animal as it ran in terror from the first explosion and the thrash of ball bearings that flailed the surrounding vegetation.

Marturak wondered how far the noise of the explosions and the ensuing automatic fire had carried. He hoped like hell that he hadn't given their position away but, as with every other aspect of this absurd chase that had them stumbling about virtually blind, he couldn't be sure. 'Allah!' he cried in desperation at the top of his voice. A flock of birds which had only just resettled in the treetops overhead were again frightened into the sky.

The sergeant knew he was going to have to replan, but what in God's name to do next? He paced around the small clearing considering the limited options, his men stepping out of his way. Perhaps the ploy of passively setting an ambush was flawed from the beginning. One thing he was reasonably sure of was that he had the two passengers bottled up. He had the noose in his hand; he just had to tighten it.

Marturak had sixteen men left from the original deployment, including the soldier who had lost three fingers from his left hand to the weapon wielded by one of the survivors. The man was in a lot of pain but a low dose of morphine helped, and he could still hold and discharge his weapon. Marturak decided to divide his force into pairs, providing eight separate opportunities to make contact with, and kill, the objectives. If his men struck serious opposition – which he doubted, but then nothing would surprise him on this job – the two-man team was a reasonably effective weapon – one man could advance under the covering fire laid down by the other. He would have preferred three-man teams but concern about spreading his force too thinly across the jungle swung his mind against it. Marturak gave each pair a compass heading to follow and established an RV, the place where his two men had been left behind after the cobra strike.

Silently, Marturak cursed their lack of equipment, in particular the lack of inter-section comms. He'd been told that this op had to be strictly emissions free, except for the scheduled broadcasts. Marturak completely understood the need for security. The Qantas plane, the elimination of civilians – it was the kind of mission that would either set him up for life if he succeeded, or get him killed if he failed. A sudden pang of objectivity made him realise that having him killed would be the safe option for his superiors, no matter what the outcome of this mission. The op was black and would have to remain so forever. It would be prudent to consider some kind of insurance policy, he decided. Marturak was vicious, but he was no fool. *The disk.* He tapped it in his webbing once to make sure it was still there, and found himself reassured by its presence. It was something only he knew the existence of and it might prove to have considerable value.

Suryei and Joe were again searching for a tree they could climb so that they could get another fix on their bearings. The hunt proved fruitless. Trees that were big enough to get them above the canopy had no branches low down, just broad, smooth trunks, gigantic living columns that appeared to support the green roof overhead, and they provided no purchase whatsoever.

They had just decided to keep moving in the direction they thought was the correct one when the distant pulse of the twin explosions, followed by a large number of popping noises, bounced off the canopy overhead. Both Joe and Suryei guessed correctly what those sounds were. They glanced at each other anxiously, and for a number of reasons. The blasts confirmed that people with guns and other explosive devices were still in the jungle and obviously still searching for them. Of more concern was that neither Joe nor Suryei had the slightest idea from which direction the sounds originated. The jungle fractured and splintered sound so that it appeared omni-directional, virtually surrounding them. For all they knew, they could be walking straight towards the source, and certain death.

'Shit,' said Suryei, looking left and right and then turning slowly in a complete circle attempting to pinpoint the direction of the explosions.

'I reckon it came from down there,' said Joe, indicating off to their right.

'Are you sure? Sounded to me like it came from just up ahead. Or maybe from over there.' Suryei gestured up the ridge to their left. 'How far away?'

Joe shrugged, spinning around, unsure, rattled. It had been more than twelve hours since their last contact with the soldiers and the rubbery dimension time had taken on added to his disorientation. It felt like they had been wandering around in the jungle forever, certainly more than three days, perhaps because surviving the jungle was a moment-by-moment proposition that took every ounce of concentration, obliterating any other reality. The crash of exploding ordnance was a blunt reminder that their pursuers were determined. And close.

To make matters worse, if that were possible, Joe and Suryei were running on empty. They had slept very little and eaten next to nothing, which had brought them to the brink of physical and mental exhaustion. If giving up had been an option, they would gladly have taken it. But it wasn't.

'Come on, this . . . way,' said Suryei, panting, sucking in the hot, wet air.

Whether or not he agreed with the direction, Suryei wasn't sure. Joe was also too tired to argue. Any decision could be wrong. Any decision could be right. Frowning, Suryei picked her way soundlessly past Joe towards a dense thicket of matted tree ferns. She ducked low with a grunt and disappeared inside.

Java, 0745 Zulu, Friday, 1 May

Achmad Reza pulled in to the centre of a small village. There was an open concrete building with seats inside where an old lady sat mending clothes. Several small children played noisily with a plastic missile, making loud rocket-type sounds. Scrawny chickens scratched for food on the ground around them.

The building, painted various shades of dirty white, green and blue, as if the people who had applied the paint had been unable to make up their minds on the colour, matched an adjoining shop. Bottles of water, Coca-Cola and Heineken beer lined the shelves outside. A blue light set in an electrified grille hung on the wall beside the darkened doorway and fried insects that became too adventurous. Several other small buildings with dark, glassless windows sat beyond. A small group of men squatted in a wired enclosure and fussed over a large roos- ter, cooing and patting it. The animal seemed comfortable with all the attention, holding its proud head high, red neck stretched.

As he drove slowly past, Reza saw a young woman lean- ing on the outside corner of the building occupied by the old woman and the children. He gathered from a slight movement of her head that he was to follow her. He glanced in the rear-view mirror. He saw a couple of bikes carrying laughing children, but nothing sinister.

Reza parked his old Mazda beside two other equally decrepit vans in a cleared area by the roadside, and cau- tiously walked towards the building the woman had disappeared into. He paused at the doorway, wiping the sweat from his forehead with an old, folded handkerchief he always kept in his pocket for the purpose, and stepped nervously into the dark interior.

His eyes adjusted slowly to the dimness. The small, one- room house was home to a family. Inside, there were two sets of bunks, a table, matting and cushions on the beaten earth floor. The aroma of potent spices filled the air. The home was neat but there was little room to spare for anything other than the people who occupied it.

A very old woman sat on some cushions in one corner. She sang quietly and tunelessly to herself and seemed oblivious to his presence. The young woman kneeled beside her. She wore a thin, bright yellow cotton sundress that complemented the copper colour of her skin. Her hair was thick and black with highlights that caught the sun pouring through the glassless window. A hint of lavender underpinned the smell of chilli and dried fish.

'Don't mind the old bag. She has Alzheimer's,' said the young woman in a disrespectful way that took him by surprise and threw him even more off balance.

'Were you followed?'

'I don't think so.'

She looked Indonesian yet spoke English with an Australian accent. Her black almond-shaped eyes never left his. Reza wondered if this woman was as dangerous as she was beautiful.

She answered his questions before he had time to get them out. 'My name is Elizabeth. I work for the Australian government. I sent you the photo.'

At that moment, Reza knew he'd been set up, used as a pawn in a game he had no knowledge of. He'd thought the photo had originated from within the TNI, but now he knew it had not. The questions lined up in his head, each fighting so hard to be asked first that none succeeded. 'What . . . what is this all about?' he stammered lamely.

'You tell me. We know your air force shot down a Qantas jumbo. We know the air traffic controller, the man who first reported the disappearance of the Qantas plane,

Abe Niko, died in a wonderfully timed accident yesterday,' she continued. 'We also know that there are Indonesian soldiers in the jungles of Sulawesi trying to kill any Australians who might have survived the crash of the Qantas plane.'

Achmad Reza's mouth had opened involuntarily in shock. A roaring sound filled his ears and he found it difficult to breathe. He sucked at the air, taking small, feeble breaths like someone on their deathbed, his chest constricted.

The woman casually lit a Marlboro, dragged deeply on the cigarette and blew the smoke into the sunlight. It swirled into a pattern of blue fingers. She seemed to be enjoying herself. 'We know that two of the conspirators are the Generals Suluang and Kukuh Masri.'

Suluang and Masri. That was odd, thought Reza, struggling to find some solid ground in a world that had suddenly tilted on its edge. Weren't theirs the units brawling in the streets of Jakarta?

'What we don't know is whether all this is something secretly sponsored by the Indonesian government. That's where you come in,' she continued, flicking the ash from her cigarette out the window.

Reza felt dizzy. 'Are you Indonesian?' he asked.

'Indonesian parents. They migrated to Australia before I was born. That makes me a hundred percent Aussie.'

'You're a spy?'

'If you like,' she said, examining the end of her cigarette.

Reza had no idea why he was being chosen to be some kind of go-between. *Is that what I am?* Certainly there were many others more qualified, better connected. He hesitated before asking the next question. 'What . . . what do you want?'

'We want you to . . . we call it throw a spanner in the works.'

Reza was familiar with the expression, and he recalled the chaos he'd caused in the parliament. 'I think I've already done that.'

The woman drew elegantly on her cigarette and blew the smoke into the air between them before continuing. 'My government can't contact yours through the usual channels because, of course, if your government has anything to do with this, then all we'll get is denials. And if we go charging in with unsubstantiated accusations . . .' She let the thought hang.

The Australians were right. 'Do you know why the plane was shot down?' he asked.

'No. But that is *the* question, isn't it?'

'You said there were soldiers hunting for survivors. Do you know if there are any survivors?'

'Yes, we believe there are two,' she said, stubbing the cigarette out on the floor before flicking the butt out the window. 'We are working on getting them out.'

That could only mean Australian soldiers on Indonesian sovereign territory. Uninvited. Reza felt decidedly uncomfortable.

'Think of it as a rescue,' she said, smiling, reading his concern and enjoying his obvious discomfort.

'Who's going to rescue Indonesia?' Reza said, sweating profusely.

'You are.' Her eyes held his.

Somewhere east of central Sulawesi, 0745 Zulu, Friday, 1 May

The V22 pulled a two-g turn, bringing Wilkes out of a dream that left him restless and disturbed. He opened his eyes. The men were edgy, fidgeting with gear and straps and ropes, like a football team getting set to play a final. The V22 bucked through low-level turbulence. If Wilkes had peered through the small fuselage porthole, he would have seen the choppy green surface of the Banda Sea barely five metres below.

Wilkes went through a mental checklist, going over his equipment and the ROE: *kill the bad guys, rescue the good guys*. The fact that he would soon be snuffing out human lives didn't concern him. He was a soldier and the enemy were soldiers. That's what soldiers did – they killed each other. That he was up against Kopassus – the Indonesian equivalent of the SAS – gave the exercise a vaguely competitive edge. Wilkes had no doubt who would come out on top. He wasn't over-confident – the Indons were well trained, ironically by the Australian military. But his men probably had the edge in continued training and the latest equipment. And given the circumstances of this mission, his men also had the certainty that right was on their side. But right or wrong, they would function as he knew they would – with calm, professional efficiency. If things did get nasty, Wilkes reminded himself, he couldn't be in better company. *Bring it on*.

The sergeant surveyed his men. There wasn't any talking going on – the intercom system didn't allow them privacy. They sat in their own world, lost in their own thoughts, most likely doing what Wilkes had been doing, going through their gear and trying to visualise the mission. There was expectancy. They actually liked doing this shit.

Wilkes felt a presence beside his shoulder. He glanced up. McBride knelt beside his seat with an A3-size photo in his hand. The captain wasn't smiling.

'What is it?' said Wilkes, wary.

'A few priorities have been rearranged upstairs and we've got a proper military sat on this for you now,' said the marine. That made Wilkes wonder. How did this man know the intel they'd been using up till now *hadn't* been military?

'This baby's got keyhole resolution in the visible light and infrared spectrum. It also has x-ray capability. It can map radio waves, even do a spectroscopy analysis. This is one serious motherfucker piece of equipment.

'What we got here is an infrared image of your search area. The satellite has been programmed to scan for temperatures up to and including one degree either side of 98.4, emanating from sources within a certain mass range; the idea being that you'll get a photo that will register human presence without it being cluttered by hotspots or ghost images that turn out to be monkeys, pigs, and so on. Anyway,' said the captain, handing him the photo, 'take a look.'

Something told Wilkes he wasn't going to like what he was about to see. The worry creasing the captain's forehead told him as much. Within a couple of seconds of examining the photo, Wilkes was wearing a similar expression.

The photo was extraordinarily clear. The satellite it came from was indeed an astonishing piece of equipment.

He took the black and white A-4 photocopy of the pic he'd been shown at the briefing back in Dili out of his top pocket, and compared it. The information presented by the new, colour A3 had totally and utterly changed. If the identical lat and long coordinates hadn't been in the left of the new photo, he would have sworn that it was a view of a completely different area.

The smudged dots previously identified as the Kopassus soldiers waiting in ambush for one of the two sets of contacts had disappeared. The jungle was now alive with pairs of distinct, hard-edged markers. Now it was impossible to tell which of the contacts were his survivors. Wilkes studied the two utterly different photographs and couldn't make sense of the information.

He shook his head. 'Jesus . . . Can we get another pass at this before we go in?' he asked hopefully.

'No, I've checked on that already.'

Wilkes had half an idea. 'Can you blow this one up to A3?'

'That I can do,' nodded the marine, taking the creased A4 sheet of paper up towards the aircraft's comms suite.

Wilkes glanced up from the A3 sheet on his lap. The men were all looking his way. 'What's happening, boss?' said the expression on Ellis's face beside him.

Wilkes gestured that he wasn't sure.

The captain returned with the old A4-size image blown up to A3 and handed it to Wilkes. He laid the new satellite intel over it. He lifted the top sheet up and down a few times and the hint of a smile curled his lips. 'You got a pen or pencil?' asked Wilkes. He took the pencil and drew a series of arrows and circles on the photos.

'Okay,' said Wilkes, 'I think I've made a bit of sense out

of this.' McBride sat in the vacant seat beside Wilkes. 'This is the first photograph. We started with this bunch of contacts here, assuming that it was an ambush line. These two contacts over here were apparently on the move, and these two over here weren't.' He indicated the position on the old photo.

'Let's take a look what's happened.' Wilkes lifted the top photo up and down and the photos came alive. Now the captain could suddenly see which of the contacts had moved, and had a few hints about the direction they had moved in, since the first photo was taken.

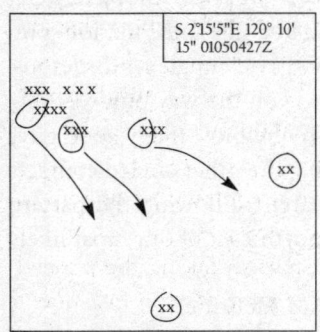 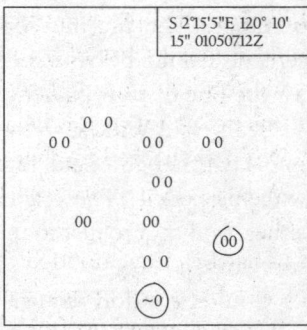

The original B&W   *The revised colour intel*

'The ambush has broken up. The Indons are now fanning out across the jungle in twos.' Arrows Wilkes had drawn on the photos showed the direction they were headed in. 'These two sets of contacts here, and here, are the mystery players,' he said, circling each pair with the pencil and doodling several question marks. 'One set is friendly, the other is not. Trouble is, I'm still not sure which is which. All I can do is take a punt. Keep your eye on these two, the pair down the bottom,' he said as he did his little animation trick again, lifting the top sheet up and down.

'Yeah,' observed McBride, 'they're stationary.'

'The only contacts that are,' agreed Wilkes. 'Any idea why one of the two dots that make up this stationary duo down the bottom would be fainter than the rest?'

The captain shook his head. 'Can't say with any certainty. It's a temperature thing. Could be someone who's sick enough to put his or her body temperature almost out of the scanning range, accompanied by someone who's okay. Could also be someone who has recently died where the core body temperature hasn't dropped completely out of range.' The marine considered the information presented. 'Could be your people. The jungle's murderous. Maybe one of your passengers is on the way out.'

'Yeah,' said Wilkes, 'so they're the most likely good guys – this pair here,' he said, tapping the other circled contacts with his pencil. 'These fellas aren't following the pattern either. And they're just to the north-east of our most likely survivors.'

'Could be Indon scouts?' said McBride.

Sergeant Wilkes was not too keen to make assertions about who was friend or foe on such scant information, but he had to make a decision. 'How long till you set us down?'

The captain checked his watch. 'Fifteen to twenty at the most. There's quite a bit of wind out there. Once we get up into the hills and it starts swirling about . . . ? Hard to know whether there'll be a headwind or a tailwind.'

'Tell the avos to set us down here,' said Wilkes, indicating a position on the photo midway between the two sets of mystery contacts. 'Also, a few copies of these would be good. I can hand them out to the lads.'

'Yes to the first,' said McBride. 'And I can do better than copies on the second.'

The American again disappeared forward to the comms desk. A minute later, a video screen flickered into life and the first of the two satellite photos appeared.

'Bastards have left the in-flight entertainment a bit late, haven't they?' quipped Morgan over the intercom.

The marine handed the sergeant a remote. 'Press this button to change views. There's a laser you can use as a pointer, here,' he said, indicating another button. Wilkes pressed it. A red dot appeared on the ceiling.

'Incoming!' joked someone, the dot reminding all of them of laser sniper scopes.

Wilkes shifted between the images a couple of times to get the hang of the technology, and began briefing his men on the revised intel.

The V22 climbed steeply as it crossed a deserted white sand beach and rose above the palm covered hill rushing to meet them. The Osprey banked forty-five degrees right and lifted towards a deep ravine cut between two towering cliffs. The whine of the turbofans crashed off the volcanic faces and ricocheted throughout the valley.

Inside the V22 Osprey, the air-conditioning was turned off. Time to acclimatise.

Central Sulawesi, 0758 Zulu, Friday, 1 May

Suryei ran her hand over Joe's back. Blood seeped from the innumerable weeping sores left by an army of leeches. Her dirt-blackened thumb flicked the lighter's small friction

wheel until the gas caught. It was now on the highest setting but the flame flickered low. She managed to sizzle one
last grey-black tube the size of a small cucumber, sending
it spinning to the ground before the Bic went out for good.
She put it in her pocket. If she managed to escape from
this with her life, she'd recycle the lighter into a good
luck charm.

'I'll pick the rest off with my fingers.'

'I can take it,' said Joe, forcing a smile.

They had climbed a low ridge in an attempt to confirm
their bearings but, again, it proved a useless exercise. Joe
hoped they were going in the right direction but feared
that they were just turning blind circles, going nowhere.
They could wait an hour or so and see which way the sun
dipped, but that was a luxury. Staying in the one place
might come with a mortal head wound. Several times they
had heard, or imagined they'd heard, footsteps behind or
beside them in the dense bush. They had to keep moving
in the direction they thought was the right one. Without
proper bearings it was a flawed plan, but its simple purpose was giving them a goal to strive for, even if that was
just to put one foot in front of the other.

Suryei was starting to doubt her ability to go on. The
muscles in her legs ached so badly from the constant effort
of walking that she dared not stop in case they cooled
down and cramped solid. But they had to rest, even if only
for a few minutes every now and then, to remove the
swarming, crawling parasites that hitched a ride and
feasted until they dropped off, bloated.

Joe found a large tick behind Suryei's ear that hurt her
like hell when he removed it. It was so drunk with her
blood that the little bugger could hardly waggle its legs

when Joe held it upside down and examined it in the palm of his hand. Suryei hoped that there weren't more of them hiding in her hair and armpits. They injected a nasty poison to keep the blood from clotting. It could bring on nauseous attacks, vomiting, and the sweats: all the good stuff.

She examined Joe's scalp and found it clear. Leeches were Joe's bane. They seemed to like his blood. He had two on his skin for every one found on hers. Following him along a trail, Suryei had even watched them standing up on the ground and turning their blood-sucking mouths in his direction as he passed.

And, of course, there were mozzies everywhere. One landed on Joe's back and wasted no time burrowing its proboscis deep into his flesh. Malaria. There was plenty of it about in this part of the world. It started with symptoms that were a bit like flu, with fevers and chills. Things went downhill from there. They had warned her about it on East Timor.

She felt okay, all things considered, but it was impossible to know what was happening inside her body. People often came down with diseases weeks after they arrived home, which meant that both Joe and she could have something now and not know it: dengue fever, filariasis, viral encephalitis. She knew all the names. She shivered, wondering what the tick had left behind after having had its fill.

'How're you feeling, Joe?'

Given the situation, Joe thought it an odd question. 'I could do with a holiday,' he said.

'No, I mean, do you feel sick at all?'

'I'm alright,' he said. 'Why?'

'If we don't get out of here soon the wildlife will kill us even if the soldiers don't.'

Joe swatted ineffectually at the miasma of insects around them. A couple of mozzies landed on his arm. He squashed them against his skin, leaving a smear of blood. 'Yeah,' he said, 'know what you mean.'

Joe looked up at the violently swaying canopy. 'Must be blowing a gale up there.' It was breathless as usual at ground level. A cloud drifted across the sun and took the ferocious burn out of it. Joe unshouldered his rucksack and dug around for a bottle of water. They were all empty.

'I'll carry that for a bit if you like,' said Suryei, holding her hand out for the rucksack. Joe thought about protesting, but then handed it over. Joe swung his axe through the air a couple of times. It felt good to have unrestricted movement, and he was now used to the weight of this souvenir from the 747. It had become his link with reality, reminding him that there was a world out there that he'd been wrenched from only days before. His axe. He swung it again. It was actually a pretty useful weapon, as one of the soldiers he'd introduced to it could attest. He swung it again and felt a vague primal surge.

'Er, Conan?' Suryei was looking back at him impatiently from the edge of some thick, chest-high grass. 'Can we go now?'

Central Sulawesi, 0834 Zulu, Friday, 1 May

A red light illuminated. Minus one minute to the drop. It had been a good twenty minutes since the LM had helped the men locate their ropes and loop them into their wrap-racks. The MAG would fast-rope down together in one wave. It was necessary to get the soldiers out and off quickly so that the V22 could leave the area pronto. Hovering stationary over the drop zone would make it an easy target for forces equipped with portable, hand-held Stinger missiles, or even just well-aimed rifle fire.

The designated LZ approached, the coordinates of which had been nominated by Wilkes and punched into the Osprey's nav com. The pilot repositioned the switch that fixed the angle of the nacelles on the wingtips and they began to rotate to the vertical. The Osprey's flight computers countered the aircraft's natural tendency to alter its altitude as the thrust vectors changed, feathering the aircraft's control surfaces to maintain level flight. The resultant forces slowed the aircraft, bringing it to a hover twenty metres above the swirling canopy. Total flight time from the *Kitty Hawk*: just one hour and fifty-five minutes.

The Jump Jets cruised high overhead, sweeping the area for bandits, conserving fuel. They were capable of hovering with the V22, behaving like helicopter gunships, but only for the briefest period. In hover mode, the AV-8's wings provided no lift whatsoever, so an enormous amount of fuel was burned to keep the aircraft aloft. Besides, there was no point putting more aircraft than necessary in the hover position vulnerable to ground fire. The pilots hoped the EA-6B Prowler had done its job, blinding Indon radar. Three Super Hornets might well be orbiting fifteen minutes away but if a flight of F-16s jumped them now, they'd be thirteen minutes too late.

The wind made it difficult to maintain position. The

Osprey slid left and right, bobbing high and low as thirty-knot winds knocked it about. Wilkes gave his men the signal and they leapt forward into the air from the V22's ramp. From the ground, the soldiers might have looked like baby spiders jumping clear of their mother. Their heavy packs swung below them, attached to their abseiling harnesses with karabiners, so that the weight of their gear didn't hinder their control and manoeuvrability, or break their legs when they hit the ground.

The men dropped to the canopy and hung suspended above it. They lowered themselves slowly through the uppermost leaves and branches until they could see a clear path to the ground fifty metres below. When each man was satisfied that his progress wouldn't be impeded, their journey down continued.

Suddenly, a wind gust that would have measured more than forty-five knots lifted the Osprey several metres and shouldered it aside. The men, still attached to their ropes fastened to the buffeted aircraft, were pulled through branches like floss through teeth.

Kevin Gibson was unlucky. He was threading his way through the fork in a heavy branch when his rope pulled him up, then dropped him. The fork caught the lower lip on his helmet as he fell through the narrow opening. The additional weight of his pack hanging from his abseil harness ensured that his neck snapped cleanly, cutting his spinal cord. Gibson wouldn't have had time to notice anything amiss before St Peter was giving him his room number.

Wilkes could see that Gibbo was in strife. The man was swinging forward on his rope in that odd way, arms hanging limply. He then bashed into a tree trunk twice but did nothing to prevent the impact either time. After the second collision, the tension on his rope released and Gibbo fell the last fifteen metres, accelerating rapidly.

None of the men shouted out when they saw him fall. It would not have been a smart thing to do. If enemy troops were in the immediate vicinity, the noise of the aircraft would have had them searching the canopy overhead.

Wilkes's eight remaining men arrived safely, meeting at the base of a hardwood giant. They instantly fed the rope through their wrap-racks to release the tension, so that the V22 pitching around in the wind overhead wouldn't bounce them off the ground. They then released the kara-biner that secured the wrap-racks to their harnesses, and the umbilical cord of the webbing that attached them to their packs.

Wilkes checked his men, counting heads as he went while snippets of conversations he'd had with Gibbo flashed into his mind.

'Jesus Christ, Gibbo,' said Ellis, bending over the body of his friend and comrade. They were drinking buddies, both single and loving it.

The others knelt beside the fallen trooper and gave him a minute of silence out of respect. He was a good soldier, one of *them*.

Wilkes kept to the schedule for the moment, ignoring his fallen comrade. He clicked the 'send' button on his TACBE three times, the agreed signal that they were on the ground and released from their ropes. Almost immediately the ten ropes, dangling from the canopy like strands of black spaghetti, rose up through the trees. The ear-splitting noise of military jets and turbofans receded quickly. It would be smart to vacate the area as quickly as possible.

Gibbo's body would probably have to be left behind, but in the meantime they didn't want to telegraph to the enemy any more than was absolutely unavoidable that foreign troops were in the house. Burying it would stop scavengers being attracted, a gathering of which might be an invitation to any Kopassus in the area to investigate. Deny the enemy as much intel as possible, for as long as possible.

Wilkes turned, taking in their position. There was no point burying Gibson here. They had to put some jungle behind them and the LZ as a first priority. 'Morgan, you and Littlemore divvy up his pack. Mac, you and Beck carry him between you till we find a spot to cache the gear.'

Robson was already fashioning a crude stretcher for the body. 'Silly bloody prick,' he muttered. The bastard should have been more careful. They all knew the risks involved and embraced them readily, but that didn't make it any easier when one of them carked it. And Gibbo had been popular. He was the tallest man in the group, the rest being more compact types. He was unbeatable in the line-outs when the rugby season was on.

With Gibson's gear divided and the body aboard a stretcher fashioned from saplings and rope, the MAG moved off through the jungle with an easy, practised rhythm, despite the weight on their backs. Wilkes noted that there were plenty of small spiders' webs strung across the spaces between the grasses and fern trees, an indication that these tracks hadn't been travelled recently. Half a kilometre from their LZ, the men came across three enormous hardwoods that formed almost an equilateral triangle, with a copse of waist-high ferns in the centre. The ground was high, reasonably dry, and soft – the perfect place to cache their gear and bury the body.

Chris Ferris and Greg Curry freed their trenching tools and dug the depression to the required depth. The men went through their rucksacks and removed duplicated gear. They placed it in heavy-duty plastic garden bags to protect it against moisture and dirt and lowered the bags into the hole. Gibson's body went in last. The men needed to be able to travel fast and light. If they succeeded quickly in their mission, the gear would be left to the worms.

'Come back for you later, bud,' said Ellis, tossing a handful of soil on the mound.

Ferris topped off the cache with a claymore set to explode upwards should the hidden mound be disturbed by unfriendlies. The exercise took seven minutes. They were practised.

Now, loads considerably lightened, the men were ready for business. The order of march was different this time. Wilkes formed his men up in a line abreast to sweep through about sixty metres of jungle. Each man confirmed that his field radio was both transmitting and receiving by answering a quick roll call.

Wilkes swept the area. He picked out cicadas, birds, spiders and even stick insects. His brain processed the images and noted any colour or movement at odds with its surroundings. Untrained eyes found it almost impossible to differentiate military camouflage from the surrounding vegetation, especially if the wearer was stationary, but Wilkes's eyes were sharp and well trained. They registered the pattern and recognised it for what it was – man-made. Wilkes would have made a good sniper, except that there was a little too much waiting around in that profession for his liking.

This jungle was beautiful, virgin. Wilkes breathed in the heavy, moist air. It was easy to imagine that they were the only humans in this, a primordial forest. The jungle was a good place to be if you knew your craft. He saw a fishtail palm. It looked a bit like the sago palm, only it had a couple of beards covered in tasty-looking fruit that hung from its umbrella of fronds. The fruits were extremely poisonous, but a sago-like pulp could be extracted from the palm's trunk. You had to *know*, and it was as simple as that.

The palm towered thirty metres towards sunlight that burned through a hole in the canopy left by a giant tree which, succumbing to termites, had crashed to the jungle floor, flattening many smaller trees as it fell. He paused beside the monstrous fallen trunk and noted the position on his GPS. At a pinch they could use this place to RV with the V22 later. Indeed, it was not that far from the spot the V22 had set them down, nor from their cached gear.

He wondered what foods the survivors of the air crash had been living on. It would be easy to die of starvation in the jungle if you had no idea where to look for food. But most likely you would die of poisoning, the desire to eat overwhelming the fear of the unknown. Many things that appeared edible could kill painfully. He trod on some fungi that looked suspiciously like *Amanita phalloides*, the death cap mushroom. Wilkes knew his fungi – had to, it was part of essential survival training – but it was easy to get it wrong. Species that were edible often had deadly cousins and it was not always easy to tell the two apart.

The jungle was alive with sound. Cicadas screamed, birds sang, macaques hooted and squealed, and the ground rustled with movement. It took some getting used to – filtering the noise so that anything man-made could be distinguished. It was nearly an impossible task. The soldiers they were up against were professionals, like themselves. They knew, as did Wilkes's men, how to move through the environment without announcing their presence. Perhaps, Wilkes hoped, providing their LZ had been out of earshot, they would still hold the trump card of surprise, the opposition believing they had the jungle to themselves.

Wilkes's men moved soundlessly to the edge of the clearing made by the fallen giant and melted into the bush, their senses tuned and sharpened by hard experience. They were the hunters now.

There was something familiar about the area, but Suryei couldn't put her finger on it. She thought she must have been imagining it – one grove of ferns looked like every other grove of ferns. There was nothing on the ground to indicate that they'd been in this area before. Perhaps it was a combination of details – a tree next to a rock beside some tall palms on an area of ground that sloped away from a sharp rise. Whatever it was, there was something about this place that *felt* familiar. And dangerous.

Suryei slowed her pace and held up her hand for Joe to stop. There was something, something not right . . .

The trail narrowed somewhat beside a hardwood giant and sloped steeply. They picked their way down, careful not to make any noise or slip on the muddy carpet of rotting leaves. At the base of the rise the trail flattened out and then widened into a small clearing with two towering trees standing in it.

Suryei noticed an odd shape on the ground, like a giant

cocoon. The cocoon moved and groaned. And then she realised why the area had been so familiar. There was the thorny bush in the centre of the clearing where they had rested on the first night, a lifetime ago. The cocoon was a man wrapped in a blanket. Joe and Suryei remembered the events of that morning as if from an old movie. This was the man who had urinated on them and then been bitten by the cobra. He didn't sound well.

'Let's go,' said Joe, feeling more vulnerable than usual in this familiar place.

'Hang on,' she said, her curiosity getting the better of her judgement.

Suryei approached carefully and bent over him. He groaned again. He was lying on ground that had been cleared of leaf litter. The man was conscious enough to open his eyes but evidently had trouble focusing them. Eventually his bloodshot eyes met hers but there was not a shred of recognition in them. He was no longer a soldier. The snake's venom had reduced him to a basic level of consciousness. His lips were black and cracked; a track of dried spittle ran away from the lower corner of his mouth. The man's tongue, dry like the head of a lizard, moved over them continuously.

Suryei signalled to Joe. He was reluctant to step into the open, away from the protective cloak of the jungle. He made his way nervously over towards them.

'Water. He'll die otherwise,' said Suryei going for one of the bottles in Joe's rucksack. Fortunately, they had only just refilled them and the water was still cool.

'Cobra venom dehydrates,' Suryei said quietly. She dripped some water on the man's tongue as it flicked out, cracked and swollen. He responded, groaning a dry, hoarse sound. She poured a little more water into the man's mouth. His Adam's apple moved up and down then spasmed as he coughed weakly. The coughing stopped. More water. The lizard came out again to drink.

'He's in a bad way,' Suryei said. 'We should leave some water and go.'

'Go, yes. Good idea,' said Joe, anxious to be far away from this place.

A sound came from behind them. It was a metallic sound. The jungle didn't make noises like that. Joe and Suryei both glanced over their shoulders. A man stood in the clearing, smiling. Joe looked down the barrel of a gun for the third time in as many days. He was still failing to find the experience a pleasant one.

The soldier gestured at them with the weapon to move away from his comrade on the ground. They moved slowly. Joe realised that both their hands were raised in the air. It had been an automatic reaction. They shuffled step by step off to one side, presenting their armpits to their captor.

The soldier with the gun nervously took their place beside the cocoon. He glanced down quickly and noted the plastic water bottle on the ground at his feet. He picked it up and said something in Indonesian. 'He wants the rucksack,' said Suryei. The soldier shouted and aimed his weapon, the point between Suryei's eyes the target. Suryei turned her head away and dropped her hands in front of her face to protect it. He yelled again. Her hands went up quickly. Joe slowly took the rucksack off his shoulder and tossed it at the soldier's feet. The man kicked it. Several bottles fell out along with Joe's axe. The soldier picked it up and tossed it out of the clearing. Joe heard it thud against a tree and drop to the ground. Several birds flew up screeching, marking its landing place.

The soldier then turned the muzzle of his automatic towards Joe and carelessly fired a round from the hip. The bullet spun Joe around as if he'd been hit a glancing blow by a car. He was on the ground, his mouth full of leaves and moss, before he realised that he had been shot. He couldn't move, shock rendering his muscles useless. The soldier then turned the weapon towards Suryei, daring her to move. She didn't.

Joe found it difficult to breathe. A rib had fractured close to his spine, the slug breaking it off cleanly as if a hammer and cold chisel had clouted it. The bullet had been deflected slightly by the collision. It drilled under his right lung and tore an exit hole in his back the size of a punnet of strawberries. Blood oozed out both holes and pooled under his belly. It felt warm, as if he'd pissed himself. He would have made a joke about it if he could have found the breath, which he couldn't. There wasn't any pain yet, but he knew it was there. Oddly, he could see it, building up like water behind a logjam. Soon he knew he would hurt like he'd never hurt before. The world went from full colour to grey and white and Joe slipped away into a little black box in his head.

The soldier toed Joe's shoulder but the body on the ground was inert. He considered putting another bullet into it anyway to make sure, but something caught his eye. From the side he could see one of Suryei's breasts inside her shirt. He wondered what it would feel like cupped in his hand. The urge to do exactly that distracted him. Oddly, he looked around the clearing in case anyone could see him taking advantage of the situation but it was empty except for the two bodies lying on the ground and this woman in front of him. He smiled. He could do whatever he wanted with her and no one would stop him.

Keeping his weapon trained on her head, the soldier slipped his free hand inside her shirt. She was breathing heavily and he managed to delude himself that it was excitement induced by his touch that had made her nipples hard.

He unbuttoned his fly and his penis sprang from the opening expectantly. Her breasts were quite large, he noted, swallowing. The soldier took one of her raised hands and wrapped it around the organ jutting from his jungle greens. Suryei had no choice. He took his knife from its sheath, letting his rifle slip to the ground.

He placed the point of the dagger against her navel and told her to take down her pants. Suryei wanted to take the knife and cut off the disgusting thing in her hand but she was afraid. At least try, she demanded to herself. He was going to rape her then kill her anyway – of that she was certain. *Damn it, go out fighting!* Something in her eyes must have given the thought away because he thrust the knife into her stomach harder. The point pierced her skin and blood oozed down towards the top button of her pants. The soldier moved the knife down and sliced off the button, then he pushed her hard so that she sprawled on the ground on her back.

The soldier was so drunk with lust and power he had convinced himself that she wanted him. His tunnel vision failed to catch Joe struggling to his feet, or his fist as it smashed into the side of his jaw, breaking it. The soldier's eyes rolled back in his head as if there was suddenly something of great interest painted on the inside of his skull, and then his legs dropped out from under him.

Joe smiled. Laying the arsehole out felt good but the effort hurt like a bitch. The smile turned to a wince and he collapsed onto the ground unconscious beside the soldier.

They all heard the distinctive crack of the carbine. It came from a patch of low ground. The sound bounced around but they were reasonably sure of its source. Wilkes estimated the distance at less than 100 metres. He gave the direction of the shot his best guess and double-checked it over the communications with his men. They all agreed.

An effort was required to fight the tendency to rush forward. That's where training and experience was so important. They could run straight into an ambush. The men took their weapons off safety and rested their fingers outside the trigger guards. They moved ahead in twos and threes, leapfrogging each other, then covering the advance of the men behind them, weapons off safety, scanning the jungle ahead and to the sides for movement.

Suryei picked herself up off the ground and realised that she was hot with anger. She wanted to pick up the man's gun and shoot him, empty its bullets into him, stick the barrel in his side and let the hot lead penetrate him. Somehow she resisted the urge and instead swung the weapon into the trees by its barrel. She heard it clatter through branches to the ground somewhere unseen.

The eyes of the man laid out by the snakebite darted left and right. He had either become suddenly aware of reality, or the activity around him had provoked delirium – probably the latter, Suryei decided, when she looked at him more closely. There was still no comprehension in his eyes.

She dropped beside Joe and put her ear to his chest. His

heart beat strongly. A large amount of rich purple blood had seeped from the raw holes in his body. He opened his eyes, blinked a couple of times and said, 'Ouch.' Suryei was so relieved she didn't know what to do. So she got up and ran around in a circle before retrieving a bottle of water from the rucksack. She put it to Joe's lips. He shook his head, declining to drink.

'Rather have a Coke,' he said, wincing. 'Oh, fuck that hurts . . . just help me up.' Suryei put her arm behind Joe's back and helped him sit. His stomach muscles were gone. Breathing felt like someone was chopping into his abdomen with a tomahawk. The pain was really starting to come on with a rush now. Neither Suryei nor Joe had enough medical experience to know whether the wound was serious, so they both just assumed that it was. The assumption was reasonable. If he didn't get proper medical assistance soon, he would die, if not from blood loss then from secondary infection. Already, insects were swarming gleefully at the fresh source of food that had suddenly presented itself.

The soldier Joe had knocked out now started to move slowly. The actions were lethargic, but becoming less so, like an animal that had been frozen beginning to thaw. The man cried out when the bones in his jaw separated, sending a spike of pain to his brain that went off like a hand grenade. The bone had fractured, dislocating across the complex lattice of nerves on the side of his jaw. A couple of teeth had also been broken off at the root, exposing raw nerves. Any movement was agonising but all the soldier's training told him that he had to get up and surmount the situation he now found himself in if he was to have a chance of surviving it. He sat up. He wanted to scream but he knew the pain in his jaw would increase many fold if he did.

Suryei watched him drag himself up on an elbow, grunting in agony. She didn't know what to do. Should she hit him, kick him? Beat him with the empty rucksack? *Why did I throw away the gun?* And then Suryei saw the knife speared into the ground. She ran to it and picked it up as the man got to his feet. He approached her, staggering. *What do I do with this thing?* Suryei had never killed a man. She froze. The soldier slowly peeled the blade from her grip, each finger giving up one at a time.

And then the soldier did something unusual. He grinned. Not at her but past her, over her shoulder. Suryei followed his line of sight, knowing that she wouldn't like whatever it was that could be so good it cut through his pain and put a smile on his face. Two Indonesian soldiers stepped into the clearing and began scouting around the edges, weapons up and ready. They moved quickly through the area, searching for anything hidden. When they were satisfied that the people in the clearing were isolated, the soldiers returned to their starting point, a little more relaxed but weapons still on Joe and Suryei. Suryei looked at Joe. There was nothing more they could do. The soldiers' eyes were vacant, black, reptilian. There was death in them.

Suryei didn't feel panicked about dying. It was like being back in the car with the lights coming over the hill, moments before impact. There was nothing more she could do to prevent it happening. She was resigned to it. They had fought well, and lost. Suddenly, a small red dot appeared like a third eye in all three of the soldiers' foreheads and the men crumpled to the ground as if their bones had been sucked clean out of their bodies.

A small movement in her peripheral vision caught her attention. Another two soldiers stood up in a thick clump of bush that bordered the clearing. There was no one there, and then there was. And there was something different about these two men. They wore different uniforms and their faces were heavily painted in camouflage colours. She recognised the helmets worn by the troops in Dili – the Kevlar ones. One of the men wore a floppy hat made from camouflage material. And then she realised. They were Australians. Australian soldiers. Suryei didn't know whether to laugh or cry. One of the men put his finger to his lips for her to be quiet.

Suryei turned to look at Joe, to see whether he'd also witnessed what she'd just seen. He hadn't. He'd slumped forward and was leaning against a tree for support. She noticed that the man with the broken jaw now had the same red dot between his eyes, and he was lying sightless on the ground. He was dead, and that made Suryei feel good.

Within thirty seconds, the little clearing seemed surrounded by soldiers. She counted nine of them. A stocky, powerfully built man strolled up to her and smiled.

'Sergeant Thomas Wilkes. We're Australian. Your name, please.' He was friendly but efficient – businesslike. Perhaps it was the hard battleship grey colour of his eyes, but something in her was aware that this man was perhaps even more dangerous than any of the Indonesians. She hoped knowing her name wouldn't put him offside.

'Suryei Hujan. The man on the ground there is Joe Light,' she said. 'We were both passengers on the Qantas plane. Joe's been shot.' Her potted history seemed stupid when she heard it – terribly inadequate – but she didn't know what else to say. Two other soldiers were already kneeling beside Joe, assessing his wound. The sergeant pulled a wad of paper from a shirt pocket and checked her name against it.

'Suryei Hujan, seat 51F. Joseph Light, 5A. Any other survivors that you know of, Suryei?'

'No, we're it. There was an old couple but these bastards,' she indicated the Indonesian soldiers lying inert on the ground, 'shot them.'

Suryei realised that she was blubbering. The tears streamed down her cheeks and out through her nose. Standing there in the jungle, hungry, half naked, every inch of exposed skin cut and bleeding, the burns on her forearms now weeping suspiciously with a yellowish fluid, swaying with exhaustion, was the happiest moment of her life. She put her head on the soldier's shoulder and cried tears of release.

Wilkes put his arm around the woman and squeezed her reassuringly. Her small body heaved with sobs.

'How's he doing, Stu?' asked Wilkes, wanting an answer on the condition of the other plane survivor, sitting on ground stained red with his clotting blood.

'Okay, I think, boss. The bullet has worked its way through. The exit wound's messy. Broken a rib . . . lung is only nicked. Lucky fucker – could be a hell of a lot worse. Going to hurt like crazy, but. Given him a shot of morphine, some antibiotics. He's a fit bugger by the looks of him. Should be able to move with a bit of help after I strap him tight.'

Wilkes took a quick look at the exit wound and knew exactly how Joe would be feeling. He'd taken a bullet in almost exactly the same place when on patrol in the first days of INTERFET. He was up on the border of West Timor when the first round fired by the militia ambush had hit him in the chest and exited below his shoulder blade. A fusillade had then poured into their position. He could see men aiming their weapons and firing at him from thirty metres away, the dirt kicking up all around him. Miraculously, he wasn't hit again. It all happened in slow motion. Then, suddenly, one of his men was on the ground, blood gurgling from both sides of his neck.

'Got a time on that?' asked Wilkes, getting his mind back on the job at hand.

'Gimme five.'

'What about that bloke?' asked Wilkes, indicating the Indonesian soldier on the ground with the wild eyes.

'Dunno, boss.'

'He was bitten by a cobra,' said Suryei, wiping her eyes, getting herself back under control.

'He must have been given some antivenom or he'd have carked it by now,' said Stu. 'What'll I do with him?'

The man was obviously in a bad way. There was not much more they could do for him. 'Give him food and water and leave him for his own people.'

'You've got food?' grunted Joe.

Wilkes turned to Robson and Curry. 'Sure. Cough up, you blokes. And don't hog your chocolate,' he said.

'Already on it, boss,' said Curry.

'As in Cadbury's?' asked Joe. Curry found some chocolate in his pack and held it under Joe's nose. He breathed deeply. It smelled glorious. But then the morphine kicked in and he vomited. 'On second thoughts . . .' Joe said between heaves, changing his mind. Robson shrugged and put his rations back in his pack.

'James. Get on the blower and see if you can get us a lift out of here pronto,' said Wilkes to Littlemore, who was already in the process of laying out the Raven's aerial. It came wrapped tightly around a small but heavy lead sphere. He fired it up into the upper reaches of the canopy with a rubber sling provided especially for the purpose. The extended aerial gave the radio a phenomenal range. Without it, transmission was limited to a handful of kilometres.

The sound of the crack from the FNC80 that wounded Joe was carried up the ravine to the Indon force fanned across the ridge line. The shape of the valley guaranteed that there was no confusion over its point of origin.

Captain 'Sandman' Elliot shook his head with disappointment. Goddam it! The turnaround of the V22 Osprey and its AV-8 escort couldn't have come at a worse time. The special ops boys on the ground must have completed their mission – whatever it was – in lightning quick time.

Sandman had taken the lead as the flight had penetrated Indonesian airspace. His job was to blast enemy radar with massive bursts of energy – weld them with electrons – so that it was blinded, allowing his flight to pass unseen into the viper's pit. Only, there was a slight problem. His number two engine had just suffered an overheat with the needle going right off the dial, and he'd had to throttle it back to idle. There was no choice. He had to turn for home, whether he liked it or not. Correction. He'd have to plot a course to the Philippines. He'd never risk trying to limp all the way back to the Carrier Battle Group down in the Arafura Sea. It was just a little too far away on one engine, and he didn't trust this bucket to keep him out of the water.

He cursed and slapped the Perspex canopy with the back of his hand. These Prowlers were great for prying but they flew like bags of shit. He called in his situation and reviewed his position in relation to the tanker, the V22 and the AV-8s. Having no electronic warfare on this sortie could get messy. The Indon air force would investigate the presence of foreign military planes in its airspace if it detected the incursion. He doubted the country had a full array of ground-based air defence radar, but Indonesia could certainly have some kind of coast watch. Whatever, like it or not, his countrymen were on their own.

Sandman was halfway through briefing his three-man crew on their situation when the AWACS informed him that there was another Prowler on exercise nearby. It was forty minutes away, and could replace him in the flight, giving the mission back its cloak of invisibility. Forty minutes. That wasn't so bad. Those damn AV-8s were probably low on fuel. Again. Most likely they would need to RV with the KC-135 and take on a load. By the time they were back over Indon territory, the replacement EA-6B would have just about arrived. The AV-8s and Osprey would just have to fly low until it did. A slight delay. No sweat.

Sandman turned away feeling a little less glum. He was still pissed at having to bug out and miss the show, but at least he wouldn't be leaving anyone in the crapper.

James Littlemore broke off the transmission. 'We got maybe an hour to kill, boss.'

'What's their bloody story?' snapped Wilkes, annoyed. The MAG's objective had been completed. It was time to go and every minute they spent loitering in enemy territory could be disastrous.

'Gremlins,' said Littlemore, still hunched over the radio. 'One of the aircraft has had engine trouble. Plus the Harriers need juice. They're RV-ing with a tanker in twenty minutes. It'll take ten to fifteen for the lot of them to refuel . . . around fifty-plus minutes to get their arses back here.'

There was absolutely nothing Wilkes or anyone else could do about it. 'Are they okay with our revised RV?' he asked.

'Gave them the coords, Sarge. They said no problem.'

'It would be nice to know where those other Kopassus boys are at. Have we got any fresh intel on that?'

Littlemore shook his head. 'Didn't ask.'

The Americans would have passed on any further information for sure if they had it. Still, it often paid to check. Wilkes walked the inside perimeter of the clearing, focusing his senses on the jungle outside it, while Littlemore re-established communications.

'That's a negative on a fresh satellite pass, boss,' said Littlemore, disappointed, when Wilkes returned.

Wilkes was not aware of the satellite's period, but he was reasonably sure another pass would have been made by now so it was worth the ask. And they had to update Canberra when contact was made with any survivors anyway. 'Give Canberra a call and see what they've got.'

'The sat phone's out, boss. Deader than Kurt Cobain.'

'What's the story?' asked Wilkes.

'Dunno. It's not batteries,' shrugged Littlemore. 'The jungle canopy might be acting as a shield . . . Could be the phone, but I checked it twice back at Dili.'

'Have you tried hitting it?' Morgan chipped in.

'Violence and microprocessors go together like fish and chocolate, Smell,' said Littlemore. 'But I did give it a little tap – nothing.'

The satellite phones were their only secure communications link. Wilkes was not keen about using the AWACS as a relay station. If anyone was listening in, their presence would be known. A message to Canberra would have to wait until they were outside Indonesian airspace.

Wilkes went through the odds of further meetings with the Kopassus in his head. In all, there'd been twenty contacts illuminated by the sat. Two were the survivors Joe and Suryei, the one with the odd heat signature must have been the man incapacitated by snakebite, and they'd just taken three more out of the game. That left a maximum of fourteen Kopassus troops to contend with. Nine against fourteen. Shit odds in a game of footie, but the difference here was that the Indons weren't aware that the SAS were on the field.

'Okay, let's fuck off out of here,' said Wilkes, getting edgy. 'This place is soon going to be crawling with nasties.' Every Indon soldier within earshot would be zeroing in on their position, and he was unsure of the direction they'd be coming from.

Wilkes had noted from the Indons already taken out that the Kopassus weren't wearing comms, so it was likely that the rest of them didn't know shit from shinola, but they would have heard the shot from the FNC80 just as they had. Wilkes's Warriors should have been gone from this location already. 'How you going there, Beck? Can we move out yet?'

'Just about, boss.'

'We've got to hoof it. If they can't walk, carry them.'

Suryei's cuts and abrasions were being seen to. The burns on her forearms had been bandaged in a way that would keep the insects off while allowing the air to circulate. Her forearms throbbed hotly under the bandages. 'I'm fine,' she said, finding that her smile came easily. Beck produced a hypodermic syringe and swabbed her skin before driving in the needle. 'Antibiotics cocktail,' he said. 'The cut in your belly. You don't know where that soldier's knife has been, but you can bet it wasn't sterile.' Suryei nodded. 'Those burns on your arms don't look too good either.'

She crouched beside Joe, who was lying on a groundsheet. He had stopped vomiting. 'How you going?' Suryei asked.

'Can't feel a thing,' said Joe dreamily. 'My brain tells me I should be in pain, but nothing's getting through. I know it's there. Very weird. You should try this stuff.' Joe brought his hand up to his face and turned it slowly in front of his eyes as if it was something strange and foreign. 'Unreal . . .' he said.

'Can you walk?'

'Baby, I can fly.' Joe struggled to his feet, helped by Suryei.

LCPL Ellis came up to Suryei and held out his hand. 'This might come in handy, Miss,' he said. In his palm was the button the Indonesian soldier had sliced off. He'd found it next to the snakebite victim. 'I've got a needle and thread too.' He produced the items from one of the many pouches hung on his belt.

Suryei realised that her pants were open at the front and that someone, unnoticed, had draped a camouflage shirt over her shoulders. Joe was also now wearing an Australian regulation army shirt. She looked around. A couple of the men had stripped down to khaki singlets. 'Thanks,' she said, accepting the offer.

'You'll have us knitting tea cosies next, Ellis,' said Wilkes, humour and impatience mixed in equal measure. 'We don't have time for that.'

Ellis nodded and produced a small tube from his medical kit. He put a few drops of the liquid on the open flaps of her pants. 'Don't get this on your fingertips or it'll stick them together,' he said quickly. 'Superglue – originally developed for battlefield wounds . . . liquid stitches.'

And then Suryei was aware that the mood in the clearing had suddenly changed. Within an instant, all the Australian soldiers, except for Corporal Needle-and-thread and the medic, had disappeared. The medic put his finger to his lips for them to be quiet. Then he cocked his head to the side, concentrating. He nodded and spoke softly into a small boom mike which, until now, had been folded back away from his mouth.

Several pairs of Indonesian soldiers, including Sergeant Marturak, converged on the clearing where they'd left one of their number to care for the snakebite victim. The men met up unexpectedly in the thick jungle drawn by the sound of the gunshot, and the surprise rendezvous, coupled with their nervousness, nearly resulted in a firefight. Had they been aware that enemy soldiers were also in the immediate area, they would almost certainly have started shooting at each other.

The Indon soldiers were wary. Nervous. Three days in the jungle tracking a foe that had eluded their best efforts – and killed or incapacitated a number of their comrades – had made them tense. And cautious.

There was a single silenced shot, *phut*. One of

Marturak's men fell, and then suddenly the jungle was alive with the sound of automatic FNC80 fire.

One of the Indonesian soldiers walking in a crouch beside Marturak collapsed forwards into fern trees as a small fountain of blood plumed from the back of his head. Marturak's surprise only lasted an instant. He dropped to the ground with the rest of his men and emptied his magazine in what he thought was the general direction of the shot. He then changed magazines.

Were they under friendly fire? Another of his men fell down beside him, much like the first, with one shot removing half his skull. The shot *sounded* different. It wasn't like the familiar noise made by his soldiers' weapons. The combination of confusion and stress was not allowing his brain to draw the correct conclusion that perhaps these weren't his own men firing on them. He called out again to cease fire but his words were cut to pieces by a thirty-round burst fired by one of his men off to the left.

The blanket of fire put down by the familiar-sounding FNCs was reducing in intensity. Marturak realised that his men were being cut down. He worked towards what cover he could find on his belly, snaking through razor grass. It was impossible to see what was going on. He had to keep his head down or lose it. Moving constantly meant survival. If he stayed where he was, he would eventually be encircled and death would pour in from all sides. Marturak glanced left and right. He had a man on either side of him that he could see. They were his men. Beyond that, he had no idea what was left of his force.

Retreat was the only answer. Was it possible that the two survivors from the plane crash had found themselves weapons and were now hunting them? No, impossible. He then reminded himself that the fire coming from unseen sources sounded different. It wasn't Indonesian issue, whatever it was.

That meant there were other soldiers in the jungle. Marturak tried to piece together the action of the last few minutes. His men had fired possibly upwards of three hundred rounds, yet he had heard only several of the deadly 'popping' sounds. Silenced weapons. He was aware that at least two of those shots had found targets. Head shots.

Marturak's mind was starting to work now and the picture it was painting did not augur particularly favourably for his future health and well-being. It had to be some kind of Special Forces group. But whose? He called to his men that he would cover their retreat to trees ten metres behind. He came up on one knee and sprayed the jungle ahead of him in a forty-five degree arc. He kept the trigger squeezed against the guard until the magazine ran dry. He dropped flat to the ground and fumbled with another magazine. Silence. Perhaps he'd been lucky, taken the opposition by surprise and killed the lot of them.

Marturak worked his way backwards to the trees on his stomach, as quietly and as quickly as he could. The chest-high growth was good cover. His feet pushed against something immovable. Swinging himself around, Marturak came face to face with two more of his men. He couldn't recognise either of them because their faces were missing. Marturak was cornered and he knew it. It was pure luck that had saved him from sharing the fate of the handful of men now lying silently in the grass around him.

It was the first time in his career as a soldier that he felt helpless. Worse than that, he was paralysed with fear. If he stayed where he was, he would be surrounded – if he wasn't already – and slaughtered. If he tried to fight it out, he would end up like the rest of his men. When he realised exactly how limited his choices were, Marturak's temper snapped, breaking his paralysis.

He had been after two pathetic survivors, civilians, for well over forty-eight hours. They were unarmed, untrained (as far as he knew) and they had managed, somehow, to make him look like an amateur. He had failed in his mission. If he ever made it back to Jakarta alive, he was certain he wouldn't stay that way for long. The men he worked for would see to that. Marturak thumbed the selector switch to single shot. He couldn't remember how many rounds were left in his magazine; in the excitement, he'd lost count of the number of shots he'd fired. He expelled the magazine, placing it inside his shirt, and fitted a fresh mag with one oiled movement.

Marturak bit a large chunk out of his lower lip and blood filled his mouth. The pain worked. It sent him into a rage. The scream filled his throat and he sprang to his feet, weapon ready for killing. But just as quickly, the scream died, strangled. Marturak was surrounded, literally ringed by soldiers, high-tech camouflaged warriors, weapons zeroed at his head. Suicide suddenly seemed a pointless option. Marturak flung his rifle away from him as if it was poisonous. Holding onto it would definitely end his life. It was bald reaction.

One of the soldiers moved forward. His weapon was different to the others'. It was a sawn-off shotgun and blue smoke snaked lazily from the black pit pointed at his head.

Shotgun blasts. Marturak realised now why he couldn't recognise the mashed faces of his comrades. He raised his hands slowly, interlocking his fingers behind his head.

He examined the soldiers who had so adeptly surrounded, cornered and slaughtered his men. They were young, serious, but far from nervous, as his men would have been if the roles had been reversed. These soldiers were cool, calculated professionals. No emotion, just business. It wouldn't take much for one (or all) of them to pull their triggers and kill him in cold blood. Again, if the positions had been reversed, he wouldn't have thought twice about it and he didn't expect them to either. His hunch was right. They were Australian SAS. The way they carried themselves and did their job made them instantly recognisable. Marturak had trained with these people before, and even fought against them in a skirmish on the border of West and East Timor. He remembered that battle vividly. He'd managed to shoot one in the head as the man stood over his fallen comrade, yet still the soldier had stood his ground and kept firing. He'd been fighting against the Australian occupation forces with the militia and had barely managed to escape with his life. Yes, they were good.

Marturak talked to them, quietly at first. He knew they probably wouldn't understand Indonesian but if he somehow forced his humanity on them, there was a slight chance that they would find it harder to kill him. That's what the TNI psychs said. Now he played that card for all it was worth.

Marturak clasped his hands together in front of his face in the universal gesture of prayer and babbled pathetically, beseeching, pleading. He almost made himself sick grovelling like this. Such antics had never deflected him from a chosen course of action, namely, to pull the trigger. But he needed time. It was all about time. The stocky soldier who appeared to be the leader – he couldn't be sure because none of the men carried any insignia of rank – ignored his pleas. The soldier stuck the barrel of his shotgun above one of Marturak's wrists and forced it down, gesturing at him to put his hands behind his back. Another soldier, one he couldn't see, held his fingers interlocked together and secured his wrists tightly with a nylon lock-tie while a third soldier patted him down, removing his sidearm, grenades and knife. A muzzle jabbed him in the back and he was walking forward, a captured prisoner in his own country.

Getting his mind back into gear took a couple of minutes but the shock of capture passed as he began assessing the situation, sifting through options. He knew he had more men out there in the bush. They would have heard the shooting. They had a radio, and they were in Indonesia. It was their home. He needed time to turn it around on these invaders. These . . . Australians (he mentally spat the word). In the meantime, he had to stay alive, so he prayed for mercy and tried to squeeze tears out of his eyes.

Wilkes couldn't speak Bahasa, but he didn't need to. The man was obviously begging for his life. Wilkes was not a cold-blooded killer. He had not been specifically ordered to slot this man. But he also had absolutely no idea what to do with him. Slotting him seemed his only option. Perhaps an alternative would present itself.

Coombs came up to Wilkes and revealed the contents of a rucksack belonging to one of the dead Indonesian soldiers. 'Looks like black boxes to me, boss. From the plane.'

That was a find. The people back home would be interested in those, big time.

Marturak walked into the small clearing pushed in front of his captors, head bowed and hands behind his back. The SAS soldiers filed in behind him. Beck and Littlemore stood to meet the advancing party, as did Suryei, while Joe stayed on his back, hypnotised by the canopy swaying high overhead. Marturak saw more of his men laid out next to each other on the ground, their shirts pulled over their heads to hide the gore from view. It took every ounce of willpower not to scream with rage at the sight of his men slaughtered by these fucking Australian pigs. He tried not to look at the bodies. It was important to keep intact the cloak of meekness he'd managed to pull over himself.

Then the woman, one of the survivors he'd failed to hunt down, came up to him and spat in his face and that was the end of his composure. He staggered forward in an attempt to shoulder-charge her, but having his hands tied behind his back upset his balance. Marturak tripped and ploughed head first into the ground, dirt filling his mouth. He struggled to get his feet under his body until a hand grabbed his shirt firmly by the collar and hauled him up.

The woman stared at him defiantly. She appeared to be Indonesian. This was one of the people who'd made him and his men look stupid. Her companion was on the ground, wounded by the look of him. Good.

Suryei feared this man. He'd come to represent for her all the senseless brutality of a nation, the torment of East Timor – the graves, so much destruction. He had pursued them through the jungle in order to kill them. She looked at the bodies being lined up on the ground, and thought about the men who probably lay dead beyond her view in the jungle. It struck Suryei that her and Joe's survival was nothing more than sheer good luck. The odds of living through the plane crash had been staggering, but then there was the jungle and this bunch of killers to contend with. The soldier didn't even know her. The soldier's hate was mindless. He inhabited a brutal world she wanted no part of. With that fresh realisation, she turned her back on the invective streaming from Marturak's mouth and quietly sat beside Joe.

There were more Indonesian soldiers out there some-where. Wilkes glanced at his watch. Just on forty-nine minutes till extraction. It would take them a good thirty-five minutes to reach the RV – the place where the felled hardwood had torn a huge gash in the canopy, large enough for the V22 to drop in and lift them out. Better to take it slow and careful. It was time to move. Now. Any Kopassus within cooee would have been drawn to the gun-fire at a run.

'Stu, you ready?' he asked.

'When you are, boss.'

'How about Joe there?' he said, nodding at Joe, who was staring up at the canopy, smiling.

'Having a wonderful time, by the looks of things. He'll be right.'

'Okay, fuck-knuckles, let's blow,' said Wilkes quietly into his boom mike. 'Stu, stay with the civilians. James, you've done bugger-all on this job. Make yourself useful and take the point. Get your machete out and cut us a path. Gary, you and Coombsy ranger for us. Mac, you take the rear. If anyone takes the easy way down our trail, let them know they're making a big mistake. We don't want any surprises and we've still got quite a few unfriendlies out there.' Wilkes had no idea where the Indons would be coming from, but if they came across an obvious path cleared through the jungle, they just might follow it. That would be handy, because knowing where the Indonesians were would make dealing with them that much easier.

'No wukkas, boss,' said Mac Robson, checking the ammo box on his Minimi and moving off at the trot.

'What do we do with blubber-mouth here?' asked Ellis, gesturing at the Indonesian prisoner.

Wilkes had momentarily forgotten about the Indon sergeant. He sized the man up and again considered the alternatives. The Kopassus soldier was an ugly son-of-a-bitch, that was for sure, with the skin on his face so badly pockmarked it had the appearance of a dirty golf-ball. He tried not to let the look of the man influence his decision either way. The humanitarian side of him considered leaving him behind to care for his own man, the snakebite victim. The SAS soldier in him thought that he should at least take the man with them so that their identity, strength and position weren't passed to his Kopassus mates, if they happened to stumble across each other. The soldier won the internal debate. 'He comes with us. Tell him any funny business and we send him to Allah,' said Wilkes simply.

The woman stepped up to within centimetres of the Indon soldier, yelled something at him, then turned and walked away.

Wilkes pulled her aside. 'You speak Bahasa. What did you say to him?'

'That if he doesn't behave you'll stick your shotgun up his arse and pull the trigger,' she said coolly.

Wilkes cleared his throat involuntarily. 'That's about right, Suryei, thanks. We're moving off now to our rendezvous. Getting airlifted out in forty-six minutes. You could give us a hand by staying close to Joe and helping him. He's going to need it. We're not going to race, but I want to get there with time to spare to set up a few defences, just in case.'

'Ah, what's your name again?' enquired Suryei, embarrassed, aware that in the surprise of the arrival of the Australian soldiers, she'd forgotten it.

'Tom will do,' said Wilkes. 'And this is my merry band of wankers.' Several men laughed out loud.

'If there's one thing Joe and I can do after three days in this place, it's move through the jungle. Don't worry about us.'

'Okay.'

Suryei suddenly realised that she had no idea how long they had been marooned here. 'What day is it?'

'It's Friday. Thank God.'

'Are you sure?'

'All day . . .' said Tom with a smile.

Suryei couldn't believe it. It was only Friday? So much had happened. She had left Sydney on the Tuesday afternoon, and the plane had crashed in the early hours of Wednesday morning, just two days ago. Unbelievable.

Suryei saw the soldier talk softly into the wire in front of his mouth. The mood in the clearing changed. Joe was lifted to his feet, supported by the soldier who'd dressed his wounds. Joe was obviously shaky, swaying on rubbery legs. Suryei went over to him and put her arm around him carefully, supporting him. He gave her a wan smile. Before she realised exactly what was going on, they were picking their way through the jungle again. Only this time it was different. The soldiers ahead were blazing the trail, and they knew where they were going. She felt safe with these people. They were *her* army. She felt good, secure, and Joe was doing better than expected.

As they walked, Wilkes reached up and plucked a piece of fruit, seemingly from out of the air, and gave it to her, smiling. He made a peeling gesture. She removed a portion of the skin and took a small bite. Whatever it was, it was sweet and delicious. She knew when they'd found the jackfruit that they were probably surrounded by food, and the soldier had just proved it. A small shiver went through her. It was good to be alive – a tangible thrill.

And then it hit her. The plane crash. The old couple shot dead. Finding Joe. Fire. Running. Death. And the awful question: why? Had the Qantas plane really been shot down because Joe had hacked into the Indonesian general's computer and stolen invasion plans? Christ Almighty! The invasion! She couldn't believe that she'd forgotten the most important thing.

Shit, it was more than important. And yet it had completely slipped her mind. Purely surviving had overwhelmed everything. One breath at a time. One step at a time. And why were Australian soldiers here in Indonesia fighting, shooting Indonesian soldiers? Jesus! Had it already begun? Were Australia and Indonesia at war? One country's soldiers didn't go into another country and kill that country's soldiers unless they were. The thought sent a shudder down her spine. She kicked herself for being so self-absorbed.

'I need a radio or a phone or something,' she blurted to Wilkes. 'I know why the Indonesians shot down our plane.'

Wilkes was taken aback. He had been expecting her to say that she liked the breadfruit. 'How do you know the Indonesians shot it down?'

'Because we found one of the plane's engines in the jungle, blasted off the wing. There was an Indonesian missile still stuck in it.'

Jesus. Wilkes was genuinely surprised.

'Are we at war with Indonesia?' she asked nervously.

'Not when we left East Timor,' said Wilkes, frowning.

That's something at least, thought Suryei. 'I have to use your radio.'

'We already know Indonesia shot the plane down,' Wilkes said, attempting to calm her.

'You know? You knew? How long have you known?'

'About a day, maybe more.'

'Then why has it taken so much time to get to us?'

'Hang on, you asked how long it has been since we knew the plane was shot down. Not how long we've known about survivors.'

'Okay, then when did you know about us?'

'About as long as it takes to stuff us into a plane and get us here – a few hours, no more.'

Suryei chewed her lip. 'Are you here because of Joe?'

'Eh?!' He looked at her, puzzled.

Suryei desperately wanted to tell the soldier everything, but she was afraid. Perhaps if they knew what Joe had done, these men would be less inclined to bring them to safety.

Wilkes felt she was holding something back. Suryei had become silent. 'If you want to talk to anyone in Australia, you'll have to wait. We've got a satellite phone but it's not working. Something to do with interference from the canopy.'

340

Suryei had no reason to doubt the man. He was on her side. Still, a powerful feeling of unease swept through her. How much time did they have? Or had time run out? And who was she going to call anyway? It wasn't as if she knew the Prime Minister . . .

Suryei watched Joe pick his way carefully through the jungle, leaning on a soldier. The morphine had wrapped him in its protective sheath. 'How long will the morphine last?' asked Suryei.

'Depends on the person – their sensitivity to the drug, body weight, the level of pain. I'd say Joe's got forty-five minutes, maybe an hour, before he comes back to earth. And he will land hard. That wound is going to hurt.'

Central Sulawesi, 0930 Zulu, Friday, 1 May

The steep bow of the prahu sliced through the murky brown coastal waters just beyond the reach of the mangrove trees. Wyan, one of three Wyans on the pirate vessel, was counting the number of sharks churning the water in the boat's lazy wake. He lowered the bucket into the water to give it a rinse. It had contained various scraps from the kitchen and it was coated with a layer of evil-smelling slime. No sooner did the bucket touch the water than he had to yank on the dirty orange nylon cord it was suspended on, lifting it out of reach of snapping grey heads.

Wyan almost lost his footing as the captain turned the wheel sharply to port to keep the prahu hugging the edge of the mangroves. Something was wrong with the boat's radar. It had mysteriously stopped working. One minute it was fine, the next it presented a barrage of static. One of the other Wyans, the one from Bali and the boat's electrical expert, pronounced that something was terminally wrong with the unit's sealed components, so they had turned it off. A pirate vessel without radar was naked, so they were lying low, hugging the coast. It would be bad to run into an Indonesian patrol boat. His brother in the air force wouldn't be able to help him then.

Wyan thought about that. It was funny; two brothers, both so different. One a pirate, the other a pilot, an officer in the air force. And so serious his older brother was too. It was almost like his little brother Wyan was an embarrassment. But who, at the end of the day, brought home more money? Wyan thought that that was the reason his older brother was always so angry with him. It wasn't because he was a pirate. It came down to money. Everything always did. A large tiger shark bit one of the smaller grey-blue ones and blood swirled through the brown murk. The water boiled with swishing tails and fins and teeth.

The prahu rounded the point just clear of the mangroves and the air was full of mechanical thunder. Wyan ducked as an aircraft roared low overhead, barely clearing the boat's stubby radio mast. The plane was gone before anyone in the wheelhouse or below decks could run out and see what all the noise was about. Wyan had seen it, though. He'd seen enough to know that it was a military plane. He recognised it. His brother had spent most of their childhood collecting photos and books of warplanes, and the strange-looking aircraft made an occasional appearance in these as an experimental concept. What in Allah's name was it called?

The small dish on the wheelhouse caught his attention. Wyan decided to call up his brother and ask about an aircraft that appeared to be part helicopter, part fixed wing plane, that had just flown into Indonesia from the sea. Wyan pulled the satellite phone out of his back pocket, checked for signal strength, and dialled the number. The greatest pleasure about being successful, thought Wyan, was being able to afford the latest gear.

The MAG made its way cautiously to the edge of the clearing around the giant fallen tree. This was their revised RV with the V22, but they wouldn't move into its centre until the transport home arrived. They would be asking for trouble out there in the centre of the clearing. The group took a few minutes to thoroughly reconnoitre the area from the cover of the tree line.

They had made good time. Fifteen minutes plus or minus two minutes until pick-up, Wilkes calculated. Enough time for a little defensive work, especially in their rear. He gave the appropriate instructions quietly into the boom mike and directed the core of his group – Joe, Suryei, Curry, Coombs and the Indonesian soldier – to the protective cover of a dense copse of trees. Ellis and Beck crouched, removed their rucksacks and extracted a stack of slim, curved grey claymores. Robson trotted in, took four of the mines, then the three soldiers left in different directions to position them for the greatest defensive effect.

'Have I got time for a brew-up, boss?' asked Robson over the comms. Wilkes glanced up at Mac and gave him a quizzical look. And then he realised what Robson was about and gave him the thumb's up, shaking his head with a half-smile.

Mac quickly checked his pack to ensure he had everything he needed, then dashed to the trail they'd hacked into the bush.

Wilks surveyed the clearing from behind an ancient, half-rotted hardwood. It was not quite as spacious as he had remembered, but big enough, he hoped, to get the V22 in. The wait was making him edgy. They weren't here for a picnic, after all. He observed that there was fuck-all cover out in the middle of the RV. Withdrawing to the aircraft would be a tricky exercise if the Indons had their shit together. Wilkes's men could easily be surrounded here and cut down. A couple of well-placed snipers would do the trick. They'd be firing from the dark into the light and they'd be virtually invisible. If the positions were reversed, he wouldn't think twice about it. He looked up at the sky. Dusk. The night would come down fast.

Was there anything good about this place? Wilkes turned around slowly through 360 degrees, considering their position. Well, at least they didn't have to make their way back to the crash site of the Qantas plane, as originally planned. The Indon soldiers would have to find them, and that wouldn't be easy; the jungle was some of the thickest he'd ever seen. It would be helpful if the Indons took the easy way and wandered up the track they'd slashed in the jungle. The claymores Robson was positioning would provide a warm welcome, and alert the Australians to any advance in their rear.

Also, there would be enough room in here to launch grenades from the M203s, without worrying about the ordnance being deflected back at them. Again, thinking negatively, if the Indonesians had grenade launchers, the open space would work for them too, and for exactly the same reason. Wilkes frowned. The more he thought about it, the more this place was bad news.

He sighted down his Minimi machine gun, resting the short barrel against the tree. He had an unobstructed field of fire across the clearing and into the trees on the opposite side. He had two other Minimis in the group. He'd keep one back for roving fire. The other he'd position twenty-five metres along the tree line, providing a wider field of fire than if just one of the Minimis had been employed. Morgan could rove with his H&K sub-machine gun, pitching in where needed.

Wilkes wondered whether he was being paranoid but decided that he was just being careful. He was still alive and kicking after all these years of soldiering and he intended to stay that way. Furthermore, something told him that this mission was perhaps the most important of his career. He was going to get these two civilians back in one piece, even if it killed him. He smirked at himself for his own poor choice of words.

Beck caught Wilkes's eye away to the left and gave a nod. The sergeant held up seven fingers. Seven minutes till pick-up.

Robson returned.

'Mac, take your Minimi down there,' he said, pointing to another large tree.

'Easy, boss.' Robson checked his weapon and sprang through the jungle, avoiding clear space. He lay down on his stomach behind a rock and scanned the tree line.

Automatic fire cracked unexpectedly from the edge of the clearing opposite, and the tree beside Wilkes's face exploded in a cloud of pulverised wood. He turned to look quickly over his shoulder and saw Coombs go down, shot, then Curry. The woman, Suryei, was next. She spun on her heels and fell over Joe, who was lying on the ground. The copse of trees provided absolutely no cover from gunfire directly opposite. It happened so fast. Wilkes dropped to one knee. He watched for the muzzle flash amongst the black and raked the area with a quick burst to see if it would be returned.

Geysers of dirt rose from the ground in front of Wilkes. One of the slugs splintered as it hit a small outcrop of rock, a fragment burrowing into the skin at the point of Wilkes's chin. It flayed the skin from his jaw and opened up his cheek before exiting below his temple. Blood gushed down his arm and made the stock of his Minimi slick. Wilkes was in shock. 'Shit, I'm hit!' he said. He shifted his weapon to his left hand and brought his right hand up to hold the side of his face together. The pressure stopped the bleeding. Wilkes retreated, finding cover behind a rock. Beck joined him.

'Cool, boss,' he said, checking the wicked gash.

'Yeah, yeah. Don't tell me, chicks dig scars,' said Wilkes.

'Team it with an eye patch,' Beck advised, closing the wound with a couple of drops of superglue.

Wilkes felt no pain. There was too much adrenaline in his system.

Flashes. Slugs slapped through the foliage by Beck's shoulder. There. Wilkes could see them off to one side of the clearing. The Indonesian position was vulnerable to a grenade. It took a second for the sergeant to react. He ran the five metres to Coombs, who was lying on the ground groaning, and exchanged his weapon for the wounded man's M4 propped against a tree. Ellis's Minimi fired into the foliage concealing the enemy. Robson did the same from behind his rock.

Wilkes's men were quick to recover their equilibrium. They formed pairs and began firing and moving through the tree line around the edge of the clearing, one covering the advance of the other. The hostile bursts of fire slowed quickly, the attention of the enemy diverted, and no doubt surprised, by the speed and focus of the counterattack.

Bang. A claymore went off in their rear. Screams. Some Indons had run into their perimeter security. Robson smiled.

Wilkes freed M203 grenades from Coombs's chest webbing. He cracked the launcher, fed in a round, and waited for muzzle flashes to provide him with a target. There, a tracer round originating from behind a particularly dark bush opposite.

Wilkes launched the grenade, the butt kicking against his shoulder. The round arced towards the trees, spinning, the revolutions arming the fuse. *Boom.* A vicious smudge of grey smoke appeared behind the trees he'd fired into. Wilkes chambered another round and squeezed the trigger. Kick. *Boom.* A scream. Muzzle flashes, twenty metres further left this time. The M4 kicked again. *Boom.* Morgan was running at a tangent to the hot area, hoping to outflank the Indons. His weapon was not shouldered. It was next to useless to run and fire, it slowed the shooter down and made aiming impossible. Morgan would find cover, locate the enemy, and then hopefully pick them off from an angle they'd least expect.

Littlemore was kneeling at the tree line, putting down covering fire while Morgan ran. Quick bursts. He counted off the rounds in his head. He always packed magazines with tracer second to last. When he saw it fired, he changed magazines. That way, he wouldn't get caught without any change in the till. Tracer. Magazine empty. Release. New mag. Quick bursts. Tracer.

Now Littlemore was up and running around the edge of the clearing, towards the trees opposite. Wilkes could see Chris Ferris also taking cover behind a hardwood blanketed in luxurious, thick moss. Enemy fire was all around him. He watched Ferris pop his head around the trunk. Once. Nothing. Twice. Nothing. He then turned and broke cover, unexpectedly coming round the other side of the tree. A spray of bullets answered his move but the rounds found only air. Ferris was too quick, too wily.

Wilkes made his way back to Coombs and the others. Coombs had been hit in the leg. Fortunately, the blade of his machete had deflected the bullet, but the force of the round had been the equivalent of having his leg thumped with a sledgehammer. Coombs thought his femur was broken. Wilkes gave it a cursory check. It wasn't, but Coombs wasn't going to be ballroom dancing anytime soon. Curry, however, looked bad. Shoulder wound. The woman was okay. He thought she'd been shot, but it was just her reaction to the incoming fusillade. She had wasted no time dropping to the ground – that had probably saved her life.

But the prisoner was gone.

Mac had also moved back to check on Coombs, Curry and the crash survivors. He gave Wilkes a reassuring nod. He fired off a burst from his Minimi at the muzzle flashes, showering Suryei and Joe with hot, spent cases.

Experience had kicked in. Panic was gone. *Boom* – an explosion from the opposite side of the clearing. A scream. Another claymore. Another scream.

Wilkes liberated his shotgun, checked that the magazine

was full, and joined Ellis, Ferris and Littlemore as they moved into the trees to mop up the remnants of the Indon force. It took a precious minute for their eyes to adapt to the lower light back in the jungle proper. Ferris had first contact. There were six, possibly seven Indonesian soldiers left. An M34 white phosphorous grenade exploded in the middle of a group of three. Littlemore had thrown it, unseen behind him. *Boom.* The flash caught Ferris by surprise and momentarily blinded him. The damage to the Indons was infinitely worse. A mushroom cloud of smoke rose quickly to the canopy above on a pillow of intensely hot air. An M26 grenade followed the incendiary ordnance. Insurance. *Boom.*

Ferris's sight recovered from the flash of the M34 grenade in time to see a pair of Indons on the move, over to the left. He relayed the observation over the comms. Wilkes set up the attack. Advance. Cover fire. Split the angles. Move. Fire. Split. Advance. The Indonesians sprayed the jungle blind, firing at trees. The SAS moved. Split. Covered. An M34 grenade lit up the trees. Screams. Ellis and Wilkes cut off two more Kopassus. A blast from a large-bore shotgun echoed through the trees, followed by a couple of two-shot bursts from silenced M4s. Phut-phut, phut-phut.

Marturak had run blindly when the shooting started, trying to find effective cover. He then made his way around to the opposite end of the clearing. One of his own men had bailed him up after a tense moment in the growing gloom and nearly shot him as one of the enemy. A few terse words had ended the confusion. His restraint had been cut and he'd picked up a weapon lying beside a dead comrade and continued to move around the perimeter of the clearing.

That was barely ten minutes ago. The SAS had been brutally effective and now, he knew he was the last.

The pattern of gunfire told a deadly tale. Two-shot bursts. To the head, no doubt. The coup de grace. And now there was silence. Except for the crash of his own heart against his ribcage, the jungle was eerily quiet. Marturak dropped his weapon and waited. He caught movement in the corner of his eye. It occurred to him that these people never seemed to come from the direction anticipated.

He turned and saw four soldiers with their sights on his head. This time he was going to die, no arguing, and no begging. And then he remembered the disk, the one he'd taken from the computer in the plane. He had no idea what was on it, perhaps nothing, but these men didn't know that. Would they spare his life for it?

He moved his left hand slowly inside his webbing to pull out the disk. Slowly. Steady. He held it in his right hand and wiggled it to attract attention.

'Bondi Beach,' he asserted. 'I love Sydney.' There was more in that vein. Marturak felt stupid saying it. He'd never been to Australia and didn't know anyone who had. But it was survival. He wasn't even sure there was a place in Australia called Bondi Beach, the name just popped into his head. The soldier with the smoking shotgun came forward and took the disk from him. Marturak smiled and put his hands together in a prayer of thanks.

'Very important. Sydney!' he said, smiling, all teeth. He watched the soldier frown at the disk and turn it over, examining it. It was obvious the Australian had no idea of its significance. The stocky soldier, the one Marturak took to be the leader, gave a small shrug then placed the disk in his breast pocket.

'I'm from Melbourne,' Ellis said to the Indonesian as Wilkes turned away. There were two quick shots and the Indonesian crumpled to the ground. Wilkes turned back, frowning. 'What . . .?!' Ellis said, shrugging playfully. 'Had to make sure, boss.'

Robson wheeled, disappearing into the trees to investigate his earlier handiwork. It took him five minutes to slip through the undergrowth to the small clearing he'd found off their trail. The closer he got, the stronger the smell of freshly brewed coffee became. He wondered how many Indons had fallen for the bait. Upon reaching the clearing, he waited on the edge amongst the trees and listened. Silence, except for the coffee still bubbling away. Two dead soldiers lay opposite. Undoubtedly they had been drawn by the aroma of Robson's favourite mocha blend, expecting to surprise the unknown enemy happily taking a break. Robson wondered whether they'd had time to realise their mistake before they met their maker.

He checked the mines he had personally set and found the Indons had only tripped one. Three were left. He disarmed them and repacked them in his rucksack, not wanting to leave behind explosive devices that an innocent person might stumble on fatally in the future.

Robson walked soundlessly to the brew, turned off the stove and packed it into his rucksack. Pouring a little cold water into the pot to cool the contents, he quickly tossed back the coffee, grounds and all. It was bitter. Burned. Oh well, better than instant. He heard aircraft approaching. It was time to leave.

The clearing filled with noise and wind as the V22 descended slowly through the darkening sky, carefully, through the hole in the canopy, rotors clearing the thrashing foliage by less than a metre. The rear door was down. McBride and the LM, both lifelined to the fuselage, waved at them to hurry aboard. Above, an AV-8 blocked the sun as it screamed overhead.

Ferris and Robson helped Suryei and Joe aboard the instant the aircraft's wheels settled tentatively on the spongy ground. The shriek of the turbines tore at Suryei's eardrums.

Ferris and Robson then immediately turned back, jumping off the ramp to cover the MAG's retreat. Wilkes and Littlemore carried Curry aboard between them, while Morgan half-carried the hobbling Coombs. Beck leapt on and then Ferris and Robson climbed on last. Where the fuck was Ellis? Wilkes had seen him running through the jungle earlier. Where had he gone? Wilkes was starting to feel a tightening in his stomach.

And then he saw Ellis running awkwardly across the clearing from the far end, something large and green over his shoulder. It was Gibbo's body. Ellis arrived at the rear door just as an enormous explosion threw a mushroom cloud into the air. 'The rest of our shit!' yelled Ellis over the engine noise. He'd blown up their cache, denying Indonesia the opportunity of parading any gear in front of the media. The LM helped Ellis and Wilkes inside with the body. He said something into his boom mike and the aircraft lifted off immediately, the rear door closing on the jungle as the V22 rose tentatively through the opening in the canopy.

McBride shouted into Wilkes's ear above the noise, 'Joe Light, alive! Amazing!'

Sergeant Wilkes nodded and pushed past, concerned about his men.

Curry's wound was bad. The bullet had shattered the clavicle and was still lodged in his shoulder. He was losing a fair bit of blood and his skin was grey-white. Beck did what he could with field dressings, but there was nothing they could do without an operating theatre and an orthopaedic surgeon. He immobilised the shoulder and gave Curry a shot of morphine. The LM had the wounded soldier carried to a stretcher fastened to a bulkhead, and strapped him in. Gibbo's body was also secured in the same way. He gestured to the soldiers to take their seats, belt up and put their headphones on.

Suryei watched the men load the bodies on stretchers and realised again how much had been sacrificed by these men to keep Joe and her alive.

'Ferret Handler. Six bandits. Six bandits. West. Eighty miles. Angels Twelve. Heading zero-niner-zero.'

'Ferret Leader. Roger that. Request bandit type and weapons intel.'

'Bandits inbound F-16. BVR capabilities negative.'

'Ferret Leader.'

Let's get ready to rumble, Captain Pete 'Toad' Sanders said to himself. The call came from an Airborne Warning and Control System, an aircraft with enormously powerful radar, orbiting well outside Indonesian airspace and out of enemy missile range. Its job was to provide the flight over

Indonesian territory with Airborne Control Interception – letting the good guys know what the bad guys were up to without the fighters having to turn on their own radars.

The ACI provided by the AWACs had just painted a picture that made Toad's scrotum tighten with fear. And, if he'd been asked, a whole lot of excitement. Uncle Sam had spent millions training him to dogfight, and he was finally getting a chance to put that training to good use.

Six enemy aircraft, F-16s, were inbound from the west. They were at angels twelve or 12 000 feet, on a course that was taking them due east. West to east. Toad was tracking north. He checked his own display to verify the call. There they were, closing at roughly twenty miles a minute off his port wing, at a range of eighty nautical miles. Six against two. Not terribly good odds on paper. In reality, however, they were heavily stacked in the AV-8s' favour.

Out in front of the AV-8s was the replacement EA-6B Prowler. The Americans turned towards the Indonesians. Almost immediately, the pods on the Prowler's wings would begin blasting them with so much energy they'd be stumbling around like Ray Charles. Totally blind.

The guys in the AWACS had said that the bandits were BVR negative, which meant they didn't have beyond visual range missiles. That was a relief. Fire-and-forget over-the-horizon missiles were expensive and only America and her best buddies had access to them. They weren't even available on the black market. It meant the aircraft closing on them had nothing smart they could launch at them and then bug out. The Indons would have to get up close and visual and use AIM-9 heaters – heat-seekers – and guns.

Indonesia was not a rich nation. They'd be running older F-16A Falcons, planes that had been superseded more than ten years ago by F-16Cs with numerous upgrades, including more powerful engines and weapons. Toad and his wingman were up against aircraft that, while not quite museum pieces, were not far from it. Their AV-8Bs, on the other hand, were the upgraded Harrier 11 Radar type, AV-8s with more powerful Pegasus engines, avionics, and the OSCAR on-board computer, which made life in the cockpit about as difficult to manage as playing a Nintendo game. Toad's weapons systems could define who was friend or foe, acquire targets, as well as arm and deploy the aircraft's weaponry, and do it all in the same instant. Once on its way, the AMRAAM missile's own systems would take over, directing the warhead to the target. Toad didn't even have to keep the target painted or illuminated in any way. Once launched, the missile was its own extremely smart, extremely deadly master.

Toad checked his ordnance by setting the correct mode and toggling from one weapons station to the next; two Advanced Medium Range Air-to-Air Missiles and a couple of AIM-9M missiles, the new, more intelligent heaters with a longer range, and a 25 mm fuselage-mounted machine gun loaded with HEI, high-explosive incendiary shells. His wingman was similarly armed. The V22? Zip. Not even a spitball. Toad glanced left and right and was reassured by the sight of his own AIM-120 AMRAAMs. Seeing them snuggled under his wing gave him an enormous sense of security.

Toad wondered what would be going through the minds of the F-16 pilots. The poor bastards would be shitting bricks. Their threat indicators would be frying like eggs on a skillet under the barrage emitted by the EA-6B. Those Prowlers were bloody frightening. Get too close to one of them while it was emitting and you could forget about ever having any children. It was highly unlikely that the Indons would have experienced anything like the EW they were now being subjected to. It meant that they were literally heading into the unknown, against an unknown enemy of unknown strength from an unknown origin. It was a fighter pilot's nightmare.

Less than four minutes to intercept. He was running passive, emitting no radar waves. Given the probable state of confusion in the cockpits of the Indonesian F-16s, he was being overcautious. But why take the risk if it was avoidable? The AWACS was providing intelligence on the F-16s rushing towards them, then beaming the ACI straight into Toad's aeroplane. He was getting all the information he could have asked for, without giving his existence away by emitting his own radar energy to get it. His threat indicator had all six bandits. Closing speed, 1.9 Mach.

Toad banked sharply and took in the terrain below. The dominating feature was the threatening cone of a huge volcano that rose from the jungle around ten klicks to the south. It towered into a duvet of cloud.

The V22 sucked negative gs as it hugged the contour of a ravine and plunged into a deep volcanic channel. Suryei just managed to pull a bag from the seat pocket in front of her and place it under her mouth before her stomach let go. The extreme movement recalled the terror of the final moments of QF-1, and the memory of it now made her gag with fear. The SAS men were all clipping in their shoulder straps and the negative-g strap between their legs. Suryei followed their example between stomach convulsions.

Toad checked his fuel pressure. Barely enough, but so what else was new? Fuel load was the AV-8B's Achilles heel. The aircraft's range, or lack of it, was a bit of a joke. He was carrying external tanks and they'd been topped off three times by KC-135s yet, despite the numbers they'd been flying to ensure best range since the last fill, he'd burned a high percentage of the aircraft's juice already.

Major Loku Shidyahan rolled his F-16 left and right, trying to pick out anything unusual against the green of the jungle below. He had the eyes in his head but nothing else to help him find the intruder. His radar was being jammed. The major had never experienced it before but he'd read enough about it to know it was happening to him and his flight.

His younger brother, Wyan, had phoned him out of the blue to ask him whether Indonesia had anything that sounded suspiciously like a V22 Osprey, because one had just flown in from the sea at wave height and disappeared inland. Of course we haven't, he'd said. It was an American plane being tested by their army and marines. As it happened, Shidyahan had just read a performance review on them that suggested they were too dangerous and would probably never see service. His brother's enquiry was just another coincidence in a day full of them. Hasanuddin AFB had been experiencing all kinds of unusual radar interference, but couldn't trace the problem to its source. And then the call had come from Wyan. There was definitely something odd going on. There were also the orders from the top to be particularly vigilant. Why? The major had no idea but he had enough muscle at Hasanuddin to get a flight of F-16s fuelled and airborne to investigate.

His brother had provided an estimated heading and speed of the suspected intruder but the plane would most likely have altered course once it had made landfall. In short, the V22 could be just about anywhere. The major wished his country had the resources to afford blanket radar coverage. With its tens of thousands of islands, having that kind of support would make the air force's job so much easier. He rolled left and right again. Nothing. A gnawing in his gut told him the radar interference hid a malignant force. He gave brief instructions into his oxygen mask and the flight made a descending turn to the left, and decelerated.

Toad's threat indicator showed the Indons making the turn. It was decision time. The Prowler had reached the agreed point where it, too, would turn away from the inbound flight of F-16s, and hightail it out of the area. Almost immediately, the Indonesians would get their radars back and the three intruders would be revealed on their scopes. The Indonesians were fifteen miles out. Toad and his wingman held the tactical advantage. He selected the AMRAAMs and his wingman did the same.

Toad, being the flight leader, chose the two leading aircraft in the approaching formation, as his wingman knew he would. Toad's OSCAR confirmed that the two leading aircraft had been targeted. He watched the Prowler turn away on his scope. As it did so, Toad thumbed the fire button. One, two missiles away. The AV-8's airframe rocked with the energy expended by the departing ordnance. OSCAR calculated time to impact.

Toad's wingman had targeted the next two closest F-16s. As Toad manoeuvred his aircraft out of the way, the wingman popped up from behind and launched his missiles.

They had launched a total of four AMRAAMs between them.

On his radar, Major Sanders saw the effect on the F-16s of the missile launches. The enemy formation split, aircraft spearing left and right in a deadly dance of evasion. The AV-8s pumped, turning aggressively through 180 degrees, to resume their sweeping fore and aft of the Osprey still hugging the treetops below.

Major Shidyahan happened to be peering at his radar display when the storms of electrons sweeping across it broke up. He saw three contacts, bandits, turning away and four inbound foxes, missiles, heading towards his flight. He instantly began to sweat. Inbound missiles! Who fired them? Where did they come from? What were they? He hoped and prayed that they would be something old and inaccurate. An equally assertive voice within him told him not to be stupid. The missiles would be coming in at Mach three. No time to think. He jerked his control stick back and the F-16 bucked, clawing for altitude. No, he wanted the ground, not sky. He pushed the stick forward. His shoulders strained against the straps and blood gushed into his brain as the F-16 hit four negative gs.

A warning horn went off in his phones from the threat indicator. *Beep. Beep.* The missile was hunting for him. The tone changed. *Wah-wah-wah.* Now it had found him. He threw the F-16 through a 90-degree left turn and pulled back into a climb. Blood rushed to his feet. His vision narrowed, blackout imminent. He released pressure on the stick, allowing a little blood back into his brain to restore sight, then jammed the stick back again.

Condensation formed at the wing roots, pressure waves squeezing the vapour out of the air. *Wah-wah-wah.* The horn might be the last thing he'd hear. Shidyahan jinked right. Then left. *Wah-wah-wah*. He looked behind him. He could see the trail left by the exhaust of the missile's solid rocket propellant. A deadly white finger reaching towards him. *Wah-wah-wah*.

Two towering, converging volcanic cliffs reared in Major Shidyahan's forward view. He was going to drill into them. Faced with a certain, violent death, he screamed. Unconsciously, he flicked the F-16 into a knife-edge turn and pulled the control stick back hard. The vertical volcanic rock wall seemed to suck the F-16 towards it. His vicious manoeuvring forced the AMRAAM to go stupid when its sensors lost the target against the noise of the ground. The missile slammed into the cliff behind him, the concussion wave from the ensuing explosion tossing the F-16 into a yaw.

Major Shidyahan sucked in the oxygen to steady his nerves. Sweat dribbled down his forehead into his eyes and stung them. He scanned his instruments. No damage, Allah be praised. As his aircraft climbed smoothly away from the rockslide caused by the AMRAAM's impact, he fought to regain control of his body and tried to think through the implications of the battle in progress. He radioed his position and situation quickly to Hasanuddin AFB. They asked him to clarify. He ignored the request. Aviate, navigate, communicate, he reminded himself, the three most important things for a pilot to remember, in their order of importance. Remembering the maxim from his early training days reassured him. But where was the avoid-incoming-missiles-at-all-costs bit? he asked himself, elated by his improbable escape from certain death.

Shidyahan pondered the origin of the enemy aircraft

he'd seen on his screen. Given that they were probably somehow related to the sighting of the Osprey, and that the Osprey itself was only in service with American forces, that meant he was up against the US army, navy or air force. The United States of America, shooting missiles at him within the airspace of his own country!? Shidyahan's fear turned to anger. He tightened his shoulder straps.

Three bandits winked out on Toad's radar screen. Two. Three. Four. Where was bandit number one? Shit. Bandit one must have outrun its AMRAAM. And the pilot in that plane had had less time to react than the other three. Yes, there he was, number one, painted on his display. He must have gone low. And survived. He silently toasted the F-16 pilot's good luck and obvious skill. The bastard should buy himself a lottery ticket, Toad thought.

On his display, Toad saw the three surviving aircraft turn towards him. Shit, he thought, that was definitely not a good sign. Those guys would be seriously pissed. He wished he had more AMRAAMs under his wings, or more aircraft in his flight. It was time to bug out. Carefully. Museum piece or not, the F-16 was a formidable enemy in the right hands, even an F-16A armed only with AIM-9s and guns. And, as he'd just witnessed, at least one of those guys could fly it. That meant their training was probably pretty good across the board.

He was checking his weapons stores again; a couple of AIM-9Ms and the gun, just as the picture presented on the small screen display went blank. What the hell . . . ? The transmission to the AV-8s from the AWACs had suddenly been cut. Just when I need them most, those bastards break for lunch, Toad fumed. He was in the process of cursing them out loud when he saw why the link had gone down. He'd just put the towering volcano between himself and the AWACS, and one thing radio waves would not penetrate was solid rock. He checked his fuel stores. Christ, they were getting marginal. His flight was now being stalked by a force that was numerically superior, and on their home turf. And he'd lost his link to the AWACS. Definitely time to bug out, thought Toad. But where the hell was that slow-mover, the V22?

The V22 accelerated to around 100 knots as it barrelled into a volcanic channel. The pilot swung through a tight turn in the channel at sixty degrees angle of bank. The bend in the channel tightened, forcing the Osprey to make a tighter, higher-g turn. The wall of the channel edged closer to the outside wing, threatening to clip it, and then suddenly it widened, allowing the aircraft to slip through unscathed. Ahead, the walls narrowed again. The pilot and co-pilot hoped the channel would lead away from the volcano, rather than snake back towards it.

It was difficult to know what was going on. Suryei couldn't rely on her inner ear for bearings at all. She couldn't see a horizon line; the window was small, revealing little detail. At one stage she was convinced they were flying nearly straight up, and then the aircraft felt like it was falling backwards. It was a very awkward motion, and bad news for her stomach. Suryei retched bile. She had never suffered from airsickness before and it was not a pleasant feeling.

A flash of green coloured the small window diagonally opposite. The blue of the sky followed. Then black rocks. She worked out that the aircraft was banking savagely through a narrow passage. Suryei wondered if there'd be any warning before they hit a mountain. Probably not, she thought, if they hit it head-on.

She remembered looking into the muzzle of the Indonesian soldier's rifle and knowing that she was about to die. Her attitude at the time had been one of resignation to her fate. She remembered feeling beyond fear. Death had failed to panic her. It was the same now. Airsickness, however, was something else entirely. The thought of dying gave her some relief. Her stomach convulsed, but nothing came up.

The V22 jinked violently up and down, then banked sharply left. It was a wild ride and Suryei found it an effort keeping her head from lolling about uncontrollably. The pressure was on her shoulder straps – they were holding her down in her seat. Her stomach felt light, as if it was trying to find its way up and out of her mouth. She retched again dryly into the bag. She was then forced the other way, driven into her seat, the air forced out of her lungs and her eyeballs squashed into their sockets. She tried to lift her hand out of her lap and found it impossible. It seemed to weigh four or five times more than usual. Suryei tried holding her breath to stop the heaves. It didn't help and she vomited through her nostrils instead.

Toad called up the V22 and got the aircraft's position. They were all participants in a game not unlike chess, where the individual pieces were capable of moving in specific and particular ways. The slow-mover was somewhere directly below him. Now, where were those bandits? Then just as quickly as it went down, the display on his screen came back up.

Shit! The F-16s were coming up behind the V22! Jesus, they'd managed to get there damn quick. Toad immediately rolled inverted and fed back pressure into the stick. His wingman followed. The AV-8s both pulled five-g half loops and accelerated towards the F-16s. The V22 Osprey was his responsibility. He was there to protect it, which meant getting it back on friendly ground in one piece; and with its cargo alive and kicking. There was a time to fight and a time to run. With no BVR missiles left, it was definitely time for the latter, but not until the V22 was secure.

Unfortunately, while the AV-8s could sprint away at the speed of sound, around 580 knots at sea level, the V22 had its balls hanging out at around 270 to 280 knots. With a top speed of well over 1000 knots, an F-16 would mow them down. There was no alternative but to engage the Indons and either try to shoot them out of the sky or persuade them to go home. Toad and his wingman were above and behind the F-16s. With a bit of luck, the Indons' radar might not have picked them up.

As only Murphy's Law could predict, Major Shidyahan crossed over the end of the channel at the same time as the V22 exited it. Shidyahan's eyes went wide at his sheer good fortune when he looked over the nose of his Falcon and saw the V22 sitting in his one o'clock low position like a fat grey cockroach waiting to be stomped on. He selected heaters and went for a tone. He couldn't get one. The angle was rear three-quarter. Perhaps the thing's engines weren't radiating enough heat for a lock. Shidyahan toggled through to gun mode. He had to be quick. His mind calculated angles and speeds. With a little deft feathering of the throttle, he might just manage to get off a burst of cannon into the odd-looking aircraft before overshooting it.

The V22 shook as a handful of 20 mm shells ripped into it and exploded, punching jagged holes in the fuselage and across the upper wing. The V22 staggered and the engine pitch heaved to a different, desperate note. Oil and smoke exploded with a ball of orange flame from the port engine. The sudden change in torque loadings threw the aircraft into a temporarily divergent flight path. The odd motion brought the paper bag back in front of Suryei's face. She took a quick look around. No one seemed hurt, but she could see blue sky through the ragged holes in the ceiling.

Toad did a conversion turn, another half loop, putting his AV-8 on an F-16's tail. The Indon was already pulling up into a high-g yo-yo, positioning itself for another run at the Osprey. Whatever damage it was capable of causing on its first pass was done and there was nothing Toad could do about it. He swore and hoped that the V22 was not in a terminal state.

Suryei's eyes nervously flicked over the V22's interior. The SAS soldiers were all in their seats. Astonishingly, one of them, Ellis, Lance Corporal Ellis – yes, that was his name – was asleep, a little drool running from one corner of his mouth onto the headrest. She wanted to kick him awake.

On the flight deck, the pilots quickly brought the aircraft back under control. They realised they'd been hit when a ribbon of tracer arced across the nose of the plane and the airframe shook with impacts. This was the first time the V22 had seen action, let alone received battle damage. They were now way outside the aircraft's test envelope, charting territory only explored in simulation. How she would perform in the real world was a mystery that would now be revealed. The instruments indicated that the port engine was next to useless. Oil pressure was nonexistent and the temps were well into the red. Fuel pressure was dropping. Fortunately, the starboard engine appeared to be running sweetly with temps and pressures all normal.

The co-pilot shut the port engine down while the captain went to full power on the remaining turbofan. A shaft running through the Osprey's wing automatically transferred power from the good engine to the failed engine's rotor, preventing the torque imbalance that would have made the aircraft virtually impossible to fly.

The Osprey's pilots were surprised at how well the aircraft took the damage. The flight computers had assessed the radically altered static and dynamic loads on the aircraft and adjusted the outputs to the control surfaces accordingly. They'd had this sort of scenario in the simulator, of course. It was reassuring, and somewhat surprising given the plane's uncertain flight test history, to know that, for once, reality was presenting nothing different to the virtual.

The engine nacelles had only just finished transitioning to the horizontal position, the V22 approaching its cruising speed, when the aircraft took the hits. The Osprey had immediately dived for the nearest cover, a deep ravine at right angles to its track, and in the opposite direction to that of the three F-16s that ripped through the air overhead.

Going on the offensive was Toad's only alternative. No communication with the Osprey was necessary; they could all see each other on their radar screens courtesy of the AWACS. Unseen by the Indon pilots, he accelerated quickly to the AV-8's maximum velocity and shot under the F-16s as they climbed. The AV-8s reached a low escarpment with an overhang just as the F-16s completed their 180-degree course change, flying inverted high overhead. Toad and his wingman threw their thrust vectors into reverse, bringing their aircraft to such a violent negative-g stop that their eyeballs felt as if they would be plucked out of their sockets. Toad hovered there with his wingman, hidden from the F-16s by the overhang, and watched horrified as their fuel levels dropped before their eyes, the AV-8's Pegasus engines gulping through the juice like dehydrated athletes after a long race.

Major Shidyahan was feeling angry and vengeful and, he had to admit, also pretty damn good for the first time all day. He had an enemy to shoot at, at last. And he also knew pretty much where that enemy would be – somewhere in his slipstream. He didn't care who they were. They had fired on him, murdered his comrades, wrecked his squadron's beautiful F-16s. He would kill them for it.

The F-16 was responding well to his commands. Today, Major Shidyahan was at one with the aircraft. Had he not just evaded a deadly AMRAAM? He would be the toast of his squadron tonight. Maybe even a little secret alcohol perhaps? He had time to reflect on the hero's welcome he would receive as the F-16's nose came around. The V22 was just where he knew it would be, in his sights, even though it was trying to evade him by diving down another channel. This time, there'd be no overshoot. He selected heaters and closed for the kill.

Shidyahan throttled back. He wanted to make absolutely sure this time, but then the fear that every fighter pilot gets of something hiding in his six, in the blind spot behind him, filled him with a moment of paranoia and made the flesh on the back of his neck tingle. He glanced around, straining as he tried to take in as much sky as possible. The Falcon's bubble canopy provided panoramic views, but when a threat could come from any quarter, the view was never perfect.

The F-16 roared over the ledge shielding Toad and his wingman from sight. Toad smiled as the F-16 shot past. The hunted was now the hunter. He'd lost the ACI from the AWACS again but this time he was prepared for it. He made a brief call to his wingman to sort out targets. When they were both a suitable distance behind the F-16s, they selected their AIM-9s, and counted down from three. At zero, both brought their missiles' infrared targeting systems to bear on the opposite outside F-16s, which they chose for maximum weapons separation. It took less than a second for the locked-on tone to sound in their headphones, indicating that their missiles had chosen a target. Toad and his wingman pressed the fire buttons on their control side sticks simultaneously. The missiles instantly accelerated from their wingtip rails.

The two targeted F-16s had time to make panicked half-turns away from the centre aircraft before the high-explosive warheads in the AIM-9s detonated behind their engines. The lock tone provided by the F-16s' threat indicators barely gave the pilots any time to react, let alone begin effective evasion. Toad watched both aviators eject as their crippled aircraft nosed forward and broke up in the sky, rolling over into fireballs and spraying the canopy below with liquid flame and molten aluminium.

Major Shidyahan bugged out of the engagement. He had flown in with five other aircraft, the pride of the TNI-AU, with men he had loved and respected as fine aviators, professionals and warriors. Now, most of those comrades were dead, and all the aircraft except his had been shot down. Shidyahan was filled with rage and frustration. He was against a force with superior weapons and tactics and he felt he had no choice. Whatever these people – these Americans – were doing illegally in Indonesian airspace, he was powerless to prevent. The major executed a 180-degree turn just as his engines started sucking vapour. *Fuel!* He couldn't remember hearing the low-fuel warnings in his headphones. He tried to gain as much height as he could but his airspeed was low. There was no alternative and he pulled the ejection handles. The bubble canopy blew off and rocket charges blasted the major's seat clear of the doomed aircraft.

'Ferret Leader. Ferret Rotor. We have cannon shell damage and falling fuel gauges. We will need a tanker in approximately thirty minutes.'

Jesus! The V22 had indeed taken hits. 'Roger that, Ferret Rotor,' Toad responded. This sortie was going to hell, just as things were starting to look up.

'Ferret Handler. Bandits. Bandits. Bandits. Seven. Repeat seven. West. Eighty-five miles. Angels ten. Heading zero-niner-zero.'

Toad wished he hadn't tempted the Big Feller Upstairs by blaspheming. Things were about to get really fucking hot.

The call from Ferret Handler, the AWACS, sounded mighty familiar. It was almost identical to the call that had announced the arrival of the previous flight of F-16s. Only this time there were more bandits, and he had only one missile left, and merely a heater at that.

They really had to get the hell out of Dodge now. Toad's eyeballs stood out on stalks when he checked his fuel pressure. It was touch and go whether he'd even make it back to the tanker, let alone a friendly carrier deck. He looked across at his wingman and got a hand signal for low fuel from him. Fuck-all ordnance, fuck-all fuel. They wouldn't last another round of air-to-air combat.

'Ferret Rotor. Are you airworthy?' Toad enquired.

'Affirmative, Ferret Leader. Some damage. One engine gone. She's flying well but losing fuel.'

'Ferret Rotor. Time to go. Do you have a maximum estimated cruise speed?'

'Estimate cruise two-fife-zero . . .'

Toad was impressed. The V22 had taken hits, lost an engine, and had who knows what other damage, yet it was still capable of flying at 250 knots, only a handful of knots shy of the maximum cruise speed available when both engines were turning. Toad had that clammy feeling on the back of his neck. The fresh Indon fighters could jump them at any time, and probably would. There was nothing they could do about it, except fly as low and as fast as they could, hugging the ground where radar was least effective. And keep their fingers crossed.

Toad saw on his screen the seven bandits approaching from the west at 3000 metres. About three minutes remained to interception. Toad guessed that they would be able to survive the first pass – maybe – but the V22's goose was cooked. Their options had run out. It was goodnight.

Then six new idents appeared on the screen, closing on the group of fighters from the east at frightening speed. The Indonesian planes scattered like chaff before them.

Toad looked up and saw six missiles cross the sky 1000 metres above him from right to left: AMRAAMs. Jesus – a beautiful sight.

'Finger-lickin', this is Hound dog inbound from the east. Apologies for the dee-lay,' drawled the thick Louisiana accent.

Major Toad Sanders was up for Colonel and the word was out. Colonel Sanders. He smiled. It wasn't the first time he'd heard jokes about changing his call sign from Toad to Finger-lickin', or even Secret Herbs and Spices, for Christ's sake!

Three new idents appeared on Toad's screen, inbound at phenomenal speed. Super Hornets. The navy's new all-purpose attack fighter. A beautiful plane. In fact, Toad had to admit that he would have welcomed even a few determined Cessnas.

The Indonesian fighters were dispersing, the fate of the last flight of F-16s having stolen their bravado. They departed as quickly as full afterburner could take them. Two AMRAAMs found their marks. The other four timed out, but their job was done.

Three F/A-18Es lined up beside the AV-8s and saluted Toad and his wingman. Toad acknowledged the salute from the naval aviators with a wave. Navy dweebs. At that moment, he loved every damn one of the sons of bitches. They would take over the duty of sweeping for the V22. The Super Hornets peeled away from the formation. Toad radioed the tanker to stand by. It was unlikely he'd make it unless the tanker could meet him inside Indonesian airspace. As it was, he'd be flying on fumes, and his wingman was in the same shit.

As the Indonesian coastline slid behind the V22, its passing was acknowledged by the Australians with relief. But the news wasn't all good. Curry was dead. Beck had been out of his seat as soon as the plane had stopped bouncing through the sky. He'd worked feverishly by Curry's side for a minute but couldn't do anything for him. Shrapnel from one of the exploding shells had entered his skull behind the ear, severing the spinal cord before exiting.

Suryei looked on helplessly. There was no justice in it. The man was an easy victim, held down by straps in the stretcher so that death couldn't miss. She looked up at the flapping fabric around the holes in the aircraft's ceiling and tempered her criticism of the fates. Most, if not all of them, had been bloody lucky. They could easily have been blown out of the sky, or a shell could have found her. Joe opened his eyes and forced a smile. 'The feature over yet?' he asked, sweat sheening his forehead.

Joe was always ready with a quip, thought Suryei. She liked that. Mostly, she reminded herself. 'How you feeling?'

'Only hurts when I breathe.' Joe shifted slightly in his seat, the pain disfiguring his face.

'You want another shot?' she asked.

'No thanks. Gives you bad dreams. Been in a plane crash, shot at . . . Bloody scary.' The aircraft hit a pocket of turbulence jolting Joe in an awkward way. The pain almost made him pass out. 'Well, maybe a bit later,' he said, grunting with the effort needed to keep the pain under control.

Wilkes returned to his seat, sliding in beside Suryei. He was angry about losing Curry. Angry at himself, although he knew that wasn't very logical. What could he have done? It was just bad luck. At least Curry would have died instantly.

Wilkes reflected on the mission. It had already taken on the perspective of a dream half remembered. The whole thing seemed surreal, vicious.

Suryei was frowning, examining the blood and dirt crusted on Wilkes's face. He felt her eyes on him. 'I'm okay,' he said, before she could ask. He'd completely forgotten about his own wound. His nerve endings were still numb from the shock. 'Cut myself shaving.' Wilkes looked across at the bodies of Curry and Gibson, rocking gently with the motion of the aircraft. He recalled their faces. Gibbo and Curry. They'd been mates. All the men in his section were mates. They risked their lives together, drank together, lived and died together. It was difficult losing people you were close to, but he'd lost them before and, no doubt, he'd lose more in the future. But that knowledge did nothing to ease the regret.

More than a few men had died on this day, and not just Australians. The Indonesian soldiers and airmen – they were just doing their job. It was their territory and they were just defending it against uninvited intruders.

McBride appeared beside Wilkes. Neither of the men had their headphones on. There was now a lot of noise in the cabin caused by the airflow ripping through the holes in the fuselage. The cacophony gave them privacy. 'Everyone else okay, mate?' shouted the captain.

There's that word . . . 'mai-yt'. Jesus, the Yanks sure knew how to murder the English language. There was something about this captain that didn't fit, things he'd said. McBride had known his identity when they'd arrived at the carrier – so right from the first, something had been wrong about this bloke. Also, he seemed more informed about the mission and what had led up to it than a captain in the Marines had a right to be. *We've got a proper military sat on this for you now . . .* Wilkes was not even aware that the satellite intelligence he had in his possession was anything other than military. And then there was that comment as they'd come aboard just now: *Joe Light, alive! Amazing!* What was so special about Joe? Wilkes decided to go fishing. 'What have you got to do with all this, McBride? You're not a Marines captain, are you?'

McBride's smile disappeared, as if a cloud had passed over his face. He held Wilkes's stare. 'Yes. And no.'

'What does that mean?'

'It's not important.'

'Bullshit! What can it hurt, Charles – Chuck – if that's your real name?' Wilkes knew he was right. The captain, if he was a captain, was more than likely some kind of agency spook. But whose? 'Look,' he said, holding his temper in check, 'there are more than four hundred dead people back there. I've lost two men. I want to know why they had to die. I've got a feeling you have the answer to that. So tell me! What the hell's going on here?' It wasn't often that Wilkes got angry, but he was working himself up to it.

What would it hurt? thought the captain. There wasn't much he could or would divulge about the NSA, but there was nothing really preventing him from giving up his cover. And the sergeant had a point. He'd certainly earned the right to know more than he did. 'Look, Sarge, there ain't nothin' sinister goin' on here. The name really is Charles McBride. Once upon a time I was a Marine looey working in special ops. Now I'm National Security Agency.'

'Well thank you, Chuck. Nice to meet the real you,'

said Wilkes sarcastically. 'What's the NSA's interest in this shite?'

'We unravelled this puzzle – one of our guys back in Maryland. I'm out of Canberra, keeping an eye on things for SIGINT, Stateside. We don't usually get involved at this level, on the ground so to speak but, well, call it a reward for being on the ball. Fact is, all this caught everyone napping. The US has been building up its intel infrastructure throughout Asia over the last couple of years – since all those religious crackpots came out of the woodwork – but it seems we've still got a few gaping holes to fill. And a few lessons to learn. We should be able to put a country like Indonesia under the microscope and prevent this kind of thing from happening, but obviously we can't. Yet.' The captain shrugged.

'A stable Indonesia is important not just to the region, but to the world. A Muslim nation that's actually *friendly* to the West? No one wants *that* boat rocked. Now, if the wrong regime gets in power . . .' he raised his eyes to the ceiling, 'it could do a hell of a lot of damage throughout the rest of Asia, and the Muslim world. And that interests the hell out of us.'

Wilkes looked McBride over. He wasn't sure what answer he was expecting, but at least his hunch was proved right.

'He can tell you more than I can,' said the captain, nodding at Joe.

'I need to use that radio.' Wilkes looked around: it was Suryei. He saw the determination on her face, the grit that had kept the woman alive and out of the rifle sights of the Indonesian soldiers.

'I'm sorry, Miss, but there are no radio broadcasts, and

especially not until we're clear of Indonesian airspace,' said McBride, weighing in.

'No, *I'm* sorry but *you* don't understand.'

'Suryei, I know I said you could use the radio, but I have no clearance for that use.' Wilkes's tone suggested that argument was pointless. 'There are obviously security issues involved here that go way beyond my mission parameters.'

Suryei's temper flared. Jesus Christ! She hadn't survived the last three days to be patted on the head and told to run along. But then she thought that maybe these guys had their reasons for doing things. They did this stuff for a living. She calmed herself down and thought things through. Suryei wasn't sure about the American. But the Australian sergeant? She liked him. And she trusted him. Hadn't he just risked his life for her? Suryei wanted to pass on her knowledge, unburden herself, make someone else responsible. What she knew was too much for one person to keep secret. And who, exactly, was she going to call anyway? She didn't know anyone in power, except maybe her former editor. Jesus! She kicked herself. Of course, the paper!

'There's nothing stopping you from telling us,' Wilkes said.

Fair enough, thought Suryei. She could tell the man who'd saved her life. She owed him that much at the very least. Images from the past three days swam before her eyes. 'The plane crash. Surviving it was just luck. Then the Indonesian soldiers arrived. I thought they were there to rescue us. I told you – they shot an old couple in cold blood, survivors like Joe and me. I ran . . . Joe . . . ' It wasn't coming out quite as controlled as Suryei had hoped. She took a deep breath and steadied herself.

'Joe and I, we found one of the engines from the plane

in the jungle. We saw remains of a missile inside it – an Indonesian missile. Joe freaked. It suddenly all made sense to him.'

'What made sense to him?' asked Wilkes.

'*Why* the plane was shot down, the Indonesian soldiers hunting us. When Joe was back on the plane, he'd hacked into the Indonesian army's computer and found something they obviously wanted to keep to themselves. Somehow, the Indonesians traced the call back to the Qantas plane.'

McBride didn't know where to look. This conversation was getting dangerously close to US national security issues. He'd been briefed on COMPSTOMP. Its continued secrecy was imperative.

'What did he find?' Wilkes asked.

'Plans to invade Australia.'

'Shit!' said Wilkes.

'That's why they blew us out of the sky.'

McBride felt hot, sweat flaring on his forehead. The 747 had been shot down as an indirect result of the NSA's desire to earn an income outside of government funding. So many people were now dead because of that. He felt the urge to apologise, but couldn't. It was a desire and a failure he would have to live with. 'Have you any idea how much the authorities in Australia will want to put Joe through the wringer?' he said instead, changing the subject.

Suryei wasn't listening. She was seeing the invasion map Joe had described to her. Strangely, she visualised it in her head as if she'd been the one who'd found it. Australia was gone. In its place was Selatan Irian Jaya, Southern High Victory. When? When would the invasion begin?

Parliament House, Canberra, 1010 Zulu, Friday, 1 May

The lights had already been lowered in the theatrette when Niven entered and his eyes were only now adjusting to the gloom. A rear projection screen television sat on the stage. A rectangle of yellow light blazed as Greenway entered. He was a couple of minutes late and mumbled an apology, but Lurch hadn't missed anything.

The screen flashed into life. The videocamera had been positioned so that its view took in Roger Bowman, Australia's ambassador to Indonesia, sitting beside a man propped up in a hospital bed. The patient's head was heavily bandaged and his eyes were a rich red from burst capillaries. What skin could be seen was bruised the colour of a plum. The corners of the man's mouth were set grimly downwards.

The men in Canberra leaned forward in their seats expectantly. This was one videoconference they *hadn't* expected. But as Bowman had just finished explaining, the doctors had told him that the human brain was an unknown quantity. No one had expected the general to come out of his coma for some time but, once the anaesthetic had worn off after the operation, his eyes had miraculously popped open. The general was groggy, but even that was wearing off quickly.

He had demanded to talk to Bowman who, of course, was particularly keen to hear what the Indonesian officer had to say for himself. Fortunately, it didn't seem that the man's memory had been impaired in the least.

Bowman cleared his throat. 'We got that security detail you sent over, Spike. I've had the general moved back to the embassy, against doctor's orders I might add. There were too many people sniffing about for my liking and it's difficult to explain the presence of half a dozen armed Aussie soldiers in a local hospital.'

Bowman paused and checked his notes. Satisfied that he'd completed the housekeeping, he cleared his throat again and cut to the chase. 'General Masri has asked for asylum and protection in Australia, for himself and his boy, as quid pro quo for enlightening us on what the hell has been going on,' said the ambassador.

The Prime Minister was angry. 'Jesus, I damn well want to hear what the bastard has to say for himself before I start handing out any bloody bonuses.'

Masri considered that before nodding.

The Australians had hastily decided to tell the general a little of what they knew, to throw him off his guard. Blight began. 'General, we are already aware that your air force shot down our 747,' he said. 'Did your government know anything about that?'

In heavily accented English, Masri replied, 'No. The government knew only what General Suluang told them, which was nothing.'

A wave of relief surged over the PM. Niven whistled at the audacity of Indonesia's military, but he was also relieved to have unequivocal confirmation of Griffin's belief that Jakarta was not involved in the act.

'The plane was not part of the plan. I did not agree with it,' Masri said.

The men in the room in Canberra exchanged glances. The word 'plan' was intriguing. 'What "plan"?' asked the PM, getting the question in first.

Masri looked around him, shifting his red eyes left and

right, as though he was about to pass something illicit in the street. 'The plan to take back political control of Indonesia.'

'A coup d'etat? That's what this is all about?' asked Niven incredulously.

Masri nodded. 'Traditionally it has been the·armed forces that have guided Indonesia. We have enjoyed a certain amount of respectful fear, which has helped to keep our country united. East Timor put an end to that. Your country put an end to that –'

'What complete crap!' Blight said angrily. There was no excuse for this cowardly, murderous act.

The Indonesian general ignored the Prime Minister's outburst. 'And that is why we planned a limited invasion of Australia.'

'What?!' exclaimed Niven and the PM in unison. Greenway and Griffin leapt to their feet as if something had bitten them.

'Jesus Christ, what . . . how?!' asked Griffin, his brain going into shock.

There it was, thought Niven: the motive. The Indonesian generals had murdered the passengers of QF-1 to keep their outrageous plan hidden.

'Invading Australia would be good politically,' Masri continued calmly.

'Good politically?' said the PM apoplectically, fighting a mixture of disbelief and outrage.

'The army has become the people's enemy. In some areas, the army has even become afraid of the people, because the people are no longer afraid of the army. Provinces in Indonesia are threatening secession. There is much killing and lawlessness.'

'How could invading Australia possibly help your domestic problems?' Griffin asked, horrified, but knowing at the same time that there was a mad logic to it.

'The army must regain face within our own country. To achieve that, we need a focus *outside* Indonesia. You think you are part of Asia when it suits you to think that way. But you are full of yourselves. You patronise us. You act like moral policemen. Look at East Timor. Bali too. You didn't even trust us to root out the criminals, even suggested using your troops to hunt terrorists in Java! You think you have the right to behave this way. Why? You think you are superior, because you are *white*!' Masri almost spat that final word.

'We aren't bloody racists. Your inferiority complex is in your own bloody heads.' Blight was working hard to keep his temper in check.

'See? It is always our fault.'

'But we're not invading *your* country!' said Blight, exasperated.

Niven fought back a wry smile. As they spoke, it was the Australian armed forces that were doing the invading, on the ground in Sulawesi.

'Then what do you call sending troops to East Timor? It was part of my country, not yours,' said Masri, face calm, belying the anger underlining his words. Niven thought he looked positively demonic with those deeply bloodshot eyes.

Blight breathed heavily, heart pumping like an old diesel motor.

'If we launched an attack against Australia, our people would applaud it. They would once again be proud of Indonesia. And the military. And perhaps it might also teach a lesson to the provinces that want to secede. Such an action – bold and decisive – would establish a context for our return to political as well as military pre-eminence in Indonesia. Fear and respect would be restored. And the army would no longer need to suppress its own people.'

'Yes, but at the bloody expense of killing ours,' said the Prime Minister in dismay. The Indonesian soldier showed no reaction. This was a mad scheme cooked up by lunatics and criminals. Australia's actions in East Timor could not be blamed for it. East Timor should never have been part of Indonesia's empire and the Australian government of the day had merely righted an old wrong by supporting its desire for independence. And now East Timor had that – nationhood – those actions had been vindicated.

'Are the plans for the invasion well advanced?' asked Niven, getting back to military specifics.

'Yes.'

'Was there a firm date?'

'No.'

'You couldn't take the whole country. What were the aims?' continued the air vice marshal, morbidly fascinated.

'It was to be a limited invasion. We planned an amphibious attack against Darwin and an airborne assault on Townsville. We would neutralise your military assets in both places, humble your arrogant Ready Reaction Force.'

Everyone witnessing this bizarre confession wanted to believe the general's story was nothing more than that, a fantastic story, a fairy tale, but it was horrifyingly real, as the friends, family and relatives of the passengers of flight QF-1 would be able to attest.

'Assuming the attacks were successful and you achieved these aims, what next?' asked Griffin.

'We would demand one thing, and one thing only, before a full withdrawal.'

'And that would be . . . ?' The PM cocked his head. This would be interesting. He had to admit he was intrigued.

'A guarantee that Australia will never again become involved in the internal politics of Indonesia.'

'What . . . ? Is . . . is that bloody all?' asked the PM, stunned, as was everyone else in the room. When he saw on the face of the general that it was indeed 'all', a hot anger filled him. 'You mean you'd invade our goddam country, kill I don't know how many people, just to get a goddam bloody assurance we'd gladly give you anyway?'

'Yes.'

'That is absolutely fucking crazy. Why?' continued the PM, experiencing a kind of sensory overload.

'For the effect it would have on our own people. As I said, it would re-establish the military's strength.'

The Australians sat back in their seats, their minds clouded with outrage. It was true – had to be true. Here was one of the conspirators laying it all out for them. Indonesia planned to invade Australia! That was bad enough, but the reason for it? Nothing more than a bit of a show for their countrymen. The irony was that, if not for the crashed Qantas plane and the deaths of all those innocent people, they never would have found out about it until it was too late.

The men let the incredible tale sink in, and struggled with their own thoughts.

'Who else was in your merry band, general? Who were the other co-conspirators?' Niven wanted to know. Something would have to be done about neutralising them, and damn quickly.

Masri swallowed and appeared nervous. No matter what the circumstances, giving up comrades was painful. 'Besides myself and General Suluang, there was Lanti Rajasa, Colonel Javid Jayakatong, Admiral Sampurno Siwalette, and air force Colonel Ari Ajirake.'

Niven pinched the bridge of his nose and closed his eyes. He knew nearly all these men by reputation. They were good soldiers, members of the Indonesian parliament, and commanded a considerable chunk of Indonesia's armed forces between them. The exception was Lanti Rajasa. He was a policeman and not a soldier.

'How would you deploy your invasion forces? You don't have the assets for a major amphibious landing,' said Niven, curious about how the Indonesians intended to pull off that aspect of their plan.

'Ah . . . you are talking about conventional assets.' There was the barest hint of a smile on the Indonesian general's lips. 'In World War 1, the French delivered its troops to the Western Front in the cabs of Paris. Japan invaded Indo-China on bicycles in the Second World War. And Indonesia, as you know, has fishing boats. Many thousands of fishing boats.'

Suddenly, Niven knew exactly how they'd pull it off. And it was so bloody obvious, all the musings by defence academics and strategists had failed to consider it. 'Jesus . . .' he swallowed. The navy could barely cope with half a dozen slow, leaking refugee vessels at any one time. A flotilla of such boats – they would only need a few hundred or so – would swamp Australia's coastal warning systems. It would be impossible to determine which boats held troops and which did not; many would obviously be decoys. The new, over-the-horizon Jindalee radar would certainly provide information about the closing flotilla to Australia's armed forces, but there simply wouldn't be enough defence to go round. In a sense, there'd almost be too much information. The navy and air force would be overwhelmed.

The diverted Australian forces would be thrown into confusion, allowing the TNI-AU to drop paratroopers into Townsville. The aircraft would come in low, then pop up near the coastline, disgorging their soldiers. Divers could easily mine the navy ships bobbing unknowingly in Darwin harbour. It would probably all happen at night, or in the early morning, when reaction times were at their slowest. The Indonesian plan would probably succeed at the cost of possibly thousands of Australian lives. But they wouldn't be able to hold those positions for long. Their supply lines would be way too long and Australia would have the home-soil advantage and, hopefully, assistance from the US. But for a couple of days, maybe three or four until the home defences could rally with the help of a US Carrier Battle Group . . . yes, the TNI could do it.

'The border of East and West Timor would be very active too. Another diversion,' the general added.

'Of course,' said Niven distantly, his mind seeing clouds of parachutes in the skies over Townsville.

'Did you consider that the sort of action you're talking about would make your bloody country a pariah in the civilised world?' asked the PM, having difficulty believing educated men could formulate such an outlaw strategy. 'What do you think would happen to your trade links with other countries after you've invaded us?' The more the PM thought about it, the more indignant he became. 'The whole thing's bloody absurd . . . '

The general visibly stiffened. 'We've bounced back from the crash of '97. And we don't need direct links with the West for prosperity. We have trade through organisations and groups like ASEAN. We are Asian *and* Muslim. We have our own networks. We don't need Europeans to get on our feet.'

Masri appeared to sigh. 'I do not think much of your understanding of the situation, Mr Blight,' he said. 'Your country is too full of its own self-importance to see the world as it really is. You think America would rush to your aid?' From his tone, the general obviously believed that it wouldn't.

Blight felt uncomfortable, but he didn't take the general's bait.

'The US wants a stable Indonesia. That's its first priority. It talks democracy, but it wants stability more. Indonesia is a democracy at the moment, but this so-called freedom threatens our very existence. There are forces within that want the nation torn apart. And the government won't do anything about it, because it doesn't have the required strength. Religious fundamentalism is growing in voice and action. You have felt the effects of that yourselves. And, as you know, many provinces now openly demand secession. A strong military hand is the only answer. Indeed, it is in your interest. We would stop this disintegration. We see no other way. You might not like having a strong military government in the region, but what is the alternative?' Masri let the thought hang in the air before continuing. 'America would realise this, and do nothing.'

Griffin cleared his throat uncomfortably. He'd talked about Indonesia going down this path. He felt like he'd almost willed it to come to pass, but at the same time knew that was ridiculous.

'It sounds to me like you don't regret any of this. So why did you turn yourself over to our embassy?' asked Niven calmly.

'It was the attack on the Qantas plane,' said Masri, looking down at his hands. All at once, his demeanour changed from a proud general to that of a deeply disillusioned man.

'General Suluang told us a file containing invasion details was stolen over the Internet. The terrorist was traced to the plane. He had the aircraft shot down to keep the plan a secret.'

'You, personally, would happily invade Australia but not shoot down a plane?' said Griffin, that particular piece of logic seeming dubious to him.

'Yes, I'm a soldier and soldiers don't kill civilians. I'm tired of killing civilians. I'm a patriot, not a murderer,' said Masri, becoming more agitated. 'That's why I agreed to the coup – because I saw a way to end the bloodshed between my men and the people of Indonesia. But what Suluang did was murder and I wanted no part of it. That's why I've turned my back on him and the rest – why I'm here, talking to you. And there is something else you should know.' He slumped back down against his pillows, head forward, a ruined, beaten figure.

'And what's that?' asked the PM, ready for anything.

'There are survivors.'

'We know,' said the PM, relieved that it wasn't yet another bombshell. 'You told our ambassador after your car accident. You were semiconscious.'

Masri suddenly appeared disoriented. 'Did I also tell

you that Suluang's Kopassus are trying to find and kill them?'

'Yes,' said the PM.

Masri looked around nervously, unsure of what he might or might not have said when he was lying outside the embassy. 'General Suluang sent Kopassus to the crash site to secure it; to remove evidence of missile damage, and to ensure there were no witnesses. There were two survivors.'

Niven realised that his own mouth was slack. He swallowed. The general's confession was an astonishing window on desperation. He fought back the desire to sneeze and gave his nose a good blow into a tissue instead.

The Australians had agreed amongst themselves before the videoconference that they would not reveal to the general the dispatch of SAS troops to Sulawesi.

There was silence in the room. The general sat propped up in bed facing the camera, the bruised skin on his round, smooth face turned the consistency of putty by the videocamera's resolution. His eyebrows drooped over soft brown eyes and, despite the heavy bandage covering most of his head, the overall effect was surprisingly avuncular. Mao – Niven was aware of the general's nickname, and he could see the similarity. It was a friendly face. But appearances could be deceptive.

'Roger, I think we need to talk things over here for a bit,' said Blight, trying to get his head around some of the practical issues now facing Australia and, more specifically, the men gathered with him in front of the monitor.

'Okay, Bill. And General Masri . . . ?'

The general. What the hell were they going to do with the bastard? wondered Blight. He considered that before answering. 'General, for what it's worth, I think your plan was despicable. You're nothing more than a mass murderer.' He paused, fighting with himself. 'However, and I'm kicking myself for saying this, I also have to thank you for coming to us with this information. If you cooperate with us, you'll get asylum. But, I stress, that cooperation would be unconditional.'

The general nodded rigidly, with some obvious degree of discomfort that wasn't just physical.

'Roger, we'll get back to you when we have some bloody idea what to do next,' said Blight.

The ambassador nodded. 'I'll let you know if anything else turns up,' he said before the screen went blank.

There was a chorus of sighs in the room, as if everyone had been holding their breath.

The lights came up and the men squinted painfully.

'There's your motive – invasion. It almost makes a crazy kind of sense now,' said Niven.

'Yep,' said Griffin.

'Jesus. Where do we begin?' said Sharpe, shaking his head.

'We have the names of Masri's co-conspirators,' said Griffin, sifting through the interview. 'That's a start. It explains a lot, actually. Now we know why the TNI have been exercising pretty much constantly over the past year. And of course, the unstable political situation throughout Indonesia is ripe for military unrest. What's so bloody fantastic is the scope of the coup.'

'We're going to have to act fast,' said Niven. 'We have to assume their plans will be drastically brought forward. Things will start to unravel for these bastards very quickly now, and we can help that along. They're going to get desperate. And the only card we have to play is surprise.'

The Commander in Chief stood and resisted the temptation to stretch. An unexpected presence in the corner of his eye caught his attention. Niven had assumed that they were alone in the darkened theatrette, but they were not. It was Parno Batuta, the Indonesian ambassador, sitting up the back in the gloom, mopping the sweat from his face.

Niven turned back and caught the PM's eye. There was the slightest of smiles on Blight's lips and then it was gone. He'd been told the PM was a shrewd operator. Niven examined the ambassador's face again and knew Blight's gamble had paid off. Batuta's shock was transmuting to anger. The Australians would need to liaise with Jakarta on this treachery, and devise a counterattack against the Indonesian officers. In Batuta, they now had a willing emissary.

1500 feet AGL, Banda Sea, 1040 Zulu, Friday, 1 May

It all fitted together for Wilkes. The Indonesian army had been robbed of its dirty little secret and subsequent events were merely the attempts to stop it becoming common knowledge. He found the audacity of it almost impossible to believe, despite his experiences in East Timor where he'd witnessed the Indonesian military's behaviour first hand. But that was quite a few years ago, he reminded himself. Indonesia was supposed to be a different country now. The government was far more accountable – not like the Indonesia of old – and less inclined to resolve conflicts with a big stick. Wilkes found it difficult to believe they'd be capable of such obscene behaviour.

A war against a country as powerful and resourceful as Indonesia? It would be a bloody, vicious encounter. Australia's arsenal, if not state-of-the-art, was reasonably sophisticated. And its army was a professional force widely regarded for its fighting abilities. But it was comparatively small. Indonesia's army, however, was large. Certainly much of its equipment was old by Australia's standards but it could still do a hell of a lot of damage.

He pitted the two countries against each other in his head. It was a frightening thought. And if Suryei was right, it was far more than a thought. It could well be a reality.

The authorities back home must know what was coming their way. But maybe they didn't. Perhaps that's why he'd had such a feeling of disquiet at the briefing back in Dili – too many unasked questions, and too many questions without answers. What the hell, he shrugged. Having the extra information wouldn't have made this gig easier, or more difficult. And maybe they didn't know anything back home. If that was the case, then he was in charge of a most precious cargo.

Wilkes's fingers unconsciously went to his breast pocket and felt the hard outline of the plastic inside it. The disk surrendered by the Kopassus sergeant. He'd completely forgotten about it. The soldier had thought it important – important enough to hope it might secure his life.

Joe's side hurt badly. His body had cramped into the shape of the seat, his bones moulding to its contours. Any movement – any – was agonising. Every twitch from the aeroplane as it rode over air currents made him feel he would scream. He remembered the Australian soldier who'd fixed him up back in the jungle. That bloke had been very offhand about his wounds. He hadn't exactly said, 'Get up, ya bludger, it's only a flesh wound,' but almost. Christ. The morphine had worn off. At least, he hoped it had worn off. If he felt this bad with morphine still acting on his system, well, it didn't bear thinking about. He wondered if he should ask for another shot, but he didn't want to act the girl's blouse in this company. Just bloody well grin and bear it, he told himself. He forced himself to shift his body to a different position in the hope that he would find a more comfortable place in the seat. He didn't. The pain made him cross-eyed. Unseen by him, the wound in his back opened and a cup of crimson blood oozed out.

When Joe opened his eyes again after several minutes of keeping them squeezed shut, he saw Suryei, an Australian soldier and a black man hunched together. The soldier pulled out a disk from his breast pocket. Seeing it almost made Joe smile.

'Where'd you get that from?' he asked, trying not to grunt with the effort required to block out the stabbing sensation that shot through his side with every word. Christ, it seemed like every part of his body was somehow connected to his broken rib. He tested the theory and gave his eyelids an experimental blink. To his profound surprise, the action didn't hurt.

There was a fair bit of noise in the cabin, but Wilkes heard Joe's question above it as if there had been silence.

Joe gestured for a closer inspection of the disk but stopped a few inches into the movement when the pain caught. The sergeant leaned across and placed the disk in Joe's open hand.

'That's mine,' said Joe, to the astonishment of the soldier. 'All my rewritables are blue.' He turned it over. 'My trademark, see?' he said, indicating a logo on the reverse side, a caricature of Albert Einstein with dreadlocks and a nose-ring made from a lightning bolt.

Wilkes gave him an odd look.

'My on-line sign is Cee Squared, as in $e = mc^2$.' Joe read their concentration as confusion. ' "Cee" is the co-efficient for light. My name's Joe Light. Cee Squared, light?'

'Yeah, got it,' said Wilkes, vaguely resenting being spoon-fed the connection. 'The disk. What's on it?'

'Don't know. Could be anything. Where'd you find it?' asked Joe.

'On the people shooting at you.'

Jesus, thought Joe, his brain working at half speed. It must have been picked up at the crash site. No, the Indonesians must have actively *searched* for it. They must have known which seat he'd occupied – easy information to obtain. The Indonesians could have done a little hacking of their own and lifted it from the Qantas server. But how had they known Joe Light had done the hacking? Was it feasible, possible, that the call had been traced? Not only that but his identity known? No it wasn't, he told himself. Or was it?

Wilkes and Suryei reached for the disk. 'Is this *the* disk? The one you saved the map to?' asked Suryei.

Joe shrugged slightly and squinted with the pain-spike the movement caused. He hoped like hell that the disk was blank. If it held the information he'd lifted from the TNI general's server, there was no way he'd ever be able to convince himself that his actions – and his actions alone – hadn't caused the horrible deaths of so many innocent people in the plane crash. The fact that finding the general's plans might also have prevented a war was too abstract. Too many ifs, buts and maybes.

The four hundred passengers left behind in the Indonesian jungle were an awful fact – unequivocal, irrefutable. It aided his conscience immeasurably to speculate that just maybe something else could have caused the crash. He didn't want to have to carry around the terrible burden of so many innocent deaths for the rest of his life. 'Can you run it?' he asked, hoping they couldn't.

Wilkes nodded and handed the disk to McBride. 'How about it?'

The captain paused, uncertain.

'Look, pal,' said Wilkes impatiently, sweat, dirt and blood combining with the wicked gash on his cheek to give him the appearance of some kind of horror film creature. 'All of us are cleared for this kind of stuff. As for Joe and Suryei here, I think they've paid their dues. So don't give me any of your top secret national security crap, okay?'

McBride took the rebuke on the chin. Wilkes was morally right, although his own superiors would no doubt think differently. He shrugged mentally, and tapped the disk on his thumb while he walked from sight into the forward comms compartment. Wilkes instantly regretted handing over the disk. This American spook could switch it, wipe it – anything. He didn't know much about the NSA or how it operated beyond the fact that it was enormously powerful, and apparently all-pervasive.

A dull white square of projected light appeared on the bulkhead that doubled as a screen. Static scrambled across it. The soldiers all looked up, expectantly. A few floaters drifted lazily down the screen. The audio channel came to life with a bottomless atmosphere. The air in the V22 was charged with electricity. The men craned their necks from side to side to get a better view over the heads in front. After a pause, a violin hummed a single high note and held it for several seconds. A chord of music from an electric guitar crashed through the headphones and the speaker boxes hidden throughout the aircraft. Then the vocals came, screamed by a man who sounded as if he was in agony.

Take my life on the point of your knife,
Show me a war, the World Bank's whore,
Where you come from, man, is full of sin.
Who do you thank,
when you're shot point blank?
Blood soaked earth, yeah, blood soaked earth . . .
    whoa, blood soaked . . .

The music fell abruptly to silence, the wall of sound seeming to echo through the aircraft. The soldiers, who had, until a moment ago, been drifting in and out of their own thoughts, were sitting forward in their seats, puzzled, their senses assaulted by the thrash coming through their headphones and the speakers. McBride put his head round the corner and apologised for the one hundred decibels of heavy-metal rock and roll. 'Sorry, guys,' he said almost comically.

The American made his way back to Wilkes, Suryei and Joe. He handed the disk to Wilkes. 'Just a bit of audio streaming. Nothing else on it.'

Joe held his hand out for the disk. Wilkes intercepted it and turned it over, examining it again.

'I was listening to that track in the plane before . . . you know . . .' Joe stumbled over his words. He tried to remember the hour before the 747 began its dive. Where had he saved those files to? It was possible that they were indeed captured on the disk in his hand, but saved as background, a little trick he'd learned from the games fraternity for concealing cheat codes. A battle raged in his conscience. The side of certainty ultimately won. Joe had to know.

'Paper and a pen . . . ' he grunted.

McBride provided him with a notebook and pencil. With obvious discomfort, Joe scribbled a DOS command on it and handed it back. 'Try that.'

Joe stared at the empty square of projected white space on the bulkhead and hoped it would stay that way.

Something flashed up and then disappeared, a ghost image. Floaters again drifted slowly from top to bottom. And then, suddenly, there it was. The map.

It depicted South-East Asia and northern Australia. Rough arrows drawn in black squeaker pen flashed dramatically here and there. Darwin and Townsville were obvious areas of interest, for that's where many of the arrows ended. Notes were hurriedly scribbled in the margin in Indonesian, none of which Joe understood. Australia was called Selatan Irian Jaya, Southern High Victory. He knew that much. Joe swallowed, drily. Suryei was transfixed. Wilkes, McBride and the rest found it hard to believe their eyes.

Ellis caught Wilkes's attention, gesturing at him to put his headphones on. Wilkes briefly put his ear in one of the cups.

'Suryei,' he said, tapping her gently on the shoulder,

breaking into her amazement, 'I've just been told we're out of Indonesian airspace. But I'm afraid I can't allow you to call anyone.'

Suryei nodded. There was no point arguing. She had the biggest story of her life, but it wasn't hers to tell. There was plainly much at stake for both Australia and Indonesia. The implications of spreading her knowledge vicariously through the media would profoundly affect events in ways she did not want to be responsible for. Truth, black and white. Grey. How would the papers deal with the astonishing revelations? Besides, she had done her bit. She had survived against impossible odds, and so had Joe. They had somehow managed to escape death many times; perhaps, the fates had ruled, just so they could bring the facts out of the jungle.

Now Wilkes and McBride had those facts. She was absolved of further responsibility. They could be the messengers now.

The realisation that she was no longer responsible for protecting the truth had a profound effect on Suryei. Suddenly, she felt bone-weary. She understood that expression for the first time in her life, because she was exhausted right to her core. It was almost impossible to move. The chair was warm and comfortable and she felt safe. Joe was next to her, eyes squeezed tightly shut, a grimace distorting his mouth. She wanted to put her arm around him and comfort him, only she knew doing so would probably make him scream. Every muscle in her body ached. Her eyes were hot and dry. She allowed herself to close them and was instantly asleep.

When the news of the rescue came through, a feeling of triumph swept the room. Something positive, at last. But the handshaking and the smiling had subsided quickly. Too many people had died over the past few days for overt expressions of joy. And two more Australians had lost their lives, members of the SAS. Apparently, the butcher's bill on the Indonesian side was far worse.

The survivors had been found and both were reasonably healthy. Remarkable, considering their ordeal. More astonishing was the twist that one of those survivors was the young man who had started this deadly snowball rolling, one Cee Squared, Joe Light. What were the chances of that? Somehow, one in around four hundred didn't seem to do the unlikely event justice. That was a bonus. He was a fact of life the non-believers within the DPRD wouldn't be able to deny. Not only that, there was apparently an overview of the invasion captured on disk, the very thing the 747 was shot down to keep secret. It was an incredible stroke of luck.

There was no doubt in Niven's mind that Joe Light was a hero. If not for him, perhaps the first indication of the invasion would have been the fishing boats swamping the northern Australian coastline.

'This isn't a triumph, Air Vice Marshal,' said Sharpe. 'It's a bloody disaster.'

'What's on your mind, Phil?' Niven asked, distracted.

'What are you going to do with these survivors?'

'Ever heard the phrase, "and they lived happily ever after"?'

'Don't be naive. I'd be thinking very carefully if I were you about the wisdom of letting someone like Joe Light loose on the national media.'

'I'm afraid he's right, Spike.' Blight had his arms folded – the body language said it all. 'The details of the last three days – the reasons for the crash – have to be kept out of the public domain.'

'Bill, I don't think it would be possible to keep it quiet,' said Niven, his respect for the Prime Minister on the verge of dissolving.

The CDF knew he wouldn't win the political argument against the Prime Minister. He wondered how much Sharpe had been in the PM's ear. If these men were thinking cover-up, survivors presented a problem. What were they going to do with them? And then the penny dropped. *Jesus Christ, we've just lost more men to keep the poor bastards alive!*

'Sir, you're not suggesting –'

Blight read his mind, horrified. 'Jesus, man!'

'Well then, what?' asked Niven bluntly. They'd all been through a lot over the past few days and the polite formalities had been dispensed with.

'Frankly, I don't know, but the national interest has to be considered here.'

'We're not the bad guys,' said Sharpe. 'We just need some kind of contingency plan.' Niven glanced at Sharpe who was behind the PM as he drew a finger across his throat, smiling. It took a supreme effort of will for Niven to ignore him.

'Spike, what do you think the Australian people will demand if the full horror of this gets out?' Blight asked. 'Over four hundred people dead, a Qantas plane shot down, plans for invasion . . .'

Niven realised the PM's fear. 'They'd want to even the score,' he said.

Blight nodded slowly. 'Revenge.'

Niven surprised himself that he hadn't considered what was so obvious. The very thing they'd just managed to avert might happen anyway. And what if Australia and Indonesia did slug it out? Aside from the destruction wreaked by the conflict itself, would that then make Australia a target for Islamic terrorists from all over the world? 'Okay, I see your point, Bill.' Blight was right, yet, in Niven's view, he was also morally wrong. What about the truth? There was no perfect solution. There were too many possibilities and variables, no matter how things were handled, and all of them had potentially dire consequences attached. Perhaps secrecy was the right way to go. Sharpe grinned behind the PM's back. Niven just wished he didn't have to agree with *him*.

The fate of Flight 007 on Sakhalin Island flashed into his brain again. The realities of the incident had been buried somehow – that was obvious to him now. But why? There was supposedly a well-known outspoken anti-Communist congressman on the flight. At the time, both sides were seeking détente. Had he been silenced to make peace a reality?

If the aircraft *hadn't* crashed into the sea as reported but had actually made it to the military base on Sakhalin itself, around 270 passengers and crew would have been spirited away. If that was the case, what had happened to them? Where were they now? If one passenger had turned up alive, questions would have been asked about what happened to all the rest. The fact that very little wreckage and only four bodies were found made that theory quite plausible. Images of frightened passengers swam in his mind – men, women and children being herded off to some unknown fate, their lives and dreams terminated because of some foreign policy manoeuvring.

We don't have anything like that kind of problem here, Niven reminded himself – just two people. 'If you don't mind, Bill, I'd like to handle it,' Niven said. If he took over, Niven reasoned, then at least it'd be done right. Two fine Australian soldiers had paid the ultimate price to protect the survivors. He didn't want that sacrifice to have been for nothing.

'Thanks, Spike,' said Blight. 'I was hoping you would.'

Sharpe placed a hand on Niven's shoulder and said quietly in his ear, 'Me too, Spike. I can think of no one better to screw over if things get fucked up.'

Niven shuddered, and not just because of the physical contact with Sharpe. Lying went against his grain even if, in this particular instance, there was a reasonable argument that doing so served the national interest. And then there was the problem of making that lie stick. Would it be possible to pass off the plane crash as some kind of bizarre accident? Alternatively, what if there was no attempt to hide the truth? Could there be advantages in that? Indonesia had to face up to the reality of its fractious military establishment once and for all. The world condemnation that would follow when the full story was known might force all kinds of changes on Jakarta. Perhaps the fate of QF-1 might be just the right catalyst. Niven wrestled with the competing voices in his head, and a small part of him was thankful that the decision about which way to jump had been taken out of his hands.

Niven glanced around the room quickly sizing up the

men he'd followed the crisis through with over the past three days. Griffin and Greenway were nodding as Blight and Sharpe spoke to them, drumming up support no doubt. Griffin caught the nervousness on Niven's face and came over. He said, 'The PM just told us . . . I know you, and I can see this sticking in your throat. Spikey, for what it's worth, Lurch and I think the PM's right. Can't see any other way.'

'There's always another way, Griff,' said Niven obstinately.

'Okay, forget about Australia and Indonesia and the geopolitical issues at stake. Try and look at it from the two survivors' point of view. They're going to want to return to some semblance of a normal life. Find some way to make that possible for them, because if all this ends up in the media, I guarantee they'll be dead within the year – think what juicy targets they'd make for extremists.'

'Yep, okay . . . that hadn't occurred to me, Griff,' said Niven. 'And the PM's reasons are valid too, I suppose. Frankly, I'm just not happy about doing another Sakhalin Island here. And y'know, no matter what we do to prevent it, it'll all come out sooner or later.'

'Too many loose ends?'

'Uh-huh.'

'Well, let's hope when it does we're all retired,' Griffin said, forcing a smile. He knew Niven was right. And when it all boiled down, the reason for the cover-up was simply to protect people's lives. 'Come on, Spike, let me get you a drink. Lord knows we deserve one.'

'Thanks, Griff, but I'll take a rain check if you don't mind. I've got a bit of planning to do and once I start drinking I don't think I'll want to stop.'

'Know what you mean. Care to bounce anything off me?'

'Actually, yes.' Niven's mind was already racing with a plan half formed. An invasion was imminent unless something could be done about Suluang and the rest. Leaking the satellite photo of the crash to the Indonesian parliament just before releasing it to the Australian media had been a clever ploy. Blight's idea. The impression was that the photo had come from a source within the TNI – more factional infighting? And then there was allowing Batuta to join the team at the videoconference, where General Masri gave up his story. Another Blight masterstroke. A risk, of course, because in reality the PM couldn't have known for sure exactly what Batuta did or didn't know. Blight had gambled that the diplomat was completely in the dark, and won. No doubt about it, the man was an excellent strategist. Now they knew exactly where the Indonesian government stood, and a counter-move could be made with some confidence. Perhaps the PM was also right about these next uncomfortable steps.

A videoconference would need to be set up as soon as possible between Batuta, Blight, and the President of Indonesia and his foreign minister. It would then be up to Batuta to convince his President to side with Canberra against the common enemy. At least Canberra had something to work with now, facts they didn't have even a few hours ago, some certainty. The Indonesian politician, Achmad Reza, the man Griffin had chosen to reveal the satellite photos of QF-1 to the Indonesian parliament, was a further asset they could harness.

Niven's plan was chancy and violent, but there wasn't much time up their sleeves for subtlety. Suluang had to be on the back foot. But there were a couple of major details Niven as yet had no answers for. The first was to find a reason for the 747's crash. It couldn't be attributed to human error. With all the press coverage the incident had received, the public was now very well informed. The fact that aircraft didn't just disappear from ATC screens without good reason had been widely canvassed. He saw no way around bringing Boeing into the loop. The manufacturing giant would thoroughly investigate the wreckage and the chances of it agreeing to attribute the cause of the crash to mechanical or systems failure were nil. Neither Boeing nor the world's carriers could afford a crisis of confidence in the popular aircraft. Secondly, there was Joe and the woman – what was her name . . . Suryei? How to protect their identities?

'Griff, if I remember correctly, you said that one of our people was Suluang's lover?'

'Well, yes . . .'

The CDF was so caught up in his thoughts, he failed to realise his cold had disappeared.

Jakarta, 1100 Zulu, Friday, 1 May

Sketchy news had just reached Suluang by phone of several F-16s involved in some kind of crash or mid-air collision in Sulawesi, but the report was unconfirmed. Hasanuddin AFB was in a flap. All planes were up, but they hadn't as yet located the missing aircraft or recovered the pilots. But it wasn't unusual to lose fighters through training accidents and other mishaps – that much he did know. Suluang wondered whether he was being hopeful or delusional. Something was wrong, definitely wrong. The 747 was located, the world was watching, and yet he was blind, attempting to plan in a vacuum.

And then there was Sergeant Marturak. Static, a distant crackling on the appointed frequency – that's all they'd received from him when they'd tried to make contact. Marturak had not called in at the appointed time. Another missed communication meant the problems were continuing. More reasons to be anxious. Marturak had been due to report and confirm that the crash site was secured at last, meaning the two survivors had joined their fellow passengers. But that communication had not been received. *What in Allah's name was going on?* There was no contingency plan because the operation had been hurriedly cobbled together and executed. Perhaps Marturak's radios had somehow been disabled. If he heard nothing within the next hour, he would dispatch another team of Kopassus troops to the area.

The problem with that, of course, was that the net was widening. Already too many people knew too much. Sooner or later there would be a leak and that was a real danger. Masri had deserted the cause after the last get-together, lost his nerve. How many others would lose their resolve with the uncertainties building? The government's internal security would be digging around, hunting for irregularities. Lanti Rajasa would take care of that, should it become an issue. But he wouldn't be able to keep the dogs at bay for long. And he wouldn't be able to help at all if their plan was revealed. Rajasa would be one of the first to be isolated, excluded from the loop. Not true, he told himself. He would be – Suluang.

General Masri still hadn't been found. His disappearance was Suluang's main concern. Bigger, even, than not hearing from the Kopassus, or that satellite photo. Masri could be dead, lying face down in a paddy field somewhere. Suluang hoped he was, because if he wasn't, then he could also be somewhere talking to the wrong people. Again, he hadn't heard anything. The hit had been ordered on Masri and the hitman had himself been killed. Masri, though, had disappeared. Vanished. And so had his driver, one of Lanti's people. The plan, the beautiful plan, was unravelling fast. *There are too many variables. Get out now!* There were countries he could disappear to and live like a sultan on the money he had salted away over the years.

And yet, a competing voice told him he was panicking unnecessarily. That there was nothing to worry about. Elizabeth always had that effect on him, the ability to block out reality; a safe harbour. She'd called him forty minutes ago at the barracks to tell him that she had rented a room at a five-star hotel, and filled the bath with bubbles. She did that occasionally. Suluang had things on his mind that demanded attention, but the thought of Elizabeth naked but for lavender suds was utterly distracting. Reluctantly, after telling her he was too busy, he'd capitulated. Perhaps, he had reasoned, the diversion would do him good. *One last time?*

Suluang was glad that he'd given in. He lay back on the crisp linen sheets in the cool, darkened room. The woman's body was exquisite. She was young, with breasts that strained against the thin fabric of her dress. Her waist was narrow and her legs long and straight. He really should talk to his uncle about including more such delicious items on the menu. What a find she was. He'd been sleeping with her, when the opportunity presented itself, for some time now. He doubted that he'd ever slept with such a beautiful woman before. And she had a dirty mind. The woman looked like an angel, but fucked like a whore.

Elizabeth smiled at the man lying on the bed. It wasn't her real name, of course. She wore names, identities, like masks. When she was done with this assignment, she'd write the name on a piece of paper and throw it in the bin. The ritual helped clear her mind so she could adopt a new mask the next time it was needed.

No matter what the assignment, Elizabeth loved sex. Indeed, the more the better. She didn't care who the man was as long as he was healthy, preferably not fat, and had a decent-sized organ. And not necessarily in that order, she thought. In the lexicon of modern neuroses, Elizabeth was a sex addict. She knew what her body demanded, and she satisfied that demand at every opportunity. She'd never suffered the indignity of having to fake an orgasm, no matter who she happened to be in bed with. She couldn't understand women having problems reaching that glorious plateau. It was so easy for her. She often wondered if men had the same attitude to fucking that she did. It would be an interesting thesis – she'd certainly enjoy researching it.

Choosing a wardrobe had been difficult for this job. Ultimately, she'd settled on a range of cotton sundresses. They were cheap but, with the right colour and length of hemline, could be very sexy. She liked the ones with buttons down the front best of all. She could keep them buttoned to the collar at work. Afterwards, the buttons could be undone to the appropriate depth. And when the sun was just so in the sky, the cotton fabric hid nothing while covering everything.

Elizabeth leaned against the side table, one of her long brown legs parting the sky-blue dress to her thigh. She undid the buttons at her chest, her golden skin glowing. She hadn't even started and already she could see that the general was ready for her. This man was too easy. The dress fell from her shoulders, crumpling at her feet. The general swallowed dryly.

He was hard when she lifted the sheet to straddle him. Suluang felt the cool fabric of her panties against the heat of his skin. His excitement thrilled her and she sensed her own wetness.

Elizabeth rode him. The general's thrusts felt good. She moved on him, positioning her body for the most pleasure. And then, like an engine on a cold morning, her orgasm began to catch, the pleasure exploding in a ball of light and heat between her legs. She tried to keep the feeling going forever. But inevitably its power subsided and she was left with the man beneath her, spent, useless.

Suluang looked up at her with a smile on his lips, the usual triumphant smile most men wore afterwards. It said, 'Yeah, baby, I'm good.' Elizabeth didn't mind that. Leaving the man confident in his prowess was part of *her* power. Elizabeth smiled back and slid off, reaching for her Marlboros on the bedside table. She walked towards the bathroom, through the sun, in a swirl of grey-blue smoke. Suluang marvelled at the highlights that flashed blue-black in her hair. The woman disappeared behind the closed bathroom door. He heard the tap running in the bath. Ah, bubbles, he thought.

Suluang closed his eyes and let his head fall back on the pillow. He thought that he could probably become quite attached to this woman, even though she was perhaps only just half his age. And only a waitress. How could she afford a room in such an expensive hotel? he wondered. Maybe his uncle was also receiving 'favours'. He shouldn't allow himself to get so attached.

A small click that came from another world distracted him, made him open his eyes.

He looked into the small black hole of a silencer attached to a Glock. He shifted focus to the pale green eyes behind it. He noted that, with only one ear, the man's head appeared lopsided. Suluang wondered how he'd lost it. The gun made the sound of a cork coming out of a champagne bottle. At the instant the bullet smashed into his skull, Suluang's mind registered blinding pain before closing down forever.

Vince had fired into the target's mouth, up into the brain. He'd resisted the temptation to follow his first shot with one more round. Two shots to the head. Once ingrained, SAS training was hard to overcome. This was not to look like a professional hit. With the man's brains all over the bed head, he didn't need to check the carotid artery but did so anyway, out of a sense of professionalism. There was no pulse.

The air smelled tangy and salty, the combined perfume of sweat, sex and propellant. Vince's nose twitched. He retrieved the small brass shell casing, rolled it between the dead man's thumb and forefinger, then let it fall to the carpet. Next he removed the gun's silencer, pocketing it, and placed the gun on the carpet close to the bed after pressing it into the man's hand to ensure the stock was marked with the proper fingerprints. Forensics would fail to turn up evidence that supported suicide, such as grains of gunpowder burned into the skin of the general's hand, but

Vince knew that sort of inspection would take a couple of days to process. By then, he would be long gone. Vince could hear the water running in the bathroom – Elizabeth. There was no reason to disturb her. Each knew what had to be done. He went to the door of the hotel room and placed the hole in the side of his head against it. There was no sound from the hallway on the other side. Vince was out and gone, just another European tourist in a five-star Jakarta hotel full of them.

Elizabeth exited the bathroom, dressed and ready to leave in a tan Chanel suit. Her hair was up and she wore expensive make-up. The young waitress was gone. In her place was a sophisticated businesswoman, a marketing director or an advertising executive, perhaps, from a big multinational agency. The man she'd left alive not ten minutes ago was now very dead, as she knew he would be. She was impressed – Vince worked quietly. White sheets, red blood, brown skin: very artistic. She observed that her g-string was still dangling from the general's fingers. She shrugged. What would it hurt to leave it? She wondered if it would cause a stir. At the very least, it would give the police something tantalising to put under their microscopes. The thought made her smile, exciting her. Elizabeth, not her real name, left the suite without a backward glance.

Sydney, 1230 Zulu, Friday, 1 May

ABC Radio 702: 'In news just to hand, it has been announced by the Indonesian government that two survivors have been found at the crash site of the Qantas 747. The names of the two survivors, believed to be a man and a woman, have not been released. The survivors were found early this morning by an Indonesian air force rescue team flown in after the location of the site was revealed by a spy satellite.

'The Indonesian government has invited Australian military and civilian aviation authorities to investigate the causes of the crash.

'Qantas Flight QF-1 was bound for London via Bangkok when it disappeared from air traffic control screens three days ago. The flight was fully booked, and it is believed over four hundred people are likely to have perished in the tragedy. The majority of the flight's passengers are thought to have been Australian, and Thai nationals returning from Australia. The crash brings to an end Qantas's fatality-free safety record.

'It is now believed that the location of the downed plane was known for at least twenty-four hours by several Indonesian military leaders, but withheld by them in the hope of embarrassing the Indonesian government prior to attempting a coup d'etat.

'One of those implicated in the cover-up and failed coup was General Suluang, Commander in Chief of the TNI, the Indonesian army, who was found dead in a hotel room earlier today after committing suicide. His death has sparked further tensions between rival military factions in Jakarta where a standoff . . .'

Jakarta, 0235 Zulu, Saturday, 2 May

The operation had been underway for at least an hour and it was running like a Rolex. General Kukuh Masri sat propped in an APC. He moved his bandaged head to an angle that lessened the hammer that pounded in his brain despite the cocktail of drugs he'd been dosed with. In his mind, Masri went over the strategy devised by the Australians with himself and members of the Indonesian government. His partners in the coup were all, by now, more than likely dead. They would not have seen their deaths coming.

Suluang was already removed, found in a hotel room with his brains staining the walls. Suicide was the initial verdict. There was no note. There would be no national mourning. He would be found a traitor to Indonesia, as would Rajasa and the others. The coup would be announced, the perpetrators rooted out and that would be that. Case closed.

Masri would be proclaimed a hero for delivering the traitors to the Indonesian people. Then he would retire quickly and quietly leave Indonesia, never to return. The truth about his involvement would eventually come out, but by then he would be long gone. The thought saddened the general. He loved Indonesia and didn't want to leave it, but there was no alternative because he also loved living. Masri was just thankful that he was needed to subdue Suluang's men. Otherwise, he too might have ended up in a lonely hotel room sucking a pistol like Suluang.

He forced his mind back to the present. Soldiers had been exchanging fire for the last thirty minutes. Each shot seemed to make the hammer in his head pound harder. The soldiers in Suluang's regiment were besieged by the same men they'd overwhelmed the day before, almost exactly twenty-four hours earlier. There was more noise than anything else – more bark than bite – plenty of expended ammunition. There were a few casualties, but no serious attempt to kill or maim had been made by either side. The soldiers on both sides of the barricades knew the outcome of the 'battle' before it started. Suluang was gone, shot by his own hand, and nothing would bring him back. The snake's head had been removed. The firefight happening around Masri was more an expression of grief by Suluang's men than anything else, the snake's body writhing in shock.

Understandably, Masri thought, Australia had had a large say in how the operation would go. He was aware that simultaneous manoeuvres were in full swing against other regiments and squadrons loyal to the traitors he had given up to the government. The air force squadrons, unlike the army units, would surrender without a fight because their battles were fought in the sky. They would be overrun on the ground. The rogue naval squadrons would also be surrounded and neutralised. The cancer had to be removed.

It was time. Masri said a few brief words into the intercom and the APC rolled. The mechanised cavalry rumbled forward. They arrived as a phalanx at the front gate of Suluang's barracks and brought their guns to bear on various structures within the gates.

Masri looked down with surprise at the blood that suddenly welled from under his arm. He wondered what was going on, but only for an instant. A stray, ricocheting FNC80 round had found a gap in the Kevlar plates of his body armour. It bored through his chest and severed the aorta. He died with a look of surprise on his face, slumped like a stuffed doll in the APC's hatch.

White flags appeared at the gates of the barracks and

the soldiers met and embraced, smiling, just as they had done the day before when the roles of victor and vanquished had been reversed.

Jakarta, 0235 Zulu, Saturday, 2 May

A-6 was finished with this business. Maros in Sulawesi, and now Jakarta. Enough was definitely enough. She craved normality. But at that moment what she wanted even more desperately was sleep. It had been a long night and she couldn't remember the last time she'd been horizontal.

A-6 had arrived in Jakarta in the early hours of the morning from Maros, after being urgently summoned there to the Australian embassy. They briefed her on the coup. Indonesia, they said, was on the verge of falling to extremists in the military. They also told her about the plane, the Kopassus, the survivors in the jungle, each new twist and turn raising the bar of her astonishment considerably. When the briefing had finished, she was speechless. But once the reality of it had started to sink in, A-6 began to feel proud of the small but not insignificant part she'd played in helping to unravel the plot, and prevent it from coming to pass. The knowledge fortified her for the role the Australian ambassador, Roger Bowman, pressed on her.

She'd been asked to help take members of Jakarta's powerful student body through an overview of the plot. A-6 was not a negotiator or a diplomat, but she had been drafted into this particular enterprise, she'd been told, because she looked and talked like an Indonesian, conveying the facts with an integrity that a white Australian public servant could never hope to match. She had conducted the meeting jointly with Achmad Reza, an Indonesian politician she'd never met or heard of before. The students seemed to trust him, however, holding him in high regard.

Achmad Reza sat somewhat dazed by events as he sipped sweet tea at a cafeteria inside the parliament and reviewed the last few hours in his mind.

Standing in front of the student delegation, armed with satellite photos and the alarming contents of the disk showing Australia redrawn as part of Indonesia, Reza had felt well out of his depth. At stake was nothing less than the future of Indonesia and even, conceivably, the stability of the world. Redressing this evil was too much responsibility for one man to shoulder. His countrymen had plotted and killed in an outrageous bid for power. The ultimate outcome of their actions was beyond his ability to predict. All that could be done now – all anyone could do – would be to ride events as they bucked and kicked sickeningly to a conclusion.

He had agreed with the Australians that the truth would have to remain hidden. Peace in the region depended on it. Unsurprisingly, it hadn't taken much to convince the ruling party about the need for outright secrecy, because everyone was in a collective state of mortification at the evidence revealed. It gave Australia an upper hand in the relationship between the two countries, and that mildly concerned Reza, but then he realised that the two countries were entering into a conspiracy and each was dependent on the other. The Australians and Indonesians all agreed that the traitors had to be purged. The coup had to be made public. Using the student body as the conduit for this news had been his idea. It seemed logical. They were party neutral and, as such, regarded by the wider population as being concerned more for the welfare of their country than politicking.

The young Indonesian woman who'd assisted him with the briefing of the students had been extremely nervous. He wasn't given her name. She'd been introduced to him as an Australian public servant. Quite obviously, she was a spy of some kind, but vastly different to the other young woman, the unnerving one called Elizabeth, who'd anonymously passed him the photo and later met with him in the village. This woman was refreshingly unsure of herself, almost frightened by the situation she found herself in. Reza had warmed to her instantly, because he knew exactly how she felt.

The angry noise outside the building reached in and bounced around the stone courtyard. Reza sipped his tea as various politicians and bureaucrats rushed past, for the most part no doubt hurrying to quieter, more secure places. The students had obviously decided that a show of solidarity, a stand against the forces determined to return Indonesia to the bad old days, was necessary. He was stunned at the speed of their reaction. They were well organised.

At first the student delegation he met with in the early hours of the morning had had trouble accepting what Reza revealed to them about Suluang and the rest. They preferred to believe that they were being used as unwitting pawns in some dangerous deception. But the taped interview with General Masri in his hospital bed was utterly convincing. Masri had been somewhat of a national hero and his confession shook them.

The police hadn't been brought into the loop for obvious reasons. Lanti Rajasa, the country's top policeman and a traitor, might have been tipped off and that would have been a disaster. The result was the conflict outside. Policeman versus student. Reza hoped that no one would get hurt.

He sighed and quaffed the remains of his tea. Perhaps the students were right and the demonstration outside was necessary, the open conflict a first important step in the healing process. Indonesia would never be the same again, of that he was certain. At the very least, the constitution would have to be redrafted to redefine the role of the armed forces. They could never again be allowed to act as financially autonomous satraps in far-flung provinces. The practice entrenched powerful expectations that ran counter to the nation's best interests. Yet Indonesia needed a strong army if it was to prevent disintegration. How could they possibly afford it? The conundrum caused Reza to have a premonition of deeply troubled times ahead.

A roar spiked through the blanket of the chanting and the bullhorns. Reza decided to leave the security of the parliament's inner sanctum and join the melee outside. The students believed in a free Indonesia, and so did he. That, at least, was simple, uncomplicated, noble; and his soul needed sustenance. Reza gently placed his cup on the delicate saucer and stood up gingerly. He knew it was risky, but his place was out front with the students.

Out on the street, A-6 was amazed at the speed of the

student response. Hundreds of belligerent police with batons and riot shields were forming lines, eyeing ranks of students wearing crash helmets and scarves tied around their mouths. Just as frightening, many students wore no protection at all. Behind the student lines was the Indonesian parliamentary building. Angry young men and women with loud-hailers bellowed that the parliament needed protection. Police vehicles rushed back and forth in the no-man's land between the opposing forces, rocks and other projectiles popping off their armour plating. She watched horrified as several students fired volleys of ball bearings at the police with homemade slingshots. Tear gas was returned. Things were spinning out of control.

A-6 glanced down at her foot. Under it was a flyer with the large black headline 'Traitors!' in Bahasa. Moving her shoe revealed mug shots of several high-ranking officers. More tear gas canisters were launched into the student ranks. It quickly became difficult to see anything clearly, as much for the tears that filled her burning eyes and throat as for the thick white smoke that swirled in the square. Several cars attempted to gain access to the parliament. The students were gathering excitedly around one of them.

Jakarta, 0235 Zulu, Saturday, 2 May

Lanti Rajasa had woken around midnight with an uneasy feeling. He'd been expecting a call from Suluang with an update from the Kopassus at the crash site. The call hadn't come through, leaving a sour lump in his belly that made sleep troubled. He gave up trying just after three in the morning, got up, showered and dressed, and left the car park of his apartment building in his black Mercedes. He had his driver cruise the hot, dusty sprawl of Jakarta, driving aimlessly for hour after hour with no set destination, while he pondered a course of action.

His initial thought was to go to the parliament, keep his ear to the ground, try to contact Suluang and some of the others and make a decision on the basis of what they told him. Then Rajasa suddenly realised the source of his unease: he was the head of the police but he did not know what was going on. That was unthinkable, and it set off an array of alarms in his head. There was only one possible reason for this lack of intelligence, and it didn't bode well for his future health and happiness. Was he purposefully being kept in the dark, starved of information, cut off for a reason? How quickly things appeared to be falling apart.

Suddenly frightened by this insight, Rajasa changed his mind. He would go to the parliament as he'd planned, but instead of contacting anyone he would go straight to his office, shred anything dangerous, wipe his hard-drive and clean and trash his email folders. He would then get on the first plane out.

It was now morning, just after nine-thirty. The sky was grey and, as usual, heavily polluted. The sight of students clashing with police had become so commonplace that it scarcely raised his interest when he arrived at the parliament. The students manning obstacles, petrol drums filled with bricks and burning rubbish, were stopping the cars at the entrance gate. Several masked faces appeared in the windows and Rajasa saw their eyes bulge first with surprise, then with anger as they recognised him. The front passenger door was flung open and his driver was pulled from the car. A poster titled 'Traitors' with the faces of himself, Suluang and the others was placed against his window and the cause of the riot was now obvious to Rajasa. He was no longer disinterested, he was afraid.

The car rocked violently from side to side. Rajasa rolled about inside helplessly, screaming obscenities. Young faces were pushed against his window yelling, spitting. A brick crashed into the bulletproof glass window beside him and bounced harmlessly off. Rajasa felt reassured by that. But then the Mercedes was pushed up onto its balance point and rolled over on its roof. He could feel and hear the bodywork being pounded by bricks and sticks. Rajasa smelled petrol and any feelings of invulnerability he may have had evaporated. Somehow the fuel tank had been punctured. One of the students lit the petrol and the flames spread quickly.

The students pulled back as the fire took hold and the heat became intense. Rajasa could see the orange tongues licking at the windows outside while inside, the car's interior filled with smoke. The fuel tank exploded, sending a shockwave through the vehicle that killed Rajasa long before the flames reached him.

A-6 had seen enough. Through her hacking cough and watering eyes, she'd witnessed the mob burn a man alive in his car. She wondered who the victim was. It was getting impossible to breathe and the widening melee, increasing in ferocity, made it likely that sooner or later she'd be dragged off by the police or hit by student missiles filling the air. She staggered down a side street, gagging, eyes weeping uncontrollably from the gas, more than ever ready to leave the espionage business, and Indonesia, behind her.

The radio journalist sat in the press lounge at Kingsford Smith Airport. Other journalists from across the media spectrum surrounded her. This was the best show in town, without a doubt, and there was genuine expectation in the room.

The two survivors of QF-1 were coming home. They'd spent a couple of days in hospital recovering from their ordeal, and were likely to be physically and mentally exhausted for a while yet. The journos had been instructed to keep their questions brief and not to overstress them. This could be one of those great survival-against-all-odds stories the public ate up.

Here in this very room, the survivors, both in their twenties, would be reunited with their families. It promised to be quite an emotional scene. Amongst all the sadness of so many people lost, everyone hoped some joy would come out of the reunion about to take place.

The RAAF Hercules transport which had brought the two home was taxiing to its holding point on the apron. Several medical staff rushed to the door as its engines spooled down. The door was flung open and a knot of people instantly formed at the base of the mobile stairs. A young woman appeared at the doorway of the aircraft, smiled and stepped into the sea of doctors, nurses and officials. A man followed, head bandaged, and joined the turmoil.

The radio journalist switched her view to the monitor. It was already happening up there on the screen. Bloody TV bastards always got first access. No doubt a report was going out live on the networks, interrupting children's shows, soap operas, and home-shopping programs. The thought really annoyed her. The brief flash the journalist managed to get of the young woman standing at the doorway of the plane surprised her. She was beautiful. Asian.

A door opened behind the dais, diverting the journalist's attention from the TV screen, and several worried-looking people filed in. The parents, obviously. One set was Indonesian. The radio journalist checked her briefing notes. That's right, she remembered now. The girl who'd survived was Indonesian, an Australian citizen but born in Indonesia of Indonesian parents. The girl's mother had a tissue out and was dabbing an eye. The energy levels in the room surged. Double doors off to one side banged open and the two survivors, surrounded by medicos, RAAF personnel, diplomats, cameramen and Qantas execs, burst in. The parents were instantly on their feet, rushing to comfort their children. Flashes went off, video lights blazed. It was beautiful.

Elizabeth had been given the new name of Tuti Murthi, and she was feeling tense about it. This was a serious acting job. Being Suluang's lover was comparatively easy. The people looking at her with sympathetic faces wanted facts, tears, *feelings*.

Tuti had been well briefed, as had the agent playing her fellow survivor, Vince, the man who had helped her deal with Suluang. So were the alleged parents up on stage, who were as much Tuti's parents as she was a QF-1 survivor.

They had to put on a good show. They would all have to endure the spotlight for a couple of days, then it would be announced that a magazine had bought exclusive rights to their story. The tale would be written, pictures taken, then they'd all beg to be left alone to get on with their lives. She'd get on a plane and disappear.

The journos were getting ready to ask their questions. Tuti was not going to enjoy this. She looked forward to the moment when she could write the name on a piece of paper, screw it up, throw it in the bin, and move the hell on.

Niven watched the show on TV. All the major networks covered it, interrupting their regular shows with the reunion. The two stand-ins were doing a great job. There was a tap on the door.

'Come,' said Niven.

'Good, hoped you'd be watching,' said Griffin as he put his head round the door. 'Mind if I sit in?'

'No, take a seat.'

Griffin sat and smiled at the news report. 'This was a great idea. Yours?'

'No, actually. It was Joe's – Joe Light's.'

'You're kidding,' Griffin said.

'Seriously. Had it completely figured out. He pointed out that, as the passenger manifest hadn't been released, all we had to do was take his and Suryei's names off it and, bingo, it could never be proved they were on the flight.'

'Shit, that's clever. So simple. The guy should be working for us.'

'Funny you should say that,' said Niven.

Joe and Suryei had been put on a plane home. Flying wasn't something either of them was keen on, but they weren't given a choice. Fortunately, the flight had been uneventful, even boring, and she decided that boredom was a good thing when it came to flying. Thankfully, after her apprehension had faded, sleep had come. Counselling had been a big help. At least now she could close her eyes without the nightmares invading the darkness. But she knew they were in her head somewhere, dreams that made her sweat with fear.

The aircraft was now descending. Suryei glanced at Joe, asleep in the seat beside her. She'd given up trying to analyse her feelings for him, and they'd both needed the intimacy while recovering at a facility she guessed was in Hawaii. At first it had been painful, even difficult, finding positions to make love that didn't aggravate either her injuries or Joe's, especially when they'd had to find out-of-the-way places for privacy.

The bandages were off her forearms now. The burns had been worse than she'd thought. They'd given her skin grafts at the hospital and the results were astonishing. Another week and it would be difficult to see how badly she'd been burned. She saw in her mind the flames that had caused the injury, but the truly ghastly details had been packed way down deep in her subconscious where the nightmares lived.

Both Suryei and Joe had contracted a mild case of malaria in the jungle, fortunately the kind with no long-term effects or damage that couldn't be treated easily with drugs. A few of Joe's scratches had become septic, but even the nastiest of them was now healing well.

For Joe, not surprisingly, the broken rib was causing the most problems. The bullet had torn up the muscles in his shoulder pretty badly when it had exited, and he still grimaced when he moved the wrong way. It would be a good three months with plenty of physio before he was fully fit and back in the gym.

Joe and Suryei had seen the papers from Australia while they were recovering. The pictures of the two 'survivors' were everywhere. The woman playing her was pretty. The man had an ear missing, an injury the papers said was sustained in the crash.

Joe's clever idea to take their names off the passenger list would allow them to return to some semblance of a normal life. Suryei gazed out the window. She went overseas so often that her friends no longer asked where she was going or when she'd return. And these days she worked freelance, so there was no employer to answer to. But her family could prove difficult. They'd been worried sick about her and would be waiting at Arrivals. When Suryei had phoned her parents to let them know she was still alive, they had first gone into shock. Anger had followed. Then joy. They'd thought she was dead. The itinerary she'd left them had listed QF-1 as her outbound plane. Qantas had refused to tell them whether their daughter was in fact a passenger on the flight, but Suryei's silence had confirmed their worst fears.

Suryei's explanation of all this had been thoroughly constructed and rehearsed beforehand. She would say that she had changed arrangements at the last minute, getting on an earlier flight with a different carrier. At Bangkok, she'd headed straight for the jungle. She'd still be there, deep in the hills with her camera, if not for an accident with a kerosene lamp that had burned her forearms. She'd known nothing about the Qantas plane until she'd returned to Bangkok. She had then called her parents immediately, knowing they'd be worried.

The Australians and Americans at the recovery facility had provided both Joe and Suryei with relevant hotel and credit card accounts and receipts to cover their last couple of weeks. Their flight details had been amended on the Australian immigration server. Suryei had even been supplied with rolls of film exposed with rare shots of wildlife unique to the jungles of Thailand. Her story would stack up.

Joe's was not as tight, but then it didn't have to be. He had no one close enough to worry about him, just a father who lived in Perth, on the other side of the country. If anyone asked, he would say that he'd decided to holiday in Malaysia, travelling up to Thailand instead of going to England. A last-minute change of plans. He'd done that plenty of times before. No big deal. What's all the fuss about?

In a month they'd both be taking up work in the US. Joe had been 'offered' a job within the NSA at their HQ in Maryland. Suryei had also signed with the local bureau of a national news service they both suspected of being just another strand of the NSA's intelligence-gathering net. They had been given time to get their things in order and would be back on a plane again in a month's time. Suryei made a mental note to check whether going to the States by sea was possible.

The aircraft lurched as the flaps extended fully. Suryei's

hand unconsciously went to the Bic lighter suspended on a simple silver chain from her neck. As she'd promised herself, she'd made it into a good luck charm. She rubbed her fingers against the smooth plastic and slowly rolled the friction wheel under her thumb, finding the action reassuring.

There were plenty of instances of people who had missed planes, trains or boats, and had avoided death because of it. And just like them, Suryei would marvel at her lucky escape. She smiled at the thought. Very few people would ever know exactly how close to the truth that was.

The wheels of the 747 hit the runway hard. The jolt made Suryei jump. Joe woke with a start. 'Jesus!' he said, eyes wide, expecting the worst.

Sydney, 0800 Zulu, Monday, 18 May

ABC Radio 702: 'A spokesman for Boeing Corporation revealed today preliminary findings into the crash of Qantas Flight 1 that killed a total of four hundred and ten passengers and crew, ruling out terrorism as a possible cause. It is believed that the section of the fuselage called the Electronics and Equipment Bay, which houses vital junctions for the aircraft's hydraulic systems, was struck by a small meteorite.

'A Boeing investigator says such a missile could have been travelling at close to 60 000 kilometres per hour, vaporising the section of the plane it struck. The investigator says the wreckage of the plane recovered from Sulawesi is consistent with this theory.

'A spokesman for Boeing says the chances of an aircraft being hit by a meteorite are around a hundred million to one but that, given the number of jets flying and the many millions of air miles flown each year, a strike by a meteorite was just a matter of time.'

Author's note

Time is a difficult beast to tame when writing a book like this, where events are happening in different time zones simultaneously. For example, something can take place in the morning in Sydney, Australia, and affect events in Hawaii the morning of the day before.

To help overcome the confusion, I've adopted the standard twenty-four hour Greenwich 'clock'. This was previously known as Greenwich Mean Time (GMT), and is now officially called Coordinated Universal Time (UTC). In military parlance, however, the letter designator for this clock is Z, or Zulu.

If I were to adhere strictly to form, 10 am on April 28 in Sydney (Eastern Standard Time) should be written 28041200Z (Sydney is +10 hours UTC).

Once you get used to reading time in this fashion, it's actually less confusing than it might at first seem. But it becomes less so when juggling several time zones at once. In order to cut down on the mental arithmetic, I've omitted the local times in the section headings. But for the sake of general interest, the local times of the major places in this story are:

Sulawesi – UTC plus 8 hrs
Bali – UTC plus 8 hrs
Hawaii – UTC minus 10 hrs
Maryland – UTC minus 5 hrs
East Timor – UTC plus 9 hrs
Jakarta – UTC plus 7 hrs
Canberra – UTC plus 10 hrs

MORE BESTSELLING FICTION AVAILABLE FROM PAN MACMILLAN

Matthew Reilly
SCARECROW

IT IS THE GREATEST BOUNTY HUNT IN HISTORY

FIFTEEN NAMES
There are 15 targets, the finest warriors in the world – commandos, spies, terrorists. And they must all be dead by 12 noon, today. The price on their heads: almost $20 million each.

ONE HERO
Among the names on the target list, one stands out. A Marine named Shane Schofield, call-sign: SCARECROW.

NO LIMITS
And so Schofield is plunged into a headlong race around the world, pursued by a fearsome collection of international bounty hunters – including the 'Black Knight', a notoriously ruthless hunter who seems intent on eliminating only Schofield.

The race is on and the pace is frantic as Schofield fights for survival, in the process unveiling a vast international conspiracy and the terrible reason why he cannot, under any circumstances, be allowed to live . . .

He led his men into hell in ICE STATION. He protected the President against all odds in AREA 7. This time it's different.

Because this time he is the target.

COMING SOON

SWORD OF ALLAH

DAVID A ROLLINS